WESTHAMPTON FREE LIBRARY
7 LIBRARY AVENUE
WESTHAMPTON BEACH NY 11978

The Best American
Mystery Stories 2001

GUEST EDITORS OF
THE BEST AMERICAN MYSTERY STORIES

1997 ROBERT B. PARKER
1998 SUE GRAFTON
1999 ED MCBAIN
2000 DONALD E. WESTLAKE
2001 LAWRENCE BLOCK

The Best American Mystery Stories 2001

Edited and with an Introduction
by Lawrence Block

Otto Penzler, *Series Editor*

HOUGHTON MIFFLIN COMPANY
BOSTON · NEW YORK 2001

Copyright © 2001 by Houghton Mifflin Company
Introduction copyright © 2001 by Lawrence Block
All rights reserved

No part of this work may be reproduced or transmitted in any form or by any means, electronic or mechanical, including photocopying and recording, or by any information storage or retrieval system without the prior written permission of the copyright owner unless such copying is expressly permitted by federal copyright law. With the exception of nonprofit transcription in Braille, Houghton Mifflin is not authorized to grant permission for further uses of copyrighted selections reprinted in this book without the permission of their owners. Permission must be obtained from the individual copyright owners as indentified herein. Address requests for permission to make copies of Houghton Mifflin material to Permissions, Houghton Mifflin Company, 215 Park Avenue South, New York, New York 10003.

ISSN 1094-8384

ISBN 0-618-12492-6

ISBN 0-618-12491-8 (pbk.)

Printed in the United States of America

DOC 10 9 8 7 6 5 4 3 2 1

"Things That Make Your Heart Beat Faster" by Jennifer Anderson. First published in *The Missouri Review*. Copyright © 2000 by Jennifer Anderson. Reprinted by permission of the author.

"Lobster Night" by Russell Banks. First published in *Esquire*. Copyright © 2000 by Russell Banks. Reprinted from *The Angel on the Roof* by permission of HarperCollins Publishers, Inc.

"Prison Food" by Michael Downs. First published in *Witness*. Copyright © 2000 by Michael G. Downs. Reprinted by permission of the author.

"In the Zone" by Leslie Edgerton. First published in *High Plains Literary Review*. Copyright © 2000 by Leslie Edgerton. Reprinted by permission of the author.

"The Paperhanger" by William Gay. First published in *Harper's Magazine*. Copyright © 2000 by William Gay. Reprinted by permission of the author.

"A Book of Kells" by Jeremiah Healy. First published in *Mary Higgins Clark Mystery*. Copyright © 2000 by Jeremiah Healy. Reprinted by permission of the author.

"Erie's Last Day" by Steve Hockensmith. First published in *Alfred Hitchcock's Mystery Magazine*. Copyright © 2000 by Steve Hockensmith. Reprinted by permission of the author.

"Under Suspicion" by Clark Howard. First published in *Ellery Queen's Mystery Magazine*. Copyright © 2000 by Clark Howard. Reprinted by permission of the author.

"Her Hollywood" by Michael Hyde. First published in *Alaska Quarterly Review*. Copyright © 2000 by Michael Hyde. Reprinted by permission of the author.

"Family" by Dan Leone. First published in *Literal Latté*. Copyright © 2000 by Dan Leone. Reprinted by permission of the author.

"Blood Sport" by Thomas Lynch. First published in *Witness*. Copyright © 2000 by Thomas Lynch. Reprinted by permission of the author.

"Carnie" by David Means. First published in *Witness*. Copyright © 2000 by David Means. Reprinted by permission of Georges Borchardt, Inc.

"Tides" by Kent Nelson. First published in *The Georgia Review*. Copyright © 2000 by Kent Nelson. Reprinted by permission of the author.

"The Girl With the Blackened Eye" by Joyce Carol Oates. First published in *Witness*. Copyright © 2000 by The Ontario Review, Inc. Reprinted by permission of The Ontario Review, Inc.

"Easy Street" by T. Jefferson Parker. First published in *Easy Street*, by T. Jefferson Parker, ASAP Press. Copyright © 2000 by T. Jefferson Parker. Reprinted by permission of the author.

"The Big Bite" by Bill Pronzini. First published in *The Shamus Game*, edited by Robert J. Randisi, Signet. Copyright © 2000 by the Pronzini-Muller Family trust. Reprinted by permission of the author.

"Missing in Action" by Peter Robinson. First published in *Ellery Queen's Mystery Magazine*. Copyright © 2000 by Peter Robinson. Reprinted by permission of the author.

"The Face-Lift" by Roxana Robinson. First published in *The Atlantic Monthly*. Copyright © 2000 by Roxana Robinson. Reprinted by permission of the author.

"Big Ranch" by John Salter. First published in *Third Coast*. Copyright © 2000 by Nathan Walpow. Reprinted by permission of the author.

"Push Comes to Shove" by Nathan Walpow. First published in *A Deadly Dozen: Tales of Murder from Los Angeles*, edited by Susan B. Casmier, Aljean Harmetz, and Cynthia Lawrence, Uglytown. Copyright © 2000 by Nathan Walpow. Reprinted by permission of the author.

Contents

Foreword

THIS IS THE FIFTH VOLUME in this series of *Best American Mystery Stories* from the distinguished publishing house Houghton Mifflin, and, I don't know, but it may well be the best yet.

There are quite a few authors here who were previously unknown to me, just as there are among those on the honor roll — the other distinguished mystery stories of 2000. Many of the genre's more familiar names are not present in this collection, either because they failed to write short stores this past year or because some of these new voices simply produced superior work. This is, for all of us who are serious readers, whether of mystery fiction or of any fiction at all, a very good thing. It's a comfort to know that the pipes remain full, and that the future of the story is secure.

I've noticed one major change since I became the series editor five years ago: That first year, there were a handful of stories published as electronic originals. The next year there were a few more. This year I probably saw 250 to 300 of them, keeping the total number of stories examined well beyond a thousand.

To be frank, most of the electronically published stories are not terribly outstanding. Not much editing occurs on many sites in the e-publishing world, and often not much selectivity, either, so it's not surprising that the vast bulk of those stories have nothing original or stylistically compelling about them. However, and this is significant, not a single story in the 1997 volume even made it to the honor roll. This year several did, and several others were pretty close. I can conclude only that more and more good material will show up on these sites among all the dross, and it won't be long before a story, or more than one, cracks the ice and makes it into the book.

Some things don't change much. More of the stories are crime or suspense stories — stories of character and motivation — than detective stories. This is probably because the pure detective story may be the hardest kind of short fiction to write. On the other hand, it may be that younger authors are more interested in delving into personality and psychology than in puzzles. Either way, this phenomenon gives the anthology a range that would be impossible if all the tales were of observation and detection.

The other thing that doesn't change much is that this year's guest editor, Lawrence Block, has selected a story by Joyce Carol Oates, who breaks her own record by appearing in this annual for the fourth time. In case you missed it, she was also nominated for another National Book Award, her sixth, for the brilliant *Blonde,* a novel about Marilyn Monroe. Eighteen of the other authors all make their first appearance in *Best American Mystery Stories,* the exception being Peter Robinson, who brightens these pages for the second time.

Lawrence Block, who has had stories in two previous volumes, was named a Grand Master by the Mystery Writers of America for his lifelong achievements in the world of mystery fiction. He is a former president of that organization and a multiple winner of the Edgar Allan Poe Award in both the Best Novel and Best Short Story categories. As guest editor, he was ineligible to have a story selected for this volume. It would, after all, be a mite unseemly for him to select one of his own stories, however worthy.

I'm sure you will agree that it was worth that sacrifice when you read his amusing introduction and revel in his selections. I wish he could have found room for one or two stories that I loved and he didn't, but there you are. Immediately after I got his list of stories for the book I called him to say that I had done my own rankings and, astonishingly, eighteen of my top twenty stories were on his list. I can only commend his superb taste.

No volume in this series should ever be published without my sincere expression of gratitude to Michele Slung, the fastest and smartest reader on the planet, without whom this book would require three years to compile. She examines literally thousands of stories to determine if they are mystery- or crime-related, and *then* makes a determination of whether they are good enough to be seriously considered. You will find several listings, both among selected stories and those on the honor roll, from what may be defined as arcane sources for this genre, and that is a tribute to her own detective skills in ferreting out worthwhile fiction for these pages.

Also, a word of thanks is due to the editors and publishers of small magazines in every part of the country who favor us with subscriptions and submissions. None of these people works for the money, but purely for the joy of contributing to the creation and dissemination of fine writing.

The definition of a mystery story that I have used throughout my somewhat lengthy professional life is any work of fiction in which a crime or the threat of a crime is central to the plot or the theme. If the work is by an American or a Canadian, and has been first published in an American or a Canadian book or periodical, it is eligible for consideration for this book. If you are an author, editor, publisher, or someone who cares about one and would like to submit a story, please do so. Send a tearsheet or the entire publication to me at The Mysterious Bookshop, 129 West 56th Street, New York, New York 10019.

To be eligible for the next volume, the story must have been published in the calendar year 2001. If it was first published in electronic format, you must submit a hard copy, as I have not yet mastered that machine in the corner, the computer, though I am taking lessons and may soon enter the twentieth century (and yes, I know we are finally in the twenty-first). The earlier your submission arrives, the greater the chance that I'll love it. For those 135 submissions I got during the last ten days of 2000, I found it a little harder to find the love in my heart that caused me to give up holiday merriment to lock myself in and read, read, read. Be warned.

O.P.

Introduction

THE AMERICAN MYSTERY SHORT STORY, it is my pleasant duty to report, is in very good shape.

Were you to skip this introduction and go directly to the stories themselves, you'd discover as much on your own. And, I must say, every impulse but that of ego leads me to urge you to do just that. The stories, to be sure, are why we're all here.

They are the best of this year's crop, and the crop itself was a bountiful one. And they were written, each and every one of them, for love — love of the ideas that propel them, love of the characters that inhabit them, love of the pure task of dreaming imaginary worlds and putting well-chosen words on paper (or the screen, or what you will).

This introduction, on the other hand, was written for money. It's part of my job as guest editor, which consists primarily of reading the year's fifty best stories as selected by Otto Penzler with the assistance of Michele Slung and choosing twenty of that number for this volume. Having performed that happy task, I'm further required to string together a hundred sentences with the aim of producing something that will serve to introduce twenty fine stories, which, truth to tell, need no introduction. My words, however, will help to justify the presence of my name on the book's cover, and will also help me earn my fee.

Should I apologize for my mercenary motive? I think not. I am guided, after all, by Samuel Johnson's immortal words: "No man but a blockhead wrote but for money."

*

Would the good Dr. Johnson's words echo so resoundingly in my soul, I have often wondered, had he picked some other word? A dimwit, say, or a palpable ass, or a clod or a clown or a numbskull? "No man but a witling, sir, wrote but for money." It has, I submit, every bit as good a ring to it, and it leaves my own innocent surname well out of it.

Ah, well. It has always seemed to me that the precise meaning of Johnson's utterance is subject to interpretation. Perhaps he is saying that the person who writes in the happy anticipation of anything *beyond* financial reward is playing the fool. If you expect to make a name for yourself, or achieve literary immortality, or change the world, or pile up brownie points in heaven, then surely you're a blockhead — because money's all you can truly hope to gain for your efforts.

Because, certainly, Johnson himself was nowhere near as mercenary as the quoted sentence makes him appear. He wrote for money, unquestionably, and he might well have stopped writing had they stopped paying him, but he wrote also with the clear intent of adding to the world's store of knowledge and enhancing English literature. Indeed, his dictum works every bit as well, and sounds just as likely to have been uttered by him, if we take it and turn it on its head, to wit: "No man but a blockhead wrote solely for money."

And who can argue with that? There are easier ways to make a living — almost all of them, come to think of it — and few less likely ways to amass a fortune.

Back to our twenty superb stories, and the twenty blockheads who've written them. Where, you may ask, do I get off calling them that? How can I be so sure money was not what got them written?

Simple: There's no economic incentive these days to write short stories.

Without getting trapped in history, let me just state briefly that it was not ever thus. In the 1920s, top slick magazines paid top writers as much as $5,000 for a short story. (That's the equivalent of what in today's purchasing power? $100,000? More?) In the '30s and '40s, the pulp magazines assured any genuinely competent writer of a market for all the short fiction he could turn out — at a low word rate, to be sure, but enough to constitute a living wage.

No more. It may be technically possible to make a living writing short fiction, but I know of only one person who does so, year in and year out. (That's the extraordinary Edward D. Hoch, whose remarkably fertile imagination has proven to be a limitless font of short story ideas.) Short stories, for most of us, are hard to write and hard to sell, and the ones that sell don't pay much.

So why write them?

Some of us don't. When I began writing professionally, shortly after the invention of movable type, most aspiring mystery writers broke in by publishing short stories in magazines. Within a decade most of those magazines had vanished, and often enough a writer's first novel was that writer's first published work. Nowadays it's increasingly common for writers who have achieved some recognition for their novels to be invited to contribute short stories to original anthologies, and frequently this has induced them to write short fiction for the first time.

I myself began as a writer of short stories. The young writer I was could not possibly have sat down and written a novel right off the bat. I had to write and publish a couple dozen short stories before I was ready to attempt something longer.

As soon as I could, I began writing novels, and it is the novel that has kept bread on my table over the years. But I never stopped writing short stories, and hope to go on as long as I have breath and brain cells available for the task.

Why?

Because it's satisfying. Because the short story, for all the hard work involved, is as close as this trade comes to instant gratification. Any novel I've written has had stretches in it not unlike trench warfare. Short stories, sometimes written at a single sitting, rarely taking more than a week overall, are less of a drain and more of a kick.

Because it's liberating. I can turn my hand to themes and backgrounds and types of characters in a short story with which I would not feel comfortable spending an entire novel. I can take chances, knowing that failure means I've wasted days, not months or years.

Because it's fun.

I suspect the authors of these twenty stories found the business of writing them to be satisfying, liberating, and fun. I certainly had fun reading them, and I trust you will as well.

I think you will be struck, as I was, by the richness of these stories, and by the extraordinary variety — of theme, of mood, of style — to be found here. The only commonality, really, aside from their excellence, is that all of these stories are crime stories — which is to say that a crime or the threat of a crime is a central element in each of them.

The variety this affords is boundless. At the same time, however, I submit that crime is a defining element in a way that various topical themes are not. People have put together anthologies in which all of the stories are about dogs, say, or take place on shipboard, or involve children, and this sort of theme can make for a successful collection, but the common feature does not define the stories. Crime is somehow more generic — which, I suppose, helps explain why the mystery is very much a literary genre, and an enduring one.

It is, as you'll see, one with a very broad canopy, a house with many mansions.

You may also be struck by the number of unfamiliar names in this volume's table of contents. Two thirds of the writers whose stories I've selected are men and women whose names and work are new to me.

And this suggests to me that the short story — the mystery short story — is still the door through which many new writers emerge.

I think that's a good thing. The whole mystery genre, we shouldn't forget, originated in the short story. That, after all, is what Poe wrote.

And here are twenty hugely talented writers following in his dark footsteps. You have a treat in store for you. Enjoy!

LAWRENCE BLOCK

The Best American
Mystery Stories 2001

JENNIFER ANDERSON

Things That Make Your Heart Beat Faster

FROM *The Missouri Review*

IF I WERE A PAINTER this is how I would paint the Napa Valley: not like those gallery scenes of mustard in bloom or harvest-ripe fruit, but this ghostly silver secret landscape, the vines dormant and white with frost, the moon full, jackrabbits scattering across the roadway before me like mercury beads. Once I was a police officer for a very short time in Saint Amelia, an exclusive postage stamp of a town, and acquired an intimate knowledge of this landscape, four miles square, in the darkness of graveyard shift. Our uniform patches were comical — not authoritarian stars or eagles but orchid-hued grapes set against streaks of orange and green vineyard, glossy and enameled in appearance, which is how I thought of the town. I ached for sleep, longed to hold my sleeping husband's body, drove the same streets over and over, turned at the same boundaries, waited for something to happen. Like a pinball moving constantly, bouncing against its limitations.

When my shift ended, I would hurry to my home in the city of Napa, thirty minutes south. My husband and I couldn't afford to live in Saint Amelia; none of the cops who patrolled there could, except a couple of old-timers who'd bought property way back when. I'd race daybreak to my bedroom with tinfoil-lined windows, where I could preserve the illusion of night and sleep. Desires — for sleep, for my husband, for something unnameable — converged. My husband, a young assistant winemaker, smelled of bleach, wet cement floors, the brackish tip of a wine-soaked cork, wet stainless steel, sweat, oak, sun. When he'd been working in the limestone wine caves, which bloom with multicolored fungi and mold, his hair and skin would be infused with a heightened artificial scent of roses. When he slept, his skin was so warm, like chocolate left in the sun just as it reaches melting point, beaded with moisture. I wanted to press as many of the planes of my cold body against his as possible, quadriceps to hamstring, stomach to back, jaw to jaw. I'd undress and place my gun on my nightstand under an open book, and then, just as I'd fold back a corner of the blankets, dancing with joy inside like someone about to enter a hot bath, his alarm would go off, the third or fourth snooze alarm, the one that meant he was late.

In our twenties we were broke and blue, and my police job was important to us for the health insurance. The Napa Valley had lost its bucolic charm, and in moments of desperation I tried to talk my husband into moving to Czech Republic, Argentina, South Africa, any other winemaking region in the world where opportunities might exist for a young, ambitious American with talent but no connections. Napa Valley winemaking was a kind of Hollywood, which ironically is where my husband first worked; he had a film degree. Idealistically, he insisted that the job could be learned only by hands-on experience, that winemaking degrees were worthless. So we were outsiders from the start in a closed, incestuous industry where the demarcation between insider and outsider felt absolute. Then, at about the same time Saint Amelia hired me, he was hired as the assistant to a "cult" winemaker who had waiting lists to buy his mythic, perfect cab. We were still broke — but with a difference. We were on a path to the inner circle, my husband assured me, if we played things right. He'd spontaneously belt out, "I've got a golden ticket!" and then worry that if he appeared too happy, the gods might snatch it away.

Our primary form of entertainment when we were alone was telling each other stories that demystified the Valley. He'd tell me about tanks of white accidentally pumped into tanks of red and then say, "This is a small valley. Talking ruins careers." He'd warn me that people might try to milk me for information. "Oh, please," I'd say. "You didn't have to sign a confidentiality agreement like I did." I'd tell him about the mystery of the naked dead man, found face-down in front of a winery chateau. It was assumed at first that he'd leaped — or been pushed — from the third-story window. (In fact, as near as anyone could tell, he'd woken from a drunken sleep and mistaken the French doors, which opened on a thirty-foot drop, for the guest bathroom.) And I'd tell him the whole collection of pervert-in-the-vineyard stories the other cops liked to tell me on uneventful shifts. At first I thought they were teasing me, but I learned that every city, large or small, always has one crime, the sex crime. In the month before I'd been hired, two women — both lived in exclusive homes backing onto vineyards — reported waking in the night to find a strange man in their beds, touching them. At the first sign of struggle he disappeared into the darkness like some malevolent vineyard spirit, leaving them to wonder if they'd only dreamed.

I couldn't believe they'd hired me. I couldn't believe they'd given me a real badge and a real gun. I started working day shift during a hot week in November, the air heavy with decaying grape must, and everything seemed tinged with the erotic, from the creak of my new leather belt to the voice of my field training officer, Ken, a voice that made me think of the word *patina*. My first week on the job was grace week, a time to ride along and observe, free from daily scores and penalties, while Ken drove. Ken showed me secret roads through vineyards, hidden mansions, shortcuts through the gravel pit, all of which were routine to him but exhilarated me. He showed me places where chanterelles could be picked after rains. At first daylight he showed me the "snail lady" creeping through her neighbor's dew-laden yards, plucking snails and sticking them to her arms, chest, cheeks, until, heavily barnacled, she brought them home to mesh crates, fed and cleaned them and sold them to restaurants. I sometimes felt like a girl cruising with her boyfriend, and when Ken drove me to the secluded Upper Reservoir and commented on the quality of light on the water and the ivy-tangled ruins of a ghost winery, I had a sudden ludicrous and sickening image of us embracing, the hard shells of our body armor knocking, our utility belts bristling about us like porcupine quills.

I bought a special purse with a hidden Velcro holster to carry off duty. At first I was terrified that the gun would accidentally discharge; after a while I would have forgotten it was in my purse, except for the ever-present weight. I could shoot pretty well for someone who'd never shot before academy, but I didn't enjoy it because of the noise (it made my heart pound) and an irrepressible fear that the gun would malfunction and blow my hand off. Sometimes my husband reverently polished the grips with a chamois and said, "You're so lucky," but the gun was a burden to me, a burden complicated by the trivial nature of most calls in Saint Amelia — "10-91, hummingbird loose inside La Dolce Vita Cantinetta. RP requests assist." I'd been trained in tactics at the Napa Valley Academy by members of the San Francisco SWAT team, and many of the things they'd stressed — never shake hands, for example; someone could be preparing to use a wrestling maneuver on you — would not make sense in Saint Amelia. I would observe Ken, to my chagrin, routinely standing on curb edges, rocking on the balls of his feet, hands in his pockets, arms folded or clutching a soda, instead of planting his feet in a balanced ninety-degree stance, hands ready.

As I drove the city my second week, I felt — how shall I put it? — sex and death all around me. It might seem overwrought, as though I'm making it up. But that's the way it was from the beginning. Saint Amelia never hires. It's "antigrowth." Then an old-timer had a sudden embolism, and I became L-7. During lunch they showed me a videotape of his funeral, and the dispatcher wept and said, "No one can ever replace Tony, ever." (Folks I met would sometimes say, "So you're the one replacing Tony.") Tony's death had motivated another old-timer to retire, so they were down two officers, but I was the only new hire. Everyone seemed jittery and full of tough posturing because the vineyard pervert was still at large. Graveyard shift had just taken a report from a woman who'd had sex with him because she thought her husband, home early from a business trip, was waking her in the middle of the night, lifting her silk jersey gown, disordering her Frette scalloped bedding that smelled of lavender. And in the course of things, she'd had the incredibly creepy realization that it wasn't her husband. When she screamed and kicked, he vanished out a sliding glass door and into the vineyard. And she couldn't describe him.

"You're lucky," Ken told me. "This is a good opportunity to learn that we don't often have." He had me read sex-crime reports and review sex-crime codes and rape protocol. Then one of the old-timers, Hash, cleared out a vineyard encampment of migrant farm workers, and the cops said that probably takes care of our pervert, just wait, we won't hear anything more about him. The police blotter was either dull — towed car, barking dog, lost bicycle — or mildly comical. Even when violence was involved, the paper took a lighthearted tone, such as the time two men flashed semiauto pistols in a restaurant and grabbed a bottle of wine, not even an expensive one at that. But I could feel him out there still, anonymous and concealed, especially now that I'd seen Saint Amelia's secret landscape.

Something else was making all ten sworn officers — four dispatchers and two half-time community service officers — jumpy. I knew city buildings had recently been rekeyed, and when I asked why we had to bring the shotguns and AR-15s in from the cars during shift change, leaning them against the wall by the briefing table piled with Thanksgiving pies and breads from supportive citizens, Ken told me. Second Sergeant Donald had been fired, had sued and appealed and lost, and had now taken his case to the state supreme court, flexing the atrophied muscles of his law degree (he'd never been able to pass the bar), and they hoped he wasn't disgruntled. Bit by bit, during the first weeks of my employment, I learned the story from the gossipy dispatchers: in the locker room, Second Sergeant Donald had drawn his gun on an officer who was having an affair with Donald's wife. The officer having the affair was called "Little Buddy," though no one called him Little Buddy to his face — they called him Bill. Little Buddy was L-1, the officer with the most years on the force, but he was lazy, so no one liked him. The catalyst, apparently, was not the affair itself, or the divorce that followed, but the divorce settlement that awarded Donald's wife his new van, and the fact that Little Buddy had begun driving Donald's ex-wife's van to work.

That second week, when I started driving, was a comic disaster. I tried to leap out of the car to respond to a choking baby call but couldn't because my seatbelt was still on. I dropped my ticket book in a puddle. Once my awkward side-handle baton pushed up against the electric seat-adjustment buttons, gradually moving my seat forward and wedging my knees against the console while I panicked and pulled off onto the shoulder. There was a brand-new field training manual, thick as a phone book, that they'd had to come up with to comply with new state requirements. The idea was that every day Ken would cover an area of training in the book, discussing it with me as we drove; I would display competence, and both our initials would appear in columns in the book's pages. Ken never opened the book. He made me take it along, and since there was no place to put it, I jammed it on top of the radar gun. Ken was also responsible for filling out a daily performance evaluation, which rated my performance in thirty different categories on a scale of one to ten. These he filled out and turned in to the Chief at the end of most days, often asking me to refresh his memory as to what we'd done. On the day I couldn't get the radar gun out from under the book in time to lock onto a speeder, fumbling with the cord when I should have been in pursuit, he gave me low scores.

Ken, I decided, was a man in the first stages of asking himself what his life meant, and the ensuing frustration had clouded his normally passive nature. When I tried to make conversation by asking him why he'd become a cop, he said, "I ask myself that question a lot lately." His only child, a five-year-old daughter born late in his life, had just finished chemotherapy for a rare form of brain cancer. On day shift Ken mostly liked to go to the middle school, where he taught the DARE curriculum, and talk to the women teachers in the lounge during recess. They would dish up some pineapple crumble for him and ask him about his daughter's progress, all the while mooning over him and hanging on his every word. On his part, he felt their undivided attention was deserved, because his daughter's illness was the most overwhelming feature of his otherwise placid life.

Ken spoke very slowly, and my impulse was to interrupt him, finish his sentences and run curlicues around his thoughts, but he was dogged and would ignore me and complete his sentences until finally I drove silently. In this manner I learned all the details of the chemotherapy drama, and progressing from there, Ken's fixation with retirement, how far off it seemed, possibilities of what he could do, etc., like he was waiting for his real life to begin. Or like he'd been asleep, and his daughter's illness had awakened him. All week long, this is how we operated: I drove and he told stories and I listened and sometimes counseled him or even tried to rally him to inspiration. At the end of the day we returned to the PD, and I sat at the briefing table nibbling pumpkin bread while he struggled with my score sheet. He handed it to me, I scanned the column of low scores, felt the sting of humility, signed the sheet to show that I had read it, and pushed it back across the table to him.

Ken's routines were entrenched. Park by the elementary school and watch for double-parkers, he'd say. Then swing by the Exxon for his jumbo Diet Coke. Drive around a bit. Then head back to the barn so he could empty his bladder. He'd gone to get a sandwich while I ate my lunch at the briefing table one day, and when he returned, he said, "Let's go. I'm driving." A volunteer at the elementary school, he told me, had observed an esteemed male teacher, an acquaintance in fact of Ken's, fondling a boy in the classroom, placing his hand in the boy's pants and holding a couch pillow over his lap while reading a story. This had the potential to cause hysteria. Children with last names you'd recognize if you drink Napa Valley wine would have to be interviewed, lots of children, with powerful parents. After we talked with the principal, Ken drove around the perimeter of town, on quiet cul-de-sacs bordering vineyards. He drummed his hands on the steering wheel. I understood that he was not going to let me drive. "A good thing to do in situations like this is to make a list. Detailed lists of everything you have to do." "Uh-huh," I said. "Let's head back to the barn," he said.

I spent hours at the briefing room table trying to study the map of Saint Amelia; I'd say over and over to myself, "north, east even," which is how the street numbers progress, while Ken made his lists and talked on the phone in the little office off the briefing room, interminably, in his slow, low voice. He had begun conducting interviews with children in the evenings and had confirmed four victims. "The important thing in a case like this, in a city like this," Ken told me, "is not to move too quickly. We don't want to cause a panic. That's the one thing we don't want." And I said, "But we've got a molester in a classroom, who has no reason to suspect anyone knows, who will therefore continue molesting." I heard Ken in the Chief's office, trying to get out of handling the case, and the Chief saying, "You're the only one who can handle it right now, Kenny, we're all feeling the pinch."

I'll admit to you, I'm a daydreamer, and I did not make the best use of my study time because I hated memorizing code. In the office supply closet I found the old police ledgers dating from the turn of the century, written in lead pencil like a lifting fog. I stopped listening in on Ken's phone call — he was talking to someone in the FBI about accessing the teacher's hard drive — and I read them one by one with tunnel vision.

So engrossed was I that I did not glance up at the sound of the back door being unlocked, nor did I see when a stocky, bearded man, former Second Sergeant Donald, walked into the briefing room carrying a shotgun. There were some confused moments then, when the dispatcher, who saw him entering the back door on the video monitor, locked herself in the bathroom and ignored the phone. Ken pleaded with Donald to put the shotgun down, while I watched, holding my place in the ledger with my finger. Finally the Chief, who was away at a meeting, was phoned and the whole thing sorted out. The Chief, a naturalized Swede who blushed a violent crimson every time he spoke — with me, with anyone — had neglected to tell anyone that Donald had won his last appeal and was reinstated, albeit demoted in rank to patrol officer.

"I'm not saying you should have pulled your gun on Donald; that would definitely not have been good," Ken said, "but my point is, you should have reacted somehow. You should have seen him first from where you were sitting." Ken was furious with me. I didn't feel like arguing with him, saying how highway patrol guys and even plain-clothed detectives from the Sheriff's department came in the back door all the time to eat their meals or stop off and write paper, and no one ever explained or introduced themselves to me. I felt that the quickest way out of this lecture was silence, compliance. "You just sat there! Reading, or whatever," Ken said. This observation renewed his indignation. Shortly afterward, I was moved to swing shift to drive with Jason, due to the intensive nature of Ken's case.

This is when it started, I think, when it was decided that I did not *see*, that I lacked the faculties of a trained observer. That my competence as a police officer was fatally flawed by an inability to process details of the concrete, physical world around me, and that only a plan to ensure that I remarked on every car parked in a red or blue zone, every expired reg tab, every loud muffler or tinted windshield, could potentially redeem me.

Jason, or Baby Cop, as he was known, looked like he was twelve years old. His wife had just given birth to their first child, and he handed out Hershey bars with customized wrappers that said, "Here-she-is," giving me extras "to keep my blood sugar up." It was his first time as a field training officer, and he wanted me to like him. "Ken tells me you really need to work on your observation skills," he said. "What we'll do — maybe later — is work on some observation techniques," he said. "I'll name an object, and you call out when you see it," he said. "For example, can you tell me right now where this is: a giant tomato?"

"Are you serious?" I said, mildly offended. "That's Pizzeria Pomodoro."

"Good, very good," he said, like I'd just performed a trick surprisingly well. "Can you give me the address where there's a lawn jockey?" he said, upping the ante.

"No clue," I said. Oh, he was pleased to have stumped me. He beamed.

"We'll work on it some more later. Don't worry about it. It'll come."

Jason told me I really should get the brass snaps changed out on my belt so that all the snaps were uniformly silver, as directed in the dress code. Also, I might want to invest in a matching pen-and-pencil set like his, to wear in my pocket. He recommended using a mechanical pencil. Pencil, Ken might have neglected to tell me, as traffic was not his thing, was necessary for writing comments on the back of tickets. He asked to see my ticket book. "This is kind of a mess," he said. "Let's see if we can fix this." He showed me how he'd arranged his ticket book, where he'd taped his cheat sheet and kept his Qwik-Codes and his crayon for marking tires. After I promised to change my snaps all to silver, buy a pen-and-pencil set, and reform my ticket book, Jason seemed to relax. "It's a shame Tony can't be here to train you," he said, referring to the deceased who'd made my hiring possible. Tony had been the senior training officer.

That first swing shift I put on my rain suit and rubber boots, checked my radio, readied the car, scanned the police log, and waited to go. I sat at the briefing table clutching my FTO manual for an hour before I realized that the Chief and Sergeant were both away, and therefore the pace would be slower. My heart sank as the sun disappeared, as surely as any lost hiker's. I had wanted to drive during the precious remaining hours of daylight, to acclimatize my eyes before plunging into the wet darkness. Jason talked three hours with Rolando, who was halfheartedly trying to catch up on reports at the computer. Rolando and Jason were the newest hires, and their favorite topic, when they were alone, was what the depart-

ment would be like when all the old-timers retired. When Rolando
and Jason were not talking about the future of the department,
they talked about women. Jason always initiated these conversations and gradually drew Rolando in. Once Rolando actually sali-
vated and smacked his lips as he described an Italian girlfriend of
his who had "the most gorgeous black peach fuzz" all over her arms
and legs — like a connoisseur describing a stinky cheese or a wine
made from mummified grapes.

My best work as a police officer always involved investigations or
writing reports, both of which I could do independently and efficiently, unlike traffic stops. Which means I did not fit the profile
of the average officer, I inverted it. For example, after we'd arrested Wexler for felony possession of firearms, I followed my gut
and found it was an invalid arrest, then let the Chief and Deputy
DA know so they could prepare for his lawsuit. Wexler was another
pervert, which had me thinking Saint Amelia had more than her
share of perverts per capita. I remember an old priest who moved
from Chicago to the Napa Valley telling me once that he believed
the low crime rate must be directly related to the extreme physical
beauty of the place. I wonder now if the beauty tempts perversion,
like Blake's "Sick Rose."

Wexler, who frequented the Saint Amelia library to view Internet
porn, had been kicked out one day for masturbating while watching a high school girl read. Because the girl had been totally un-
aware and the librarians hadn't actually seen what he was doing under his magazine, there was no victim and technically no crime.
Wexler made a scene at the library, then at his psychologist's office,
and finally in the PD lobby, where he wanted to file a complaint
against "those whore-librarians." When I reported for swing shift, I
found the Chief, dispatcher, CSO, and day-shift sergeant crowded
behind the lobby door, peering through the dispatch window at
Wexler talking to Donald in the lobby. They were quietly and glee-
fully laughing at Wexler, whom they likened to a werewolf, because
of his bushy hair and beard, and a unicorn, because of a large, bul-
bous growth on top of his head. "Look," they told me, "it's like a
second head."

While we were gawking at Wexler, who reeked so alarmingly of
garlic that the scent had infiltrated the ballistic glass that separated

us from him, his psychologist called and said she felt afraid for her safety. Wexler had offered to "show her what he'd done at the library," and when he began unzipping his pants (he had impulsivity issues), she told him to leave. Wexler left her office enraged, twice ousted by women in one day, and she knew he owned a gun or possibly guns.

The dispatcher ran him for rap sheets and gun licenses, and when she found he'd been convicted of felony battery against a police officer in another state ten years before, the Chief said, "Bingo" and claimed the arrest as mine. Everyone wanted to know when the arrest would take place, if I was nervous, seeing as it would be a rite of passage: my first felony arrest. A jolt of testosterone had just affected everyone in the room but me. I felt no aggression toward this disheveled man with his girlish wrists; I felt nausea, at the unpleasant thought of having to touch him. I was also conscious that watching a six-foot brunette cuff and search a petite perverted freak might appeal to the other officers as something interesting to watch.

By eight P.M. we had a signed search warrant for Wexler's third-story apartment over a garage in a gated Seventh-day Adventist compound outside Saint Amelia. Jason, with whom I normally drove, was on his days off, and Sergeant Tom, with whom I drove on Jason's days off, was tied up with a traffic collision. So the group consisted of the Chief (whose call-sign was A-1, like the steak sauce), Donald (who felt he'd established a good rapport with Wexler), a deputy (since it was county jurisdiction), and me. We learned from Wexler's landlord that he was away at a Sex Addicts Anonymous meeting and would probably be home at nine-thirty or ten, which was great because we could get him separate from his guns, and the plan was to wait. I rode with Donald, who'd scouted the place, which was difficult to find at night. I noticed that Donald's hands trembled visibly, and I wondered if he was on medication or just especially nervous.

It was dark with our headlights off, and I remember looking up at the stars while we waited for Wexler. The only sound was the landlord's two rottweilers barking behind the gate. Donald had the idea that he and I should get Wexler's landlord to let us into the apartment to observe the layout and scan for weapons, which I was not happy about, legally and because it meant negotiating the rottweilers, but we did it anyway. Wexler's landlord doubtfully watched us as we checked drawers and closets for weapons. "He's a sweet man," the landlord said. "He wouldn't harm a fly."

It was like looking at a physical manifestation of Wexler's crazy yet ordered mind. In the entry room were three bare cots, but Wexler slept on the floor in the second room, on a pillow made of plastic grocery bags, hundreds of them stuffed one inside another. On his kitchen counter were myriad plastic bags of lentils and dried beans secured with rubber bands, carefully spaced in rows. And dominating the room was a huge, walk-in gun safe, locked. We went back to the cars, and everyone was burning to know, speculating on what might be in that safe — not only what weapons but what dark evidence of perversion. Videotapes, maybe. At ten-thirty we left, as our warrant was not endorsed for night service.

The next day I reported early for my shift. Jason and Donald and the deputy and I were to attempt the arrest during daylight. Wexler's landlord said he was home, so the plan was for the landlord to call Wexler when we arrived and get him to come down on some pretense. But when the time came, Wexler's phone rang and rang. "Maybe he's got it unplugged," the landlord said. "His car's here." I looked up that narrow flight of stairs to Wexler's third-story apartment, and then I followed Jason, who was behind Donald, single file up those stairs. Donald drew his gun and held it behind his leg, and then Jason did, and I looked behind me at the deputy, who had his drawn, and I drew mine and said, "Oh, I guess we're taking our guns out now," realizing as I said it how inappropriate it sounded.

"I find it interesting that I'm not sexually aroused by you because you are so much larger than me." This is what Wexler said when I cuffed him. He had been studying calculus when Donald knocked, and he answered the door amicably enough that Donald reholstered his gun and stepped inside. Donald then presented the search warrant, and, while I cuffed Wexler as a safety measure, he asked for the combination to the gun safe. You can imagine the suspense when the heavy door finally swung open. Everyone was almost disappointed to find it only contained two pistols and a shotgun, each loaded and with a round in the chamber, cocked and locked, and 105 rounds, including six loaded magazines of .45

hollow-point ammunition. "Search him now," Jason said, and then all eyes were on my searching technique.

Wexler wouldn't shut up. He kept saying, "This isn't right." I can't tell you the disgust I felt touching him, pinching and twisting his thin, grayed dress shirt, undoing his belt ("My trousers will fall to my knees," he warned me, and they almost did), grasping his bony legs, inhaling the reek of someone who rarely bathed, even patting at his snarled hair. Sweat was sheeting off my forehead as I untied his shoes from behind him. I kept telling myself, be slow, be methodical, don't miss anything, because I'd once missed a razor blade tucked under a belt during a practice search in academy. I told myself, pretend they're not here watching you, because the three cops were hovering over me, like they could scarcely keep from touching Wexler themselves. "What would you do if I reached over and brushed against your thigh? I could, you know," he said. Calmly, I said, "If you do that, I'll be forced to use a compliance technique and take you to the ground for your safety and mine." Wexler replied that he might enjoy it (that old cliché), and suddenly everyone in the room was talking, drowning out my voice. They were all unbearable and needed to fight or run or take a cold shower.

On the night of Wexler's arrest, Jason wouldn't let me eat dinner because he was so stressed about boxing and labeling all the evidence we had collected. I would have swept it all into one big box, labeled it "Wexler," evidence-taped it, and been done with it because we still had to take Wexler to the county facility in Napa. But Jason made me find just the right shape box for each item. I had to seal each box with evidence tape and sign my initials and the date, and he'd say, "Now wait. Don't touch anything! Let the ink dry." Then he'd turn around and get flustered and say, "Where did my sheet of paper go?" At the end of the night we were exhausted, and Jason couldn't find the small rechargeable flashlight that was always in our car. He swore at the thought of Hash finding out he'd misplaced gear, the teasing he'd have to endure. I told him not to be such a baby; anyway he could always blame it on me.

"Tell me something. How'd it go tonight? In your estimation."

"Well, you were there. I mean, aside from our initial approach plan not working, things went smoothly."

"How about tactically?" I said I hadn't expected Donald to suddenly head up the stairs without any discussion. "I am not happy with Donald," he said. Then he asked me if he'd heard correctly, had I said, "Oh, I guess we're taking our guns out now," as we approached? "We'll do your evaluation tomorrow," he said. "I just want you to think about something: What would you have done if I'd been shot? What if I lay on the stairs bleeding to death? Because I'm a father now."

The next day I got on the phone to the out-of-state PD that had arrested Wexler ten years earlier. I decided not to say anything to Jason about my concern that the arrest might be invalid because he always said, "If their lips are moving, they're lying." I called the correctional center where Wexler had served time, the prosecutor's office, the superior court clerk, and parole board and requested the case file, probation presentence report, and prosecutor's post-conviction sentence statement. Over the next couple nights I received faxes and learned that his conviction had been reversed and remanded for a new trial and that the court had overturned the conviction and released him; Wexler's rap sheet had never been amended to show this. Legally he was entitled to own guns. I wrote a report supplement and attached a memo to the Chief when Jason invited the ambulance crew over for pizza and eggnog. I included a copy of a court-ordered psychiatric evaluation that described Wexler as having latent paranoid schizophrenia with probability of becoming actively psychotic, so that we could work on a strategy for keeping his guns legally. If Jason had asked what I was working on, I'd have shown him. But Jason was flirting with the female EMT, showing her how his numchucks worked and, at one point, chasing her around the briefing table and putting a piece of apple pie down her blouse.

The Chief asked to speak with me in his office. Jason sat next to me. The door was open. I'd always had reason to think the Chief liked me because once or twice when he'd seen me working at the computer he'd said, "How's our future sergeant?" And when he'd hired me, he'd sounded almost apologetic about the department, as if he wanted to give me a chance to reconsider. But now he looked like someone who has been deeply disillusioned. He asked me a rapid series of questions that seemed insane in their lack of context.

"What do you like best about this job?"

"The fact that you never know what's going to happen next." I watched him turn rose-geranium pink.

"Uh-huh. And how does your husband feel about you working Christmas day?"

"He's very supportive." The pink deepened a notch.

"How would you feel if you found a dead body?"

"Horrible, I guess."

"How 'bout if I arrange for you to view an autopsy?"

"That would be great," I said. "I'd appreciate it."

"Wrong choice of words," he said dryly. "But we'll see what we can do. I'll contact the coroner and request something unholy, if possible. We may have to be patient." I was confused. Was seeing a dead body supposed to have some effect on my marriage?

The Chief began talking about the creeping darkness that invades the life of an officer, what with shift work, holidays spent away from family (Jason, for example, would miss his daughter's first Christmas), and so often observing only the negative side of human nature. "Everyone here really likes you," he said. "We don't want you to change." He paused and looked at me like he wanted a response, a signal as to how to proceed, that I was not giving him. He had the advantage, I thought, of knowing the contents of my in-depth psych profile; I wished I could have read it so I'd know which buttons he thought he was pushing. The Chief held out my performance evaluation from the night I'd arrested Wexler. When I'd searched Wexler, I'd had my gun side toward him for two minutes — Jason had counted them — when Wexler, though cuffed, could possibly have reached the gun. They were going to give me a remedial mark in my evaluation. I would have to watch a video on officer safety and then demonstrate competent searching techniques.

"Now having said that, I read your supplement on Wexler. You're working at a seasoned investigator's level in some respects. But what good is that if you don't nail your traffic stops?" He asked me why I still let potential stops pass by. Was I afraid of confrontation? Working swing shift in the nontourist season, there were not a lot of incidents, and it was true, I did sometimes throw them back, like too-small fish. "Is there anything we can do better on our end?" the Chief said, in a clipped manner, like he was wrapping things up and expected me to say no, and thanks for asking. I mentioned that no one had yet cracked my field training manual open, that

I'd never been quizzed and that I wasn't following any type of formalized training program, as were trainees I knew working in Napa, Fairfield, West Sacramento, Vallejo, Antioch, and Richmond. "We'll fix that," Chief said.

On Christmas day Sergeant Tom told me I had a rare opportunity. They'd never had a police sketch artist come in before, and he was sure I could benefit from watching because the drawing process is all about paying attention to detail. A red-headed woman in a silk dress was swiveling in her chair and licking her coffee spoon. She didn't seem like a victim. She was laughing and telling the artist, a cop from the Bay Area, how she was fixing lobster ravioli for Christmas dinner. The woman, staying in a guesthouse bordering a vineyard, woke in the night and saw a man at the foot of her bed. She yelled and chased him outside into the vineyard, clutching a high-heeled pump, which she threw at him.

"That was a stupid thing to do," the artist told her. "What would you have done if you caught him?"

"I don't know. I wasn't thinking that far ahead. I was just pissed off. I think I hit him with my shoe!"

I could see this woman being referred to as "spunky" or "a real spitfire" and felt mildly jealous. The artist had sketched a face shape and was now asking the woman to choose eyes from a book of all possible eye shapes. The woman became frustrated that she'd never find the right eyes and wanted to take a smoking break, then suddenly said, "These!" Gradually, a face emerged with long hair, high cheekbones, almond eyes. A good-looking face. "No, no, I can't remember," the woman said, looking depressed for the first time. "Look, tell me what's wrong and we'll fix it," the artist said.

I felt a constant slow, fateful pressure after that day and sometimes imagined that I was a splinter being extruded from a finger. I'd think of George Orwell's essay about shooting an elephant and how he called his police career an "unsuitable profession." Every impulse in my personality seemed in conflict with the extroverted, grounded, aggressive, sensory nature of a cop. Still I did not relent, though it occurred to me that I had become like someone who enjoys watching pigeons get fed — oh, lovely, lovely, all those crumbs — so circumscribed had the pleasures in my life become. When skinny, acne-scarred cadets, awkward in suit and tie, interviewed for the remaining trainee position, they were labeled "too aggressive," "won't stay long-term," "not enough life experience," until a bit of hope would rekindle in me that I was, after all, an adequate fit.

In January shifts rotated, and the way they described graves to me was this: Nothing happens. But if something does, it's more likely to be dangerous. My life was as silent and dark as the surface of the moon. No matter how much I slept, nights I was slow, leaden, and ill, a false vampire working against my own vigorous diurnal metabolism. All I wanted in the world was to sleep, which was dangerous. But when I drove home in the mornings, in the lightening sky, I would experience a strange kind of euphoria I don't understand, a kind of chemical surge in my blood, a prickling warmth and expansiveness, like the first chills of fever. I drove with my windows open, and the air was so sweet it was like breathing deep into a carnation. I wanted to scream things into the wind, "I love my husband," or crazy things, "I will live forever." At home, I'd fix us eggs, coffee for him, sometimes a martini for me, then I'd sleep, and dream. I ran through the streets of Saint Amelia into the moonlit vineyards, and I felt no pain or tiredness, no burning lungs or side stitches, but a kind of ecstasy of ever-growing strength, as if I could run forever. Sometimes I'd fly over the rooftops of Saint Amelia, and all the roofs of the houses would gently loosen and float away, so that I could observe the floor plans and even fly in for close-ups of the sleeping citizens.

This is how I thought of graveyards: one hundred miles, four miles square. Because I'd put one hundred miles on the car in one night, driving the same streets over and over again, in four square miles of city. Some officers, I learned, would nap most of the night, then take the car out on a large loop into county territory, so when they recorded the odometer at shift end, it would look like they'd been out patrolling. The boundaries of the city elicited frisson, but once when I wanted to take a run down Beaujolais, just out of bounds, not to poach or anything, just for a change of scenery, my training officer told me I didn't know enough details about Saint Amelia yet. I needed to go deeper, he said — even though I knew every alleyway, dead end, greenbelt, vineyard perimeter. The intimacy of patrolling, committing to memory each nuance of that highly cultivated and celebrated bit of land, seemed to me similar to the intimacy of love, with one difference: I was motivated by desire to know the geography of my husband's body, but I lacked such a motive for Saint Amelia. Ken had wrapped his investigation and moved to graveyard shift, and he asked me what kind of lock the alley door of Rita's Margaritas had. I didn't know, so we drove down the alley. "Here," he said, "turn off your alley light. See the bar lock? Look for that silhouette, and you'll know it's locked." Once or twice in ten years he'd had to wake Rita because whoever had closed had forgotten to lock up. Later that night he said, "Do you want to see something wonderful? Turn the spotlight on." I turned it on, and I didn't see anything wonderful. "Don't you see?" It was a train car in someone's backyard; chickens nested in it. Sometimes I caught Ken looking at me like someone helplessly watching a drowning woman. But how could I possibly fail — or succeed for that matter — when nothing ever happened?

I dreaded the nights when I had to drive with Sergeant Tom, which was half of the time. The first time I ever drove with him he said, "I hate fuckin' winemakers. They're all a bunch of fuckin' pricks." As a rule I adopted a tone with him that was light and full of laughter, as if everything he said was funny, and sometimes it worked and he ended up laughing despite himself. Tom's conversation was dominated by rounds, slugs, bullets, powder, deer tags, bear tags, payload, and megabytes. Eventually, nightly, he would work himself into a barely controlled rage because of the stupidity of everyone — out — there — all — of — them — fucking — idiots! The only thing we had in common was that we both liked listening to Art Bell's radio program about alien encounters from eleven to two A.M. Though it occurred to me that we were exactly the kind of nameless, faceless, expendable beat cops, driving in the middle of the night, who always find the alien ship, decide to investigate alone and are hideously crushed or exploded within the first fifteen minutes of a movie.

It is to Tom that I ascribe the ultimate outcome of my field training at Saint Amelia because Tom had rank, and he gradually decided that my time would best be spent not in patrolling the city but in learning how to pick Master Lock padlocks, cutting up pieces of rebar with giant wire cutters, fuming fingerprints with Krazy Glue, fiddling with a narcotics analysis kit, checking out his form-making software, listening to various versions of "Stairway to

Heaven" in his MIDI file collection — anything that kept me sitting at the PD briefing table or close by, such as washing the patrol car or playing with the night-vision gear in the broom closet we called our "armory." Because mind games are so much a part of police culture and training, beginning with tear-you-down-build-you-up-again academy, it was difficult for me to know whether Tom had accepted me into the lazy heart of things as one of them or cut me off. I was soon to start the shadow phase of my training, where I'd be solo in a car and a training officer would shadow me on calls. My evaluation scores were average, above average in certain areas (neatness and appearance), though they'd dipped lately, accompanied by absurd comments. "Officer hits road obstacles," for example. I hadn't hit anything, so I asked Tom what he meant. "One thing about you that really pisses me off," he said, "is your driving. You run right through potholes and over speed bumps. And you're anal about using your blinker and coming to a complete stop at stop signs. Who do you think is going to notice at three A.M. ?" But when I rolled through stops, he deducted points for that.

My one chance to escape the PD came at two A.M., when the two bars on Main Street closed. Tom liked to watch the bar patrons leave and have me try for deuces, then take a walk down Main Street and check all the business doors, which kept him from feeling too sleepy. At three A.M., we'd always head back to the PD for lunch (he always ate spaghetti or fried chicken and tapioca pudding), then read the morning papers when they were delivered. When Rolando was working, he and Tom would discuss impending salary negotiations between the Police Officers Association and the city. Occasionally they'd take these conversations into the sergeants' office and close the door. There were new educational requirements. The Chief wanted Tom, who had an AA in criminal justice from the local junior college, to go back to school for a BA. When we first met, Tom asked if it was true that I had an MA in English, and after that he would make me drive to quiet, dark places where wildlife crept in the brush, eyes glittering like moonstones, and quiz me on Vehicle Code, most of which he'd memorized, unlike the other officers, who used cheat sheets, until finally he determined that my memory was subpar. I always felt we were doing something slightly sordid, our knees almost touching, the dome light glinting off his pomaded hair and thick glasses, tinted a subtle yellow like that elementary school glue, mucilage.

One morning about two-thirty, I was driving along cul-de-sacs and side streets that border vineyards because it had been raining, and Tom didn't want to walk downtown. If I'd been alone, I might have closed my eyes for a moment under the moonlight, but I was not alone, Sergeant Tom was riding with me. It was like driving with someone who has Tourette's syndrome. Every pothole or speed bump elicited, "Fuck! Damn! Shit! Holy Mother of God!" That's why I got the idea to go down a certain unpaved private vineyard lane we almost never patrolled, because it was the one place I really didn't want to go with Tom beside me.

It was a stealthy maneuver on my part. I drove around the tiny industrial park, past the lumberyard and day-care center, and then made a hard right into the vineyards. I had been down this lane once before with Ken on an alarm call. At the end of the lane, you'd never believe it, was the most gorgeous Italianate mansion, owned by a banking family whose last name is on credit cards. That night I was possessed; I persisted in driving down the long, muddy lane, spraying gravel into the air and nearly stranding the car in the vines, waking dogs in neighboring parcels. I turned a bend, and my headlights flashed off the eyes of a huge, dead buck in the middle of the road, its antlers glistening white. "Holy shit," Tom said, jumping out the passenger's door before I'd come to a complete stop. "It's fresh. I'm calling my dad," he said, suddenly in a golden mood. "Gonna get me some venison sausage."

He told me to pop the trunk and get disposable gloves out, and I helped him drag the carcass to the side of the road. Tom got back in the car. "Turn around," he said. "It's lunchtime. I'm gonna eat and then wake up old Dad."

"What do you think killed it?" I asked, putting the car in drive.

"Some vehicle. Who the hell cares. It's good to go." He clucked like a peahen and fidgeted in his seat with pleasure. The road was too narrow to make a U-turn, so I continued on down the lane half a mile, planning to turn in the gravel half-circle in front of the mansion. But before I turned, my headlights glanced off the windows of a parked car in just such a way that I had the impression someone might be sleeping inside. The lane went on for a space past the mansion and its drive and then abruptly ended. The car was parked there, as if the driver had run out of road and didn't know what to do. "Lovers' lane?" I said.

I pulled in behind the car, a pale blue '70s station wagon with a blanket hung inside the rear window.

"What are you doing?" Tom asked irritably.

"I think someone might be sleeping inside; I'm going to run a 28."

"Leave it for day shift; it's probably a vineyard worker. I'm hungry."

"Just let me check something," I said. I called the plate in to dispatch, and she told me to hang on, the terminal was down.

"Fuck it, let's go," Tom said.

"Just a second," I said. I put the car in park, took off my seatbelt, got out, flipped on my portable radio, and grabbed my light. I gave dispatch my location, and when Rolando asked over the radio if I wanted backup, I said yes. I approached the rear on the driver's side and held my light up to windows opaque with moisture. I wasn't sure what I was seeing; dim colors inside seemed to move, like fish in a dirty aquarium. The hood was damaged and streaked with blood. My heart was pounding loudly enough to wake a sleeping man; my breathing became shallow, and I forced myself to take deep, controlled breaths; my vision narrowed to a small point in front of me. I was shivering violently, wiping at my dripping nose with my icy fingers. I moved away from the door in a bladed stance and tapped on the rear window with the light in my left hand, keeping my right hand ready.

Tom was standing off to the side of the patrol car in the shadows, his arms crossed, looking up at the sky as if asking God to help him bear the burden of riding with me. He had no idea who was in that car; if he had, he sure as hell wouldn't have let me handle things. I don't think he understood until much later, after the dispatcher had come back on the radio and the man had bolted into the vineyards, after I'd chased and tackled him and pinned him to the vineyard floor in a kind of stasis where he tried to unsnap my holster but was unable to, and I tried to get him into a carotid but was unable to. Tom cuffed him, and we jerked him to his feet, and Tom said, "Goddamnit! Goddamnit! Fuck! Fuck! Fuck!" at all of blighted creation. I was embarrassed for him; a law enforcement officer should have more self-control, I thought. I realized that he was furious not that the suspect had run into the vineyard, or that his uniform was muddy, but that I'd changed his plans. It hit me as ludicrous that he'd be so furious about missing his lunch or losing out on venison when it seemed likely we'd caught our vineyard rapist. "I'm driving," he yelled. "Rolando's doing the CHP 180 form." He said nothing to me during the drive, and when we arrived at the PD, he said, "Go eat and read the papers." He was calmer then, which filled me with dread.

At five A.M., the Chief walked in the back door, wearing jeans. The Chief never came in before seven. He and Tom went into the locker room, and when they came out again, the Chief was in full uniform. Chief drummed his fingers on the kitchen counter while his coffee brewed. He poured it slowly into a cup and walked into the briefing room, where I sat, trying to conceal the fact that I was reading the paper. "Got a minute?" Tom followed us into the Chief's office and closed the door. Perhaps we didn't have the vineyard rapist in custody after all.

Tom wouldn't look at me. His skin seemed fluorescent and waxen beside the Chief's beet-colored face.

"Have you agreed with your daily evaluation scores, for the most part?" the Chief asked.

"I don't think I'm in a position to agree or disagree," I said.

"That being the case . . ." The Chief handed me a crisp letter of termination for failure to meet the standards of the field training program. "We think you are not a confrontational person, and that's what this job's about," the Chief said. They both flinched as I hit the magazine release on my gun and then struggled to eject the round jammed in the chamber. I fumbled with it and cleared it. Had they expected me to put my loaded gun on the desk, alongside the badge?

I managed to shake hands with them both and say something completely untrue and absurdly pleasant, which perhaps proved the Chief's point. If I was the kind of trainee who ticked days off the calendar, I would have known that the date was exactly three months from the day I'd been hired, the day when I should have gone solo. We never mentioned the morning's events, never discussed the fact that I'd caught the vineyard rapist. I wonder now how long my termination had been planned. Weeks, I suppose. So that once the decision had been made, last-minute change would seem too perplexing, too embarrassing, to be feasible.

"Don't be a stranger" was the last thing Tom said.

*

For a long time I couldn't drive into the city limits of Saint Amelia without feeling panicked. This was difficult because the events of my husband's growing social calendar — tastings, dinners — were often in or around Saint Amelia. When I slept I dreamed about nameless, faceless groups of men rejecting me, or wounded men with broken backs begging me for help. I took a consulting job in San Francisco and told myself I would make more money in six months than the Chief made in a year, as if that mattered. And I tried to find solace by becoming something unattainable to the men I'd driven with — a very beautiful woman. So my nails always glistened, I painted my eyelids like a chanteuse. *Men cluster to me, like moths around a flame. And if their wings burn, I know I'm not to blame,* I'd sing along with Marlene Dietrich. I'd tuck gardenias behind my ears. But I still didn't — though I no longer needed to worry about being in a ground fight — wear earrings or necklaces or rings.

One Saturday night, about five months after my dismissal, we were invited to a party in the middle of a vineyard just south of Saint Amelia. An old couple from Texas who'd made a small fortune in forklift propane had bought the vineyard for a retirement hobby, and in a bid for authenticity they'd hired my husband's boss as consultant winemaker. Which means my husband made their wine. The party was to celebrate bottling their sauvignon blanc and merlot, and they'd invited all their kin, children and grandchildren and great-grandchildren, to help with the bottling. I didn't know anyone, and — though I was relieved that no one would ask me about the progress of my law enforcement career, something that had been a sort of *amuse-gueule* at certain dinner parties — I wanted to leave immediately. A small area was clear of vines and had been sprinkled with sawdust, tables set up and strung with lights shaped like chili peppers, campfires built, and barbecues lit. There was a table full of hard liquor, and the old Texans started off drinking glasses of gin or whiskey and Coke. One of the sons up from Los Angeles, who was asking my husband about wine-making, said, "Isn't it ironic that the *locals* drink whiskey, not wine?" and my husband, who was drinking a beer, caught my eye, and we smiled, because these folks were so obviously *not*.

We ate steaks on round tables, under a honey-colored harvest moon, which seemed out of place since it was spring. I'd made a friend at dinner, a frosted-blond daughter-in-law from Pasadena.

(We met when I asked her where the restroom was, seeing as we were in the middle of the vineyard. She said someone had stolen the vineyard workers' portable toilet — all the women were very upset — but she had Kleenex if I needed to go out into the vineyard.) I'd been cutting my sauvignon blanc with water all night, with an eye to leaving. Oh, she was just beginning. Wait till midnight, she said. About this time, several women decided to make a group trek into the vineyards to urinate. I know this sounds very strange, but you have to understand, no one wanted to go out there alone. There was some talk first about whether anyone was sober enough to drive into town to use the hotel facilities. I was sure we'd be thrown out — the big drunken group of us — if we tried. So into the vineyards we went. I caught my husband's eye on the way and thought how he'd laugh if he guessed what we were doing. I could hear him talking permits and licenses with men anxious to get their hands on the little 150-case parental wine hobby and make it grow, men salivating over the idea of owning a Napa Valley winery.

We staggered over dirt clods, under the preternatural moon. "What's this?" one of the women asked me, as if I would know by the leaf whether we were walking through merlot or cabernet or sauvignon blanc. Some of the women were making educated guesses, like "this must be merlot, the leaf is larger than the palm of my hand." I began to feel uneasy. There I was in the middle of a starlit vineyard on a cold spring night — it's funny when I think of it now — increasingly tense, irritated, sober. The women were all very drunk and giddy, holding children, tripping over the uneven soil and into each other, laughing, losing their shoes, as we walked farther from the glowing lights, Frank Sinatra's crooning, farther into the cold, green vines. I was walking with a balanced stance, my hands at a ready position, pivoting my head from side to side, forcing myself to see — what? (I thought of Ken saying, "Throw your vision out there.") There wasn't anything in the darkness. Feeling that some malignant spirit was laughing and watching for the moment we'd all drop our pants or lift our skirts and flash the vines.

RUSSELL BANKS

Lobster Night

FROM *Esquire*

STACY DIDN'T MEAN to tell Noonan that when she was seventeen she was struck by lightning. She rarely told anyone, and never a man she was attracted to or hoped soon to be sleeping with. Always, at the last second, an alarm in the center of her brain went off, and she changed the subject, asked a question like, "How's your wife?" or "You ready for another?" She was a summertime bartender at Noonan's, a sprawling log building with the main entrance and kitchen door facing the road and three large plate-glass dining room windows in back and a wide redwood deck cantilevered above the yard for taking in the great sunset views of the Adirondack Mountains. The sign said, NOONAN'S FAMILY RESTAURANT, but in fact it was a roadhouse, a bar that — except in ski season and on summer weekends when drive-by tourists with kids mistakenly pulled in for lunch or supper — catered mostly to heavy drinkers from the several nearby hamlets.

The night that Stacy told Noonan about the lightning was also the night she shot and killed him. She had rented an A-frame at off-season rates in one of the hamlets and was working for Noonan only till the winter snows blew in from Quebec and Ontario. From May to November, she usually waited tables or tended bar in one or another of the area restaurants, and the rest of the year she taught alpine skiing at Whiteface Mountain. That was her real job, her profession. Stacy had the healthy, ash-blond good looks of a poster girl for women's Nordic sports: tall, broad shouldered, flat muscled, with a square jaw and high cheekbones. But despite appearances, she viewed herself as a plain-faced twenty-eight-year-old ex-

athlete, with the emphasis on *ex*. Eight years ago, she was captain of
the nationally ranked St. Regis University downhill ski team, only a
sophomore and already a star. Then in the eastern regionals she
pushed her luck, took a spectacular, cartwheeling spill in the giant
slalom, and shattered her left thigh. The video of her fall was still
being shown at the front of the sports segment on the evening news
from Plattsburgh.

A year of physical therapy and she returned to college and the
slopes, but she'd lost her fearlessness and, with it, her interest in
college, and dropped out before fall break. Her parents had long
since swapped their house for an RV and retired to a semiper-
manent campground outside Phoenix; her three older brothers
had drifted downstate to Albany for work in construction; but Stacy
came back to where she'd grown up. She had friends from high
school there, mostly women, who still thought of her as a star:
"Stace was headed for the Olympics, y'know," they told strangers.
Over time, she lived briefly and serially with three local men in
their early thirties, men she called losers even when she was living
with them — slow-talking guys with beards and ponytails, rusted-
out pickup trucks, and large dogs with bandannas tied around
their necks. Otherwise and most of the time, she lived alone.

Stacy had never tended bar for Noonan before this, and the
place was a little rougher than she was used to. But she was experi-
enced and had cultivated a set of open-faced, wiseguy ways and a
laid-back manner that protected her from her male customers' pre-
sumptions. Which, in spite of her ways and manner, she needed:
She was a shy, north-country girl who, when it came to personal
matters, volunteered very little about herself, not because she had
secrets but because there was so much about herself that she did
not yet understand. She did understand, however, that the last
thing she wanted or needed was a love affair with a man like
Noonan — married, twenty years older than she, and her boss. She
was seriously attracted to him, though. And not just sexually. Which
was why she got caught off guard.

It was late August, a Thursday, the afternoon of Lobster Night. The
place was empty, and she and Noonan were standing hip to hip behind the bar, studying the lobster tank. Back in June, Noonan, who
did all the cooking himself, had decided that he could attract a

better class of clientele and simplify the menu at the same time if, during the week, he offered nightly specials, which he advertised on a chalkboard hung from the FAMILY RESTAURANT sign outside. Monday became Mexican Night, with dollar margaritas and all the rice and refried beans you could eat. Tuesday was Liver 'n' Onions Night. Wednesday was Fresh Local Corn Night, although until mid-August, the corn came not from Adirondack gardens but from southern New Jersey and Pennsylvania by way of the Grand Union supermarket in Lake Placid. And Thursday — when local folks rarely ate out and therefore needed something more than merely special — was designated Lobster Night. Weekends, he figured, took care of themselves.

Noonan had set his teenage son's unused tropical fish tank at the end of the bar, filled it with tap water, and arranged with the Albany wholesaler to stock the tank on his Monday runs to Lake Placid with a dozen live lobsters. All week, the lobsters rose and sank in the cloudy tank like dark thoughts. Usually, by Tuesday afternoon, the regulars at the bar had given the lobsters names like Marsh and Redeye and Honest Abe, after local drinking, hunting, and bar-brawling legends, and had handicapped the order of their execution. In the villages around, Thursday quickly became everyone's favorite night for eating out, and soon Noonan was doubling his weekly order, jamming the fish tank and making Lobster Night an almost merciful event for the poor crowded creatures.

"You ought to either get a bigger tank or else just don't buy so many of them," Stacy said.

Noonan laughed. "Stace," he said. "Compared to the cardboard boxes these guys've been in, the fish tank is lobster heaven. Four days of swimmin' in this, they're free-range, practically." He draped a heavy hand across her shoulder and drummed her collarbone with a fingertip. "They don't know the difference, anyhow. They're dumber than fish, y'know."

"You don't know what they feel or don't feel. Maybe they spend the last few days before they die flipping out from being so confined. I sure would."

"Yeah, well, I don't go there, Stace. Trying to figure what lobsters feel, that's the road to vegetarianism. The road to vegansville."

She smiled at that. Like most of the Adirondack men she knew, Noonan was a dedicated, lifelong hunter — mainly of deer, but

also of game birds and rabbits, which he fed to his family and sometimes put on the restaurant menu as well. He also shot and trapped
animals he didn't eat — foxes, coyotes, lynxes, even bears — and
sold their pelts. Normally, this would disgust Stacy or at least seriously test her acceptance of Noonan's character. She wasn't noticeably softhearted or sentimental when it came to animals, but shooting and trapping creatures you didn't intend to eat made no sense
to her. She was sure it was cruel and was almost ready to say it was
sadistic.

In Noonan, though, it oddly attracted her, this cruelty. He was a
tall, good-looking man in an awkward, rough-hewn way, large in
the shoulders and arms, with a clean-shaven face and a buzz-cut
head one or two sizes too small for his body. It made him look boyish to her, and whenever he showed signs of cruelty — his relent-
less, not quite good-natured teasing of Gail, his regular waitress,
and the LaPierre brothers, two high school kids he hired in sum-
mers to wash dishes and bus tables — to her, he seemed even more
boyish than usual. It was all somehow innocent, she thought. It had
the same strange, otherworldly innocence of the animals that he
liked to kill. A man that manly, that different from a woman, can
actually make you feel more womanly — as if you were of a different species. It freed you from having to compare yourself to him.

"You ever try that? Vegetarianism?" Noonan asked. He tapped
the glass of the tank with a knuckle, as if signaling one of the lobsters to come on over.

"Once. When I was seventeen. I kept it up for a while — two
years, as a matter of fact. Till I busted up my leg and had to quit college." He knew the story of her accident; everyone knew it. She'd
been a local hero before the break and had become a celebrity
afterward. "It's hard to keep being a vegetarian in the hospital,
though. That's what got me off it."

"No shit. What got you on it?"

That's when she told him. "I was struck by lightning."

He looked at her. "Lightning! Jesus! Are you kidding me? How
the hell did *that* happen?"

"The way it always happens, I guess. I was doing something else
at the time. Going up the stairs to bed, actually, in my parents'
house. It was in a thunderstorm, and I reached for the light switch
on the wall and *bam!* Just like they say, a bolt out of the blue."

"But it didn't kill you," Noonan tenderly observed.

"No. But it sure could've. You could say it *almost* killed me, though."

"But it didn't."

"Right. But it *almost* killed me. That's not the same as 'It didn't kill me.' If you know what I mean."

"Yeah, but you're OK now, right? No lingering aftereffects, I mean. Except, of course, for your brief flirtation with the veg world." He squeezed the meat of her shoulder and smiled warmly.

She sighed. Then smiled back — she liked his touch — and tried again: "No, it really changed me. It did. A bolt of lightning went through my body and my brain, and I almost died from it, even though it lasted only a fraction of a second and then was over. It changes you, Noonan. That's all."

"But you're OK now, right?"

"Sure."

"So what was it like, getting hit by lightning?"

She hesitated a moment before answering. "Well, I thought I was shot. With a gun. Seriously. There was this loud noise, like an explosion, and when I woke up, I was lying at the bottom of the stairs, and Daddy and Mom were standing over me like I was dead, and I said, 'Who shot me, Daddy?' It really messed with my mind for a long time. I tried to find out if anybody else I knew had been struck by lightning, but nobody had. Although a few people said they knew someone or heard of someone who'd been hit and survived it. But nobody I ever met myself had been through it. I was the only person I knew who'd had this particular experience. Still am. It's strange, but when you're the only person you know who's gone through something that's changed you into a completely different person, for a while it's like you're on your own planet, like if you're a Vietnam vet and don't know anyone else who was in Vietnam, too."

"I can dig it," Noonan said somberly, although he himself had not been in Vietnam.

"You get used to it, though. And then it turns out to be like life. I mean, there's you, and there's everybody else. Only, unlike the way it is for everybody else, this happened to me in a flash, not over years and so slow you don't even realize how true it is. Know what I mean?"

"How true what is?"

"Well, just that there's you, and there's everybody else. And that's life."

"Sure, I can understand that." He turned away from the tank and looked into Stacy's blue eyes. "It's the same for me. Only with me it was on account of this goddamned bear. Did I ever tell you about the bear that tore my camp down?"

She said, "No, Noonan. You didn't."

"It's the same thing, like getting struck by lightning and afterward feeling like you're a changed man." It was years ago, he explained, when he was between marriages and drinking way too much and living in his hunting camp up on Baxter Mountain because his first wife had got the house in the divorce. He got drunk every night in town at the Spread Eagle or the Elm Tree or the old Dew Drop Inn, and afterward, when he drove back to Baxter Mountain, he'd park his truck at the side of the road, because the trail was too rough even for a four-by-four, and walk the two miles through the woods to his camp. It was a windblown, one-room cabin with a sleeping loft and a woodstove, and one night, after stumbling back from the village, he found the place had been trashed by a bear. "An adolescent male, I figured, it being springtime, who'd been kicked out of his own house and home. Not unlike myself. I had a certain sympathy for him, therefore. But he'd wrecked my cabin looking for food and had busted a window getting in, and I knew he'd come back, so I had to take him down."

The next evening, Noonan blew out his kerosene lantern, climbed into the sleeping loft with a bottle of Jim Beam, his Winchester .30-06, and his flashlight, and waited. Around midnight, as if brushing away a cobweb, the bear tore off the sheet of polyurethane that Noonan had tacked over the broken window, crawled into the cabin, and made for the same cupboard he'd emptied the night before. Noonan, half drunk by now, clicked on his flashlight, caught the startled bear in its beam, and fired, but only wounded him. Maddened with pain, the bear roared and stood on his hind legs, flinging his forelegs in the air right and left, and before Noonan could fire again, the animal had grabbed on to a timber that held up the loft and ripped it from its place, tearing out several other supporting timbers with it, until the entire cabin was collapsing around Noonan and the wounded bear. The structure

was feeble anyhow, made of old, cast-off boards tacked together in
a hurry twenty years before, never rebuilt, never renovated, and it
came down upon Noonan's head with ease. The bear escaped into
the night, but Noonan lay trapped under the fallen roof of the
cabin, unable to move, his right arm broken, he assumed, and possibly several ribs. "That's when it happened," he said.

"What?" Stacy dipped a dozen beer mugs two at a time into cold
water, pulled them out, and stuck them into the freezer to frost for
later on.

"That's when I knew there was me, and there was everybody else.
Just like you said. It changed my life."

"No kidding. How?" She refilled the salt shakers on the bar.

"Well. I stopped drinking for one thing. That was a few years
later, though. But I lay there all that night and most of the next day.
Until this beautiful young woman out looking for her lost dog
came wandering by. And, Stace," he said, his voice suddenly lowered, "I married her."

She put her fists on her hips and checked him out. "Seriously?"

He smiled. "Well, yeah, sort of. I'd actually known her a long
time beforehand, and she'd visited me a few times at my camp, let
us say. But, yeah, I did marry her . . . eventually. And we were very
happy. For a while."

"Uh-huh. For a while."

Noonan nodded, smiled, winked. Then he bumped her hip with
his and said, "I gotta get the kitchen set up. We can pursue this
later, Stace. If you want."

She didn't answer. She started slinging bottles of beer into the
darkness of the cooler, and when she next looked up, he was gone
and a pair of road workers were coming through the door, hot and
sunburned and thirsty.

The day had been clear, with wispy fantails of clouds in the east,
promising a soft, late-summer sunset over the mountains for the
folks dining out at Noonan's Family Restaurant. It was unusually
busy that evening, even for Lobster Night. Depressed by an earlier
quarrel with her pregnant daughter over money, Gail fell quickly
behind in her orders and, after being yelled at, first by her hungry
customers in the dining room and then by Noonan in the kitchen,
where seven or eight bright-red lobsters on their platters awaited

pickup, she broke down and ran sobbing into the ladies' room. She came out, but only after Stacy went after her and promised to help in the dining room, where fifteen kids from three unrelated French-Canadian families were banging their silverware rhythmically against their glasses. Back in the kitchen, halfway into the supper hour, Donny LaPierre threw down his dish towel and told Noonan to take his job and shove it — he didn't graduate high school to get treated like an idiot for minimum wage. His younger brother, Timmy, who would graduate the following year, high-fived Donny and said, "Whoa! Way cool, D.L.," and the two walked out together.

Noonan stood at the door and bellowed, "Don't even think about gettin' paid for this week!" and the boys gave him the finger from the parking lot and laughed and started hitching to Lake Placid.

Eventually, Gail and Stacy, between them, got everyone satisfactorily served, the diners and their children quieted down, and order was restored — even in the kitchen, where Noonan, almost grateful for the chance to do it right, took over the dishwasher's job himself. At the bar, four bored, lonely regulars, men of habit, were drinking and smoking cigarettes and watching Montreal lose to the Mets on television. Stacy gave them a round on the house for their patience, and all four smiled and thanked her and resumed watching the game.

In the fish tank, the one last lobster bumped lazily against the glass. Stacy wiped down the bar and came to a slow stop by the tank. She leaned down and gazed into what she believed was one of the lobster's eyes — more of a greenish knob than an eyeball, anatomically absurd to her — and tried to imagine what the world of Noonan's Family Restaurant looked like through that knob and the thirty-gallon cell of cloudy water surrounding it and, beyond that, the lens of the algae-stained glass wall. It probably looks like an alien planet out here, she thought. Or incomprehensibly foreign, like some old-time Chinese movie, so you don't even know what the story's about, who's the good guy and who's the bad guy. Or maybe, instead of an actual place or thing, to a lobster it looks like only an idea out here. That scared her.

There must be some kind of tradeoff among the senses, she reasoned, like with blind and deaf people. If one sense is weak, another must be strong, and vice versa. Lobsters, she figured, probably can't see very well, living as they do way at the dark bottom of the sea. To distinguish food from friend and friend from foe, they would need powerful senses of smell and hearing. She brought her face up close to the glass and almost touched it with her nose. The lobster bobbled and jiggled just beyond, as if struggling to use its weak eyes and tank-impaired hearing and olfactory senses to determine if Stacy was a thing that could eat it or breed with it or be eaten by it. So much in the life of any creature depends upon being able to identify the other creatures accurately, Stacy thought. In the tank and out of it, too. And this poor beast, with only its ridiculous eyes to depend upon, was lost, was wholly, utterly lost. She reached toward the lobster, as if to pat it, to comfort and reassure.

Noonan's large hand dropped unseen from above, as if through dark water, and came to rest upon hers. She turned, startled, and there was his face a bare few inches away, his large, bloodshot brown eyes and his porous peach-colored skin with black whiskers popping through like lopped-off stalks, soft caves of nostrils, red lips, tobacco-stained teeth, wet tongue. She yanked her hand away and stepped back, bringing him into a more appropriate and safe focus, with the bar between them like a fence, keeping him out or her in, she wasn't sure, but it didn't matter, as long as they were on opposite sides of it.

"You scared me!" she said.

He leaned across the bar and smiled indulgently. Behind her, the men drank beer and watched baseball. She heard the crowd at the ballpark chitter in anticipation of the pitch. From the dining room came the low rumble of families distributing food among themselves and their hushed commentaries as they evaluated its quality and the size of their portions, praise and disappointment voiced equally low, as if both were gossip, and the clink of their forks and knives, gulps, chomps, an old man's sudden laugh, the snap of lobster claws and legs breaking.

"Stace, soon's you get the chance, c'mon out to the kitchen. There's something I want to tell you." He turned and abruptly strode to the dining room, spoke a moment to Gail, sympathetically offering to let her go home early, Stacy guessed, getting rid of witnesses, and gathered up a tub of dirty dishes left behind by Donny LaPierre. As Noonan disappeared into the kitchen, he glanced over at Stacy, and though a stranger would have thought him expressionless, she saw him practically speaking with his face, saw him using it to say in a low, cold voice, "Stace, as soon as we're alone here tonight, I'm going to take you down."

She decided to force the issue, to go back to the kitchen right now, before Gail left, while there was still a fairly large number of people in the dining room and the four guys at the bar, and if Noonan said what she expected him to say and did what she expected him to do, then she would walk out the door just like the LaPierre boys had, take off in her car, the doors locked and windows up, the wheels spinning, kicking gravel and squealing rubber as she left the parking lot and hit the road to Lake Placid.

Who the hell did he think he was anyhow, coming on to her like that, him a married man, middle-aged, practically? Sure, she had been attracted to him from the first time she saw him, when he interviewed her for the job and made her turn and turn again, while he sat there on the barstool and looked her over with genuine interest, almost with innocence, as if she were a bouquet of wild-flowers he'd ordered for his wife. "Turn around, Stace. Let me see the other side." She had actually liked his suddenness, his fearless, impersonal way of telling her exactly what he wanted from her, instructing her to wear a tight white T-shirt and black jeans or shorts to work in and to be friendly with the customers, especially the males, because he wanted return business, not one-night stands, and men will come back and stay late again and again if they think the pretty girl behind the bar likes them personally. She had smiled like a coconspirator when he told her that and said, "No *problema*, Mr. Noonan."

"Hey, you can call me Charlie, or you can call me Noonan. Just don't call me at home, and never call me Mister. You're hired, Stace. Go change the dress and be back here by six." But all that was before she told him about having been struck by lightning. Until then, she had thought it was safe to flirt with him; he was married, after all, and he was so unlike the losers she usually hooked up with that she had decided it was harmless as well as interesting to be attracted to him, and nothing could come of it anyhow; and wasn't it intelligent, after all, for a young woman to want a successful older man's attention and approval? Wasn't that how you learned about life and who you were?

But somehow, this afternoon everything had changed. She couldn't have said how it had changed or why, but everything was different now, especially between her and Noonan. It wasn't what he had done or not done or even anything he had said. It was what she had said.

A woman who has been struck by lightning is not like other people. Most of the time Stacy could forget that fact, could even forget what that horrible night had felt like, when she was only seventeen and thought that she had been shot in the head. But all she had to do was say the words, reestablish the fact, and the whole thing came back in full force — her astonishment, the physical and mental pain, and the long-lasting fear, even today, that it would happen to her again. The only people who say lightning never strikes twice in the same place have never been struck once. Which was why she was so reluctant to speak of it.

But Noonan had charmed her into speaking of it, and all at once, there it was again, as if a glass wall had appeared between her and other people, Noonan especially. The man had no idea who she was. But that wasn't his fault. It was hers. She had misled him. She had misled herself. She checked the drinks of the customers at the bar. Then, to show Gail where she was headed, she pointedly flipped a wave across the dining room and walked back to the kitchen.

When she entered, Noonan was leaning against the edge of the sink, his large, bare arms folded across his chest, his head lowered: a man absorbing a sobering thought.

Stacy said, "What'd you want to tell me?" She stayed by the door, propping it open with her foot.

He shook his head as if waking from a nap. "What? Oh, Stace! Sorry, I was thinking. Actually, Stace, I was thinking about you."

"Me?"

"Yeah. Close the door. Come on in." He peered around her into the dining room. "Is Gail OK? She's not crying or anything anymore, is she?"

"No." Stacy let the door slide shut behind her. The exhaust fan chugged above the stove, and the dishwasher sloshed quietly next to the sink, tinkling the glasses and silverware inside and jiggling the plates. On a shelf by the rear door, a portable radio played country and western music at low volume — sweetly melancholic

background music. There was a calming order and peacefulness to
the kitchen, a low-key domesticity about it that, even though the
room was as familiar to her as the kitchen of her rented A-frame,
surprised Stacy. For a moment, she felt guilty for having been so
suspicious of Noonan and so quick to judge and condemn him.
She liked his boyish good looks, didn't she? She enjoyed his smoky
baritone voice and unapologetic north-country accent, and she was
pleased and flattered by his sudden flashes of intimacy. "What did
you want to tell me, Noonan?" she repeated, softly this time.

He leaned forward, eyes twinkling, mischief on his mind, and
looked right and left, as if not wishing to be overheard. "What do
you say we cook that last lobster and split it between ourselves?" He
gave her a broad smile and rubbed his hands together. "Don't tell
Gail. I'll boil and chill the sucker and break out the meat and
squeeze a little lime juice over it, and we'll eat it later, after we close
up, just the two of us. Maybe open a bottle of wine. Whaddya say?"
He came up to her and put his arm around her shoulder and
steered her toward the door. "You go liberate the animal from its
tank, and I'll bring the kettle to a roiling boil, as they say."

"No." She shrugged out from under his arm.

"Huh? What d'you mean, 'No'?"

"Just that. No. I don't want a quiet little tête-à-tête out here with
you after we close. I don't want to make it with you, Noonan. You're
married, and I resent the way you act like it doesn't matter to
you. Or worse, me! You act like your being married doesn't matter
to me."

Noonan was confused. "What the fuck? Who said anything about
making it? Jesus!"

She exhaled heavily. "I'm sorry," she said. "You're right. I don't
know what you've got in mind, Noonan. Really. I don't know why I
said all that. I'm just . . . I'm scared, I guess."

"You? Scared? Hah!" She was young and beautiful and healthy;
she was an athlete, a woman who could pick and choose among
men much younger, more available, better-looking, and richer
than he. What did she have to be scared of? Not him, that's for
sure. "Man, you are one screwed-up broad, let me tell you." He
shook his head slowly in frustration and disgust. "Look, I don't give
a shit if you don't want to join me in a whaddyacallit, a tête-à-tête.
Suit yourself. But I'm gonna eat me some lobster anyhow. Alone!"
he said, and he sailed through the door into the dining room.

Stacy slowly crossed the kitchen to the back door, last used by the
LaPierre brothers on their way to the parking lot and road beyond.
It was a screen door, and moths and mosquitoes batted against it
and swarmed around the yellow bulb on the wall outside. On this
side of the restaurant, it was already dark. Out back, where the
building faced west to the mountains, the sky was pale orange, with
long, silver-gray clouds tinged with purple floating up high and
blood-red strips of cloud near the horizon. She decided she'd
better return to the bar. There would be a few diners, she knew,
who would want to take an after-dinner drink onto the deck and
watch the sunset.

Before she could get out the door, Noonan, his face dark with
confused anger, strode back into the kitchen, carrying the last lobster in his dripping-wet hand. The lobster feebly waved its claws in
the air, and its thick, armored tail curled in on itself and snapped
back in a weak, hopeless attempt to push Noonan away. "Here, you
do the honors!" Noonan said to Stacy, holding the lobster up to her
face. With his free hand, he flipped the gas jet below the slow-boil-
ing lobster pot to high. "Have you ever boiled a live lobster, Stacy?
Oh, it's a real turn-on." He leered, but it was an angry leer. "You're
gonna love it, Stacy, especially the way it turns bright-red as soon as
you drop it into the boiling water. It won't sink right away, of
course, because it's still alive and will struggle to climb out of the
pot, just like you would. But even while it's trying to get out of the
boiling water, it'll be turning red, and you'll see it give up, and
when that happens, it's cooked and ready to be eaten. *Yummm!*"

He pushed the lobster at her, and it flailed its claws in her face, as
if it were her hand clamped onto its back, not Noonan's. She didn't
flinch or back away. She held her ground and looked into what
passed for the animal's face, searching for an expression, some in-
dicator of feeling or thought that would guide her own feelings
and thoughts. But there was none, and when she realized there
could be none, this pleased her and she smiled.

"It's getting to you, right?" Noonan said. "I can tell, it's a turn-on
for you, right?" He smiled back, almost forgiving her for having
judged him so unfairly, and held the lobster over the pot of boiling
water. Steam billowed around the creature's twisting body, and
Stacy stared, transfixed, when from the dining room she heard the
rising voices of the diners, their loud exclamations and calls to one
another to come and see, hurry up, come and see the bear!

Stacy and Noonan looked at each other, she in puzzlement, he with irritated resignation. "Shit," he said. "This has got to be the worst goddamn night of my life." He dropped the lobster into the empty sink and disappeared into the pantry, returning to the kitchen a few seconds later with a rifle cradled in his arm. "Sonofabitch, this is the last time that bastard gets into my trash!" he declared, and made for the dining room, with Stacy following close behind.

She had never seen a black bear close-up, although it was not uncommon to come upon one in the neighborhood, especially in midsummer, when the mountain streams ran dry and sent the normally shy creatures to the lower slopes and valleys, where the humans lived. Once, when driving back to college after summer vacation, she thought she spotted a large bear crossing the road a hundred yards ahead of her and at first had assumed it couldn't be a bear, it must be a huge dog, a Newfoundland, maybe, moving slowly, until it heard her car coming and broke into a swift, forward-tilted lope and disappeared into the brush as she passed. She stopped the car and backed up to where the animal had entered the brush, but there was no sign of its ever having been there, no broken weeds or freshly fallen leaves, even.

This time, however, she intended to see the bear up close, if possible, and to know for sure that she had not imagined it. When she got to the dining room, everyone, Gail and the regulars from the bar included, was standing at the windows, gazing down at the yard in back where the land sloped away from the building, pointing and murmuring small noises of appreciation — except for the children, who were stilled by the sight, not so much frightened by the bear as in awe of it. The adults seemed to be mainly pleased by their good luck, for now they would have something novel to report to their friends and family when they returned home. This would become the night they saw the bear at Noonan's.

Then Stacy saw Noonan and several other diners, all of them men, out on the deck. They, too, stared down into the yard below the dining room and in the direction of the basement door, where Noonan stashed his garbage and trash barrels in a locked wooden latticework cage. The men were somber and intent, taut and almost trembling, like hunting dogs on point.

Stacy edged up to the window. Behind the distant mountains, the sun was gloriously setting. Its last golden rays splashed across the neatly mowed yard behind the restaurant and shone like a soft spotlight upon the thick, black-pelted body of the bear. It was a large adult male, over six feet tall on his hind legs, methodically, calmly ripping away the sides and top of the lattice cage, sending torn boards into the air like kindling sticks, working efficiently but at his own placid pace, as if he were utterly alone and there were no audience of men, women, and children staring down at him from the dining room windows overhead, no small gang of men out on the deck watching him like a hunting party gathered on a cliff above a watering hole, and as if Noonan were not lifting his rifle to his shoulder, aiming it, and firing.

He shot once, and he missed the bear altogether. He fired a second time.

The bear was struck high in the back and a tuft of black hair flew away from his chest where the bullet emerged. The crowd in the dining room groaned and cried out, "He's shooting it! Oh, God, he's shooting it!" A woman screeched, "Tell him to stop!" and children began to bawl. A man yelled, "For God's sake, is he nuts?" Gail looked beseechingly at Stacy, who simply shook her head slowly from side to side, for she could do nothing to stop him now. No one could. People shouted and cried, a few sobbed, and children wailed, and Noonan fired a third time. He hit the bear in the shoulder and the animal spun around, still standing, searching for the source of this terrible pain, not understanding that he should look up, that the man with the rifle, barely fifty yards away, was positioned out of sight above him and, because of his extreme anger, because of his refusal to be impersonal in this grisly business, was unable to kill him, and so he wounded the poor creature again and again, in the chest, in a paw, and shot him through the muzzle, until finally the bear dropped to all fours and, unsure in which direction to flee, tumbled first away from the restaurant downhill toward the woods, and then, hit in the back, turned and came lumbering, bleeding and in pain, straight toward the deck, where Noonan fired one last shot, hitting the bear this time in the center of his forehead, and the bear rolled forward, as if he had accidentally tripped, and died.

*

Rifle in hand, Noonan stomped in silence past the departing
crowd, his gaze fixed rigidly on something inside, a target in his
mind of a silhouetted bear. No one spoke to him or caught his eye
as he passed; no one looked at his back, even, when he strode into
the kitchen and the door swung shut behind him. The men who
had stood with him on the deck outside were ashamed now to have
been there. Making as little of it as possible, they joined their wives
and friends, all of whom were lined up at the cash register paying
Gail, leaving cash on the table, or paying Stacy at the bar, and
quickly headed for the parking lot and their cars. There were a few
stunned, silent exceptions, older kids too shocked to cry or too
proud, but most of the children were weeping, and some wailed,
while the parents tried vainly to comfort them, to assure them that
bears don't feel pain the same way humans do, that the man who
shot the bear had to shoot it because it was damaging his property,
and not to worry, we will never come to this restaurant again, no
matter what.

When everyone had left, Gail walked slowly from the dining
room to the bar, where she took off her apron, folded it carefully,
and set it on a barstool. "That's it for me," she said to Stacy. With
trembling hands, she knocked a cigarette loose from the pack, lit it,
and inhaled deeply. "Tell him he can mail me my pay," she said.
"The fucker." She started for the door and then abruptly stopped.
Without turning around, she said, "Stacy? Why the hell are you
staying?"

"I'm not."

In a voice so low she seemed to be talking to herself, Gail said,
"Yes, girl, you are." Then she was gone.

Stacy flipped off the lights in the bar and dining room one by one,
unplugged the roadside sign, and locked the front entrance. When
she pushed open the door to the kitchen, Noonan, standing at the
far end of the long stainless-steel counter, looked up and scowled at
her. He had cooked the last lobster and was eating it, eating it off
the counter with his hands; broken shells and the remains of its
shattered carcass lay scattered in front of him. He poked a fore-
finger into the thick, muscular tail and shoved a chunk of white
meat out the other end, snatched it up, and popped it into his
mouth. "Eight fucking shots it took me!" he said, chewing. "That's

what I get for stashing that goddamn pissant .22 here instead of laying in a real gun." He waved contemptuously with the back of his
hand at the rifle propped against the counter, and with his other
hand he pushed more lobster meat into his mouth. His face was
red, and he was breathing rapidly and heavily. "I missed the first
shot, y'know, only because I was so pissed off I didn't concentrate.
But if I'd had a real gun, that second shot would've done the job
fine. By God, tomorrow I'm bringing in my .30-06!" he declared.

Stacy picked up the .22 rifle and looked it over. She slid it into
shooting position against her right shoulder and aimed along the
barrel through the screen door and the fluttering cluster of moths
to the outside lamp.

"Is it still loaded?" she asked.

"There's four rounds left, so don't fuck with it." He yanked the
spindly legs off the underbelly of the lobster and sucked the meat
from each and dropped the emptied tubes, one by one, onto the
counter in front of him.

Slowly, Stacy brought the rifle around and aimed it at Noonan's
skull. "Noonan," she said, and he turned.

"Yeah, sure."

She closed her eyes and pulled the trigger and heard the explosion, and when she opened her eyes, she saw in the middle of
Noonan's broad, white forehead a dark hole the size of a dime,
which instantly expanded to a quarter, and his large body jerked
once as if electrocuted and flipped backward, his astonished face
gone from her sight altogether now, and she saw instead the back
of his head, and a hole in it the size of a silver dollar. His body, like
a large, rubberized sack of water, fell to the floor, spinning away
from her as it descended, ending flat on its back, with Noonan's
wide-open eyes staring at the pot rack above the counter. Blood
pumped from the hole in the rear of his skull onto the pale-green
linoleum and spread in a thickening, dark-red puddle slowly toward her feet.

She laid the rifle on the counter beside the broken remains of
the lobster, crossed to the stove, where the pot of water was still
boiling, and shut off the gas flame. Slowly, as if unsure of where she
was, she looked around the room, then seemed to make a decision,
and perched herself on a stool next to the walk-in refrigerator.
She leaned her head back against the cool stainless-steel door and

closed her eyes. Never in her life, never, had Stacy known the relief she felt at that moment. And not since the moment before she was struck by lightning had she known the freedom.

A rattling Ford pickup truck stopped beside the darkened roadside sign, and the LaPierre brothers, Donny and Timmy, leaped from the truck bed to the side of the road. "Hey, good luck with ol' Noonan, you little assholes!" the driver said, and he and a male passenger in the cab cackled with laughter. Two beery, expansive carpenters, they were cousins of the LaPierres, heading home to their wives and kids late from the bars of Lake Placid. They waved cheerfully to the boys and pulled away.

Donny and Timmy crunched across the gravel parking lot. The kitchen light and the lamp outside were still on, and when the boys were halfway across the lot, they saw Stacy through the screen door, seated on the stool by the big walk-in fridge. She was asleep, it looked like, or maybe just bored out of her mind listening to one of Noonan's dumb hunting stories.

"You think he's screwing Stacy?" Timmy asked.

"C'mon, man. Stacy's a babe. And he's ancient, man," Donny said. "It's cool she's still here, though," he added. "She likes us, and he'll hire us back just to look good."

"I wouldn't mind a little of that myself."

"A little of what?"

"Stacy, man!"

Donny punched his younger brother on the shoulder. "Yeah, well, you'll hafta wait your turn, little fella!" he laughed. He waved away the swarming cloud of moths and pulled the screen door open. Timmy entered first, and Donny, hiding his fading grin behind his hand, followed.

MICHAEL DOWNS

Prison Food

FROM *Witness*

SHELLY WOLANSKY'S DESK faced a wall, and to the right, over
the in-basket, was the only window in the prison kitchen. It was a
small window, no bigger than a cutting board, with a view Shelly
could live without: razor-wire and grim concrete walls, beyond that
acres of dead weeds bordered by cyclone fence and more razor
wire, and in the distance Route 5 and the doughnut shop where
corrections officers could buy Bavarian creme and chocolate
frosted at a 20 percent discount. When Shelly had seen it all once,
she'd seen it too many times.

Her head ached. Her desk was a mess. She untucked her shirt,
undid the top button of her pants — the waistband pinched when
she sat, the price she paid for having quit smoking — and reread
the warden's memo. He needed her to work Thursday night — the
night of the execution — to make the last meal.

The warden promised Friday off — Thursday, too, except the
few hours that night. Fine with her. Not working Friday meant she
could make Chuck's hockey tournament in New Haven, keep an
eye on him. Lord knows he needed watching, especially after the
bit two months back with that other boy's car. That was the worst,
but she didn't like the way he'd been drawing penalties on the ice,
either. Chuck's coach had said it was part of the game, that hockey
players need an attitude. "Yeah, well, he needs his attitude adjusted," she had said.

If Hank were still alive . . .

Ah, quit it, Shelly told herself. Maybe, if, maybe, if. You can't play
that game anymore. Four years is too long.

The banging pans and rattling blowers of the kitchen didn't help her headache, and when Danny, the trusty, dropped a soup pot he was washing, she yelled at him. "Sorry, Julia Child!" he shouted back. She smiled, despite herself. She liked it when people in the prison called her Julia Child. She liked what it said about how she ran the kitchen.

Shelly rolled back in her chair — inventory reports could wait — and glanced out the window. It was snowing. Somehow that made the view even harder to bear. In the distance, out past the fence, she could see little stick people waving signs. Protesters already, and the execution still two days away. All those people standing in the cold — good news for the doughnut shop.

The kitchen's fluorescent bulbs stuttered. The stainless steel shone dull in the flickering light. She needed her hands in food, needed to chop something. So she buttoned her pants, pulled on latex gloves, and stopped near a cutting board to put zucchini under the knife. She wondered what the guy would order for his last meal. Though she'd worked at the prison three years, the state hadn't killed anyone since she started. A new governor now changed all that. She figured this late-night supper would be the first of many, and that thought turned her stomach queasy.

"What's up, Julia Child?"

Danny nudged her, shoulder-to-shoulder as if they were dancing. "You're staring into space land," he said, bending around to see her face. He smiled his soda-pop smile, the smile of a con man, which he had been until an old couple turned him in. The file Shelly read had told how Danny, out on bail before the trial, stopped by the couple's house and hospitalized them for six weeks each. That tantrum earned him his spot in maximum security. Good behavior, and likely that smile, had freed him for the kitchen. That and the fact the warden liked to make the white guys trusties.

"You're not supposed to touch the staff," she said.

He ignored her and pointed at the knife. "You don't focus, you might lose a finger. What's on your mind?"

Shelly put down the knife. It was easy to see how he could bilk people — his gentle laugh, his sincere and curious face — Shelly had overheard kitchen workers confess deep anxieties to Danny. But he was scary, too, because of what he'd done. Because he was maximum. Because when Shelly looked close enough, she noticed parallel scars at his wrist and the earlobe that was missing, and when she paid attention to his voice she heard that dialect white men only speak when they've been inside the walls a long time.

"I'm cooking that guy's meal Thursday night."

"Doyle?" He laughed. "He's a mean bastard, that one."

"I don't want to know. I'm sure it was a long, long time ago."

"Hell no, Julia Child. Not long back, they let Doyle in the yard with the rest of us, and he said something to piss off some Latin Kings. You don't piss off the Kings. They stabbed him. That son of a bitch just pressed a sock over the hole in his belly so he wouldn't look weak. Later, he's walking some hall with guards on both sides, his hands and legs cuffed, and they pass the dude who stabbed him. Doyle bites off the dude's nose. And now Julia Child's making him dinner."

"Don't you have trays to wash?"

"About five years' worth, with good behavior."

Back at the sink, he worked the high-pressure hose, spraying until steam swallowed him. Having Danny around was as bad as having that window over her desk, reminders she didn't need. When she saw him, she couldn't help but see the baseball bat that broke the ribcage of the old man, smashed the old woman's arthritic hands. No matter how Danny laughed or winked, he couldn't hide his history. He wore it as plainly as he wore his blue prison shirt, untucked and buttoned to the collar, just like all the inmates.

Sometimes Chuck dressed for school the same way. "It's a style," he argued. "No big deal."

At the rink that night, Shelly nodded to other parents as she picked a spot on the splintering bleachers behind the team box. The boys skated onto the ice, greeted by hand-clapping and rock 'n' roll that gargled from the arena's loudspeakers, and Shelly remembered how earlier, when she left the prison for the rink, the protesters had sung "Amazing Grace" and shoved signs in front of her windshield as she drove out the gate. Like she had anything to do with whether the guy lived or died, like she did anything but run the kitchen and cook.

A teenage girl came and sat beside Shelly. Chuck's girlfriend. "Hi, Tina," Shelly said, friendly despite her better judgment.

"Hey."

Tina wore a fatigue jacket, and her lacquered hair hung in her eyes like a purple shield. Why is it, Shelly wondered, that high school boys love the psychos the way dogs love antifreeze? How could Chuck love this girl, who let him twist for days before return- ing his phone calls, who flirted with other guys, and who even in- vited them along when she and Chuck had a date? That's how he had wrecked his Chevy Nova, smashing the Firebird of some guy Tina was vamping. Chuck got his license revoked and two years probation. Tina never said sorry. Just after that, Shelly started hav- ing nightmares: Tina, a wedding ring on her finger, her arms open for a hug, saying, "Hi, Mom." In the dream, Shelly never knew whether to hug her daughter-in-law or spank her.

Chuck was in the goal mouth now, deflecting slap shots, mon- strous in his pads and goalkeeper's mask. Shelly stared at the mask, trying to make out what was scrawled in red across the forehead.

"What's that say?" she asked, pointing.

"Maim," said Tina.

"Maim? Like, wound?"

"Dismember. Cripple. Yeah." Tina laughed.

"It's not funny, Tina."

"I think it is."

Teenage testosterone, Shelly told herself. Same as when he plas- tered the walls of his room with pictures of hockey players brawl- ing. Same as when he stayed up late playing blood-soaked video games on his computer. But what about the night he wrecked the cars? Could she blame testosterone then? Hadn't he crossed some line? And what about "maim"?

Hank, Hank . . . when you died, he was still a boy, asking permis- sion to spend his allowance on Hershey Bars, full of please and thank you. Four years later, he's some other thing, out of my con- trol. He scares me, Hank.

But thinking of her husband settled her, because she'd seen Hank handle the worst kinds of people, from drunks in his favorite taverns to the lowlifes he dealt with every day as a Hartford cop. Sometimes she'd drive to the city and wait in the station's lobby to meet him for lunch, and he'd come in from patrol, a look in his eyes that made whatever punk he had in cuffs waddle like he had peed himself. Sometimes the punk really had peed himself. But Hank never raised a fist. Never used a club. His eyes did the work.

Hank's eyes — frightening and cold when he was angry — promised something worse than a beating if he'd ever let loose. And that look, that promise, gave her faith that nothing would ever hurt him, that he'd always come home. Foolish hope. Because the doorbell did ring one night. Not when he was at work, no. It rang late, when he'd gone out with the boys, and then it was Enfield's cops instead of Hartford's. Hank had a few. Missed a stop sign.

No. Maim wasn't funny.

Shelly stared at her son in case he'd notice her and feel chastised. For all the good it did. Midway through the third period, Chuck charged out of the goal and with his stick flattened the other team's center, doubled the kid over. The kid jumped up looking for a fight, but Chuck punched first and kept punching until the referees pulled them apart. All the time on the bench, even with the coach in his face, Chuck never removed his mask.

Game over, Shelly waited outside the locker room but kept her distance from other parents. She didn't want their small talk when all they'd be thinking is what the hell was wrong with her boy. Tina stayed near but said nothing. After a while, the coach came out, and he told Shelly that he'd have no choice: Another fight, Chuck's off the team.

"Maybe if you'd done something earlier . . ." she said.

"I'm not his father," he said. "There's a limit."

When the coach returned to the locker room, a shabbily dressed man slipped out, wearing thick glasses and carrying a notebook under his arm. Chuck appeared a few minutes later, his puffy down coat unzipped, his dress shirt wrinkled, his game-day tie loosely knotted. He hadn't shaved, and his cheeks shined with acne and exertion.

He draped his arm around Tina. They both said, "Hey."

"That took a while," Shelly said.

"I was talking to some guy from the newspaper."

"They want to do a story on you?"

"Yeah. I guess that's why he was talking to me."

Outside, Shelly unlocked the trunk of the old Buick. Chuck dropped his duffel bag with such weight that a clump of crusted, wet snow — brown with dirt and rust — fell from the bumper and splashed on the pavement.

At Tina's house, Shelly adjusted the rearview mirror so she could watch. With car exhaust drifting around them in blue clouds, Chuck tried to kiss Tina. She stepped back. They whispered, their words puffs of frozen breath. He grabbed her wrist. She yanked it away. Shelly thought of driving off, leaving them to eat each other alive.

Then Tina shoved Chuck and marched to her door. Chill air rushed with him into the Buick.

"What's with all the bad actor stuff?" Shelly asked as they drove home.

"With Tina?"

"With everything. Coach says you're off the team, you keep pulling that stuff."

"He won't. There's nobody else to play goalie."

"I don't like it anyway."

"It gives me a boost," he said. From his backpack he look a candy bar, ripped open the wrapper and swallowed in two bites. "That other team is the bad guys. You don't shake hands with bad guys. You just kick their asses."

"Your father dealt with bad guys every day. He never hit one. He —"

"— drank his way through a stop sign so maybe he's not the best role model."

"You shut your mouth."

She wanted to slap him, but she worried about the Buick skidding into a tree.

All of a sudden Chuck rose and, with a grace that seemed impossible given his bulk, pulled himself into the back seat. Shelly looked over her shoulder, and he had closed his eyes.

"You don't know anything about hockey," he muttered and said nothing else that night.

Shelly woke Wednesday morning, bleary and grumpy from too much worrying and too little sleep, wanting a cigarette for the first time in months. At work, she found a memo from the warden listing Doyle's menu: cheeseburger plain with onion slices, french fries, orange Jell-O, a glass of milk, a hard-candy mint for after. At the bottom, the warden's scrawled note: *Don't jazz it up. Give the guy what he wants.*

Her staff shuffled around the tilt grills and steam kettles, and the kitchen smelled of pesto and grilled chicken — that night's entree. *Don't jazz it up.* Fine. She could cook a cheeseburger. She'd cooked thousands of cheeseburgers, back when Hank was alive and Chuck was still a cherub. Meatloaf, too. All the basics: meat, potatoes, vegetables from a can. Now and then, on an anniversary or on Mother's Day, Hank took her someplace with candles and lace tablecloths, and they ate nice, but she never imagined she could create what appeared on those plates. Then Hank died, and she dreamed about him sitting with her at the kitchen table eating tomato soup and black bread, and he said, "You should try cooking school. It's a way to make a living."

She had always figured you needed a Rockefeller's salary and a degree from Harvard to make the dishes she saw prepared on public television. But after a few months of classes at Hartford Culinary College, Shelly learned that all a person needed to move beyond meatloaf and mashed potatoes was time to enjoy the kitchen. For hours she'd stand over the stove, the food processor, the cutting board, peeling garlic or sprinkling saffron or deveining shrimp, loving the work in a way she'd never loved anything before. She didn't graduate — money ran short — but she passed enough classes to get the job at the prison kitchen, and pretty quick she worked her way up to manager. That gave her time and money. And she had ideas how to use both.

She'd seen how people became respectful when seated before a plate of marinated pork tenderloin, and she wondered how prisoners might act if they ate chestnut soup instead of chicken-patty sandwiches, spinach fettucine instead of sloppy joes, chicken molé instead of Salisbury steak. She wasn't stupid. She didn't figure she could turn a murderer into a school crossing guard, but, she thought, maybe good food might make him a little less angry. It wasn't easy changing the menu — the cafeteria's budget wasn't so big after all — but she learned to substitute ham for prosciutto, Swiss cheese for Gruyère.

The prisoners flushed the food at first. Shelly kept trying, and eventually they started to eat what she served. Some even liked it. The warden praised her, especially when she won a state government award for initiative and creativity, but the new menu didn't change anybody's behavior. After a while, that didn't matter to Shelly. If she had to cook, she wanted to cook good food.

When she took her break, she found Danny in the snack room. He sat at a round table, reading a newspaper and picking his teeth with a plastic fork that had all its tines broken off except one.

"Just reading about your boy."

"Chuck said they were doing a story on him. I didn't know it ran already."

"Not Chuck." He slid the paper across the table. She took it, then sat and read the front-page headline:

A MOTHER'S PLEA
Begs governor for son's life

She saw two photographs, one new and in color of a sixty-ish woman with a face puckered from a lifetime of two packs a day. She held a photo of her son the murderer as a preschooler. That picture was reproduced — larger — next to hers. Probably snapped on his birthday. He wore a pointed paper hat and a short-sleeve white shirt with a dark tie. He held a stuffed lion toy. His hair was curly and blond, his skin Irish pink. The caption read: "Bobby Doyle, age five."

"Cute," she said.

"Amazing his mother sticks by him. My mother's pretty much forgotten me. I mean, she keeps proof that she had me — my badges with the Cub Scouts and a big picture of me in an altar boy uniform. Nothing after that, though. Like once I hit puberty, I vanished."

"You were an altar boy?"

"Until I stole a candlestick." He laughed. "Most guys in here will tell you they were good guys once."

"Can I take this?" she said.

Danny nodded — "You're the boss, Julia Child" — picking his teeth.

That night on her couch, chilled despite her flannel pajamas and the wool blanket wrapped around her legs, Shelly read the newspaper story to the inside pages. He had loved dogs, said his mother. Played checkers like a whiz. The article also mentioned that he had killed two girls after raping them — the daughters of his girlfriend at the time. Inside was a mug shot of Doyle: his lips curled in a frown, and his clenched jawbones pushing out of his cheeks. The

worst part was his eyes. Not like Hank's, which had been scary for what they promised. Doyle's eyes delivered, shot through with blood and rage. Shelly looked back and forth from Doyle the boy to Doyle the killer.

She started when Chuck threw open the front door, home from hockey practice. He passed her without a word — despite her "Hello" — a newspaper under one arm and his goalkeeper's mask in hand. He grabbed a bag of cookies from the kitchen, then shut himself in his room.

When she knocked, there was no answer.

"Chuck?"

"I'm busy."

"And I'm in no mood to talk to you through a door."

She twisted the knob and went in.

He whipped a jackknife at the wall, trying to stick the blade through the newspaper he had taped there. In the middle of the page was a photograph of a hockey goalie.

"What are you doing?"

He threw the knife again. It hit flat against the newspaper and fell.

"I said —"

"Getting mad."

"At who?"

"Churchill Bannerman. Goalie from Avon."

"What'd he do?"

"Nothing. It's a hockey thing." He kept throwing, missing, retrieving the knife . . .

"Give me the knife, Chuck. If you know what's good for you, give me the knife now."

He tossed it once more, missing again, then fell back on the mulch of dirty clothes covering his bed.

She folded the knife, then gathered a deep breath and looked around his room.

"Have you had dinner?"

He waved the bag of cookies.

"How about if I heat some eggplant lasagna for you."

"If it's prison food, I don't want it."

"What difference does it make?"

"If it's prison food, I don't want it."

It sounded like a dare, as if forcing dinner on him would be asking for trouble. He stared, breathing quietly if he breathed at all.

"Suit yourself," she said, and she walked out, leaving his door open. He shut it as soon as she was in the hallway.

In bed, she read the newspaper story once, then twice, while chewing the plastic cap of a ballpoint pen. She wondered about Chuck and Danny and Doyle — all good kids once — and the wonder turned to worry about how short a step it might be from knifing a wall to knifing a body. Before she turned out her bedside lamp, she buried Chuck's jackknife in a dresser drawer beneath her socks and panties.

On Execution Day, Shelly brushed her teeth and wondered whether Doyle was brushing his teeth, too, or whether he wouldn't bother. What did a man do on his last day? As he rinsed the toothpaste from his mouth, would he relive what he had done? Would he regret it? Or would he think back to happier days? She wondered about Doyle's happy days. She wondered whether he had played hockey in high school.

She found Chuck in the living room, eating chips out of a bag, gazing at cartoons on TV.

"That your breakfast?"

A nod.

"Breakfast of champions. At least sit with me at the table while I eat. Pretend we're family."

He shrugged and followed. His baggy pants, designed to make him look like a hoodlum, made him seem to her only a boy in man's clothes. He wore his cap turned so the bill faced sideways, and he'd left the price tag attached. He looked silly.

"We've been reading in current events class about the execution," he said. "Some of us thought we'd go watch."

Shelly popped a prison omelet into the microwave. Leftovers from the day before. She punched the buttons on the microwave, playing its one note over and over. "Watch what? You won't see a thing."

"We thought we'd carry signs: 'Bobby Doyle Fan Club.' It'd be cool." His face opened a little, and he dropped into a chair. He fiddled with the corner of the kitchen table where the laminate was peeling, picking at it with his fingernails.

"I want you home. We've got to be up by five for the tournament."

"But isn't that wild? Right after midnight — the Witching Hour — and the dude's dead. Pffffit. Nada. Our teacher told us they'll strap him to a table shaped like a cross." He smiled. "A nurse is going to swab the spot where they'll give him the IV, like he needs to worry about infection. They paralyze him. That's how he'll die. And because he's paralyzed, his organs and stuff won't relax, so he won't shit himself. Nice and clean, no screaming or anything. Like he falls asleep. Lullaby, little Bobby." He stopped talking and looked at her. "Hey, Mom."

"Hmm?"

"Microwave's beeping."

Shelly opened the oven door to stop the sound, but left her food inside.

"Chuck, you don't shock me, OK? Do a 'Bobby Doyle Fan Club.' I don't care. Just don't do a Bobby Doyle."

"Mom . . ."

"Look. I'm working tonight. I'm making his last meal. And I don't want to talk about this anymore."

"You're making his last meal? That's totally cool."

"You think it's cool?"

"Totally. It's so messed up. I mean, what a waste of food, right?" He plunged a hand into his bag of chips, shoved a few in his mouth. "I bet he won't get leftovers."

Shelly parked on the street outside the Hartford Public Library waiting for the doors to open, her worry over Chuck stewing into anger. She checked the Buick's ashtray for stubs, found only a few wisps of ash, and wanted to blame Chuck for that, too.

Inside the library, her mood worsened with the nausea she got spinning microfilm back to the murders.

BRISTOL — Whoever raped and killed the two Williams sisters earlier this week first bound them with phone cords and stuffed their mouths with aluminum foil, police said yesterday.

Shelly's throat tightened, a sympathetic gag.

Bite marks on the foil indicate that the girls — Nancy, 13, and Kim, 11 — were alive when their mouths were stuffed, and probably raped after that, according to Homicide Detective Glenn Falzarrano of the Bristol Police De-

partment. Each girl was then shot through the head with a .38 caliber handgun.

Falzarrano asked that any information that could lead to an arrest be given to his office immediately . . .

A helpful librarian interrupted to show her a feature article a national magazine ran about the murders. "A lot of people have been asking this week," the woman said.

The magazine reveled in awful detail. The girls, the prosecutor had told the jury, "writhed like earthworms in their own living room." The police caught Doyle hiding in the ruin of a stone farmhouse near Litchfield where he had killed a stray dog for food.

But the article also offered Doyle's history: Cub Scout through his bear badge, a pole vaulter at Bristol Central High, later an exterior detailer in a body shop. Reliable, his boss had said. A good eye for colors. Along with all that, a photograph of Bobby in high school with some friends in a cellar, surrounded by dumbbells and barbells and concrete, the boys skinny in tight T-shirts, each trying to look threatening, trying so much they looked sweet.

And there were school pictures of the girls. Nancy, the older, had dark, feathered hair, braces on her teeth, and spare shoulders that looked too slight to support her neck. Kim, also a brunette but with a lighter tint, squeezed her lips shut as if smiling would be an act of surrender. Shelly looked for a long time.

A whiz at checkers, his mother had said. And he had liked dogs.

The house was quiet, Chuck not yet back from practice, but he had been home for lunch and left a carton of milk on the counter to spoil. She poured the milk down the sink and decided that she needed music during dinner, something to drive away images of Bobby Doyle with those sisters, their mouths packed with aluminum foil, the last taste on their tongues. Country, maybe. Some twangy, seductive voice. She touched the power button on the radio.

Ripping heavy metal guitars and barking voices slammed from the speakers. She panicked, punched the power off. Caught her breath. That damn kid. That little shit.

She reheated chicken fettucine and sautéed vegetables, then let them steam in front of her, and remembered how she and Chuck used to share dinnertime. She'd make meals, even reheated ones from the prison, and mother and son would sit at the table with place mats and napkins and food in serving dishes, everything presented like she learned in cooking school. He'd ask about the prison, but she wanted to hear what happened at school. As he got older and as her exhaustion grew at the end of each day, sometimes she wouldn't remember place mats. Sometimes she'd heat leftovers and want to watch sitcoms from the couch. Then sometimes became always.

The fettucine and vegetables stopped steaming so she returned them to the fridge, thinking that maybe Chuck would have stayed a gentle kid if she'd kept putting out place mats, if meals had remained special. Food, she thought, should always be an occasion.

On the road to the prison that night, the Buick's heater blowing loud dry air at her, she squinted at the glare from approaching headlights and kept her left foot at the ready above the brake pedal. It wouldn't do to die on the way to make the last meal for Doyle, that son of a bitch.

She figured she'd cooked for him before without realizing it. Guards must have brought him trays of her food from the cafeteria where the rest of the population broke bread. Now she pictured Doyle eating that cheeseburger with onion slices, the Jell-O, the french fries. She imagined him wiping his mouth while the corrections officers watched. Maybe some family would be there. A brother, his mother. Certainly his mother, who would wear bright colors — a polka-dot blouse of pink and blue, bangles and bracelets on her arms as if at a family picnic. They'd sit in the brightness of the death-row visiting room, painted white and lit by the bald glare of a 120-watt bulb. He'd have chains around the ankles of his slippered feet. A tattoo of a spider would creep up his neck from out of his shirt, the strands of web like a collar. He'd lean against the wall of cinderblocks, fold a napkin around his fries, wink, and say, "Maybe I'll save these for tomorrow."

Cheeseburgers. Jell-O. Fries. Not a green vegetable in the whole damn meal. That outraged her for some reason she couldn't explain, made her move her foot away from the brake pedal and press harder on the accelerator as if she might catch Doyle crossing the road and run him down. No green vegetable. The bastard.

Stomach queasy, fists tight on the steering wheel, she remembered how Chuck had laughed at her for feeding a man who would be dead, laughed at the waste of food, but that wasn't what bothered her. She would have made glorious food for Hank had she known she was going to lose him. She would have baked a sour cream apple pie laced with walnuts and a hint of almond; she would have mixed a cranberry chutney to spread over hickory-smoked ham; she would have set a table of crystal and china and silver, and brought sparkling mineral waters and wine and strong Dutch coffee when he finished — an unforgettable farewell of flavor and grace.

But God, she couldn't remember. What had she fed Hank before he died? The protesters marched now in front of the chain-link gate — a line of nuns and children and grown-ups with umbrellas — who refused to budge until she honked. Cold rain pattered her as she stepped from the Buick, one hand clenching the collar of her raincoat, and she turned to watch the protesters light candles that the wind blew out, then try to light them again. A short distance away, TV crews huddled near their vans, occasionally turning their camera lights on the protesters who would then shout and wave their homemade posters: MURDER BY THE STATE IS STILL MURDER! and THOU SHALT NOT KILL! but the writing bled in the drizzle.

She had never approached the prison alone. Even on her first day of work, she joined a group of new employees who had gathered in the parking lot for orientation, and every day since then Shelly had walked through the employee gate with others, talking to the person next to her about weather, TV shows, kids. In a group, it was easy to ignore the towers, the harsh lights, the emptiness of the yard, the paranoia of a place where nobody breathed without someone else's say-so.

At the entry door, behind a bulletproof glass shield, sat a night-shift corrections officer Shelly didn't know, whose cold voice crackled from a speaker to demand her employee ID. She passed surveillance cameras, walked down noiseless hallways, through doors that opened with an echoing, teeth-shivering buzz, until she reached the kitchen, which glowed blue in a twilight of hazard lamps and pilot lights. No blowers rattled.

She unzipped her wet coat, shook it, then hung it over the back of her desk chair. Light through the window caught her attention. Not just the prison lights, but the TV lights that shined on the protesters, and the headlights of cars driving on Route 5, and the colorful neon of the doughnut shop. Shelly shivered and felt hungry for a plain doughnut, drowned in coffee. She flipped on the kitchen's fluorescents, then found a new message tacked to the bulletin board, scrawled in Danny's handwriting. "Welcome to The Last Chance Kitchen," it read. "If the food don't kill you, the state will." Shelly crumpled the note and dropped it in the trash.

The Jell-O would need time to set, so she broke out a box of it, boiled water, then mixed the water in a bowl with the orange powder. She splashed in ice cubes and shoved it in the freezer. Those protesters. What did they know about the people inside these walls and whether those people should live or die? Had they ever worked beside someone like Danny? Had they ever feared someone like him? Two more swings of that bat, or an ambulance stuck in traffic, and he might have been the guy strapped to a table tonight.

In the walk-in refrigerator, she found ground beef, defrosted, and brought that back to the work counter beside Stove #2. The stupid bastard. That was the crime on this night, wasn't it? that Doyle could pick out his last menu when so many others — decent people, kids, old people, young girls, fathers — couldn't plan for a last taste of something salty or sweet, tart or creamy or bitter or all of those in one dazzling mouthful. She imagined Hank in the tavern that night, cracking peanuts and letting the shells drop to the foot of the barstool. Beer on his tongue, and a bump, too. Scotch. Fire for the throat after a long day on the street corralling those punks. Ah, but you had it easy, Hank. Just had to keep yourself from killing them. You never sat beside them in the break room. Never cooked for them. Could you have done that? Could you talk nice to a girl who made a cat toy out of your son? Could you live with Chuck, knowing that when he smashed that other boy's car, the boy was in it, arms across his face to shield against the shattering glass?

Would you cook for your son?

Those girls. Those poor, frightened girls.

Shelly sliced the onions. She turned the knob on the grill to 275. Then, with kitchen scissors, she snipped a sheet of aluminum foil into bits. Like confetti for a party.

We do what we've got to do, Hank. We do what we've got to do.

Shelly swept the shredded foil from the counter into her hand, then littered the meat with it, rolled and slapped it into a patty filled with so many shining reminders that Bobby Doyle would get some in every bite, or spend his last hours picking it out.

Maybe she'd lose her job. Maybe he'd squeal that someone had messed with his cheeseburger. This worried her a moment, but then she remembered what Danny had said about the knife wound and the sock and Doyle not wanting anyone to think that they could get to him, that he was weak. The burger sizzled on the grill, and when she flipped it the foil had burned black and greasy.

When all was ready, she placed the hot foods in the portable warmer, and set the Jell-O in a little cooler. She phoned for a corrections officer, and a stocky young fellow arrived a few minutes later. "Some night, ain't it?" he said as he leaned over the hot pot, pushing it out the door.

"It's awful quiet for a place where so much is going on," she said. "Makes me want to sing just to hear a human voice."

"You do that," he said. "Could use a song myself."

As he headed down the hallway, she tried to find a tune, but nothing came to mind. She listened instead to the shudder as the hot pot wheels rolled.

When she arrived home — late, having stopped for gasoline and cigarettes — the house was dark, not even a porch light, so she figured Chuck was already asleep. At the front door, as she searched her key ring, she flinched at the sound of breathing and the creak of the porch swing.

"Hey, Mom," Chuck said.

Through the dark, she could just make out Chuck on the swing and someone else beside him.

"You could've said something earlier," she said.

"Could've," Chuck said. "Would've scared you no matter what."

"Who's that with you?"

"Tina."

"Hey, Mrs. Wolansky."

Shelly waved and went inside. With measured steps, she walked to every room — even Chuck's — and turned on every light in the house before closing her bedroom door. She opened a window, though it let the cold in, and placed an ashtray on the sill. She smoked one cigarette, then another, waiting for a phone call or a knock at the door, but nothing broke the silence. She undressed, put on a flannel nightgown, then slipped between the sheets and shivered.

A few hours later, still long before dawn, Chuck dropped his duffel bag into the Buick's trunk and sat in the back seat. He carried his "maim" mask, which had been in his hands since he left his room that morning.

"So, is he dead?" Chuck asked, pulling the mask over his face. Looking in the rearview mirror, Shelly read "MIAM."

"I suppose. I thought we'd pick up a newspaper to find out."

They stopped at the doughnut shop on Route 5. While the woman behind the counter worked hard to look at her register and nowhere else, Chuck, in his mask, ordered three chocolate frosteds and a pint of chocolate milk. Shelly ordered a plain doughnut and a cup of coffee, regular. With the change on her bill, she bought a newspaper from the box out front, its headline heavy and black: DOYLE DIES.

There on the sidewalk, she read by neon light how he lay on the table, headphones over his ears and a portable CD player attached to his belt. He would not look at the mirrored panel behind which the witnesses sat: the uncle of the girls, the prison warden, two reporters, and the prosecuting attorney who tried him. He was listening, the report said, to Pink Floyd when he died: "The Great Gig in the Sky."

"He didn't eat much," the warden was quoted as saying. "Just a few french fries. A bit of a cheeseburger."

Shelly stood, silent for a moment, not reading, not thinking, surprised that she felt sorry for Doyle, surprised at her grief and regret. She inhaled quickly, by reflex, then remembered that Chuck waited inside, that she had also ordered a doughnut and coffee. The food seemed more than she could stomach.

Inside, Chuck sat in a booth, the mask off his face now and set on the table. He had eaten a doughnut and a half. "So?" he said.

"He's dead." She sat across from him on the cracked red vinyl.

"And he ate your food? Man, you're just about famous, huh?"

"Chuck, leave it alone." She wiped her eyes.

"Hey," he said. "What's wrong?"

"What's wrong? What's wrong." She turned to face the fluorescent lights, then to the racks of doughnuts behind the counter. Finally, she stared out the plate window at the prison across the highway, at the search lights, the fencing, the concrete. A monster of a building filled with monsters. Danny. Doyle. The worst kind of people. She wanted to close her eyes, but the prison filled the window frame, demanding that she look, that she see. The worst kind of people.

"What's wrong is you used to be such a nice kid, you know, and I worry about you now. I do. Geez, I hate crying."

"So stop."

"I had a hard night, OK? Do me this favor. Scratch that word off your mask. Shake hands with the other team. It's hard enough making meals for all those punks in jail. I can't make them for punks at home, too."

He started to laugh.

"I'm not kidding." The words choked out of her. "You wear that mask again, you can eat junk food the rest of your life. Eat salty chips until your insides dehydrate, I don't care."

"Like you ever cook for me anyway." He chomped on a doughnut, chocolate smearing the cusps of his frown, that frown he wore to play the dangerous man. He was no such thing, she thought. He wasn't even in his mother's league.

She slapped him, so fast, so hard he dropped the doughnut. The frosted side stuck to the floor.

"That's exactly who I cook for," she said, her palm stinging. "For the last three years, every day of the week in that god-awful place cooking. For who else? Rapists? Murderers? Grow up, Chuck. I've cooked for you."

Other customers stopped talking, and Shelly knew they stared, worrying they might have to get involved. The bell on the door jingled as a couple of day-shift corrections officers arrived for their morning treat and waved at Shelly, but she ignored them. Chuck shifted nearer the wall, away from her.

She saw how the mark of her hand blotched his pale cheek. Just that quick she could turn on him. Just that quick she could hurt him. Lord help her. She remembered Hank's face, remembered those moments when his eyes revealed and held back such fury, and now she wanted to kiss each eye in gratitude because she understood, she knew, the rage and violence Hank had smothered.

When Chuck lifted his face he looked scared and angry, and Shelly wanted above all else that he would turn out more his father's son than his mother's, that he would learn to put down the stick and to sheath the knife. She stood, hand in purse feeling for car keys, but Chuck stayed seated, fingers at a loss, twisting the bottom of his game-day tie.

LESLIE EDGERTON

In the Zone

FROM *High Plains Literary Review*

I TOLD MANNY the whole story. We were staying in on a Saturday morning while everyone else went to the movie. Sat up at the front table, playing double sol and eating Keebler's Chocolate Chips and smoking tightrolls, Camels. Doing the prison day-off thing.

"I was hung up on her, bro," I said, trying to explain it to him. "She owned my ass."

"I been there," he said, and the way he said it I knew it was true.

"We were broke up and I was taking out some other ladies," I went on. "One weekend, a Sunday, I must have had four different babes come over, different times, got laid each time. I was having a ball, but it was crazy. No matter how much fun I was having, I still couldn't get Donna out of my mind. I was fucked up, man.

"Anyway, the last chick left about eleven that night, and I went to bed. To sleep."

Manny cracked up, leaned back in his chair and laughed with his head tilted back and his mouth wide open.

"I guess you weren't gonna pound your trouser worm," he said.

"I guess not. I was just getting asleep when the doorbell rang, and I got up and it was Donna. 'I got to talk to you,' she said.

"'Fuck, Donna,' I said. 'I'm just about asleep. We're over, sugar. Why don't you just leave me alone.' 'No,' she said, 'I've really got to talk to you.'

"'Well,' I said, 'I'm just about asleep, and if I don't go right back to bed I won't be able to. I oversleep and lose this job, my P.O.'ll violate me.'

"'Okay,' she said, pushing her way in. 'You go back to bed. I'll come with you and we'll talk in the morning. It's really important.'"

I looked over at Manny. "You know how it is when you're just about asleep? I told her, 'All right, come on in, but we're not doing anything, Donna. I just want to go to sleep.'

"Well, she came in and I went back and climbed in bed and she came in a minute later and crawled in with me, buck naked. I meant what I said, though — I wasn't going to fuck her. I turned over and closed my eyes, tried to get to sleep again. About five minutes later the doorbell rang again.

"It was a girl I'd seen a couple of times that week. Patsy. 'Patsy,' I said, 'I've got company.' 'Oh,' she said. 'Well, that's cool, I guess. I'll see you tomorrow then.' And she left.

"When I came back into the bedroom, Donna jumped up and asked me who that was. 'Nobody,' I said, 'just a friend. She's gone.' Donna ran to the front door and must have seen her walking away. She came back, and she was hot.

"'You fucking that girl,' she said. I said, 'No, I'm not, but that's none of your business anyway. We're broke up,' I said.

"'That's it,' she said, slamming around and throwing her clothes on. 'I'm outta here.' 'That was the original idea,' I said back to her, and she went out, just about busting the door.

"That's it, I'm thinking, and went back and lay down. But then I thought I heard voices and got up and opened the door, and sure enough, there's Patsy sitting in a chair by the pool and Donna's giving her the business, screaming at her.

"'Donna!' I yelled down. 'Get your ass out of here right now or I'm calling the cops.' I didn't say anything to Patsy even though I knew she didn't have a clue what was going on, but I knew Patsy was cool. I figured if I said anything to her that'd fire Donna up again and I'd just tell Patsy the next day what went down and she'd understand. Well, they both get up and head for their cars. Patsy always parked on one side of the complex. I watched for a minute, saw Donna was heading in a different direction, and went back inside. I lay back down, but then I got to thinking — I know this bitch — Donna — I better be sure she's left.

"I went to the front door again, and sure enough, Donna's dogging Patsy, walking right behind her, yapping at her. I ran out of the apartment along the catwalk. All I had on were my jockeys. There's a little space where you can look out at the parking lot, and I ran to that. Patsy's up against a car and Donna's got her face right up in

Patsy's. I ran downstairs and around the corner and just as I came around the corner, I see Donna's fist come back and she smacked Patsy. She smacked her hard, dude. I never seen a *guy* hit another guy the way that broad hit her. I ran over to them and just as I got there Donna's raising her hand to smack Patsy again. Only she wasn't hitting her. She was stabbing her. It really didn't register, though. I got there just as she was coming down with the knife and I grabbed her arm with one hand and Patsy with the other and shoved them apart. Donna went down on her knees and then started coming up, trying to cut me. I ducked my stomach back and at the same time she missed I grabbed the hand with the knife and hit it against my knee. This all happened fast, man. Really fast.

"She lost the knife when her hand hit my knee and my first thought is . . . *find the knife.* I know if I get the knife first she can't hurt me. We're both scrabbling around looking for it — it was dark in that parking lot — and I find it first. It was this big-ass switchblade — in fact, I gave it to her a long time ago as a present — and I find it and pick it up and she sees I've got it and she takes off running. I'm standing there with this switchblade and I tried to close it and couldn't 'cause it's bent in two-three places. I just stand there until I see the reflection of her lights go on in the other parking lot and hear her tires burn out, and then I walk over to Patsy, who's standing up against a car.

"Well, this sounds weird, but it's the truth, Manny. I've got this knife in my hand and everything but it still doesn't dawn on me that Patsy's been stabbed. It just happened so fast. Patsy didn't know she'd been cut either.

"I walk up to her and say, 'Are you all right?' She's got this white silk blouse on and chinos and I see little tiny sprinkles of blood on the blouse, looked like somebody'd sprinkled red salt out of a shaker, or tabasco sauce . . . yeah . . . more like tabasco sauce. 'You been hit,' I said. 'You got a nosebleed.' 'No,' she says, 'she missed me. I ducked and she hit me in the back.'

"She turned around, and man! Her whole back was solid red and blood was running down her pants like she was peeing herself. 'You been stabbed,' I said, what had happened finally dawning on me. 'I have?' she said. She didn't even know it herself."

Just then the dorm hack came by, motioned at us to come over. He was taking the count. Even though he knew us, he made us tell him our names and he read the numbers off our shirts, made check marks on his clipboard, and then left, probably to take a nap downstairs where his desk was.

We went back and sat down at the table.

"You sure you want to hear the rest of this?" I asked Manny.

"Fuck, yes," he said, grinning. "This is some wild bitch!"

I went ahead with the story.

"Well, I wanted to take her over to Charity Hospital, but she said no. She wanted us to go up to my apartment and get a better look at where she'd been stuck. We climbed up the stairs, and I'm thinking she's not that bad, being as how she can go up stairs and all. When we get to my apartment I took off her blouse and all I can see is an entry wound about this big [I held up my fingers to show about an inch and a half or so], so my mind says the knife only went in a couple inches and hit a bone. That's what bent the blade, I'm thinking. Anybody knows you can bleed a lot from even a small cut. The blood's not running anymore, it's kind of just bubbling a little. I bandage her up with a bath towel and some electrician's tape I had, and then she says maybe I ought to take her over to the hospital as she's feeling a little woozy. That's smart, I tell her, and we go downstairs.

"I drive her over to Charity and pull up to the emergency room entrance and the rent-a-cop comes out and they get a wheelchair after I tell them the score and wheel her in.

"I tell the rent-a-cop what's gone down, and he calls the real deal, and when that guy gets there, a uniform, I tell him the same story and give him the knife. I tell him where he can probably find Donna. 'Look over at the Godfather in Metairie,' I say. 'How's the girl got stabbed?' he asks, and I tell him I don't know, I don't think it's that bad, and give him my reasoning about hitting the bone and all. 'But check with the doctor,' I said.

"Well, he doesn't check with the doctor, just leaves, and they pick up Donna the next morning and all she gets charged with is simple assault, not assault with a deadly weapon or attempted murder or any of that, only I don't know none of this until the next day.

"About an hour after I bring Patsy in, I'm sitting by my lonesome in the waiting area and in comes this lady and man. The man looks exactly like that guy used to be on *Miami Vice*, the TV show? You know, the captain? The one with all the acne scars? Remember? Anyway, this lady comes over to me, no howdy-do, nothing, and she says, 'If my little girl dies, you die, and this guy will kill you.' She means the scarface with her. It must be Patsy's mom, I guess, which it is, and I try to explain how it isn't my fault — that if it wasn't for me Patsy probably would be dead as Donna was fixing to stab her again when I broke it up.

"'Don't matter none,' she says. 'If she hadn't been at your place, she wouldn't have got stabbed to begin with.' I guess she'd already talked to the cops or the hospital or somebody, got the lowdown on what happened. You couldn't reason with her. This guy she was with, later I find out he's connected, would've done what she said, terminated my ass. Him I never talked to. In fact the whole time, the four hours we sat there the only ones in the waiting room, he never said a word to me or her. Just sat there mugging on me with no expression on his face. It was creepy.

"I went to the john a couple of times and each time I'm thinking, Should I just take off now, go to California or something? See, I was convinced that if Patsy died her mom meant business. There was no doubt in my mind. The only thing kept me there was I still thought Patsy wasn't hurt all that much.

"Shit. It was serious all right. Along about daybreak this doctor comes out to talk to us. 'We think she's gonna make it,' he says to Patsy's mom, 'but it's still a little shaky.' Turns out the knife went all the way in, almost came through the other side. It did hit a bone, and that's what saved her. 'We were looking to see if the blade hit the lung,' he said. 'If it had even nicked it, we couldn't have saved her. Her lungs would have filled up with blood and she would have basically drowned.' As it was, they ended up giving her six units of whole blood and the doc said she died on them twice and they had to bring her back from the dead. They had to wait until the blood clotted and moved away from the lung to get a clear picture. The x-ray showed it had missed, but how he didn't know. It was a miracle.

"For her *and* me. Once we found out she was out of the woods, we all left. Before we did, her mom turned to me and said, 'You're still on the hook, Mayes. She might still die. If she does, you're dead, Mister.'

"Way it turned out, Patsy came through fine, although she was a little sore."

"So why'd you try to kill yourself? I don't get it."

"Wait a minute. I'm getting to it." I saw Manny was getting antsy now that the bloody part was all over, so I speeded up a couple of the in-between details and cut to the grand finale. "Patsy gets out of the hospital, sore but OK, and we even started dating kinda heavy, although we had to fuck real easy or else open up her wound again. Her mom decides she likes me, and she tells me what she told me in the hospital was for true — I'd'a been dead meat if her darlin' daughter'd croaked. She says she's glad she didn't 'cause now she likes me, but somehow that didn't make me feel a whole lot better. She's an okay enough gal, but every time I see her I still get a little nervous.

"Anyhoo, a couple weeks go by and then I start getting phone calls at work from Donna. She don't say hello, kiss my ass or nothing when I pick up the phone, just starts talking like we hadn't ever stopped. 'I drive by your work every day when I get off,' she says, 'and I point my gun at you while I'm going by. One of these days I'm pulling the trigger, motherfucker.' The first time or so she pulls this I just sort of laugh it off, but after a solid week of these kinds of conversations I had enough and called the district attorney. 'Nothing we can do,' he says, 'until she does something, but I made a note of this and if she ever actually shoots at you or anything like that we'll pick her up.' That made me feel about as good and safe as finding out I got blood in my urine. I thought once or twice that maybe I ought to do her before she does me, but when I start scheming about how to carry that off, I realize I'm still fucked up over her."

"You still fucked up over this crazy bitch after the shit she done?" I didn't realize Manny's eyes could get that wide. The way he looked and the way he said it made me think maybe it was me that was crazy. "How can you even want to be on the same planet with her?"

"Because I'm stupid?" I wasn't a hundred percent joking. I stared at the end of the cigarette I had going. "Yeah. It's somethin', huh? Go figure. You want me to lie about it?"

"Naw, man. It's just . . . well, I don't figure you to be pussy-whipped, that's all."

"You wait, Manny. Anyway, I didn't know what to do. I knew she was just about wacko enough to pull some stunt like that — drive by and shoot me — it wouldn't be hard — I'm working in front of this big plate glass window two feet from the street — and then I get this phone call from her."

"What'd she say?" He was all ears.

"She said, 'I just want to tell you why I came over that night.'"

"That's right. You said she said she wanted to talk to you about something."

"Yeah. What it was, what she said was that she was pregnant and that she murdered it. That's the words she used."

"You mean —"

"Abortion. She had an abortion. Man, I'm death on abortions! She knows that, the bitch!" Thinking about it all over again brought on some of the same feelings I'd had then.

"I started thinking about this baby boy — I *know* it was a boy — and man, I lost it. I started drinking then, went out and bought a bottle of Jack and hit it hard. I'm thinking all kinds of things. You know, 'what coulda been' kinds of things. Me and her. Me and her and our baby boy. I just kinda went out of my skull. It probably didn't help I laid up in this motel room out on Esplanade for three days doing nothing but slugging down Jack and going crazy in the head. That's when I did it."

I told him about the Norelco razor cord and it breaking when I tried to hang myself with it. I didn't know why I was telling Manny all this. Maybe to get it all out, make me feel better. Only it didn't. Make me feel better, that is. I felt worse. I felt just like I had during those three days, only I didn't have any whiskey to help take the edge off. I know one thing — if I'd been on the bricks right that minute I wouldn't be qualifying for any of those white poker chips they give out at AA.

Time I went to bed that night I'd got it back under control somewhat. Only thing is I kept seeing Donna's fucking face, and I hated the way I felt. Like I still wanted us to be together.

Ain't that some shit?

If having Donna on my mind wasn't enough, that fucker Boles came back, the one I stabbed up on the roof of the laundry. You'd think a guy had thirty-some laundry-pin holes in him would have sense enough to check outa this sorry life. I was cutting a guy's hair when Manny came over and told me. He'd been up front, talking to the guard on duty that day. They'd put him in the infirmary.

The guard thought he'd be there at least a week before they put him back out in the population and gave him limited duty. Proba-

bly put him in the library for a while, the guard told Manny. That
made sense. Put an illiterate in charge of Angola's priceless Zane
Grey paperback collection.

There was no question I had to get to him. It was obvious he
hadn't snitched on me yet, but I knew it was only a matter of time.

It's hard to move around in prison. In movies, it seems like guys
come and go pretty much as they want. All they have to do is bribe a
guard or some trusty. That might be the case in Tinseltown, but at
Angola it was a different story. You couldn't take a crap without a
pass. And what're you supposed to be bribing guards with? Packs of
cigarettes?

I was still trying to cook up a scheme when the situation changed
just three days later. For the better. Boles got released from the
infirmary, and just like that guard had predicted, he was put in the
library. He'd be much easier to get to there. I just had to dope out a
way to get there without getting caught. That meant I couldn't get
a pass to the library since that'd leave a record on somebody's pass
sheet.

The smart thing to do was get to Boles quick. He was still weak
from his wounds. Also, he hadn't talked yet. If I waited too long
he'd not only be stronger and harder to take down but he might
have a change of heart and snitch me out.

My man Dusty came through, though. Just like in the movies.

"I got something for you," he said when we came in that night
from chow.

"What?"

"You got to fix that guy over at the library, right?"

He knew I did.

'You told me you might need some help sometime with this guy."

I was surprised he remembered, and then I wasn't. Dusty was no
lame-o.

"So what you got?"

"Here."

He put a piece of paper in my hand. It was a pass. "Free-walkin'"
passes, we called 'em. Only trusties got this kind of pass. It allowed
you free movement wherever you wanted to go inside the walls.
The best thing was it didn't have your name on it. A solid gold pass,
especially for what I needed it for.

Dusty told me one other thing.

"Do it tomorrow morning," he said. I wanted to know why then. "'Cause, stupid, you're gonna need an alibi maybe, and I can give you one. I've got to take the barber-shop towels over to the laundry, and I'm going to ask for you to help me. You got twenty minutes to do it in. I got a friend at the laundry I already talked to. He's gonna say you came in with me, dropped the laundry off."

It's things like this let you know who your friends are.

All I did that night was have one nightmare after another. Practically every night I had a dream — nightmares most of the time — while I was behind bars. On the bricks I never dreamed.

I woke up after about the tenth dream where I was being chased by Donna with her fucking knife, my heart beating like I'd been doing amyl nitrate poppers, and I'm laughing like somebody in the squirrel factory, and there was some fucker in the back of the dorm ripping out these horrible sobs.

I felt the sweat chill as I threw off my blanket. I yelled, "Somebody put a dick in that asshole's mouth!" I barefooted it over to the window and looked out and the cooking crew was heading across the quad to the mess hall in their whites so I figured it was four-thirty since that's when they went over to start destroying breakfast.

There was no use trying to get back to sleep. They'd be rousting us for wake-up in another hour anyway, so I went and got my shaving gear and took a shower and shaved, brushed my teeth. Nice, I thought. You could actually take a shit without ten thousand guys screaming ten feet from you. I'd have to remember that and get up early from now on.

I sat on the stool longer than what I needed, just thinking. About the dream and Donna and Boles and all kinds of shit like that. Just sat there getting madder and madder. It wasn't like I was building a hard-on so's I could jack up Boles later on. I never needed that shit. You know, get mad so I could jump on somebody. That kind of shit's for punks. The best way is to not even think about it. Just do it.

That's the onliest way to do anything major. Specially when you got a choice, got two roads you can take. Like I could whack out Boles or I could do something else. Like nothing. Just not do it at all, see what happened then.

Fuck that. Boles was going down. I couldn't believe a guy could get stabbed that many times and still live. What was he, some kind

of vampire? Thirty-some holes this punk gets with a straightened-
out laundry pin and he's over working in the library like he just got
over the flu. I shoulda put a wooden stake through his mother-
fucking heart is what I shoulda done, prevented all this happy
horseshit.

It's like a stickup. Most outlaws I talked to got busted 'cause they
planned too much. Figure out what to do if this happens, that happens. The best way is not even know you're gonna do it till it happens. Like, you're in a supermarket buying a deck of butts, whatever, and on the way out you see all the checkout girls heading with
their money trays to the office on account of the next shift is there.
Before you walked in, robbing somebody maybe was the last thing
on your mind. You see that, all them trays stacked up on the desk in
the office, the safe open, and the smartest thing you can do is walk
over, pull out your piece, and tell the guy in the tie to bag it up,
hand it over. Zip, boom, bang, you're out of the place and cruising
down the road before you even know what you did. Just like that.

I never once in my entire life got caught on a job when I did it
like that. The ones I keep getting busted on are the ones where you
cased and planned and schemed for eleventeen years before and
always — *always* — the one little thing you never thought of happens and the next thing you know is you're trying to wipe black ink
off your fingers with that one little paper towel they always give you
and you feel you're waking up from a bad dream. Into one that's
worse.

I'm thinking all this and then I just did it. Dropped a sheet over
all them other thoughts about Donna and even Boles and just went
into another part of my mind.

We were walking out of the dorm after breakfast and Manny was
saying something to me. In fact, he was almost screaming before I
noticed anything.

"What?" I said, wondering why he was yelling at me, and then
Dusty, who was walking with us, said, "Leave him alone, Manny.
He's in the zone."

He gave me a look and took a quick glance around, and then his
hand touched mine and I knew what it was. I slipped it into my
shirt. Without looking I could feel it was a knife, a regular hunting
knife, not some piece of shit that had been jury-rigged from a piece

of metal from one of the shops. This was a serious killing weapon. What he did, what I had in my hand, registered, not in the front part of my mind but in the back, where I was.

We got to the barber school and I just went on back to stand behind my chair instead of screwing around with the others. A couple of the guys walked by, said something, and I just nodded. I don't have a clue what they said to me.

Then Mr. Dillsie came to the door of his office and yelled at me to come up front, help Dusty with the towels. I could see Dusty behind the glass. There were five large sacks. I grabbed three of them and Dusty the other two and we went out the back door.

"Run," Dusty hissed, once we were out of sight of the school. "You gotta book, man!"

We ran all the way to the laundry and his man was standing outside waiting for us. "You got fifteen minutes, maybe twenty," Dusty said. "Go!"

I threw down my sacks and took off again, heading up toward the quad, around the chow hall, and luck was with me. I didn't pass a single guard, only one inmate. I kept my head down and I don't think the guy even noticed me. The library was two buildings down from the chow hall and nobody was on the walk in front of me. Clear sailing. This was the best time. There shouldn't be anybody else in the library except the librarian for at least another hour.

There wasn't.

I went in quick, closed the door behind me. I could feel the knife where I'd put it under my shirt, the handle stuck down behind my belt.

At first I thought nobody was there, and then I heard something sounded like a book drop back in the office. I walked back and went into the room. He was there, bending over. He straightened up, a book in his hand, and looked at me.

"Boles," I said. I could see the fear in his eyes.

"I didn't snitch you out, man," he said, laying the book down on the desk in front of him and stepping back. He moved kind of stiff-like, and I guess I would too, if I had that many holes in me.

"I know. I couldn't be here if you had, could I?"

I pulled out my knife.

"Why you gonna do this?"

"You know why."

He took another step back and was up against the wall. I started toward him.

"Oh, man." His voice broke. He put his hands up, palms facing me, and began edging along the wall toward the door. "Man, you're safe. I'm not gonna tell who did me. If I was gonna tell, I'd'a already done it. I'm sorry for what I did to you, man. We're even. Don't you see we're even?"

In a way, he was right. I'd had the same thought myself. The pain I'd put him through almost certainly matched what he'd done to me. In one way the score was settled.

I didn't even feel the same anger I had when he'd raped me. The day I'd shanked him up on the laundry roof the mad had disappeared, vanishing a little bit with every hole I put in him until it was all gone. There was no revenge left in my heart, none at all. It was just pure-d empty of everything, all malice.

I walked over to him and he just stood there. I don't think his knees would let him move. His eyes told me that. I stopped inches from him. His hands went down to his sides.

"You won't talk? Ever?"

"Oh, man! No! I swear t'God! You're safe, man. I just want to do my time, get the fuck out of here, that's all."

I believed him. I could hear it in his voice.

"You don't even know my name, do you?" I said.

"No." He was telling the truth.

"My name's Jake Mayes," I said. Then I stabbed him. Who knows why? Just like that. It started in easy enough, then hit something solid so that I had to push harder on the handle before it went all the way in. I looked him in the eyes the whole time. It seemed like it lasted for hours, us standing there, and his eyes changed, just the least little bit, in realization of what was happening, I guess, and his eyelids started to quiver like he was trying to keep from blinking, as if once he blinked it was all over, and then all the bones just seemed to go out of his face. I reached up with my other hand, grabbed his shirt, and eased him on down to the floor. His eyes were still open. He hadn't blinked, but he was dead.

I got back to the laundry and Dusty was still there talking with his friend. I knew I had been gone longer than I should have.

"What you doing?" Dusty said, when I came up. 'You're walking like you got all the time in the world, moron. C'mon, let's get the fuck out of here."

The other guy turned and went back inside the laundry and we started walking back to the barber school. On the way, Dusty asked me questions. "You get rid of the knife? Anybody see you?"

Back at the school I had a customer waiting for me. Dusty did too. The guy wanted a flattop. I got out the triple-ought blade, rinsed it in the sterilizing solution. When I got done, I stepped back and looked. It was the best flattop I had ever cut. It was a fucking masterpiece, it was. You could land a plane on that flattop. I just laid down my clippers when the steam whistle blew. I knew what that meant. I looked over at Dusty and he at me and he held his hand down low so nobody else could see and gave me a thumbs-up. I just nodded. Ice cold, that's the way I felt. Frosty. Peaceful. When that whistle blew, something happened inside. Time, as a concept, just disappeared. Just blew away in the wind, went over the wall.

A couple months later, my old rappy Bud came down from Kenner after his trial and Dusty got him into the dorm with us. It was Kimmie he'd killed, got him sent back, but he told us it was an accident. She was giving him some grief, yakking that he was always out too late, lame crap like that, and he tapped her.

"I didn't even hit her that hard," he said. "I hit her lots harder lots of times. It was just a freak accident."

"Fucking life's a freak accident," I said, and we all laughed: me, him, Dusty, and Manny. We were all outside on the ballfield, sitting at one of the picnic tables, eating Oreos and smoking tightrolls, playing dominoes.

This is as good as it gets, I thought, looking around. I saw a bird fly up to the wall and then it was gone, flew over the side. That was all right, I thought. Good fucking riddance. This was OK too, sitting out in the grass with my buds. The green, green grass of home. No fucking broads hassling us, just good friends sitting around, having us a ball. I started to think of Donna but got that shit out of my mind. Thinking about broads is what fucks up your time in here. All I want to do now is my time.

Eight more years, thanks to Boles. Yeah, they found out it was me. Fuck it. Like I give a shit.

I can do eight years and snooze all the way through it, now that I got Donna out of my skull.

Got my head on right, now. I'm in the zone, man, the zone we all been looking for since the minute we were born. In the zone, you're a man nobody fucks with. You're the fucking Master of the Universe. People step aside when you walk by. You stare at any motherfucker you want, all day long, you feel like it. Cracks me up, way these chumps try and become invisible, they see me coming down the tier walk.

Invisible *this,* I say in my head when I walk by, and then I do whatever the fuck I want, whatever I feel like doing. Just what-the-fuck-ever. *Just like that,* amigo.

WILLIAM GAY

The Paperhanger

FROM *Harper's Magazine*

THE VANISHING of the doctor's wife's child in broad daylight was an event so cataclysmic that it forever divided time into the then and the now, the before and the after. In later years, fortified with a pitcher of silica-dry vodka martinis, she had cause to replay the events preceding the disappearance. They were tawdry and banal but in retrospect freighted with menace, a foreshadowing of what was to come, like a footman or a fool preceding a king into a room.

She had been quarreling with the paperhanger. Her four-year-old daughter, Zeineb, was standing directly behind the paperhanger where he knelt smoothing air bubbles out with a wide plastic trowel. Zeineb had her fingers in the paperhanger's hair. The paperhanger's hair was shoulder length and the color of flax and the child was delighted with it. The paperhanger was accustomed to her doing this and he did not even turn around. He just went on with his work. His arms were smooth and brown and corded with muscle and in the light that fell upon the paperhanger through stained-glass panels the doctor's wife could see that they were lightly downed with fine golden hair. She studied these arms bemusedly while she formulated her thoughts.

You tell me so much a roll, she said. The doctor's wife was from Pakistan and her speech was still heavily accented. I do not know single-bolt rolls and double-bolt rolls. You tell me double-bolt price but you are installing single-bolt rolls. My friend has told me. It is cost me perhaps twice as much.

The paperhanger, still on his knees, turned. He smiled up at her.

He had pale blue eyes. I did tell you so much a roll, he said. You bought the rolls. The child, not yet vanished, was watching the paperhanger's eyes. She was a scaled-down clone of the mother, the mother viewed through the wrong end of a telescope, and the paperhanger suspected that as she grew neither her features nor her expression would alter, she would just grow larger, like something being aired up with a hand pump.

And you are leave lumps, the doctor's wife said, gesturing at the wall. I do not leave lumps, the paperhanger said. You've seen my work before. These are not lumps. The paper is wet. The paste is wet. Everything will shrink down and flatten out. He smiled again. He had clean even teeth. And besides, he said, I gave you my special cockteaser rate. I don't know what you're complaining about.

Her mouth worked convulsively. She looked for a moment as if he'd slapped her. When words did come they came in a fine spray of spit. You are trash, she said. You are scum.

Hands on knees, he was pushing erect, the girl's dark fingers trailing out of his hair. Don't call me trash, he said, as if it were perfectly all right to call him scum, but he was already talking to her back. She had whirled on her heels and went twisting her hips through an arched doorway into the cathedraled living room. The paperhanger looked down at the child. Her face glowed with a strange constrained glee, as if she and the paperhanger shared some secret the rest of the world hadn't caught on to yet.

In the living room the builder was supervising the installation of a chandelier that depended from the vaulted ceiling by a long golden chain. The builder was a short bearded man dancing about, showing her the features of the chandelier, smiling obsequiously. She gave him a flat angry look. She waved a dismissive hand toward the ceiling. Whatever, she said.

She went out the front door onto the porch and down a makeshift walkway of two-by-tens into the front yard where her car was parked. The car was a silver-gray Mercedes her husband had given her for their anniversary. When she cranked the engine its idle was scarcely perceptible.

She powered down the window. Zeineb, she called. Across the razed earth of the unlandscaped yard a man in a grease-stained T-shirt was booming down the chains securing a backhoe to a lowboy hooked to a gravel truck. The sun was low in the west and blood-red behind this tableau and man and tractor looked flat and dimensionless as something decorative stamped from tin. She blew the horn. The man turned, raised an arm as if she'd signaled him.

Zeineb, she called again.

She got out of the car and started impatiently up the walkway. Behind her the gravel truck started, and truck and backhoe pulled out of the drive and down toward the road.

The paperhanger was stowing away his T-square and trowels in his wooden toolbox. Where is Zeineb? the doctor's wife asked. She followed you out, the paperhanger told her. He glanced about, as if the girl might be hiding somewhere. There was nowhere to hide.

Where is my child? she asked the builder. The electrician climbed down from the ladder. The paperhanger came out of the bathroom with his tools. The builder was looking all around. His elfin features were touched with chagrin, as if this missing child were just something else he was going to be held accountable for.

Likely she's hiding in a closet, the paperhanger said. Playing a trick on you.

Zeineb does not play tricks, the doctor's wife said. Her eyes kept darting about the huge room, the shadows that lurked in corners. There was already an undercurrent of panic in her voice and all her poise and self-confidence seemed to have vanished with the child.

The paperhanger set down his toolbox and went through the house, opening and closing doors. It was a huge house and there were a lot of closets. There was no child in any of them.

The electrician was searching upstairs. The builder had gone through the French doors that opened onto the unfinished veranda and was peering into the backyard. The backyard was a maze of convoluted ditch excavated for the septic tank field line and beyond that there was just woods. She's playing in that ditch, the builder said, going down the flagstone steps.

She wasn't, though. She wasn't anywhere. They searched the house and grounds. They moved with jerky haste. They kept glancing toward the woods where the day was waning first. The builder kept shaking his head. She's got to be *somewhere*, he said.

Call someone, the doctor's wife said. Call the police.

It's a little early for the police, the builder said. She's got to be here.

You call them anyway. I have a phone in my car. I will call my husband.

While she called, the paperhanger and the electrician continued to search. They had looked everywhere and were forced to search places they'd already looked. If this ain't the goddamnedest thing I ever saw, the electrician said.

The doctor's wife got out of the Mercedes and slammed the door. Suddenly she stopped and clasped a hand to her forehead. She screamed. The man with the tractor, she cried. Somehow my child is gone with the tractor man.

Oh Jesus, the builder said. What have we got ourselves into here?

The high sheriff that year was a ruminative man named Bellwether. He stood beside the county cruiser talking to the paperhanger while deputies ranged the grounds. Other men were inside looking in places that had already been searched numberless times. Bellwether had been in the woods and he was picking cockleburs off his khakis and out of his socks. He was watching the woods, where dark was gathering and seeping across the field like a stain.

I've got to get men out here, Bellwether said. A lot of men and a lot of lights. We're going to have to search every inch of these woods.

You'll play hell doing it, the paperhanger said. These woods stretch all the way to Lawrence County. This is the edge of the Harrikan. Down in there's where all those old mines used to be. Allens Creek.

I don't give a shit if they stretch all the way to Fairbanks, Alaska, Bellwether said. They've got to be searched. It'll just take a lot of men.

The raw earth yard was full of cars. Doctor Jamahl had come in a sleek black Lexus. He berated his wife. Why weren't you watching her? he asked. Unlike his wife's, the doctor's speech was impeccable. She covered her face with her palms and wept. The doctor still wore his green surgeon's smock and it was flecked with bright dots of blood as a butcher's smock might be.

I need to feed a few cows, the paperhanger said. I'll feed my stock pretty quick and come back and help hunt.

You don't mind if I look in your truck, do you?

Do what?

I've got to cover my ass. If that little girl don't turn up damn quick this is going to be over my head. TBI, FBI, network news. I've got to eliminate everything.

Eliminate away, the paperhanger said.

The sheriff searched the floorboard of the paperhanger's pickup truck. He shined his huge flashlight under the seat and felt behind it with his hands.

I had to look, he said apologetically.

Of course you did, the paperhanger said.

Full dark had fallen before he returned. He had fed his cattle and stowed away his tools and picked up a six-pack of San Miguel beer and he sat in the back of the pickup truck drinking it. The paperhanger had been in the navy and stationed in the Philippines and San Miguel was the only beer he could drink. He had to go out of town to buy it, but he figured it was worth it. He liked the exotic labels, the dark bitter taste on the back of his tongue, the way the chilled bottles felt held against his forehead.

A motley crowd of curiosity seekers and searchers thronged the yard. There was a vaguely festive air. He watched all this with a dispassionate eye, as if he were charged with grading the participants, comparing this with other spectacles he'd seen. Coffee urns had been brought in and set up on tables, sandwiches prepared and handed out to the weary searchers. A crane had been hauled in and the septic tank reclaimed from the ground. It swayed from a taut cable while men with lights searched the impacted earth beneath it for a child, for the very trace of a child. Through the far dark woods lights crossed and recrossed, darted to and fro like fireflies. The doctor and the doctor's wife sat in folding camp chairs looking drained, stunned, waiting for their child to be delivered into their arms.

The doctor was a short portly man with a benevolent expression. He had a moon-shaped face, with light and dark areas of skin that looked swirled, as if the pigment coloring him had not been properly mixed. He had been educated at Princeton. When he had established his practice he had returned to Pakistan to find a wife befitting his station. The woman he had selected had been chosen on the basis of her beauty. In retrospect, perhaps more consideration should have been given to other qualities. She was still beautiful but he was thinking that certain faults might outweigh this. She seemed to have trouble keeping up with her children. She could lose a four-year-old child in a room no larger than six hundred square feet and she could not find it again.

The paperhanger drained his bottle and set it by his foot in the bed of the truck. He studied the doctor's wife's ravaged face through the deep blue light. The first time he had seen her she had hired him to paint a bedroom in the house they were living in while the doctor's mansion was being built. There was an arrogance about her that cried out to be taken down a notch or two. She flirted with him, backed away, flirted again. She would treat him as if he were a stain on the bathroom rug and then stand close by him while he worked until he was dizzy with the smell of her, with the heat that seemed to radiate off her body. She stood by him while he knelt painting baseboards and after an infinite moment leaned carefully the weight of a thigh against his shoulder. You'd better move it, he thought. She didn't. He laughed and turned his face into her groin. She gave a strangled cry and slapped him hard. The paintbrush flew away and speckled the dark rose walls with antique white. You filthy beast, she said. You are some kind of monster. She stormed out of the room and he could hear her slamming doors behind her.

Well, I was looking for a job when I found this one. He smiled philosophically to himself.

But he had not been fired. In fact now he had been hired again. Perhaps there was something here to ponder.

At midnight he gave up his vigil. Some souls more hardy than his kept up the watch. The earth here was worn smooth by the useless traffic of the searchers. Driving out, he met a line of pickup trucks with civil-defense tags. Grimfaced men sat aligned in their beds. Some clutched rifles loosely by their barrels, as if they would lay waste whatever monster, man or beast, would snatch up a child in its slaverous jaws and vanish, prey and predator, in the space between two heartbeats.

Even more dubious reminders of civilization as these fell away. He drove into the Harrikan, where he lived. A world so dark and forlorn light itself seemed at a premium. Whippoorwills swept redeyed up from the roadside. Old abandoned foundries and furnaces rolled past, grim and dark as forsaken prisons. Down a ridge here was an abandoned graveyard, if you knew where to look. The paperhanger did. He had dug up a few of the graves, examined with curiosity what remained, buttons, belt buckles, a cameo brooch. The bones he laid out like a child with a Tinkertoy, arranging them the way they went in jury-rigged resurrection.

He braked hard on a curve, the truck slewing in the gravel. A bobcat had crossed the road, graceful as a wraith, fierce and lantern-eyed in the headlights, gone so swiftly it might have been a stage prop swung across the road on wires.

Bellwether and a deputy drove to the backhoe operator's house. He lived up a gravel road that wound through a great stand of cedars. He lived in a board-and-batten house with a tin roof rusted to a warm umber. They parked before it and got out, adjusting their gunbelts.

Bellwether had a search warrant with the ink scarcely dry. The operator was outraged.

Look at it this way, Bellwether explained patiently. I've got to cover my ass. Everything has got to be considered. You know how kids are. Never thinking. What if she run under the wheels of your truck when you was backing out? What if quicklike you put the body in your truck to get rid of somewhere?

What if quicklike you get the hell off my property, the operator said.

Everything has to be considered, the sheriff said again. Nobody's accusing anybody of anything just yet.

The operator's wife stood glowering at them. To have something to do with his hands, the operator began to construct a cigarette. He had huge red hands thickly sown with brown freckles. They trembled. I ain't got a thing in this round world to hide, he said.

Bellwether and his men searched everywhere they could think of to look. Finally they stood uncertainly in the operator's yard, out of place in their neat khakis, their polished leather.

Now get the hell off my land, the operator said. If all you think of me is that I could run over a little kid and then throw it off in the bushes like a dead cat or something then I don't even want to see your goddamn face. I want you gone and I want you by God gone now.

Everything had to be considered, the sheriff said.

Then maybe you need to consider that paperhanger.

What about him?

That paperhanger is one sick puppy.

He was still there when I got there, the sheriff said. Three witnesses swore nobody ever left, not even for a minute, and one of them was the child's mother. I searched his truck myself.

Then he's a sick puppy with a damn good alibi, the operator said.

That was all. There was no ransom note, no child that turned up two counties over with amnesia. She was a page turned, a door closed, a lost ball in the high weeds. She was a child no larger than a doll, but the void she left behind her was unreckonable. Yet there was no end to it. No finality. There was no moment when someone could say, turning from a mounded grave, Well, this has been unbearable, but you've got to go on with your life. Life did not go on.

At the doctor's wife's insistence an intensive investigation was focused on the backhoe operator. Forensic experts from the FBI examined every millimeter of the gravel truck, paying special attention to its wheels. They were examined with every modern crime-fighting device the government possessed, and there was not a microscopic particle of tissue or blood, no telltale chip of fingernail, no hair ribbon.

Work ceased on the mansion. Some subcontractors were discharged outright, while others simply drifted away. There was no one to care if the work was done, no one to pay them. The half-finished veranda's raw wood grayed in the fall, then winter, rains. The ditches were left fallow and uncovered and half-filled with water. Kudzu crept from the woods. The hollyhocks and oleanders the doctor's wife had planted grew entangled and rampant. The imported windows were stoned by double-dared boys who whirled and fled. Already this house where a child had vanished was acquiring an unhealthy, diseased reputation.

The doctor and his wife sat entombed in separate prisons replaying real and imagined grievances. The doctor felt that his wife's neglect had sent his child into the abstract. The doctor's wife drank vodka martinis and watched talk shows where passed an endless procession of vengeful people who had not had children vanish, and felt, perhaps rightly, that the fates had dealt her from the bottom of the deck, and she prayed with intensity for a miracle.

Then one day she was just gone. The Mercedes and part of her clothing and personal possessions were gone too. He idly wondered where she was, but he did not search for her.

Sitting in his armchair cradling a great marmalade cat and a bottle of J&B and observing with bemused detachment the gradations of light at the window, the doctor remembered studying literature at Princeton. He had particular cause to reconsider the poetry of William Butler Yeats. For how surely things fell apart, how surely the center did not hold.

His practice fell into a ruin. His colleagues made sympathetic allowances for him at first, but there are limits to these things. He made erroneous diagnoses, prescribed the wrong medicines not once or twice but as a matter of course.

Just as there is a deepening progression to misfortune, so too there is a point beyond which things can only get worse. They did. A middle-aged woman he was operating on died.

He had made an incision to remove a ruptured appendix and the incised flesh was clamped aside while he made ready to slice it out. It was not there. He stared in drunken disbelief. He began to search under things, organs, intestines, a rising tide of blood. The appendix was not there. It had gone into the abstract, atrophied, been removed twenty-five years before, he had sliced through the selfsame scar. He was rummaging through her abdominal cavity like an irritated man fumbling through a drawer for a clean pair of socks, finally bellowing in rage and wringing his hands in bloody vexation while nurses began to cry out, another surgeon was brought on the run as a closer, and he was carried from the operating room.

Came then days of sitting in the armchair while he was besieged by contingency lawyers, action news teams, a long line of process servers. There was nothing he could do. It was out of his hands and into the hands of the people who are paid to do these things. He sat cradling the bottle of J&B with the marmalade cat snuggled against his portly midriff. He would study the window, where the light drained away in a process he no longer had an understanding of, and sip the scotch and every now and then stroke the cat's head gently. The cat purred against his breast as reassuringly as the hum of an air conditioner.

He left in the middle of the night. He began to load his possessions into the Lexus. At first he chose items with a great degree of consideration. The first thing he loaded was a set of custom-made monogrammed golf clubs. Then his stereo receiver, Denon AC3, $1,750. A copy of *This Side of Paradise* autographed by Fitzgerald that he had bought as an investment. By the time the Lexus was half full he was just grabbing things at random and stuffing them into the back seat, a half-eaten pizza, half a case of cat food, a single brocade house shoe.

He drove west past the hospital, the country club, the city limit sign. He was thinking no thoughts at all, and all the destination he had was the amount of highway the headlights showed him.

In the slow rains of late fall the doctor's wife returned to the unfinished mansion. She used to sit in a camp chair on the ruined veranda and drink chilled martinis she poured from the pitcher she carried in a foam ice chest. Dark fell early these November days. Raincrows husbanding some far cornfield called through the smoky autumn air. The sound was fiercely evocative, reminding her of something but she could not have said what.

She went into the room where she had lost the child. The light was failing. The high corners of the room were in deepening shadow but she could see the nests of dirt daubers clustered on the rich flocked wallpaper, a spider swing from a chandelier on a strand of spun glass. Some animal's dried blackened stool curled like a slug against the baseboards. The silence in the room was enormous.

One day she arrived and was surprised to find the paperhanger there. He was sitting on a yellow four-wheeler drinking a bottle of beer. He made to go when he saw her but she waved him back. Stay and talk with me, she said.

The paperhanger was much changed. His pale locks had been shorn away in a makeshift haircut as if scissored in the dark or by a blind barber and his cheeks were covered with a soft curly beard.

You have grow a beard.

Yes.

You are strange with it.

The paperhanger sipped from his San Miguel. He smiled. I was strange without it, he said. He arose from the four-wheeler and came over and sat on the flagstone steps. He stared across the mutilated yard toward the treeline. The yard was like a funhouse maze seen from above, its twistings and turnings bereft of mystery.

You are working somewhere now?

No. I don't take so many jobs anymore. There's only me, and I don't need much. What has become of the doctor?

She shrugged. Many things have change, she said. He has gone. The banks have foreclose. What is that you ride?

An ATV. A four-wheeler.

It goes well in the woods?

It was made for that.

You could take me in the woods. How much would you charge me?

For what?

To go in the woods. You could drive me. I will pay you.

Why?

To search for my child's body.

I wouldn't charge anybody anything to search for a child's body, the paperhanger said. But she's not in these woods. Nothing could have stayed hidden, the way these woods were searched.

Sometimes I think she just kept walking. Perhaps just walking away from the men looking. Far into the woods.

Into the woods, the paperhanger thought. If she had just kept walking in a straight line with no time out for eating or sleeping, where would she be? Kentucky, Algiers, who knew.

I'll take you when the rains stop, he said. But we won't find a child.

The doctor's wife shook her head. It is a mystery, she said. She drank from her cocktail glass. Where could she have gone? How could she have gone?

There was a man named David Lang, the paperhanger said. Up in Galletin, back in the late 1800s. He was crossing a barn lot in full view of his wife and two children and he just vanished. Went into thin air. There was a judge in a wagon turning into the yard and he saw it too. It was just like he took a step in this world and his foot came down in another one. He was never seen again.

She gave him a sad smile, bitter and one-cornered. You make fun with me.

No. It's true. I have it in a book. I'll show you.

I have a book with dragons, fairies. A book where hobbits live in the middle earth. They are lies. I think most books are lies. Perhaps all books. I have prayed for a miracle but I am not worthy of one. I have prayed for her to come from the dead, then just to find her body. That would be a miracle to me. There are no miracles.

She rose unsteadily, swayed slightly, leaning to take up the cooler. The paperhanger watched her. I have to go now, she said. When the rains stop we will search.

Can you drive?

Of course I can drive. I have drive out here.

I mean are you capable of driving now. You seem a little drunk.

I drink to forget but it is not enough, she said. I can drive.

After a while he heard her leave in the Mercedes, the tires spinning in the gravel drive. He lit a cigarette. He sat smoking it, watching the rain string off the roof. He seemed to be waiting for something. Dusk was falling like a shroud, the world going dark and formless the way it had begun. He drank the last of the beer, sat holding the bottle, the foam bitter in the back of his mouth. A chill touched him. He felt something watching him. He turned. From the corner of the ruined veranda a child was watching him. He stood up. He heard the beer bottle break on the flagstones. The child went sprinting past the hollyhocks toward the brush at the edge of the yard, tiny sepia child with an intent sloe-eyed face, real as she had ever been, translucent as winter light through dirty glass.

The doctor's wife's hands were laced loosely about his waist as they came down through a thin stand of sassafras, edging over the ridge where the ghost of a road was, a road more sensed than seen that faced into a half acre of tilting stones and fading granite tablets. Other graves marked only by their declivities in the earth, folk so far beyond the pale even the legibility of their identities had been leached away by the weathers.

Leaves drifted, huge poplar leaves veined with amber so golden they might have been coin of the realm for a finer world than this one. He cut the ignition of the four-wheeler and got off. Past the lowering trees the sky was a blue of an improbable intensity, a fierce cobalt blue shot through with dense golden light.

She slid off the rear and steadied herself a moment with a hand on his arm. Where are we? she asked. Why are we here?

The paperhanger had disengaged his arm and was strolling

among the gravestones reading such inscriptions as were legible, as if he might find forebear or antecedent in this moldering earth. The doctor's wife was retrieving her martinis from the luggage carrier of the ATV. She stood looking about uncertainly. A graven angel with broken wings crouched on a truncated marble column like a gargoyle. Its stone eyes regarded her with a blind benignity. Some of these graves have been rob, she said.

You can't rob the dead, he said. They have nothing left to steal.

It is a sacrilege, she said. It is forbidden to disturb the dead. You have done this.

The paperhanger took a cigarette pack from his pocket and felt it, but it was empty, and he balled it up and threw it away. The line between grave robbing and archaeology has always looked a little blurry to me, he said. I was studying their culture, trying to get a fix on what their lives were like.

She was watching him with a kind of benumbed horror. Standing hip-slung and lost like a parody of her former self. Strange and anomalous in her fashionable but mismatched clothing, as if she'd put on the first garment that fell to hand. Someday, he thought, she might rise and wander out into the daylit world wearing nothing at all, the way she had come into it. With her diamond watch and the cocktail glass she carried like a used-up talisman.

You have break the law, she told him.

I got a government grant, the paperhanger said contemptuously.

Why are we here? We are supposed to be searching for my child.

If you're looking for a body the first place to look is the graveyard, he said. If you want a book don't you go to the library?

I am paying you, she said. You are in my employ. I do not want to be here. I want you to do as I say or carry me to my car if you will not.

Actually, the paperhanger said, I had a story to tell you. About my wife.

He paused, as if leaving a space for her comment, but when she made none he went on. I had a wife. My childhood sweetheart. She became a nurse, went to work in one of these drug rehab places. After she was there a while she got a faraway look in her eyes. Look at me without seeing me. She got in tight with her supervisor. They started having meetings to go to. Conferences. Sometimes just the two of them would confer, generally in a motel. The night I watched them walk into the Holiday Inn in Franklin I decided to kill her. No impetuous spur-of-the-moment thing. I thought it all out and it would be the perfect crime.

The doctor's wife didn't say anything. She just watched him.

A grave is the best place to dispose of a body, the paperhanger said. The grave is its normal destination anyway. I could dig up a grave and then just keep on digging. Save everything carefully. Put my body there and fill in part of the earth, and then restore everything the way it was. The coffin, if any of it was left. The bones and such. A good settling rain and the fall leaves and you're home free. Now that's eternity for you.

Did you kill someone, she breathed. Her voice was barely audible.

Did I or did I not, he said. You decide. You have the powers of a god. You can make me a murderer or just a heartbroke guy whose wife quit him. What do you think? Anyway, I don't have a wife. I expect she just walked off into the abstract like that Lang guy I told you about.

I want to go, she said. I want to go where my car is.

He was sitting on a gravestone watching her out of his pale eyes. He might not have heard.

I will walk.

Just whatever suits you, the paperhanger said. Abruptly, he was standing in front of her. She had not seen him arise from the headstone or stride across the graves, but like a jerky splice in a film he was before her, a hand cupping each of her breasts, staring down into her face.

Under the merciless weight of the sun her face was stunned and vacuous. He studied it intently, missing no detail. Fine wrinkles crept from the corners of her eyes and mouth like hairline cracks in porcelain. Grime was impacted in her pores, in the crepe flesh of her throat. How surely everything had fallen from her: beauty, wealth, social position, arrogance. Humanity itself, for by now she seemed scarcely human, beleaguered so by the fates that she suffered his hands on her breasts as just one more cross to bear, one more indignity to endure.

How far you've come, the paperhanger said in wonder. I believe you're about down to my level now, don't you?

It does not matter, the doctor's wife said. There is no longer one thing that matters.

Slowly and with enormous lassitude her body slumped toward him, and in his exultance it seemed not a motion in itself but simply the completion of one begun long ago with the fateful weight of a thigh, a motion that began in one world and completed itself in another one.

From what seemed a great distance he watched her fall toward him like an angel descending, wings spread, from an infinite height, striking the earth gently, tilting, then righting itself.

The weight of moonlight tracking across the paperhanger's face awoke him from where he took his rest. Filigrees of light through the gauzy curtains swept across him in stately silence like the translucent ghosts of insects. He stirred, lay still then for a moment getting his bearings, a fix on where he was.

He was in his bed, lying on his back. He could see a huge orange moon poised beyond the bedroom window, ink-sketch tree branches that raked its face like claws. He could see his feet bookending the San Miguel bottle that his hands clasped erect on his abdomen, the amber bottle hard edged and defined against the pale window, dark atavistic monolith reared against a harvest moon.

He could smell her. A musk compounded of stale sweat and alcohol, the rank smell of her sex. Dissolution, ruin, loss. He turned to study her where she lay asleep, her open mouth a dark cavity in her face. She was naked, legs outflung, pale breasts pooled like cooling wax. She stirred restively, groaned in her sleep. He could hear the rasp of her breathing. Her breath was fetid on his face, corrupt, a graveyard smell. He watched her in disgust, in a dull self-loathing.

He drank from the bottle, lowered it. Sometimes, he told her sleeping face, you do things you can't undo. You break things you just can't fix. Before you mean to, before you know you've done it. And you were right, there are things only a miracle can set to rights.

He sat clasping the bottle. He touched his miscut hair, the soft down of his beard. He had forgotten what he looked like, he hadn't seen his reflection in a mirror for so long. Unbidden, Zeineb's face swam into his memory. He remembered the look on the child's face when the doctor's wife had spun on her heel: spite had crossed it like a flicker of heat lightning. She stuck her tongue out at him. His hand snaked out like a serpent and closed on her throat and snapped her neck before he could call it back, sloe eyes wild and wide, pink tongue caught between tiny seed-pearl teeth like a bitten-off rosebud. Her hair swung sidewise, her head lolled onto his clasped hand. The tray of the toolbox was out before he knew it, he was stuffing her into the toolbox like a ragdoll. So small, so small, hardly there at all.

He arose. Silhouetted naked against the moon-drenched window, he drained the bottle. He looked about for a place to set it, leaned and wedged it between the heavy flesh of her upper thighs. He stood in silence, watching her. He seemed philosophical, possessed of some hard-won wisdom. The paperhanger knew so well that while few are deserving of a miracle, fewer still can make one come to pass.

He went out of the room. Doors opened, doors closed. Footsteps softly climbing a staircase, descending. She dreamed on. When he came back into the room he was cradling a plastic-wrapped bundle stiffly in his arms. He placed it gently beside the drunk woman. He folded the plastic sheeting back like a caul.

What had been a child. What the graveyard earth had spared the freezer had preserved. Ice crystals snared in the hair like windy snowflakes whirled there, in the lashes. A doll from a madhouse assembly line.

He took her arm, laid it across the child. She pulled away from the cold. He firmly brought the arm back, arranging them like mannequins, madonna and child. He studied this tableau, then went out of his house for the last time. The door closed gently behind him on its keeper spring.

The paperhanger left in the Mercedes, heading west into the open country, tracking into wide-open territories he could infect like a malignant spore. Without knowing it, he followed the self-same route the doctor had taken some eight months earlier, and in a world of infinite possibilities where all journeys share a common end, perhaps they are together, taking the evening air on a ruined veranda among the hollyhocks and oleanders, the doctor sipping his Scotch and the paperhanger his San Miguel, gentlemen of leisure discussing the vagaries of life and pondering deep into the night not just the possibility but the inevitability of miracles.

JEREMIAH HEALY

A Book of Kells

FROM *Mary Higgins Clark Mystery Magazine*

THE IRISH-AMERICAN HERITAGE CENTER was located in a red-brick building three blocks off East Broadway in South Boston. Growing up in the neighborhood, I remembered the structure as a public elementary school, but when the city fell on hard times in the seventies, the mayor and council sold a number of municipal properties to keep real-estate taxes from rocketing skyward. As I parked my old Honda at the curb, I got the impression that the Center was doing a lot better by the building than the school department ever had.

The main entrance consisted of three separate doors, the one to the left having a sign in gold calligraphy, reading TRY THIS ONE FIRST, which I thought was a nice touch. Inside the lobby area, the same ornate lettering adorned the walls, including a mural with the homily MAY YOUR TROUBLES BE LESS/YOUR BLESSINGS BE MORE/AND NOTHING BUT HAPPINESS/COME THROUGH YOUR DOOR.

On my right was an office complex, probably where the principal used to hold court. A woman sitting behind a reception counter rose when she saw me.

"John Cuddy," I said, "here to see Hugh McGlachlin."

"Oh, yes." Her expression shifted from concerned to relieved. "Please come in."

A buzzer sounded. She opened the door nearest her counter and showed me through a second inner door. "Hugh, Mr. Cuddy," she said.

A voice with just a lick of the brogue said, "Thank you, Grace. And hold any calls, if you would, please."

Grace nodded and closed the inner door behind me.

The man rising from the other side of the carved teak desk was about five-nine and slight of build, wearing a long-sleeved dress shirt and a tie. His hair was gray and short, combed a little forward like a Roman emperor's. Despite the gray hair, his face was unlined around the blue eyes, and his smile shone brightly enough for a toothpaste commercial.

A woman occupied one of the chairs in front of McGlachlin's desk, but instead of standing as well, she turned toward me while twisting a lace handkerchief in her lap. I pegged her as middle forties, with florid skin and a rat's nest of red hair. She wore the drab, baggy clothes of someone catching up on her housework, a canvas tote bag that had seen better days at her feet.

The man came around his desk and extended his right hand. "Hugh McGlachlin, executive director of the Center here. Thanks so much for coming so quickly."

I shook hands with him, and McGlachlin turned to the seated woman. "This is Mrs. Nora Clooney."

She swallowed and shook hands with me as well, hers trembling in mine.

"Well," said McGlachlin, tapping the back of the other chair in front of his desk, "I'm not sure of the protocol, but I think I'd be most comfortable using first names."

"Fine with me."

He and I sat down at the same time, and McGlachlin studied me briefly. "I didn't tell Michael O'Dell why we needed a private investigator," he said.

O'Dell was a lawyer in Back Bay who'd fed me a lot of cases over the years. "Probably why he didn't tell me."

The toothpaste smile again. "Michael is a member of our advisory board. And he assured me you were the soul of discretion and someone to be trusted."

"I'll be sure to thank him."

McGlachlin leaned back in his chair. "I think you may be just the man for the job, John."

"Which is?"

He pursed his lips. "How much do you know about the Heritage Center?"

"Only what I've seen so far this morning."

Hugh McGlachlin rose again, picking up a manila envelope

from the corner of his desk. "In that event, I think a brief tour might prove instructive. Nora?"

Clooney preceded us out the inner door.

"We incorporated as a nonprofit institution in 'seventy-five," said McGlachlin, "and moved into this building four years later. I don't mind telling you, John, the city left it quite the mess." He made a sweeping gesture with the envelope. "But thanks to some Irish-American tradesmen generously donating their time and talents, we've been able to renovate the interior a bit at a time and rejuvenate the community we serve."

I sensed that the operative word for me was *donating*.

The three of us were moving down a hallway festooned with the various crests of the thirty-two counties of Ireland, that signature gold calligraphy naming each. On the left, double doors opened onto a large and beautifully rendered country-house room, sporting an exposed-beam ceiling, slate floor, and massive fieldstone fireplace on the shorter wall. In the hearth was a cauldron suspended by metal bars over an unlit fire, an iron milk jug bigger than a beer keg to the side.

I said, "Hugh, what exactly is the Center's problem?"

McGlachlin just stopped, but Clooney seemed to freeze in her tracks. He looked up at the crests over our heads. "Would you know where your forebears hailed from, John?"

"County Kerry on my father's side, Cork on my mother's."

"Ah." McGlachlin pointed first to a shield with a white castle and gold harp. "Kerry . . ." and then to a crest with a galleon sailing between two red towers ". . . Cork."

He took a step into the room. "In both places, John, they would have broken their backs hoisting jugs like that one onto a pony cart to carry their cows' milk to town." He fixed me with those blue eyes. 'Tis a marvelous thing that we who emigrated are more fortunate, don't you think?"

"Hugh," I said, "until I know why you called Michael O'Dell — and probably why Mrs. Clooney seems nervous as a wet cat — I won't be able to tell you whether I can help the Center for free."

McGlachlin grinned this time, but without showing any teeth, and I had the feeling that despite being six inches taller and fifty pounds heavier, I'd hate to meet him in an alley. He said, "Yes, I do believe you're the man for our job. This way, please."

We took an elevator to the second floor. As I followed McGlachlin down the hallway, I tried to stay abreast of Clooney. No matter how I adjusted my stride, though, she always stayed a step behind me.

McGlachlin stopped again, this time outside a large classroom where the chairs and tables were shoved against the walls. Perhaps a dozen girls and young women were moving in a circle, their hands joined but held high. "We have step-dancing classes in here," he said, "though we also host Lithuanian folk dancing for our neighbors of that extraction. The Nimble Thimbles teach needlework over there, and every Wednesday we have instruction in Gaelic."

I nodded.

Another toothy smile. "All right, then. The next floor is one that concerns us most at the moment."

"This is our museum, John."

McGlachlin used a key to open a heavy security door in a corridor filled with construction odds and ends, plaster dust on every surface. The area at the end of the hallway was still just undefined space, only a few wall studs in place.

The security door opened into a large viewing room, glass-faced cases along two walls displaying china in all shapes and sizes, lots of pastel green "icing" on the edges of plates and pitchers.

"Recognize it?" asked McGlachlin.

My mother had a piece she prized. "Belleek."

"Very good. The finest of Irish porcelain." He waved a hand at the third wall. "And there's the loveliest collection of lace you may ever see."

I took in the white fabric spread on trays of green velvet. "You said downstairs that —"

"— this is the floor that concerns us most right now. Yes, indeed I did." McGlachlin's voice dropped to the subdued tone of a devout man entering his church. "Over here, John."

We went through a doorway into a smaller room with soft, recessed lighting. In the center was a freestanding case about two feet square. Its top, or cover, evidently had been glass, though it was hard to judge further because it was shattered into crumbly crystals lying fairly evenly on the otherwise empty green velvet.

I said, "You've had a theft."

McGlachlin looked my way as Clooney began twisting her hankie again. After glancing at her, he turned back to me. "John, you recognized the Belleek. Would you also know about *The Book of Kells?*"

"Something Irish monks did back in the Middle Ages?"

"Close enough. During the eighth and ninth centuries, Celtic scribes painstakingly copied each passage of the four Gospels onto 'paper' made from the stomach lining of lambs. Every page is an artist's palette of flowing script and glorious colors, with the original book carefully guarded at Trinity College in Dublin. However, in 1974 some reproductions were permitted — they called them 'facsimiles.' Only five hundred copies, but they are works of art themselves, down to the wormholes in the pages."

I looked at the smashed case. "And you had one of those."

"The Center purchased its facsimile in 1990 for twenty thousand dollars."

I thought back to my time as a claims investigator. "You've notified your insurance carrier."

McGlachlin shook his head. "On the collector's market now, the price is ten times what we paid, but the money is largely irrelevant: Nobody who has a facsimile is willing to part with it."

"Still, the policy would pay —"

"It's not a check I want, John. It's the book itself. There'll never be any more facsimiles produced, at least not in our lifetime. The Center needs its copy back as a matter of" — another sweeping gesture with the manila envelope — "heritage."

I looked at him. "Let me save you some time. The Boston police have an excellent —"

"Not yet, John." McGlachlin seemed pained. "I'm rather hoping this can be resolved without resorting to our insurance company or the police." He opened the manila envelope and slid a single piece of paper from it. "This was on top of the shards there."

I stepped sideways so I could read it without touching it. In simple block lettering on white photocopy stock, the words were TAKEN, BUT NOT STOLEN, AND WILL BE RETURNED.

"Who found this?"

"I did, sir," said Clooney, the first words I'd heard her speak.

McGlachlin cleared his throat. "Nora volunteers her time to clean for us. Given all the plaster dust from the ongoing renovation, it's no small task."

I looked at her. "Where was this piece of paper when you first saw it?"

Clooney glanced at her boss. "It was just like Mr. McGlachlin told you. The note was lying atop all the broken glass." The brogue was woven through her voice much more than her boss's.

"And the glass hasn't been disturbed since?"

McGlachlin said, "I've kept the room locked since Nora came to me this morning with the news."

I let my eyes roam around before returning to Clooney. "Do you clean this room the same time every day?"

"First thing in the morning, sir. Eight o'clock. It wouldn't do for visitors not to be able to see the book for the plaster dust covering its blessed case."

"And nothing was wrong yesterday at eight?"

"No, sir." The lace hankie was getting wrung some more.

I glanced around again. "Other than the locked door, what kind of security do you have for this room?"

"None," said McGlachlin. "We've been spending every available penny on the renovations."

I stared at him. "But what about visitors wandering in?"

"Access to these museum rooms is restricted solely to those of us with a key to that door. As anyone can plainly see, there's been no attempt to jimmy it or the windows, even assuming the bastard — sorry, Nora — thought to bring a ladder with him to lean against the outside wall."

I thought about it. "I can see why you haven't gone to the police."

McGlachlin sighed. "Exactly so. This had to be — is it still called 'an inside job'?"

I turned back to Clooney. "So the incident must have occurred sometime between eight A.M. or so yesterday —"

"More like nine, sir, the time I finished in here —"

"To eight this morning?"

"Yes, sir."

I looked at McGlachlin. "All right, how many people have keys to that door?"

"I do, as executive director. And Nora, for her cleaning and turning."

"Turning?"

She said, "Every day, sir, I go up to the book and turn a page."

McGlachlin pointed to the windows. "So the sun fades the ink only a tiny bit, and more or less evenly."

I looked at the shattered glass. "How did you open it?"

They both stared at me.

"The glass cover, or top. How did you open it to turn the pages?"

"Oh," said Clooney, and moved to a wall panel. She threw a switch, and the remaining structure of the glass top clicked upward.

McGlachlin went to demonstrate. "You can then lift this —"

"Don't touch it," I said. "Fingerprints."

"Ah, yes. Of course."

I gestured toward the paper he still held in his hand. "And please don't let anybody else touch that. As it is, the police will need elimination prints from you, and —"

"Harking back to what I said earlier, John, we hope we won't be needing the police, thanks to you."

I waited before asking, "Who else has keys to the security door?"

McGlachlin raised a finger. "The chairman of our advisory board, Conor Donnelly. He's a professor of Irish studies." He named the college. Another finger went up. "Conor's brother, Denis, was a generous contributor to the Center, so he received a key as well."

"Denis Donnelly, the venture capitalist?"

"The very one."

"The man kicks in enough, he gets his own key?"

McGlachlin cleared his throat again. "Given the amount of Denis's contribution, John, that would be an awkward request to deny."

"Anybody else?"

"Only Sean Kilpatrick. The carpenter donating his time to do our work down the hall."

I looked around one last time. "These museum rooms look pretty well completed. Why would Kilpatrick need access to them?"

"In the event anything went wrong," he said. "But, John, Sean's somebody who's completely trustworthy."

"Hugh, at least one somebody with a key obviously isn't."

We were back in the executive director's office, the door closed. "Mr. McGlachlin, will you or Mr. Cuddy be needing me anymore today?"

McGlachlin glanced at me, and I shook my head. "Go home, then, Nora," he said. "And tell Bill I'll be by to visit after work."

After Clooney had picked up her tote bag and left us, I said, "Bill's her husband?"

"Just so. And a fine, generous man to boot, but suffering from the cancer. You know how that can be."

Though I figured McGlachlin meant his comment rhetorically, I still pictured my wife, Beth, asleep in her hillside less than a mile away. "I do."

He shook his head sadly. "They met each other here at one of the Center's first socials. But then, we've sparked a lot of unions from our activities."

"Who else besides Nora — and you — actually knew how the cover over your *Book of Kells* opened?"

McGlachlin grew wary. "And what difference would that make, John? The case was smashed."

"That 'ransom' note — it was lying on top of the broken glass. Being a single sheet of paper, it's pretty light."

More wary now. "Agreed, but —"

"— so the note wouldn't have disturbed the broken glass under it very much, if at all."

McGlachlin seemed to work it through.

To save time, I said, "And since the glass shards were spread almost evenly . . ."

The executive director closed his eyes, ". . . the book was probably taken out of the case before the cover was smashed."

"Somebody wanted you to think that the glass had to be broken in order to take the book. So my question still stands: Who else knew about the cover mechanism?"

McGlachlin fixed me with his blue eyes. "John, I just don't know. But I do know this. Nora wouldn't know what to do with our book. And she's honest as the day is long."

I filed that with his endorsement of the carpenter, Sean Kilpatrick. "You didn't mention if Grace, your receptionist, also had a key."

"She does not. But given where Grace sits, she's in a position to see who comes and goes."

"Assuming everyone comes through the main doors."

"The other outside doors are alarmed, John. And besides, Grace tells me she saw all three of our key holders walk by her yesterday."

"Both in and out?"

"No, but each of them had either a knapsack or briefcase or tool-box big enough to hold the book."

"You have any suggestions on where I should start?"

"More a question on *how* you should start." McGlachlin paused. "So far, only Nora, Grace, and you know about what's happened."

"And given the tenor of that ransom note, you're hoping the book will be back by the time anyone else has to know?"

"On the button, John. There's an advisory board meeting here next week — five days hence, to be exact. The members have a tra-dition of reading a passage from the book — as a benediction, you might say."

"Meaning the book is taken from the case?"

"No. No, we all troop up to the room, and thanks to Nora's turn-ing the page each morning, there're always different passages to choose from."

"Anything else about this situation you haven't told me?"

"One of the reasons I'm trying to resolve things quickly." McGlachlin pursed his lips. "You see, Conor — our board chair-man — was asked by his brother, Denis, a few months ago to loan out the book for a party. Denis was giving a la-di-da affair at his home, and he wanted to have our facsimile on display for his guests."

"And what did Conor say?"

"That he'd have to put it to the Center's advisory board, which he did. And they voted not to allow the book to leave its case."

"How did Denis take that?"

"Not well. He stomped in here the next day, gave me holy hell. He thought I could perhaps permit him to borrow the book any-way."

"For a small . . . stipend?"

He nodded. "I told him I couldn't do that." McGlachlin winced. "You could have heard him yelling all over the building."

"Denis believed he should have been accommodated because of that large contribution you mentioned?"

"More specific than that, I'm afraid. You see, John, 'twas Denis's money that let our Center buy the book in the first place."

After getting McGlachlin's home number — "Call, John, any time of the day or night" — I drove from the Center to another

repository of memories. Irish-American also, but different. And
more personal.

Leaving the Honda on the wide path, I walked through the garden of stones until I found hers. The words ELIZABETH MARY
DEVLIN CUDDY have never changed, but they've become a little
fainter, the freeze/thaw of Boston winters taking their toll even on
polished granite.

"I've been asked to find a book, Beth."

A book?

I explained the problem to her. After a pause, she said, *I remember
seeing an illuminated page from it, in an art-history text, I think.*

"That would make sense."

An incredible collector's item.

As I nodded at her comment, my eye caught the plodding movement of a lobster boat down in the harbor, chugging along in the
light chop of a northeast wind that smelled of rain to come. Its skipper seemed intent on collecting his pots before the storm began
to . . .

John?

I came back to her stone. "Sorry?"

*How are you going to approach these three men without tipping them to
who you are and what you're doing?*

"It took a while, but coming here has shown me the way."

I fooled myself into thinking I could hear the confusion in Beth's
next, unspoken question.

Picture the kind of campus that would bring tears of joy to a high
school guidance counselor. The classroom and dormitory buildings were a Gothic design like the lower, auxiliary structures tacked
onto cathedrals — imposing mullioned windows, ivy winding from
the ground nearly to the roof lines.

After stopping three students with enough earrings piercing
them to fill a jewelry box, I was directed by the last to a sallow, four-
story affair. Inside, red arrows with small signs beneath them directed me to the second floor, and a receptionist swamped by students picking up exams waved me toward the office on her immediate right. The stenciling on the door reminded me of my own
office's pebbled glass, but instead of JOHN FRANCIS CUDDY,
CONFIDENTIAL INVESTIGATIONS in black, this one read
CONOR DONNELLY, IRISH STUDIES in green.

I knocked and received a "Come," repeated three times like an oft-intoned litany.

The door opened into a large office with a high ceiling and two banks of fluorescent lights suspended over the bookshelved wall. The opposite wall had five of the multipaned windows throwing as much sunshine as the day was offering onto the head and shoulders of a standing man.

Conor Donnelly scribbled in a loose-leaf notebook lying on one of those breadbox lecterns you can lift onto a table to make a podium. His shoulders were rounded under a V-neck sweater over a flannel shirt. The brown hair was thinned enough that he had resorted to one of those low-part comb-overs, the scalp showing through between the strands that were left. His bushy eyebrows made up a little for the hairline, though. As he stepped toward me, Donnelly had to shuffle around stacks of papers on the floor.

His gray eyes blinked. "You're not a student." Brooklyn instead of brogue in his voice.

"No, but I'm hoping you're Conor Donnelly."

"A fair assumption, given where you've found me." Donnelly returned to his notebook. "But these are office hours for the students, so I can't spare you much time, Mr. . . ."

"Francis, John Francis," I said, which amounted to only one third of a lie. "I'd like to speak with you about *The Book of Kells.*"

That seemed to catch Donnelly's interest, because he motioned me toward a captain's chair across from his desk, though he stayed at the lectern. "We can speak about it, but you're a good three thousand miles from the original."

"All right, *a Book of Kells,* then. I represent a collector who'd very much like to own one of those limited-edition facsimiles, and I understand you have access to such."

Donnelly cocked his head. "In a functional sense, yes. However, I'm afraid ours at the Heritage Center is not for sale."

"No matter the money involved?"

Now Donnelly frowned. "Well, as chair of the advisory board, I'd be honor-bound to entertain any serious offer — subject, of course, to board approval."

"Professor, I'm aware that the going rate for a reproduction is tenfold what the Center paid, and my client is prepared to substantially sweeten even that inflated price. Provided, of course, that you can open that glass cover over the book so she can inspect the item."

No reaction to my "cover-opening" comment, which told me Donnelly already knew of the mechanism. "Well, Mr. Francis, you're welcome to submit your offer in writing, but I must inform you, I doubt the board will approve it. We take great pride in our copy of the book, and frankly, I don't know that any owner not desperate for money would part with one of the facsimiles."

I decided to explore what might be a gambit from Donnelly. "Would it have to be the technical owner who was desperate for money?"

He looked confused. "I don't follow you."

Leaning forward in the captain's chair and lowering my voice, I said, "Or would a person even have to be desperate for money just to be interested in having himself a little — no, a lot — more of it?"

"Ah," said Donnelly, "the light dawns. A bribe, eh?"

I shrugged.

Conor Donnelly smiled and returned again to his notebook. "Mr. Francis, get the hell out of my office before I call campus security and have you thrown out."

His brother's receptionist, in a lovely office suite overlooking Faneuil Hall, told me politely, if firmly, that Denis Donnelly would not be in that day. Both of Boston's daily newspapers had run profiles on him, though, and in each story the venture capitalist's obsession with his home in Weston Hills shone through. It didn't take long to find the place — read *estate* — and once I gave the hard-eyed man at the driveway's security gate two thirds of my name and mentioned *The Book of Kells,* I was escorted by a younger hard-eyed guard up the drive and into a mansion on a par with the gold-domed statehouse on Beacon Hill.

The second guard watched me admire — without touching — a dozen paintings, sculptures, and vases in the parlorlike anteroom before a pair of gilded doors opened and a man I recognized from his newspaper photos came out from a spectacular atrium to greet me.

The financier was a glossy version of his brother the professor. A hair weave of some kind made this Donnelly look as if a lush bush had been planted in the middle of his head and was spreading symmetrically outward. He'd colored his eyebrows to match the new do, and his gray eyes had that jump in them I associate with race car drivers and serial killers. He wore a silk shirt over his rounded shoulders. A pair of painfully casual, stonewashed jeans ended an inch above some loafers, no benefit of socks.

After we shook hands, Donnelly glanced at his security man. "I'll be fine with Mr. Francis, Rick," he said, his brother's Brooklyn accent on his words too. "But advise Curt no more visitors until I'm done here."

Rick nodded, gave me a look that said, *Don't make me come back for you,* and left us.

Donnelly suggested the Queen Anne loveseat might hold me, while he sank into a leather, brass-studded smoking chair. "So, Mr. Francis, you mentioned to Curt a *Book of Kells.*"

"Actually, *The Book of Kells,* but I'm sure we mean the same thing."

A look of frank appraisal. "You want to buy a facsimile, or sell one?"

"Buy, as intermediary for a client of mine."

No change of expression. "I'm in and out of the art market quite a bit. I don't recall anyone with judgment I respect ever mentioning your name."

"It's an easy one to forget."

A grin that you couldn't exactly call a smile. "You, my friend, are trying to scam me. Why?"

"No scam. My client wants one of the reproductions, and I understand you have a brother with — shall we say — sway over one of them."

"Hah!" said Donnelly, though it came out more as a bray. "I haven't so much as spit in Conor's face for a good two months now."

I tried to look disappointed. "Why?"

Donnelly lazed back in his chair. "I'm guessing you already know. I'm guessing also that you're playing me for some reason I can't figure. But I also can't see how this bit of information can hurt me. Come along."

I followed him into the atrium room, even on a dark day spectacularly lit by a rotunda skylight. I couldn't describe the furnishings if I had an hour to write about them. Except for one piece. It rested on a pedestal in a corner, shielded from potential sunlight by a glass cover that was smoke-colored on top but crystal clear on the sides. Donnelly moved directly toward it, beckoning me.

As I looked down at the large and open book, Donnelly said, "You've never seen one before, have you?"

"No," I said, my voice a little clogged as I took in, up close and personal, the filigreed detail on the capital letter at the top of the left-hand page, the depictions of people and animals — some real, some fantastical — occupying the margins and trailing after the end of paragraphs, even just the calligraphy in the text — some version of Latin, I thought.

"My brother thinks I wanted to borrow his Center's copy just to show it off for a party here. And I did." Donnelly's voice wavered. "But once I got a look at it, even in that pop-top candy case in their museum room, something — a kind of tribal memory, maybe — kicked in. What Conor seemed to forget is that I could have had the Center's own copy by just buying it for myself ten years ago. And once he and his snotty board turned me down on the party idea, I went out last month and — quietly — bought another one."

I tore my eyes away from the pages in front of me. "For how many times the twenty thousand you shelled out for the first?"

Donnelly moved over to twin columns extruding from his wall. He pushed a button, and I looked back at the book pedestal, expecting its glass case to open the way the one at the Center had. It was maybe five seconds before the button's purpose hit me.

I heard a noise behind my back and wheeled around. The two hard-eyed security guys were standing inside the double doors of the atrium, arms folded in front of their chests. Looking a little more critically now at each, I didn't see any evident weapons.

I said to Donnelly, "That business of 'no other visitors' was code for 'hang close,' right?"

A nod with the bad grin. "And now, since you've obviously wasted my time on some sort of false pretenses, I think I'll enjoy watching Curt and Rick bounce you around a bit."

I tilted my head toward the door, my eyes still on Donnelly. "Just the two of them?"

The venture capitalist's eyes went neon. "Oh, I might jump in at the appropriate time."

I turned to Rick and Curt. "Denis, you're one man short."

Rick, the younger one, stepped up to the plate first. He extended both his hands to push on my chest, just like a demonstration of unarmed defense back in the sawdust pit when I was an MP lieutenant. I danced to Rick's lead for two steps, then reversed my feet and sent him over with a hip throw. When he landed on the floor, the sound of his lungs purging air was a lot easier on the ears than the gagging and dry-heaving that followed.

Curt was on me before I could turn back, clamping a chokehold across my throat with one of his forearms. I smashed my left heel down hard on his left instep and he cried out, lifting the foot. I hammered back with my left elbow and found his rib cage, feeling some of his cartilage separating as I drove into it.

Curt slid off me and cradled his left side with both hands, eyes squinched shut like a little kid who really doesn't want to cry but doesn't see how to avoid it. When I looked at Rick, he was still trying to give himself mouth-to-mouth resuscitation.

Denis Donnelly said, "So much as touch me, and I'll sue you and your client for every cent you've got."

I walked up to him, Donnelly apparently forgetting that those twin columns behind him significantly limited his mobility. He tried to kick me in the groin, but I caught his ankle in my right hand, then bent upward until he began to moan.

"Denis, I lift six more inches and you lose at least a hamstring, maybe an achilles tendon as well. We communicating?"

A strangled "Yes."

"OK. I was never here."

"Right, right."

"And I'm never going to have to worry about Rick or Curt or any of their successors trying to find me, am I?"

"No. No, of course not."

I left him then, but not before taking a last look at Denis Donnelly's *Book of Kells*. I'd found one facsimile, but Donnelly's arrogance seemed more consistent with his trumping story of buying a facsimile for himself than with stealing the copy he had in essence donated to the Center. Which left me just one last key holder to the museum rooms.

It was nearly dark by the time Sean Kilpatrick's carpentry truck pulled into the driveway across the street from where I was sitting behind the wheel of the Honda. When the pickup approached the garage of the modest ranch, security floods came on, bathing the front yard in a yellow glow. Thanks to the lights, I could see that his truck had a primered front fender and the tailgate was held in place by bungee cords.

As Kilpatrick got out of his vehicle, I got out of mine and began crossing over to him. At the sound of my footsteps, he straightened up and turned to me.

Kilpatrick stood about six feet, with broad shoulders and curly black hair. He was wearing a sweatshirt with the sleeves cut off at the armpits over jeans and work boots. By the time I reached the foot of his driveway, his right hand had a claw hammer in it.

I stopped short of his rear bumper. "Mr. Kilpatrick?"

"And you'd be?" A brogue heavy enough that if you didn't listen for the rhythm of his cadence, you might not catch the words themselves.

"John Francis. I understand you're doing some work over at the Heritage Center."

I'd expected him to tense even more at the mention of the place, but instead he visibly relaxed, tossing the hammer toward the passenger's seat of his pickup before wiping his right palm on his thigh and approaching me to shake hands. Up close, he had a pleasant face around a genuine smile with crooked front teeth.

"Mr. Francis, pleased to make your acquaintance. What can I do for you?"

Letting go of his hand, I said, "A client of mine is a collector."

Confusion on the pleasant face. "Collector? You mean of bills, now?"

"No. Art, sculpture, rare . . . books."

"And what would that be to me?" Kilpatrick gestured toward the truck. "I'm just a carpenter."

"But a carpenter with access to the Heritage Center's museum."

"Yes." He actually started to pull out a key ring from his back pocket, the ring itself anchored to his belt by a clasp and coiled cord. "I've got —" Kilpatrick reined up short. "Wait a minute, now. What are you saying?"

"I'm saying there's a particularly valuable book under a glass case in one of those museum rooms, and a considerable commission to be earned by the person who obtains it for us."

Kilpatrick lost the crooked smile, his face now anything but pleasant. "You're wanting me to steal *The Book of Kells?*"

"Let's not say 'steal.' Let's just say you flip open the thing's glass cover before knocking off one night, and you slip the book itself into a —"

"Boyo, if you're not out of my sight in ten seconds, I'll kick every fooking tooth in your head down your fooking throat."

No need to listen for the rhythm there to know what he meant. "Sorry to have troubled you," I said.

I turned, half listening for those heavy work boots to come clumping after me. But as I got back into the Honda, Sean Kilpatrick was still standing at the rear of his battered pickup, fists on hips and staring me down.

Even after dark, you can see the dome of the Massachusetts statehouse from my office window on Tremont Street. It's a pretty impressive effect, the gold leaf painstakingly reapplied by artisans a few years ago for what it probably cost the Navy to buy a carrier jet. But the dome also helps me to think, somehow, especially when I'm stuck.

And I was stuck fast that night.

A very valuable reproduction of *The Book of Kells* disappears from the locked room in which it's kept, the glass top of its case smashed. Most people with access to the museum know that this top opens to allow Nora Clooney to turn a page each day, but the thief smashes it anyway, maybe to deflect suspicion onto others less informed. Hugh McGlachlin, as executive director of the Center, has a key, though he's the one calling me into the matter, through a member of the advisory board, Michael O'Dell. On the other hand, reacting immediately and internally like that might be a good cover story for McGlachlin himself. Of the three people he "reluctantly" suspects, none acts suspiciously — or even smugly — about my suggesting the book could be pinched: Professor Conor Donnelly orders me to leave his office, brother Denis wants me beaten up for "scamming" him, and carpenter Sean Kilpatrick stops just short of mayhem himself when I imply he could steal the Center's copy for me.

Which, according to the note left on the broken glass, wasn't actually what had happened, anyway. "Taken, but not stolen, and will be returned." No apparent sarcasm in the words or even a double meaning.

If the one person who'd asked to borrow the book had now apparently acquired a copy for himself, who would need the facsimile only temporarily?

Then, staring at the statehouse dome reminded me of something else I'd seen at the Center. It was a long shot, but worth at least a call to a certain home phone.

After dialing, I got a tentative, "Hello?"

"Hugh, it's John Cuddy."

"Ah, John. You've found something, then?"

"Maybe, but I need to ask you a question first. Who did all that calligraphy work at the Center?"

The front door to the three-decker in Southie opened only about four inches on its chain inside. The one eye I could see through the crack seemed troubled. "Oh, my. Mr. Cuddy, how could I be helping you at this hour?"

"I'd like to meet with your husband," I said.

Nora Clooney tried to tough it out. "He's asleep. Perhaps in the morning?"

I shook my head.

She squeezed her lips to thin lines. "Then let me just pop up there, sir, make sure my Bill hasn't —"

"Nora, we both know what I'll see. Can we just get it over with?"

Her head dipping in defeat, she undid the chain on the door. "That'd probably be best, I suppose."

Terminal cancer has a certain aura to it. Not always a smell, though. More an edge in the air, a sense that something's very wrong but also irreparable. Bill Clooney's bedroom projected that aura.

His wife led me into the ten-by-twelve space. There were matching mahogany bureaus with brass handles, and framed photos of a younger couple wearing the clothes and hairstyles of the late seventies. The bed was of mahogany too, a four-poster that I could see newlyweds buying shortly after their ceremony. A set to last a lifetime.

Bill Clooney lay under sheets and a quilt, his head nestled in a cloud of pillows. There were a few wisps of gray hair on top of his head, a patchy fringe around the ears. His eyes were closed, but the mouth was open, a snoring so faint you might lose it in the hum of the electric space heater near one corner of the room. His hands lay atop the quilt, bony and heavily veined.

Centered between Clooney's throat and waist, a bed tray strad-
dled his torso. A very large book was open on the tray, a couch
cushion propping the text at an angle toward his face.

"My Bill was a graphic artist," said Nora Clooney, her voice barely
louder than her husband's snoring. "He came over from Ireland
five years before me, and he was ten years older to start with. The
charmer told me he fell in love the moment he laid eyes on me, but
I wasn't sure of him till I saw his wondrous calligraphy, after a social
at the Center that very same night. Modest about it though, my Bill
was, telling me that I'd not use the word *wondrous* for his lettering
once I saw *The Book of Kells.*"

I kept my voice low as well. "You wanted to bring the book home
so your husband could see it again."

"See it, yes sir, and touch it and even breathe it as well. But after
the terrible row between Mr. McGlachlin and that Mr. Donnelly at
the Center, I knew the board would never grant my Bill what it refused a rich man."

"You took the book out of its case before you broke the glass."

"Yes, sir." She made a sign of the cross. "I'd never have forgiven
myself if I'd damaged so much as a page of it."

"And you carried the book out in your tote bag."

"Brazen, I was. Walked right by Grace behind the reception
counter, her not suspecting a thing."

"Then why did you leave the note?"

She blew out a breath. "I thought it might keep Mr. McGlachlin
from calling in the police right away, sir. Buy me the time to let my
Bill pore over the book during his last days before I took it back to
the Center, unharmed." She turned toward her husband, and I had
the sense that Nora Clooney always looked at him this way, with the
same expression. A loving one that went beyond duty and maybe
even devotion as well.

"Every morning he was able, my Bill would come to the Center
with me. Oh, his eyes would shine, sir, watching me turn that day's
page, him feeling honored as though he was the first modern man
to look upon the work of those long-ago scribes."

I waited a moment before saying, "Nora, I need to make a phone
call."

She closed her eyes and dipped her head again. "The one in the
kitchen, please. So we don't disturb my Bill."

As I followed her down the stairs, I said, "You wouldn't know whether Hugh McGlachlin has Caller I.D. on his home phone, would you?"

From the look on her upturned face, I could tell that Nora Clooney thought I was crazy.

In the kitchen, I dialed and got that tentative hello.

"Hugh, John Cuddy again."

"John, are you calling from the Clooneys, then?"

"No," I lied, "a pay phone. I'm afraid Nora and Bill couldn't help me. But listen, Hugh, I've traced your *Book of Kells*."

"Traced it?" His voice was thick with hope.

"Yes," I said. "The book'll be back in the Center before your board meets next week."

A long pause on the other end. "John, is there something you're not telling me?"

"There is."

An even longer pause. "Michael O'Dell said I could trust you."

"And you can."

No pause at all now, but a considerable sigh. "Then I will. Good night, John Cuddy, and thank you."

As I hung up the phone in Nora Clooney's kitchen, she blinked three times before kissing the pads of the index and middle fingers on her right hand and then touching them to my forehead.

STEVE HOCKENSMITH

Erie's Last Day

FROM *Alfred Hitchcock's Mystery Magazine*

7:00 A.M.:

The radio alarm by Larry Erie's queen-size bed turned itself on. A deep-voiced announcer began telling Erie about the morning's top stories. Erie didn't really care what the morning's top stories might be, but he lay there for a while and let the announcer ramble. There was nobody there to give him a playful kick and tell him to shut that noise off. There was nobody there to make breakfast for. There was nobody there to fetch pills for. It was just him and the announcer.

7:19 A.M.:

Erie finally pulled himself out of bed and went out to the porch in his pajamas and robe to pick up the morning paper. It was cool outside, just like the cheerful people on the radio said it would be. A storm passing through in the night had left puddles on the pavement.

He scanned the yard for the little black shape that sometimes came bounding up to him from behind shrubs or garbage cans, meowing greetings at him as if he were a long-lost relative. But the cat wasn't there. Erie went back inside.

He ate breakfast sitting on the edge of the bed. It was a habit he couldn't drop even though there was no longer anyone there to keep company.

7:42 A.M.:

Erie showered, shaved, flossed, brushed, gargled, rinsed, and repeated. Then he carefully picked out his clothes. He pulled on
his best white shirt, his best suit, his favorite tie. He shined his
shoes before putting them on. He looked at himself in the mirror,
straightened his tie, smoothed a few errant hairs into place. Then
he pulled his gun off the bureau and clipped it onto his belt.

Some cops started to get a little sloppy years before they retired.
Others waited till just a few months or weeks before their last day to
start letting themselves go. Erie remembered one cop, a fellow detective, who came in for his last day in a Hawaiian shirt and ber-
muda shorts. It gave everybody a good laugh.

But that wasn't Erie's way. He was determined to make every day
of his time on the force count. Even his last.

8:07 A.M.:

Erie was reaching out to open his car door when he heard the cat.
She was hurrying up the driveway toward him, meowing loudly. He
knelt and stretched out his right arm. As always, the cat rubbed her
face on his hand several times before flopping over on her back
and stretching out her legs. He rubbed her stomach. Her fur was
long and matted.

"How do you like that, buddy? How do you like that?" Erie asked
the cat.

The cat purred.

Erie had never owned a cat, never really known a cat, never been
interested in them. He had no idea how old the little black cat was.
She'd been hanging around the neighborhood about a month.
She had grown noticeably bigger since he'd first seen her. She had
also become friendlier. She wore no collar or tags.

Occasionally Erie had found himself worrying about the cat.
Where was she sleeping? What was she eating? He'd seen her once
over by Green River Road, and the thought of her trying to cross
busy streets had haunted him for hours.

But Erie always reminded himself that he wasn't a cat person.
And he had bigger things to worry about than dumb animals.

"That's enough for today," he told the cat as he stood up. She rolled over on her stomach and looked up at him expectantly. "Nope. No more. So long."

He climbed into his car and started the engine. He backed out of the driveway slowly, keeping an eye on the cat lest she jump up and dart under the tires. But she stayed where she was, watching him, seemingly puzzled by his desire to leave this perfectly wonderful driveway and this perfectly wonderful cat.

8:33 A.M.:

On his way into police headquarters from the parking lot, Erie was stopped by three cops. They were all men he hadn't seen or spoken to in the last week. Each one stopped him separately and said the same thing.

"I'm sorry about your wife."

Erie said the only thing he could: "Thanks."

On his way past the Human Resources office a female coworker called out, "Look who's early! Hey, Larry, don't you know you're not supposed to come in before noon on your last day?"

"The early bird catches the worm," Erie said.

A uniformed officer stopped as she passed. "You don't have to worry about catching worms anymore, Detective Erie. You just head down to Arizona and catch some sun. Leave the worms to us."

8:45 A.M.:

Erie had already cleaned out his office, for the most part. The walls were bare, his desktop was free of clutter, the drawers were practically empty aside from a few stray pens and paper clips and leftover forms. So it was impossible to miss the yellow Post-it note stuck to the exact center of his desktop. It was from Hal Allen, director of Detective Services/Homicide — his boss. The note read, "See me in my office ASAP." Erie hoped it was a special assignment, a favor he could do for Allen or the department, something that would draw on his decades of experience, something that would make his last eight hours as a police officer count.

8:48 A.M.:

Erie knew he was in trouble the second he stepped into the office of May Davis, Allen's administrative assistant and official gatekeeper. He'd walked into a trap, and there was no way out.

Twenty people were crammed behind Davis's desk. Behind them was a banner reading WE'LL MISS YOU, BIG GUY! On it were dozens of signatures surrounded by drawings of handcuffs and police badges and men in striped prison uniforms. The people waiting for him, the entire homicide division reinforced by a couple of evidence technicians and some of his old buddies from other departments, began singing "For He's a Jolly Good Fellow."

Erie stood there, smiling dutifully, and took it like a man.

9:09 A.M.:

Erie endured the song and the hugs and the slaps on the back and the vanilla cake with the outline of Arizona in orange frosting. He endured Allen's speech about thirty-three years of service and one hundred and twelve murderers behind bars. He endured it all without ever saying, "What about those twenty-nine *unsolved* murders?" or "Why would I move to Arizona without Nancy?" And after the ordeal was over and the revelers had all drifted away, it became clear that he was supposed to drift away, too. There were forms to fill out and drawers to empty, right? Instead, he asked Hal Allen if they could step into his office.

"What's on your mind, Larry?" Allen was a different breed of cop. He was younger than Erie. He worked out every day. His walls weren't covered with pictures of his kids or newspaper articles about his big busts. He had his degrees — a B.A. in criminal justice, a Master's in psychology — and inspirational posters about Leadership and Goals. For him, being a cop wasn't a calling, it was a career choice. But Erie liked him and hoped he would understand.

"I was wondering if I could take back one of my cases."

"Come on, Larry," Allen said. "You're going to have to let go."

"Just for today, Hal. I just want to make some inquiries, see if I can get the ball rolling again. At the end of the day I'll turn it back over to Dave Rogers with a full briefing."

Allen shook his head, grinning. "I've heard of this condition. It's called dedication to duty. We're going to have to cure you of it. I prescribe a day playing computer solitaire followed by a much-de-served early retirement in beautiful, sunny Arizona."

"Nancy liked Arizona, Hal. We were moving there for her."

"Oh." The smile melted off Allen's face. "So you're not —"

"I don't know. We hadn't signed anything yet when Nancy took that last turn for the worse. I'm not sure I want to leave Indiana. I've lived here all my life." Erie shifted nervously in his seat. "But that's neither here nor there. I'm just asking for one more day to protect and serve."

Allen leaned forward in his swivel chair and gave Erie a long, thoughtful look as if really seeing him for the first time. "You're not going to solve your one hundred thirteenth homicide today, Larry. You're just going to end up chasing around stone-cold leads and getting nowhere."

"I love days like that."

Allen nodded. "OK. Do what you have to do. But drop by my of-fice before you go home tonight. I want to talk to you again."

Erie practically jumped up from his chair. For the first time that day he actually felt awake.

"Yes, sir," he said. "Anything you say."

9:31 A.M.:

Detective David Rogers was on the phone when Erie appeared in the doorway to his office. Rogers waved him in, said "No problem," and hung up. "The boss says you want to catch a bad guy today," he said.

"I just want to borrow back one of my cases. Is that OK with you?"

Rogers smiled and pointed at a stack of bound folders on one corner of his desk. "Pick your poison," he said. "If you insist on working your last day, I'm not going to stop you."

Erie shuffled through the case files. Did he want the fifteen-year-old crack dealer, four months dead? The unidentified, twenty-something woman found in the woods of Lloyd Park, six months dead? Or the middle-aged insurance salesman, ten months dead?

Lifeless eyes stared up at him from Polaroids paper-clipped to xeroxed autopsy reports. They looked inside him, told him, "Do something. Avenge me. Avenge *me.*"

But justice isn't for the dead. That was one of the things he had learned in his years working homicide. It's no use fighting a crusade for a corpse. It will still be a corpse even if somebody turns its killer into a corpse, too. But the family, the loved ones, *the living* — they can be helped.

He chose a file and left.

10:07 A.M.:

Unlike most of the older, lower-middle-class neighborhoods around town, Pine Hills actually lived up to its name. It had both pines and hills, though not many of either. It also had a reputation among Erie's fellow cops for producing wild kids. On Halloween night patrol cars cruised through the neighborhood as if it were Compton or Watts, and EMT crews waited on standby for the inevitable wounds from bottle rockets, M-80s, broken glass, and exploding mailboxes.

O'Hara Drive was a short crooked sloping street in the heart of the neighborhood. It was all of one block long, bracketed on each side by longer streets that curved up to the neighborhood's highest hills. From the top of one you could see the airport just a mile away. From the other you could see the county dump.

The house at 1701 O'Hara Drive wasn't just where Joel Korfmann, insurance salesman, had lived. It was where he had died, too. There were two vehicles in the driveway when Erie arrived — a silver, mid-'90s model Ford Taurus and a newer Ford pickup, red. The Taurus he remembered.

He parked at the curb and walked toward the house. All the curtains had been drawn shut. A big plastic trash can lay on its side near the foot of the driveway.

He rang the doorbell. And waited. He knocked on the rickety metal of the screen door. The curtains in the front window fluttered, and a woman's face hovered in the shadows beyond. Erie tried to smile reassuringly. He pulled out his badge.

"It's Detective Erie, Mrs. Korfmann."

The face disappeared. Erie waited again. Finally the front door opened. The screen door in front of it remained closed.

All the lights of the house were off. Candace Korfmann stood back from the door, away from the sunlight. "Hello."

"Hello, Mrs. Korfmann. I'm just dropping by this morning to ask a few followup questions. Is now a good time to talk?"

"Sure," she replied lifelessly. She was dressed in a bathrobe. Erie recalled that she was what people used to call a housewife or home-maker. She didn't have a job to give her life focus again after her husband died. And she didn't have any children to keep her busy, keep her mind from dwelling on the past, on what had happened in her own kitchen. He pictured her brooding in the darkness of the little white house all day every day, alone.

"Good," Erie said. "First off, I'm afraid I have to tell you that we haven't uncovered any new leads. But we're putting a new investi-gator on the case next week, Detective David Rogers. So don't lose hope, Mrs. Korfmann. He's a good man."

After a moment's pause she nodded. "OK, I won't."

"Good. Now, second, I was wondering if there was anything new you could tell me — any new memories or thoughts you've had that might help our investigation."

Mrs. Korfmann stared at him impassively. Standing in the shad-ows, perfectly still, she looked flat, one-dimensional, like the mere outline of a woman. Her shape — the slumped shoulders and tou-sled hair and slightly tilted head — reminded him of Nancy toward the end, when she was so weak she could barely stand. "It could be anything, even just a rumor going around the neighborhood," he prompted. "Every little bit helps, Mrs. Korfmann."

She shook her head slowly. "I don't know what to tell you. I haven't heard a thing."

"That's OK. No reason you should do our job for us. I have just one more thing to talk to you about." He pulled a card from his jacket pocket. "I'd like to give you this. It's the number of a woman I know. She runs a group for . . . those who've been left behind. A survivor support group. You might want to give her a call."

Mrs. Korfmann didn't move for a long moment. Then she opened the door and reached out to take the card. As she leaned into the light, Erie could see that her skin was pale, her eyes hollow. He noticed a slight swelling in her lower lip and a dark, bluish smudge of bruised flesh under her left eye.

"Thanks," she said.

"Sure. You take care now, Mrs. Korfmann."
She nodded, then closed the door.

10:24 A.M.:

Erie started his car. The digital clock on the dashboard came to
life. Not even an hour back on the Korfmann case, and already he
was done. He had driven across town just to stir up painful memories for a sad and lonely woman. There was nothing to do now but
head back to the office and shoot the breeze with whoever he could
find lounging around. Reminisce about the good old days, trot out
old stories and legends, do nothing. Then go home.

He shut off the ignition and got out of the car. He walked to the
house across from 1701 O'Hara Drive and rang the doorbell. An
old man opened the door. He was wearing glasses so thick Erie
couldn't see his eyes, just big, shimmering ovals of pale blue.

"Yes?"

Erie took out his badge. "Good morning, Mr. Wallender. I'm Detective Erie. You and I spoke about ten months ago."

The old man bent forward to peer at the badge. "Of course I remember you, Detective. Come on in." He shuffled ahead of Erie
into the next room. "You have a seat there and I'll get some coffee."
He disappeared around a corner. "I've got some on the stove. Every day I make a pot of coffee and drink two cups. I don't know why
I keep doing that. I pour more coffee down the drain in a morning
than most people drink in a week." Erie could hear cabinet doors
and drawers opening and closing, porcelain sliding over countertops, the hum of an open refrigerator.

"I'll just take mine black, Mr. Wallender," he called.

"Have you arrested Joel Korfmann's killer yet?"

"Not yet. That's why I'm here. I'm making a few followup inquiries."

Wallender shuffled into the living room with a mug in each
hand. He gave one to Erie. The liquid in it had the telltale hue of
coffee with skim milk. Erie didn't take a sip.

"I was wondering if you'd heard or seen anything else that might
have a bearing on the case."

Wallender lowered himself slowly into a recliner. "I've been keeping my eye on the neighborhood kids. They're always planning some kind of prank. I called the police a couple of months ago. Thought I saw a boy with some dynamite. A policeman came out. Do you know an Officer Pyke?"

"Yes, I do." The old man's vision and hearing might be shaky, but his memory was fine. "Have you spoken to Mrs. Korfmann at all? Do you know how she's doing?"

Wallender brought his mug to his lips, his hands trembling badly.

"She kind of dropped out of sight for a while there. I figured she went to be with her family or some such," the old man said. "She was gone maybe two months. When she came back, she seemed to be doing fine. I took it upon myself to drop in and chat with her from time to time."

"And her state of mind seemed good?"

Wallender shrugged. "Far as I could tell. They were always standoffish people, her and her husband both. She seemed a little friendlier for a while there, but then her young man began hanging around and she was the same old Candace again."

"Her young man? You mean she has a boyfriend?"

"I guess you could call him that, seeing as how his truck's there most nights."

"And how long has this been going on?"

"Maybe two months, maybe a little longer." Wallender's thin, trembling lips curled into a sly smile.

"Now, don't go thinking evil thoughts, Detective Erie. She needed a man around, so she found one. It's understandable. People get lonely. I know a little something about that. It's not easy living alone."

Erie tried to smile back but found he couldn't. His mouth, his whole face, felt stiff, dead. "I'm not thinking evil thoughts, Mr. Wallender. I'm just curious. That's my job."

"Sure, sure. I understand. I guess I'm curious, too. Except when it's a neighbor being curious, people call it nosy."

"Have you ever spoken to Mrs. Korfmann's young man?"

"Well, I've tried. He's not a very talkative fella. I've been over to chat once or twice when I noticed him out working on his truck. He didn't have a lot to say. Actually, he reminds me a lot of Joel — Mr. Korfmann."

"Did you happen to catch his name?"

"Ray. He didn't mention his last name. He works over at De-Rogatis Ford as a mechanic." The old man grinned again. "That's all I got out of him, chief. If you want me to try again, maybe I could get his Social Security number for you."

Erie finally found himself able to smile back. "You're a real character, Mr. Wallender."

"I certainly am," the old man said with obvious pride. "I just wish more people knew it."

10:43 A.M.:

Erie was back in his car, faced again with the drive to the station, spending the afternoon killing time, the evening killing time, the weekend killing time, the years killing time until time finally killed him.

He thought about Candace Korfmann. Her dead-eyed stare, the way she had stayed away from the light, the black eye. He tried not to think evil thoughts about Ray. But he couldn't stop himself. Good cops and social workers can smell abuse a mile away, and Erie had caught a whiff of something in the air around 1701 O'Hara Drive. Maybe he couldn't catch a killer in one day, but he sure as hell could sniff out a woman-beater. What he would do about it, he wasn't sure.

He started his car and put it in gear. As he pulled away from the curb, he noticed movement in one of the windows of the Korfmann house — a dark shape quickly replaced by the swaying of a blind. Someone had been watching him.

He drove to the intersection of Oak Hill Road and Highway 41, home of DeRogatis Ford.

11:10 A.M.:

A salesman swooped down on Erie before he could step out of his car.

"Good afternoon there! What can I help you with today?"

Erie flipped out his badge. "I'd like to have a word with whoever runs your mechanics' shop."

Sweat instantly materialized on the salesman's forehead.

"Don't worry. I'm just making a routine inquiry."

The salesman still looked panic-stricken.

"It has nothing to do with DeRogatis Ford," Erie added. "I'm trying to locate someone who may be an employee. He's not in any trouble. Like I said, it's very routine."

The salesman nodded and gave Erie an unconvincing smile. "Sure, officer. We're always happy to help River City's finest. Right this way."

The salesman led him through the showroom to a bustling garage. About eight cars were being worked on, some with their hoods up, some on hydraulic lifts. Off to the side customers lounged in a waiting room watching *The Jerry Springer Show*. The salesman pointed out a short, middle-aged Asian man leaning over an Escort's engine.

"That's Frank Takarada. He runs things back here." The salesman slipped a business card out of his shirt pocket. "If you ever want to talk cars, I'm your man. I'm here Tuesday through Saturday." He shook Erie's hand and hustled away.

Erie pocketed the card and headed toward Takarada. The mechanic noticed his approach and eyed him warily.

"Mr. Takarada, could I have a word with you, please?"

"I'm very busy. Maybe later."

Sometimes the badge-flash routine got quick results, sometimes — especially in public places when plenty of people were around — it just irritated or embarrassed people. Takarada looked like the irritable type. Erie leaned close and lowered his voice. "I'm a police detective, Mr. Takarada. I promise that I only need five minutes of your time. Do you have an office where we can speak?"

Takarada pulled a greasy rag out of one pocket and began wiping off his hands. "Come on," he grunted. He led Erie to a back corner of the garage. Auto parts in plastic bags hung from pegs on a large partition. Takarada stepped around it. Erie followed, finding a makeshift office complete with desk, computer terminal, fan, and filing cabinets covered with crinkled paperwork. A large board studded with pegs hung on the wall. Car keys dangled from the pegs.

"So what do you want?" Takarada said.

"I'd like to know if you have a mechanic here by the name of Ray or Raymond."

"Nope."

Erie felt foolish. He had followed up a blind hunch, something that had nothing to do with his job, based on the memory of a doddering old recluse. He was about to apologize and leave when Takarada spoke again.

"Not anymore. Had one a few months ago, though. Ray Long."

"What happened?"

"We had to let him go," Takarada said with mock gentility. He didn't volunteer anything further.

"This is off the record, Mr. Takarada. Just between you and me. You can be plainspoken."

"Okay," said Takarada, who seemed glad to have permission to be blunt. "He's an ass. Always was. I put up with him for two years and then —" He mimed dropping a ball and punting it.

"When was this?"

"Six weeks, maybe two months ago, something like that."

"What happened?"

"Instead of being late once or twice a week, he was late every day. Instead of being hungover some of the time, he was hungover all of the time."

"How did he react when you fired him?"

Takarada laughed bitterly. "Typical macho b.s." His voice suddenly took on a southern Indiana twang. "'Oh yeah, man? Well, I don't need this stupid job, anyway! I'm set up, man! So screw you!'"

Erie's fingers and toes began to tingle the way they always did when he sensed a break. He forced himself to relax before he spoke again. "He said, 'I'm set up'?"

"Something like that, yeah."

"Can you tell me if a Candace Korfmann had her car serviced in this shop in the last few months? She drives a silver Taurus, looks like a '95 or '96."

The mechanic looked annoyed. "I'd have to look that up."

"I would appreciate that, Mr. Takarada. It's very important."

Takarada sighed heavily. "How do you spell that?" He walked back to the computer terminal and took a seat.

Erie's mind was racing ahead of Takarada as he typed. The dealership's records would show that Candace Korfmann had brought her car in about two months ago, maybe three. Raymond Long had worked on the car. He had noticed her waiting — she wasn't an unattractive woman. He took her over to show her something, began flirting. He could sense that she was vulnerable. He got her to agree to a date. He found out she was a widow. Her husband had been an insurance agent. She had received a large amount of money upon his death. Raymond Long saw an opportunity. He wormed his way into her heart, then her home. Now he thought he ran the show. Erie would figure out a way to prove him wrong.

"Yeah, we've got a Candace Korfmann in here. Drives a 1995 Taurus, like you said."

"Does it show who worked on her car last?"

"Sure. Got the initials right here. 'R.L.'"

Erie nodded with satisfaction. "Raymond Long. This was around June or July?"

"Not even close."

"What?"

Takarada turned away from the computer. "Try May — of last year."

Erie stared at the mechanic blankly, his mind racing. His pet theory was blown.

Within seconds another one started to take its place.

He gestured at the key rack on the wall. "These are for the cars you're working on?"

"And the ones waiting out back, yeah."

"You ever work on vans here?"

Takarada shrugged. "Sure, every now and then."

Erie mulled that over for a moment. "Anything else?" Takarada was obviously anxious to get back to work.

"If you could print that out for me, I'd appreciate it." Before Takarada could groan or sigh or roll his eyes, Erie added, "Then I'll be leaving. You've been a big help. Thanks."

Takarada started to swivel back to the keyboard, then stopped himself. "So, can you tell me? Is Long in some kind of trouble?"

Erie gave the safe cop answer: "No, this is just a routine inquiry." But he knew trouble was headed Raymond Long's way. Erie hoped to deliver it himself before the day was over.

11:44 A.M.:

Erie ate lunch at a Denny's across the street from the Ford dealership. A few too many people were probably expecting him to drop by Peppy's, the diner around the corner from police headquarters. But he wanted a chance to think.

His turkey club and fries went down untasted. The file on Joel Korfmann's murder was spread across the table before him.

Erie was pleased to see that the report was neat, thorough, precise. He'd put it together himself months before.

On New Year's Eve, at approximately nine-fifteen P.M., Joel Korfmann had been bludgeoned to death in his home. The victim, age forty-one, was a Lutheran Family Insurance representative who had spent the day making calls on potential customers. In the evening he had been at the office doing paperwork. (In parentheses after this information were the words "Indicative of victim's character?" Those were code words. What they meant was, "What kind of jerk makes cold calls selling insurance on New Year's Eve? Then spends the evening doing paperwork when he could be with family and friends?") Security surveillance tapes showed that he left work at eight-forty-three P.M. It would have taken him about half an hour to drive home.

The victim's wife, Candace Lane Korfmann, age thirty-eight, spent the evening with her sister, Carol Lane Biggs, and brother-in-law, Rudy Biggs. Witnesses placed them at the Dew Drop Inn on Division Street from eight-thirty P.M. until approximately twelve thirty A.M.

Carol and Rudy Biggs drove Candace Korfmann home, arriving at twelve-fifty-five. All three entered the house. Mrs. Korfmann immediately noticed that several items — a GoldStar television, a Sony VCR, a Sony stereo — were missing. In the kitchen Rudy Biggs discovered the body of Joel Korfmann. He had been hit from behind by a large, heavy object. Forensics later concluded that he had been hit five times with the butt of his own shotgun, which was also reported missing.

Most of the Korfmanns' neighbors had been away for the evening celebrating the holiday. But a James Wallender, an elderly man who lived by himself across the street, reported seeing a dark van parked on the street near the house at approximately eight-thirty P.M. Later, Wallender said, he saw it in the Korfmanns' drive-way. (In parentheses here: "Witness seems anxious to help investi-gation." That was Erie's way of hinting that the old man might not be the most reliable witness. Sometimes lonely people were so ea-ger to please they would "remember" things they'd never seen.)

The report concluded that the victim had surprised someone in the house — an individual or individuals in the process of burglar-izing it. Seeing the house dark on a holiday, the perpetrators must have assumed the residents were out of town or would be out all night partying. It was a common scenario.

There had been no evidence when Erie had written his report. There were no fingerprints, no hairs, no tire tracks that could be linked to the crime, and the stolen items had never surfaced. And that hadn't changed. Erie still had no evidence. But he did have something new — a hunch.

Driving back to headquarters after lunch, his mind dwelled on Raymond Long. He pictured him as a young long-haired redneck with muscular arms and fiery eyes. He pictured him killing Joel Korfmann. He pictured him beating Candace Korfmann, finally killing her in a rage — or just because it suited him. He saw it all, crystal clear in his mind. Long the manipulator, Long the killer. Joel and Candace Korfmann, the victims.

The only thing that interrupted these thoughts was a stray one that crept in from another part of his brain as he maneuvered through afternoon traffic. It was the image of cars and trucks whip-ping up and down Green River Road, leaving roadkill behind them on the asphalt, on the side of the road, tumbling into ditches. He hoped the little black cat was safe.

1:10 P.M.:

At headquarters Erie checked to see if "Long, Raymond" had a criminal record. He wasn't disappointed. There were three charges of disturbing the peace, two charges of battery, two disorderly con-ducts, one assault, and the inevitable DWI and resisting arrest. Over the years he had served a grand total of fifteen months in the Vanderburgh County lockup.

The pictures came as a surprise, though. Long was thirty-seven, and he looked every day of it. He was balding, pug-nosed, and jowly. He didn't look like the kind of handsome young devil who could charm a vulnerable widow — or widow-to-be. Erie assumed he was one hell of a talker.

Erie went back to his office (accepting a number of hand-shakes and pats on the back on the way) and began calling all the U-Stor-Its and Storage Lands in town. The people he spoke with knew him, knew what he was looking for, knew the drill, but they couldn't help. No, they hadn't rented space to a Raymond Long in the last year. Yes, they'd give him a call if a Raymond Long came in.

After saying "Thanks, have a good one" for the eighth time, Erie hung up the phone and left his office. It was time to have a talk with Raymond Long.

2:17 P.M.:

There was something different at 1701 O'Hara Drive when Erie pulled up. He walked toward the house slowly, trying to pin down what it was.

The curtains were still drawn shut. The Taurus and the pickup were still parked out front. The trash can still lay on its side in the yard.

He was walking up the driveway past the pickup when he realized what it was. The truck was splattered with mud — mud that hadn't been there that morning. Erie crossed the street and rang James Wallender's doorbell.

"Hello there, chief," the old man said as he opened the door. "I was wondering if you'd come back again. Why don't you come in?"

"I'm sorry, Mr. Wallender, I don't have time to visit right now. I just wanted to ask if you'd seen any activity at the Korfmann house today."

"Well, I might have peeked out the window a time or two since you were here." Wallender winked. "Hold on a minute." He shuf-fled away, then returned a moment later with a small notepad clutched in one trembling hand. "You left here at approximately ten-forty-five A.M. Around eleven that fella Ray pulled his truck into the garage and brought the garage door down. At eleven-twenty he drove out again and was gone for a while."

"Was there anything in the pickup when he left?"

"Yeah. Something big and green."

"Green?"

Wallender checked his notepad. "Yes, green. At least that's what it looked like to me." He tapped his eyeglasses. "I have to look at everything through these Coke bottles."

"Could it have been a tarp thrown over something in the back of the truck?"

Wallender nodded. "Sure, it could have been."

"And how long was Ray gone?"

Wallender looked at his notepad again. "Forty-five minutes."

Erie extended a hand. Wallender shook it. "Mr. Wallender, by the power vested in me by the state of Indiana, I hereby declare you a junior G-man."

Wallender smiled. "I always said I wanted to be a detective when I grew up."

3:10 P.M.:

The shoes Erie had shined so carefully that morning were now covered with mud, coffee grounds, and mysterious flecks of filth. His trousers were similarly splattered, and there was a new rip where a piece of jagged metal had snagged his pant leg. Even his tie was beginning to smell bad.

Early on, there had been two other scavengers, a heavyset couple with prodigious guts spilling out from under their dirty T-shirts. They'd seen him — a well-dressed, middle-aged man picking through piles of garbage at the county dump — and stared as if he were some exotic, dangerous animal pacing back and forth in a cage at the zoo. They kept their distance, eventually driving off in a beat-up station wagon loaded with discarded toys and clothes and broken appliances.

Erie told himself he'd only look for another half-hour. If he couldn't find anything, he'd head back down to Pine Hills and have that talk with Raymond Long. Not that he was going to make much of an impression in his current condition. Maybe after another thirty minutes wading through garbage he would smell so putrid Long would confess just to get away from him.

The ridiculousness of it made him long for Nancy. He wanted to go home and tell her everything that had happened. He couldn't even tell if his last day had been sad, funny, triumphant, or disastrous without her face to gauge it by.

From off in the distance came the popping and clicking of tires rolling over gravel. More scavengers were headed up the winding back road to the dump. Erie was going to be on exhibit again. He thought about abandoning his crazy theory and just going home for a nice long bath.

And then he found it. It was underneath a big flattened-out cardboard box, the kind washing machines are delivered in. A GoldStar TV. The screen had been broken in and the plastic cracked on top, but it was relatively free of mud and grime. Erie checked the back. Even though someone had made a halfhearted effort to bust up the television and make it look old, they hadn't bothered scratching off the serial number.

Erie tore into the nearest pile of garbage, tossing trash bags and boxes aside with manic energy. At the bottom he found a Sony VCR, the top crushed as if someone had jumped on top of it. He picked it up and looked at the back. Again, the serial number was still there.

It only took him another minute of digging to find the stereo. It was nearby, underneath a pile of newspapers. It had hardly been damaged at all. There was still a serial number on the back.

That left just one item — the most important of all. Once he found that, he could call in the evidence techs to dust everything for prints and look for tracks that matched the tires on Raymond Long's truck. The tracks would have to be nearby. Erie turned around to look.

Raymond Long was walking toward him. "Is this what you're looking for?" he said.

He was holding a shotgun. It was pointed at Erie. His finger was on the trigger.

In the time it took Long to take two more steps Erie had considered five different options: dive and roll and draw his gun; charge Long and go for the shotgun; put up his hands and feign ignorance; put up his hands and try to talk Long into surrendering; run like crazy. Those few seconds were all Erie needed to realize that all his options stank. But he picked one anyway. He put up his hands and started talking.

"Don't do anything dumb, Ray. A lot of people know where I am.

If anything happens to me, they're going to know exactly who to point the finger at."

Long stopped about seven yards from Erie. At that range there was little doubt what outcome a shotgun blast would have.

"Yeah, well, maybe by the time they're pointing fingers, I'll be hundreds of miles away." His voice was full of spiteful good ol' boy bravado. But Erie could see the sweat shining on his face, the damp rings that were spreading under the armpits of his T-shirt.

Erie shook his head. "You won't make it. Wherever you try to go. Cop killers never get away. Other cops take it too personally. You'll end up right back in Indiana facing a capital murder charge."

"Don't you mean *two* capital murder charges?" Long sneered. He had a good face for sneering. It looked like he'd done a lot of practicing over the years.

"You should stop talking, Ray. You should put down the shotgun and let me take you in. That's what a lawyer would tell you to do. You haven't crossed the line yet — you haven't doomed yourself. If you put the gun down now, this could all still work out for you and Candace."

Erie knew instantly that he'd made a mistake. As soon as he'd said *Candace*, Long's sneer had turned into a scowl of rage. Erie had pushed the wrong button. Now he had to get out of the way.

Erie threw himself to the left, twisting in mid-flight so he'd take most of the buckshot in the back, buttocks, or legs instead of the face and chest. There was a boom, and a searing pain lanced his side. But it wasn't bad enough to stop him. He rolled over and came up with his gun pointing toward Long.

But Long wasn't standing there anymore. He was lying on the ground. Erie watched him for a second, stunned. Long wasn't moving.

Erie stood up and winced as a bolt of agony struck in a familiar place: his gymnastics had strained his cranky lower back. He limped toward Long, each step sending pain shooting up his spine.

Long was a mess. And he was dead.

Erie guessed that he'd bent the shotgun's barrel or jammed the chamber when he bludgeoned Joel Korfmann. He might even have used the stock to bust up the TV, VCR, and stereo. So when he tried to shoot Erie, the shotgun had exploded, sending shards of metal and wood out in all directions — but mostly into Long's body.

Erie checked the right side of his abdomen where he'd felt the sting a moment before. He'd been wounded but not by buckshot or shrapnel. His shirt was torn, and a short, shallow gash was bleeding onto the white cotton. When he'd jumped, he'd landed on something sharp.

He began walking very, very slowly to his car, trying to remember the last time he'd had a tetanus shot.

3:55 P.M.:

A patrol car was waiting for him at 1701 O'Hara Drive when he arrived as he had requested from the dispatcher.

"Geez, Larry, where did the tornado touch down?" one of the officers asked as he limped to their car.

"Right on top of me. Can't you tell?"

"What's the story?" the other cop asked.

"I need to pick somebody up for questioning. I'm not expecting any trouble, but I wanted a little backup just in case. You two just hang back and observe."

"Hang back and observe," the first cop said, giving Erie a salute. "That's what I do best."

Erie walked up to the house and rang the doorbell. Candace Korfmann opened the door almost immediately.

"I've been waiting for you," she said. She was wearing jeans and a River City Community College sweatshirt. "I'm ready to go."

She stepped outside, closed the front door, and brushed past Erie. "That's you, right?" she said, pointing at Erie's car.

"Yes."

She walked to the car quickly. Erie followed her.

"Do you want me in the front or the back?" she asked.

"The front is fine." Mrs. Korfmann opened the door and climbed in. Erie eased himself gingerly into the driver's seat and started the engine. He gave the cops watching from their patrol car an "everything's under control" wave.

"I hope you weren't hurt," Mrs. Korfmann said as Erie pulled away from the curb.

"You're not under arrest, Mrs. Korfmann. I'm taking you in for an interview, that's all. You don't have to say anything if you don't want to."

"Is he dead?"

Erie took his eyes off the road for a moment to watch her. "Yes, Raymond Long is dead. He was killed about half an hour ago."

She grunted. A long stretch of road rolled by in silence.

"It was his own fault," she suddenly announced. "He killed himself when he pulled that trigger." She didn't look at Erie as she spoke. She stared straight ahead, unblinking.

"What do you mean?"

"I filled the barrel with caulk last week." She was still staring at nothing, but tears had begun to trickle down her cheeks. "I was afraid he was going to use it on me."

"He was abusive?"

"Yes."

Erie stole another glance at her. The tears were still flowing, but her face was impassive, blank. "He was your lover," he said.

"Yes."

"He killed your husband."

"Yes," she replied without hesitating.

"He used a van from DeRogatis Ford to fake a burglary."

"Yes."

"He kept the things he took from your house and brought them with him when he moved in with you."

"Yes." She spat out the word this time. "That idiot."

"Will you repeat all this when we reach police headquarters? In a formal statement?"

"Yes."

Another mile rolled under the wheels before Erie spoke again. "Why did you go along with it?" he said. "Did you love him?"

Mrs. Korfmann finally turned to face him. That morning she had reminded him, just a bit, of Nancy. But whatever resemblance he had seen in her then was gone now, crushed with the rest of her spirit.

"Joel used to beat me, too," she said. "Ray said he would protect me."

5:25 P.M.:

She repeated everything on the record, just as she said she would. Erie stayed in the interrogation room only long enough to make sure it was all on tape. But he left Dave Rogers to prepare her statement and get a signature. He simply stood up and said, "I'm tired, Dave," and walked out.

Hal Allen was waiting for him outside. "I'd never have guessed it," Allen said. "You've been holding out on us all these years. If I'd known you could wrap up a murder case every day, I never would have let you retire."

"Too late now, boss," Erie replied. "All right if I go home?"

"In a second. I wanted to see you at the end of the day, remember?"

"Oh, right. I guess you need this." Erie slipped his badge-clip off his belt and handed it to Allen. "And this." He unholstered his revolver and handed that over, too.

"Well, yeah, we need those." Allen slipped the items into his jacket pocket. "But that's not what I wanted to see you about. Do you still carry cards for Julie Rhodes, the grief counselor?"

"Um-hmm."

"Could I see one?" Erie pulled out one of the cards. He handed it to Allen, who looked at it for a moment before handing it back.

"Here," Allen said. "I think you should use this."

5:50 P.M.:

Erie stopped at a grocery store on the way home. He found the cheapest red wine in stock and put four bottles in his cart.

But on the way to the register he changed his mind.

He found the aisle marked Pet Supplies and threw a bag of kitty litter and a dozen cans of cat food into his cart. He left three bottles of wine on the shelf next to the cat treats.

When he got home, he opened one of the cans of cat food and dumped its contents onto a small plate. He took the plate out to the front porch along with his wine, a glass, and a bottle opener. He placed the plate on the walk that led to the driveway, then eased himself down on the first step of his porch.

He opened the wine and waited.

CLARK HOWARD

Under Suspicion

FROM *Ellery Queen's Mystery Magazine*

FRANK DELL WALKED into the Three Corners Club shortly after five, as he usually did every day, and took a seat at the end of the bar. The bartender, seeing him, put together, without being told, a double Tanqueray over two ice cubes with two large olives, and set it in front of him on a cork coaster. Down at the middle of the bar, Dell saw two minor stickup men he remembered from somewhere and began staring at them without touching his drink. Frank Dell's stare was glacial and unblinking. After three disconcerting minutes of it, the two stickup men paid for their drinks and left. Only then did Dell lift his own glass.

Tim Callan, the club owner, came over and sat opposite Dell. "Well, I see you just cost me a couple more customers, Frankie," he said wryly.

"Hoodlums," Dell replied. "I'm just helping you keep the place respectable, Timmy."

"Bring some of your policemen buddies in to drink," Callan suggested. "That'll keep me respectable *and* profitable."

"You're not hurting for profits," Dell said. "Not with that after-hours poker game you run in the apartment upstairs."

Callan laughed. "Ah, Frankie, Frankie. Been quick with the answers all your life. You should've been a lawyer. Even my old dad, rest his soul, used to say that."

"I'm not crooked enough to be a lawyer," Dell said, sipping his drink.

"Not crooked *enough*! Hell, you're not crooked at all, Frankie. You're probably the straightest cop in Chicago." Callan leaned forward on one elbow. "How long we known each other, Frank?"

"What's on your mind, Tim?" Dell asked knowingly. Reminiscing, he had learned, frequently led to other things.

"We go back thirty years, do you realize that, Frank?" Callan replied, ignoring Dell's suspicion. "First grade at St. Mel's school out on the West Side."

"What's on your mind, Tim?" Dell's expression hardened just a hint. He hated asking the same question twice.

"Remember my baby sister, Francie?" Callan asked, lowering his voice.

"Sure. Cute little kid. Carrot-red hair. Freckles. Eight or ten years younger than us."

"Nine. She's twenty-seven now. She married this Guinea a few years ago, name of Nicky Santore. They moved up to Milwaukee where the guy's uncle got him a job in a brewery. Well, they started having problems. You know the greaseballs, they're all Don Juans, chasing broads all the time —"

"Get to the point, Tim," said Dell. He hated embellishment.

"OK. Francie left him and came back to live with my brother, Dennis — you know him, the fireman. Anyhow, after she got back, she found out she's expecting. Then Nicky finds out, and he comes back too. Guy begs Francie to take him back, and she does. Now, the only job he can get down here is pumping gas at a Texaco station, which only pays minimum wage. He's worried about doctor bills and everything with the baby coming, so he agrees, for a cut, to let a cousin of his use the station storeroom to stash hot goods. It works OK for a while, but then the cousin gets busted and leads the cops to the station. They find a load of laptop computers. Nick gets charged with receiving stolen property. He comes up for a preliminary hearing in three weeks."

"Tough break," Dell allowed, sipping again. "But he should get probation if he's got no priors."

"He's got a prior," Callan said, looking down at the bar.

"What is it?"

"Burglary. Him and that same cousin robbed some hotel rooms down at the Hilton when they was working as bellmen. Years ago. Both of them got probation on that."

"Then he's looking at one-to-four on this fall," Dell said.

Callan swallowed. "Can you help me out on this, Frankie?"

Dell gave him the stare. "You don't mean help you, Tim. You mean help Nicky Santore. What do you think I can do?"

"Give your personal voucher for him."

"Are you serious? You want me to go to an assistant state's attorney handling an RSP case and personally vouch for some Guinea with a prior that I don't even know?"

"Frank, it's for Francie —"

"No, it isn't. If Francie was charged, I'd get her off in a heartbeat. But it's not Francie; it's some two-bit loser she married."

"Frank, please, listen —"

"No. Forget it."

There was a soft buzzing signal from the pager clipped to Dell's belt. Reaching under his coat, he got it out and looked at it. It was a 911 page from the Lakeside station house out on the South Side, where he was assigned.

"I have to answer this," he told Callan. Taking a cellular phone from his coat pocket, he opened it and dialed one of the station house's unlisted numbers. When someone answered, he said, "This is Dell. I got a nine-one-one page."

"Yeah, it's Captain Larne. Hold on."

A moment later, an older, huskier voice spoke. "Dell? Mike Larne. Where's Dan?" He was asking about Dan Malone, Dell's partner, a widower in his fifties.

"Probably at home," Dell told the captain. "I dropped him off there less than an hour ago. What's up, Cap?"

"Edie Malone was found dead in her apartment a little while ago. It looks like she's been strangled."

Dell said nothing. He froze, absolutely still, the little phone at his ear. Edie was Dan's only child.

"Dell? Did you hear me?"

"Yessir, I heard you. Captain, I can't tell him —"

"You won't have to. The department chaplain and Dan's parish priest get that dirty job. What I want you to do is help me keep Dan from going off the deep end over this. You know how he is. We can't have *him* going wild thinking he'll solve this himself."

"What do you want me to do?"

"I'm going to assign you temporary duty to the homicide team working the case. If Dan knows you're on it, he might stay calm. Understand where I'm coming from?"

"Yessir." Dell was still frozen, motionless.

"Take down this address," Larne said. Dell animated, taking a small spiral notebook and ballpoint from his shirt pocket. He wrote down the address Larne gave him. "The homicide boys have only been there a little while. Kenmare and Garvan. Know them?"

"Yeah, Kenmare, slightly. They know I'm coming?"

"Absolutely. This has all been cleared with headquarters." Larne paused a beat, then said, "You knew the girl, did you?"

"Yessir."

"Well," Larne sighed heavily, "I hate to do this to you, Frank —"

"It's all right, Cap. I understand."

"Call me at home later."

"Right."

Dell closed the phone and slipped it back into his pocket. He walked away from the bar and out of the club without another word to Tim Callan.

Edie Malone's address was one of the trendy new apartment buildings remodeled from old commercial high-rises on the near North Side. The sixth floor had been cordoned off to permit only residents of that floor to exit the elevator, and they were required to go directly to their apartments. Edie Malone's apartment was posted as a crime scene. In addition to homicide detectives Kenmare and Garvan, there were half a dozen uniformed officers guarding the hallways and stairwells, personnel from the city crime lab in the apartment itself, and a deputy coroner and Cook County morgue attendants waiting to transport the victim to the county hospital complex for autopsy.

When Frank Dell arrived, Kenmare and Garvan took him into the bedroom to view the body. Edie Malone was wearing a white cotton sweatshirt with MONICA FOR PRESIDENT lettered on it, and a pair of cutoff denim shorts. Barefoot, she was lying on her back, elbows bent, hands a few inches from her ears, feet apart as if she were resting, with her long, dark red hair splayed out on the white shag carpet like spilled paint. Her eyes were wide open in a bloated face, the neck below it ringed with ugly purplish bruises. Looking at her, Dell had to blink back tears.

"I guess you knew her, your partner's daughter and all," said Kenmare. Dell nodded.

"Who found her?"

"Building super," said Garvan. "She didn't show up for work today and didn't answer the phone when her boss called. Then a coworker got nervous about it and told the boss that the victim had just broken up with a guy who she was afraid was going to rough her up over it. They finally came over and convinced the super to take a look in the apartment. The boss and the coworker were down in his office when we got here. We questioned them briefly, then sent them home. They've been instructed not to talk about it until after we see them tomorrow."

The three detectives went into the kitchen and sat at Edie's table, where the two from homicide continued to share their notes with Dell.

"Coroner guy says she looks like she's been dead sixteen, eighteen hours, which would mean sometime late last night, early this morning," said Garvan.

"She worked for Able, Bennett, and Crain Advertising Agency in the Loop," said Kenmare, then paused, adding, "Maybe you know some of this stuff already, from your partner."

Dell shook his head. "Dan and his daughter hadn't been close for a while. He didn't approve of Edie's lifestyle. He and his wife had saved for years to send her to the University of Chicago so she could become a teacher, but then Dan's wife died, and a little while after that Edie quit school and moved out to be on her own. Dan didn't talk much about her after that."

"But Captain Larne still thinks Dan might jump ranks and try to work the case himself?"

"Sure." Dell shrugged. "She was still his daughter, his only kid."

"OK," Kenmare said, "we'll give you everything, then. Her boss was a Ronald Deever, one of the ad agency execs. The coworker who tipped him about the ex-boyfriend is a copywriter named Sally Simms."

"Did she know the guy's name?" Dell asked.

"Yeah." Kenmare flipped a page in his notebook. "Bob Pilcher. He's some kind of redneck. Works as a bouncer at one of those line-dancing clubs over in Hee-Haw town. The Simms woman met him a couple times on double dates with the victim." He closed his notebook. "That's it so far."

"Where do we go from here?" Dell asked.

Kenmare and Garvan exchanged glances. "We haven't figured that out yet," said the former. "You've been assigned by a district captain, with headquarters approval and a nod from our own commander, and the victim is the daughter of a veteran cop who's your senior partner. We'll be honest, Dell: We're not sure what your agenda is here."

Dell shook his head. "No agenda," he said. "I'm here to make it look good to Dan Malone so he'll get through this thing as calmly as possible. But it's your case. You two tell me what I can do to help and I'll do it. Or I'll just stand around and watch, if that's how you want it. Your call."

Kenmare and Garvan looked at each other for a moment, then both nodded. "OK," said Kenmare, "we can live with that. We'll work together on it." The two homicide detectives shook hands with Dell, the first time they had done so. Then Kenmare, who was the senior officer, said, "Let's line it up. First thing is to toss the bedroom as soon as the body is out and the crime lab guys are done. Maybe we'll get lucky, find a diary, love letters, stuff like that. You do the bedroom, Frank. You knew her; you might tumble to something that we might not think was important. While you're doing that, we'll work this floor, the one above, and the one below, canvassing the neighbors. We'll have uniforms working the other floors. Then we'll regroup."

With that agreed to, the detectives split up.

It was after ten when they got back together.

"Bedroom?" asked Kenmare. Dell handed him a small red address book.

"Just this. Looks like it might be old. Lot of neighborhood names where Dan still lives. None of the new telephone exchanges in it."

"That's it?"

"Everything else looks normal to me." Dell nodded. "Clothes, makeup, couple of paperback novels, Valium and birth-control pills in the medicine cabinet, that kind of stuff. But I'd feel better if one of you guys would do a follow-up toss."

"Good idea." Kenmare motioned to Garvan, who went into the bedroom.

"Neighbors?" Dell asked.

"Zilch," said Kenmare.

Kenmare and Dell cruised the living room and small kitchen, studying everything again, until Garvan came back out of the bedroom and announced, "It's clean." Then the men sat back down at the kitchen table.

"Let's line up tomorrow," Kenmare said. "Dell, you and I will work together, and I'll have Garvan sit in on the autopsy; he can also work some of the names in the address book by phone before and after. You and I will go see Ronald Deever and Sally Simms at the ad agency, maybe interview some of the other employees there also. We need to track down this guy Pilcher, too. Let's meet at seven for breakfast and see if there's anything we need to do before that. Frank, there's a little diner called Wally's just off Thirteenth and State. We can eat, then walk over to headquarters and set up a temporary desk for you in our bullpen."

"Sounds good," Dell said.

Kenmare left a uniformed officer at the door to Edie Malone's apartment, one at each end of the sixth-floor hallway, one at the elevator, and two in the lobby. When the detectives parted outside, Dell drove back to the South Side, where he lived. When he got into his own apartment, a little after midnight, he called Mike Larne at home.

"It's Dell, Captain," he said when Larne answered sleepily.

"How's it look?" Larne asked.

"Not good," Dell told him. "Only one possible lead so far: an ex-boyfriend who threatened to slap her around. We'll start doing some deeper work on it tomorrow."

"Was she raped?"

"Didn't look like it."

"Thank God for that much."

"I'll let you know for sure after the autopsy."

"All right. How's it setting with Kenmare and Garvan? You getting any resistance?"

"No, it's fine. They're OK. They're giving me a temp desk downtown tomorrow. What's the word on Dan?"

"The poor man is completely undone. The chaplain and the parish priest managed to get him drunk and put him to bed. Jim Keenan and some of the other boys are staying at the house until Dan's sisters arrive from Florida. Listen, you get some sleep. I'll talk to you tomorrow."

"OK, Cap."

Dell hung up and went directly to the cabinet where he kept his bottle of gin.

*

At the Able, Bennett, and Crain advertising agency the next day, on the fortieth floor of a Loop building, Kenmare sat in Ronald Deever's private office to interview him while Dell talked with Sally Simms in a corner of the firm's coffee room. Sally was a pert blonde who wrote copy for a dental products account. She told Dell that Edie Malone had been employed by the agency for about eight months as a receptionist and was well liked by everyone she worked with. Sally had double-dated with her half a dozen times, twice with the man named Bob Pilcher.

"He's from North Carolina, a heavy smoker," she said. "That was the main reason Edie quit going out with him; she didn't like smokers. Said kissing them was like licking an ashtray."

"What's the name of the club where he works?" Dell asked.

"It's called Memphis City Limits. Kind of a hillbilly joint. Over on Fullerton near Halsted."

"What made you tell your boss that you were afraid Pilcher might rough Edie up?"

"That's what Edie told me. She said Bob told her he wasn't used to women dumping him, and maybe she just needed a little slapping around to get her act together. Edie wasn't sure he meant it, but I was. I mean, this is one of those guys that doesn't just walk, he *struts*. And he wears those real tight Wranglers to show off his package. Got real wavy hair with one little curl always down on his forehead. Ask me, he's definitely the kind would slap a woman around. I told Edie she was better off sticking with guys like Bart Mason."

"Who's he?" Dell asked.

"Bart? He's a nice young exec works for the home office of an insurance company down on twenty-two. They dated for a while, then broke up when Edie started seeing someone else."

"Who did she start seeing?"

Sally shrugged. "I don't know. She went out a lot."

"Have you told Bart Mason that Edie's dead?"

"Why, no. That detective in Ron Deever's office told both of us not to mention it."

"We appreciate that you didn't," Dell said. "Besides this Bart Mason, do you know of any other men in the building that Edie went out with?"

"No," Sally said, shaking her head.

Just then, Kenmare came into the room. He said nothing, not wishing to interrupt the flow of Dell's interview. But Dell rose, saying, "OK, thanks very much, Miss Simms. We'll be in touch if we need anything else."

"Do I still have to not talk about it?" Sally asked.

"No, you can talk about it now. It'll be in the afternoon papers anyway. But don't call Bart Mason yet. We want to talk to him first." When Sally left the room, Dell said to Kenmare, "Bart Mason, guy works for an insurance company down on twenty-two, used to date Edie. Supposedly doesn't know she's dead yet."

"Let's see," said Kenmare.

Going down in the elevator, Dell asked, "Anything with Deever?"

"Nothing interesting."

The insurance company occupied the entire twenty-second floor, and the detectives had a receptionist show them to Bart Mason's office without announcing them. Once there, Kenmare thanked her and closed the door behind them. They identified themselves and Kenmare said, "Mr. Mason, do you know a woman named Edie Malone?"

"Sure. She works for an ad agency up on forty," Mason said. "We used to date." He was a pleasant-looking young man, neat as a drill instructor. "Why, what's the matter?"

"She was found murdered in her apartment."

"Edie?" The color drained from Bart Mason's face, and his eyes widened almost to bulging. "I don't believe it —"

"Can you tell us your whereabouts for the last forty-eight hours, Mr. Mason?"

Mason was staring incredulously at them. "Edie — murdered —?"

"We need to know where you've been for the last couple of days," Kenmare said.

"What? Oh, sure —" Mason picked up his phone and dialed a three-number extension. When his call was answered, he said, "Jenny, will you come over to my office right away? It's important."

"Who's that?" Dell asked when Mason hung up.

"My fiancée. Jenny Paula. She works over in claims. We live together. We're together all the time: eat breakfast together, come to work together, eat lunch, go home, eat dinner, sleep together. We haven't been apart since a week ago Sunday when Jen went to spend the day with her mother." He took a deep breath. "My God, Edie —"

A pretty young woman, Italian-looking, came into the office. She looked curiously at the two detectives. Mason introduced them.

"They need to know my whereabouts for the last few days," he said.

"But why?" she asked.

"Just tell them where I've been, hon."

Jenny shrugged. "With me."

"All the time?" asked Kenmare.

"Yes, all the time."

"Like I said, we do everything together," Mason reiterated. "We work together, shop for groceries together, stay in or go out together, we even shower together."

"Bart!" Jenny Paula said, chagrined. "What's this all about anyway?"

"I'll explain later. Can she go now, Officers?"

"Sure," said Kenmare. Thank you, Miss Paula." She left, somewhat piqued, and Kenmare said to Mason, "We may need to talk to her again, in a little more depth."

"We're both available anytime," Mason assured him.

"How long did you date Edie Malone?" Dell asked.

"About six months, I guess."

"Were you intimate?"

"Sure." Mason shrugged.

"When did you break up?"

"Late last summer sometime. Around Labor Day, I think."

"What caused you to break up?"

"Edie began seeing someone else. I didn't like it. So I split with her."

"Do you know who she started seeing?"

"Yeah. Ron Deever, her boss upstairs at the ad agency."

Dell and Kenmare exchanged quick glances. They continued to question Mason for several more minutes, then got his apartment address and left.

On the way back up to the fortieth floor, an annoyed Kenmare, referring to Ron Deever, said, "That son of a bitch. He never mentioned once that he went out with her. I think I'll haul his ass in and take a formal statement."

"He'll lawyer up on you," Dell predicted.

"Let him."

When they got back to Able, Bennett, and Crain, Kenmare went into Ron Deever's office again while Dell took Sally Simms back into the coffee room.

"Did you know that Edie Malone had dated Ron Deever?" he asked bluntly. Sally lowered her eyes.

"Yes."

"I asked you if you knew of any other men in the building that Edie had gone out with and you said no. Why did you lie?"

"I'm sorry," she said, her hands beginning to tremble. "Look, this guy is my boss. I'm a single parent with a little boy in day care. I didn't want to take a chance of losing my job." She started tearing up. "First thing he asked me after you left was whether I told you about him and Edie."

"Why was he so concerned?"

"He's married."

"Did Edie know that when she was seeing him?"

"Sure. It was no big thing for her."

Dell sighed quietly. Reaching out, he patted the young woman's trembling hands. "Okay. Relax. I'll make sure Deever knows it wasn't you who told us. But if I have to question you again, don't lie to me about anything. Understand?"

"Sure." Sally dabbed at her eyes with a paper napkin. "Listen, thanks."

Dell sent her back to work and went into Deever's office, where Kenmare was reading the riot act to him.

"What the hell do you think this is, a TV show? This is a *homicide* investigation, Mister! When you withhold relevant information, you're obstructing justice!" He turned to Dell. "He's married. That's why he didn't come clean."

"I just chewed out Miss Simms, too," Dell said. "Told her how much trouble she could get into covering for him."

"All right," said Kenmare, "we're going to start all over, Mr. Deever, and I want the full and complete truth this time."

A shaky Ron Deever nodded compliance.

When they got back to the squad room, Garvan was waiting for them and a spare desk had been set up for Dell.

"She wasn't raped or otherwise sexually assaulted," he reported. "Cause of death was strangulation — from behind. Coroner fixed time of death at between nine at night and one in the morning. Best bet: between eleven and midnight." He tossed Edie's address book onto the desk. "You were right about this, Dell: It's old. Some of these people haven't seen or heard from her in three or four years. The ones who have couldn't tell me anything about her personal life. You guys make out?"

"Not really," said Kenmare. "We've got one guy who could have slipped out while his fiancée was asleep and gone over and done it — but it's not likely. Another guy, married, was at his son's basketball game earlier in the evening, then at home with his family out in Arlington Heights the rest of the night. One of us will have to go out and interview his wife on that this afternoon."

"I'll do it," Garvan said. "I need the fresh air after that autopsy. Oh, I almost forgot." He tossed five telephone messages to Dell. "These were forwarded from Lakeside. Three are from your partner, two from your captain."

"If you need some privacy to return the calls," Kenmare said, "Garvan and I can go for coffee."

Dell shook his head. "Nothing I can't say in front of you guys. You both know the situation." He could tell by their expressions, as he dialed Mike Larne's number first, that they were pleased at not being excluded. "It's Dell, Captain," he said when Larne answered. "I told you I'd check in when I had the autopsy results. Edie wasn't raped or anything like that. Somebody strangled her from behind, between nine Tuesday night and one on Wednesday morning." He listened for a moment, then said, "Couple of soft leads, is all. Very soft." Then: "Yeah, he's called me three times. I guess I better get back to him."

When he finished his call to Larne, Dell dialed Dan Malone's home. The phone was answered on the third ring. "Hello."

"Yeah, who's this?" Dell asked.

"Who are *you?*" the voice asked back.

"Frank Dell. Is that you, Keenan?"

"Oh, Frank. Yeah, it's me. Sorry, I didn't recognize your voice. How's it going?"

"Very slow. Dan's been calling me, I guess. How is he?"

"Thrashed, inside and out. But the boys and me have him under control. And his two sisters are here with him. He's sleeping right now. It means a lot to him that you're working the case, Frank. He's got a couple of names that he wants checked: old boyfriends of Edie's that he didn't like. Wasn't for you being on the case, he'd probably be out doing it hisself. Pistol-whipping them, maybe."

"You have the names?"

"Yeah, he wrote them down here by the phone." Dell took down the names and told Keenan to tell Dan that he'd see him tomorrow with a full report of the case's progress. After he hung up, he handed the names to Kenmare. "Old boyfriends," he said.

Kenmare gave them to Garvan. "Start a check on them before you go out to interview Deever's wife. Frank and I are going out to that line-dancing joint — it's called Memphis City Limits — to interview Bob Pilcher. We'll meet back here at end of shift."

Memphis City Limits did not have live music until after seven, but even in midafternoon there was a jukebox playing country-and-western and a few people on the dance floor around which the club was laid out. It was a big barn of a building that had once been a wholesale furniture outlet, then remained vacant for several years until some entrepreneurial mind decided there might be a profit in a club catering to the area's large influx of Southerners come north to find work.

Dell and Kenmare found Bob Pilcher drinking beer at a table with two cowgirl types and a beefy man in a lumberjack shirt. Identifying themselves, Kenmare asked if they could speak with Pilcher in private to ask him a few questions. Pilcher shook his head.

"Anything you want to ask me about Edie Malone, do it right here in front of witnesses."

"What makes you think it's about Edie Malone?" Kenmare asked.

"No other reason for you to be talking to me. Story's been on TV news all morning about her being murdered." Pilcher spoke with a heavily accented drawl that sounded purposefully exaggerated.

"When did you see her last?" Dell asked.

"'Bout a week ago." He winked at Dell. "She was alive, too."

"Can you account for your time during the past seventy-two hours?" Kenmare wanted to know, expanding the time period more than he had to because of Pilcher's attitude.

"Most of it, I reckon," Pilcher replied. "I'm here ever' day 'cept

Sundays from no later than six of an evening to closing time at two
A.M. Usually I'm here an hour or two *before* six, as you can see today.
As for the rest of my time, you'd have to give me specific times and
I'd see what I could come up with." His expression hardened a lit-
tle. "Tell you one thing, though, boys, you wasting good po-lice
time on me. I didn't off the gal."

"We have reason to believe you slapped her around now and
then," Dell tried.

"So what if I did?" Pilcher challenged. "You can't arrest me for
that: She's *dead,* fellers, hell!" He took a long swallow of beer.
"Anyways, one of the reasons women like me is that I treat 'em
rough. That one wasn't no different."

"So you did slap her around?"

"Yeah, I did," Pilcher defied him, lighting a cigarette. "Go on and
do something about it if you can."

"Where can we find your employer," Kenmare asked, "to verify
that you've been here the last three nights?"

Pilcher smiled what was really a nasty half-smirk. "So she was
offed at night, huh? For sure you'll have to pin it on somebody
else." He nodded across the club. "Manager's office is that door to
the right of the bar."

Pilcher blew smoke rings at the two detectives as they left him at
the table with his friends and sought out the club manager. He confirmed that Pilcher had indeed been on duty from at least six until two every night since the club had been closed the previous
Sunday.

"Brother, would I like to nail that hillbilly for this," Kenmare
groused as they walked back to their car. "I'd plant evidence to get
that son of a bitch."

"So would I," Dell admitted. "Only there's no evidence to plant.
Anyway, the timeline doesn't jibe. A second-year law student could
get him off."

When they got back to the squad room, Garvan had already returned. "Struck out," he announced. "Deever's wife puts him at
home from about ten-thirty, after their son's basketball game, until
the next morning about eight when he left for work." He turned to
Dell. "And those two boyfriends your partner didn't like: One of
them's in the navy stationed on Okinawa; the other's married, lives
in Oregon, hasn't been out of that state since last July. You guys?"

"Pilcher's a scumbag, but his alibi's tight," Kenmare said. He looked at his watch. "Let's call it a day. Thursday's a big night for my wife and me," he told Dell. "We get a sitter, go out for Chinese, and see a movie."

Dell just nodded, but Garvan said, "Go see a good cop picture tonight. Something with Bruce Willis in it. Maybe you can pick up some tips on how to be a detective."

"Up yours, you perennial rookie," Kenmare said, and left.

Garvan turned to Dell. "Buy you a drink, Lakeside?"

"Why not?" said Dell. "Lead the way, Homicide."

At two o'clock the next morning, Dell was in his car, parked at the alley entrance to the rear parking lot of the Memphis City Limits club. He was wearing dark trousers and a black windbreaker, and had black Nikes on his feet. Both hands were gloved, and he wore a wool navy watch cap low on his forehead, and a dark scarf around his neck. The fuse for the interior lights on his car had been removed.

He had been there for half an hour, watching as the last patrons of the night exited the club, got into their vehicles, and left. By ten past two, there were only a few cars left, belonging to club employees who were straggling out to go home. The lot was not particularly well lit, but the rear door to the club was, so it was easy for Dell to distinguish people as they left.

It was a quarter past two when Bob Pilcher came out and swaggered across the parking lot toward a Dodge Ram pickup. Dell got out of his car without the light going on and, in his Nikes, walked briskly, silently toward him from the left rear, tying the scarf over his lower face as he went. When he was within arm's length of Pilcher, he said, "Hey, stud."

Pilcher turned, a half-smile starting, and Dell cracked him across the face with a leather-covered lead sap. He heard part of Pilcher's face crack. Catching him before he dropped to the ground, Dell dragged the unconscious man around the truck, out of sight of the club's back door. Dropping him, he rolled him over, face-down. Pulling both arms above his head, he pressed each of Pilcher's palms, in turn, against the asphalt, held each down at the wrist, and with the sap used short, snapping blows to systematically break the top four finger knuckles and top thumb knuckle of each hand.

Then he walked quickly back to the alley, got into his car, and drove away. The whole thing had taken less than two minutes.

Be a long time before you slap another woman around, he thought grimly as he left. Or even hold a toothbrush.

Then he thought: That was for you, Edie.

The next day, Dell went to be with Dan Malone when he came to the funeral parlor to see Edie in her casket for the first time. The undertaker had picked up her body when the coroner was through with it, and one of Edie's aunts and two cousins had gone to Marshall Field's and bought her a simple mauve dress to be laid out in.

There were a number of aunts, uncles, cousins, and other collateral family members in attendance when the slumber room was opened, and groups of neighbors gathered outside, easily outnumbered by groups of police officers, in uniform and out, who had known Dan Malone for all or part of his thirty-two years on the force and had come from half the police districts in the city to offer their condolences.

Dell was shocked by the sight of Dan when the grieving man arrived. He looked as if he had aged ten years in the three days since Dell had seen him. A couple of male relatives helped him out of the car and were assisting him in an unsteady walk toward the entrance when Dan's eyes fell on Dell and he pulled away, insisting on a moment with his partner. Dell hurried to him, the two men embraced, then stepped up close to the building where people cleared a space for them to speak privately.

"Did you find those two bastards Keenan gave you the names of?" Dan asked hoarsely.

"Yeah, Dan, but they're clean," Dell told him. "They're not even around anymore."

"Are you sure? I never liked either one of 'em."

"They're clean, Dan. I promise you. Listen," Dell said to placate him, speaking close to his ear, "I did find one guy. He's clean for the killing, but he'd slapped Edie around a couple of times."

"The son of a bitch. Who is he?" The older man's teary eyes became fiery with rage.

"It's OK, Dan. I already took care of it."

"You did? What'd you do?"

"Fixed his hands. With a sap."

"Good, good." Malone wet his dry, whiskey-puffed lips. "I knew I could count on you, Frankie. Listen, come on inside and see my little girl."

"You go in with your family, Dan. I've already seen her," Dell lied. He had no intention of looking at Edie Malone's body again.

Dell gestured and several relatives hurried over to get Dan. Then Dell returned to a group of policemen that included Mike Larne, a couple of lieutenants, Keenan and other cronies of Dan's, and a deputy commissioner. Larne put an arm around Dell's shoulders.

"Whatever you said to him, Frank, it seemed to help."

"I hope so," Dell said. "Listen, Captain, I'm going to get back down to Homicide."

"By all means," said Larne. "Back to work, lad. Find the bastard who caused this heartache."

In the days immediately following the funeral and burial of Edie Malone, the three detectives on the case worked and reworked the old leads, as well as a few new ones. A deputy state's attorney, Ray Millard, was assigned to analyze and evaluate the evidence as they progressed. Disappointingly, there was little of a positive nature to analyze.

"It's too soft," Millard told them in their first meeting. He was a precise, intense young lawyer. "First, you've got the guy she worked for: older man, married, concealed the relationship when first questioned. Solid alibi for the hours just before, during, and after his son's basketball game which he attended on the night of the murder. Decent alibi for the rest of the night: a statement by his wife that he was at home. He *could* have slipped out of his suburban home when everyone was asleep, driven into the city, and committed the crime — but *why* would he have done that, and who's going to believe it?

"Second, you've got the good-guy ex-boyfriend. He's well set up with a new girlfriend, and the two of them are practically joined at the hip: live together, work together, play together. Again, he *could* have slipped out of their apartment around midnight when his fiancée was asleep, gone to the Malone woman's apartment, a relatively short distance away, and killed her. But again, *why?* Let's remember that *he* dumped *her*, not the other way around. Soft, very soft.

"Third, bad-guy ex-boyfriend. The hillbilly bouncer." Millard paused. "Incidentally, I understand that the night after you guys interviewed him, somebody jumped him outside the club and broke his nose, one cheekbone, and both hands. You guys heard anything about that?"

The detectives shrugged in unison, as if choreographed. "Doesn't surprise me," Kenmare said.

"Me either," Dell agreed. "Scumbags like that always have people who don't like them."

"Well, anyway," the young lawyer continued, "bad-guy boyfriend would be a beaut to get in court. I could try him in front of a jury of his *relatives* and probably get a death sentence — except for one thing: He's got a home-free alibi on his job. No way he could have been away from the club long enough to go do it without his absence being noticed. He's the bouncer; he's got to be visible all the time." Millard sat back and drummed his fingers. "Anything else cooking?"

Kenmare shook his head. "We're back canvassing the neighbors again, but nothing so far. We had one little piece of excitement day before yesterday when a little old retired lady in the victim's building said she'd heard that the building super had been fired from his last job for making lewd suggestions to female tenants. We checked it out and there was nothing to it. Turned out she was just ticked off at him for reporting her dog making a mess in the hallway a couple times."

"Too bad," Millard said. "The super would've made a good defendant. Had a key to her apartment, found the body, whole ball of wax. He alibied tight?"

"Very. Lives with his wife on two. They went to a movie, got home around eleven, went right to bed. He's got a good rep — except for the little old lady with the dog."

"Had to be somebody she knew," Millard said. "No forced entry, no lock picked. No rape, no robbery. This was a personal crime. She let the guy in." He tossed the file across the desk to Kenmare. "Find me that guy and we'll stick the needle in his arm."

The three detectives took off early and went to a small Loop bar, where they settled in a back booth. Dell could sense some tension but did not broach the subject. He knew Kenmare would get around to whatever it was.

"We've enjoyed having you work with us, Frank," the senior detective finally said. "We had our doubts about your assignment, but it's turned out OK."

"Yeah, we had our doubts," Garvan confirmed, "but it worked out fine."

"I tried not to get in the way," Dell said.

"Hey, you've been a lot of help," Garvan assured him. "Got me away from this nag for a while," he bobbed his chin at Kenmare.

"Listen to him," the older man said. "Wasn't for me, he'd be directing traffic at some school crossing."

"What's on your mind, boys?" Dell asked, deciding not to wait.

Kenmare sighed. "It's a bit delicate, Frank."

"I'm a big boy. Shoot."

They both leaned toward him to emphasize confidentiality. "That first night in the apartment, you commented that Dan Malone and his daughter hadn't been close for a while," Kenmare recalled.

Garvan nodded. "You said he didn't approve of her lifestyle."

"You said he didn't talk much about her after she quit college and went out on her own."

Dell's expression tightened and locked. "You're getting very close to stepping over the wrong line," he said evenly.

"I'm sorry you feel that way, Frank," said Kenmare. "It's a step that has to be taken." He sat back. "You know as well as I do that if he wasn't one of our own, he'd have been on the spot from day one. As soon as we decided there was no forced entry, no rape, no robbery, we would have included an estranged father in our investigation. But Garvan and me, we kept hoping that evidence would lead us to somebody else. Unfortunately, it hasn't."

"Look, Frank," Garvan said in a placating tone, "it doesn't have to be a complicated thing. It can be, like, informal."

"Of course," Kenmare agreed, his own voice also becoming appeasing. "Drop in on him. Have a drink. Engage him in casual conversation. And find out where he was during the critical hours, that's all."

"Sure," said Garvan, "that's all."

Dell grunted quietly. Like it would be a walk in the park to handle a thirty-two-year veteran cop like that. He took a long swallow of his drink. His eyes shifted from Kenmare to Garvan and back again, then looked down at the table, where the fingers of one hand drummed silently. He did not speak for what seemed like a very long time. Finally Kenmare broke the silence.

"It's either that way or it'll have to be us, Frank. But it's got to be done."

With a sigh that came from deep inside of him, Dell nodded. "All right."

The tension that permeated the booth should have dissipated with that, but it did not. Dell once again became, as he had been at the very beginning of the investigation, an outsider.

Dan Malone smiled when he opened the door and saw Dell.

"Ah, Frank. Come in, come in. Good to see you, partner. I've missed you."

"Missed you too, Dan."

They embraced briefly, and, Dell sensed, a little stiffly.

"I was just having a beer after supper," said Dan. "You want one?"

"Sure."

"Sit down there on the couch. I'll get you one." He turned off a network hockey game, picked up a plastic tray on which were the remains of a TV dinner, and went into the kitchen with it. In a moment, he returned with an open bottle of Budweiser. "So," he said, handing Dell the beer and sitting in his recliner, "how's it going?"

"It's not going, Dan. Not going anywhere," Dell replied quietly, almost dejectedly.

"Well, I figured as much. Else you'd have been in closer touch. Not getting anywhere on the case?"

"No. I've been meaning to drop by and talk to you about it, but I thought you probably still had family staying with you."

"My two sisters were here for a week," Dan said. "And there've been nieces and nephews running in and out like mice. Finally I had enough and ran them all off. Then my phone started ringing off the hook all day, so I finally unplugged that just to get some peace and quiet. I guess they all think I'm suicidal or something."

"Are you?" Dell asked.

Dan gave him a long look. "No. Any reason I should be?"

Dell shrugged. "Sometimes things like this are hard to get over. Some people want to do it quickly."

"That's not the case with me," the older man assured him. "I lost Edie a long time ago, Frank. I think I probably started losing her when she slept with her first man. Then every man after that, I lost her a little more. Until finally she was gone completely."

"Were there that many men?"

"You're working the case; you ought to know."

"We've only found three."

Malone grunted cynically. "You must not have gone back very far." He stared into space. "I used to follow her sometimes. She'd go into a bar and come out an hour later with a man. Night after night. Different bars, different men. It was like some kind of sickness with her."

They both fell silent and sat drinking for several minutes. Dell, who had always been so comfortable with his partner, felt peculiarly ill at ease, as if he had now become an outsider with Dan Malone as he had with the two homicide detectives. Finally he decided not to prolong the visit any more than necessary.

"How long have we known each other, Dan?" he asked.

"What's on your mind, Frank?" the older policeman asked knowingly. It had been he who taught Dell that reminiscing frequently led to other things.

"The night of Edie's murder."

"What about it?"

"I need to know where you were."

Malone nodded understandingly. "I wondered when they'd get around to it." He smiled a slight, cold smile. "Suppose I tell you I was right here at home, alone, all night. What then?"

"Tell me what you did all night."

"Watched the fights on television. Drank too much. Passed out here in my chair."

"Who was fighting in the main event?"

Malone shrugged. "Some Puerto Rican against some black guy, I think. I was sleepy by the time the main go came on; I don't remember their names."

"Neither do I," said Dell.

"What?" Dan Malone frowned.

"I don't remember their names either. But you weren't alone that night. That was the night I dropped over. We both drank too much. I fell asleep on the couch. Didn't wake up until after one o'clock. Then I put you to bed and went home. That was the night, wasn't it, Dan?"

The older man's frown faded and his face seemed to go slack. "Yes," he said quietly. "Yes, I do believe that was the night."

There was silence between them again. Neither of them seemed to know what to say next, and they could not look at each other. Malone stared into space, as he had done earlier; Dell stared at the television, as if it had not been turned off. Only after several minutes did Dell drink the rest of his beer and put the bottle down. He rose.

"I'll be going now. You won't be coming back to work, will you, Dan?"

Malone looked thoughtfully at him. "No," he replied. "I'm thinking of putting in for retirement. My sisters in Florida want me to move down there."

"Good idea. You'd probably enjoy yourself. Lots of retired cops in Florida." Dell walked to the door. "Goodnight, Dan."

"Goodnight, Frank."

Only when he got out into the night air did Dell realize how much he was sweating.

The next morning, Dell typed up a summary of Dan Malone's statement, along with his own corroboration of the alibi. After signing it, he handed the report to Kenmare. The lead homicide detective read it, then passed it to Garvan to read.

"You've thought this through, I guess," Kenmare said.

"Backwards and forward," Dell told him.

Garvan raised his eyebrows but said nothing as he handed the report back to Kenmare.

"I don't think the brass will buy this," Kenmare offered.

"What are they going to do?" Dell asked. "Suspend Dan *and* me? Open an internal investigation? On what evidence? And how would it look on the evening news?"

"The higher-ups might feel it was worth it," said Garvan.

"Worth it why?" pressed Dell. "What's the gain? The department's getting rid of Dan anyway; he'll be retiring."

"But you won't," Garvan pointed out.

"So? What have I done that the department would want to get rid of me?"

"Helped him get away with it, that's what," said Kenmare.

"*If* he did it," Dell challenged. "And we don't know that he did.

All we know is that we can't find anybody else right now who *did* do it." He decided to throw down the gauntlet right then. "You guys going to let this report pass, or are you going to make an issue of it?"

"You didn't mention this alibi last night when we were talking," Kenmare accused.

"Maybe I had my days mixed up." Dell shrugged. "Maybe I thought it had been Monday night I had dropped in; maybe Dan had to remind me it was Tuesday."

"Maybe," Kenmare said. He looked inquiringly at his partner.

"Yeah, maybe," Garvan agreed.

"You're sure Malone's retiring?" Kenmare asked.

"Positive," Dell guaranteed.

Kenmare pulled open a desk drawer and filed the report. "See you around, Dell," he said.

"Yeah," said Garvan. "Take it easy, Dell."

Dell walked out of the squad room without looking back.

That night, when Dell came into the Three Corners Club and took his regular seat at the end of the bar, it was the owner, Tim Callan, who poured his drink and served him.

"I've missed you, Frankie," he said congenially. "How've you been?"

"I've seen better days," Dell allowed.

"Ah, haven't we all," Callan sympathized. He lowered his voice. "I'm really sorry about the young lady. Edie, was that her name?"

"Yeah, Edie." Dell felt the back of his neck go warm.

"I seen her picture in the paper and on the news. Took me a few looks to place her. Then I says to myself, why, that's the young lady Frankie used to bring in here. Always wanted the booth 'way in the back for privacy.'" Callan smiled artificially. "I remember that every time I loaned you the key to use the apartment upstairs I had to make you promise to be out by midnight so's I could get the poker game started. And you never let me down, Frank. Not once. 'Course, we go back a long ways, you and me." Now Callan's expression saddened, genuinely so. "I'm really sorry, Frank, that things didn't work out between you and Edie."

"Thank you, Tim. So am I." Dell's heart hurt when he said it.

"They still don't know who did it?"

Dell looked hard at him. "No."

They locked eyes for a long moment, two old friends, each of whom could read the other like scripture.

"What was the name of that brother-in-law of yours charged with receiving stolen property?" Dell finally asked.

"Nick Santore," said Callan. "Funny you should ask. His preliminary hearing's day after tomorrow."

"Ill talk to the assistant state's attorney," Dell said. "I'll tell him the guy's going to be a snitch for me, that I need him on the street. I'll get him to recommend probation."

"Ah, Frankie, you're a prince," Callan praised, clasping one of Dell's hands with both of his own. "I owe you, big time."

"No," Frank Dell said, "we're even, Timmy."

Both men knew it was so.

MICHAEL HYDE

Her Hollywood

FROM *Alaska Quarterly Review*

THE GIRL WAS Mary Alice Bunt and they found her by the river.
My brother Wade and I thought we'd see the print her body made
but rain came and the river jumped its banks before we could find
the spot. It's a good thing the search party found her when they
did. She's liable to have been washed away and lost because everything came rushing in that brown flood: flat tires, TV antennas, a
doll carriage like one I used to push.

The dead girl before she was dead lived in Tobo. In wagon train
days there used to be a Tobo Hotel. That's how the place got its
name. It was a layover for travelers, someplace for them to steal a
breather, get a drink, maybe spend the night. But the hotel's gone
now and it's nothing but cheap trailers — one lived-in box after
the other — lined up along Tobo Road.

Mary Alice Bunt was pretty. I know this for two reasons. Reason
number one is because her picture was front-page in both morning
and evening *Dispatches*. Next day they put her picture in the obitu-
ary section, too, except smaller. Reason number two I know Mary
Alice Bunt was pretty is because Mom said so. Wade and I'd just
come home from school and there Mom was bawling her eyes out.

Her makeup wasn't smeared so I figured she hadn't been crying
long. "Always the pretty ones that die" she was saying over and over
and didn't have to say anything else because I know she was thinking I was safe as could be. Plain Jane she liked to call me, teasing
me to get me shouting my lungs that my name was Connie not stupid Jane. She got a big kick out of it and laughed like it was the joke
of the century. Even when she'd let me sit down beside her at the

vanity she'd start comparing our faces, hers with mine, and she'd always throw in "You can thank your father for that nose." The way she said it I knew I didn't need to be thanking anybody.

When Mom was crying over Mary Alice, Wade and I tried to give her a hug because that's what I thought she was expecting but she pushed us out of the way and started walking around the kitchen — her head bent a little bit to the side — moving like a statue would move if it could. I don't need to tell you that Mom was an actress at the community theater. She taught me and Wade from the very start about *drama*, which she said translated into English as meaning "larger than life." Thanks to her, Wade and I were drama experts. We'd have to be, the way she changed moods like clothing. We all remember Mom's Mary Alice act as one of her final performances because ten days later she left us for Hollywood. It's strange how those two things happened, boom-boom, one right after the other, that girl dying and my mother going away.

I didn't know Mary Alice Bunt but she was a junior at my school, two grades above me and in the same grade as my brother Wade. Wade didn't know her either but that was because Wade didn't know anybody. He wasn't smart about people or in general but I still loved him in the way you have to love dogs that can only stare at you when you've thrown a stick for them to fetch. At school the kids called Wade *LD*. He was in the special class for kids with *Learning Disabilities*. There were only three other LDs at our school. Wade and them had class in one room painted bright yellow over the cinderblocks. "Hey LD," kids said when they saw Wade in the hall. "Hey, LD, what's one plus one?" Wade was older than me but I always thought of him as my little brother. Like Mom said once: Wade's head's just not what its supposed to be. He'll never be like other kids, no matter how hard he studies or practices or tries.

When she was alive I never would've cared who Mary Alice Bunt was. Or anyone like her. And since Wade wasn't smart about people and since I didn't care about them, he and I were always together. I'd find him each lunch period standing at the front of the cafeteria, straining his neck 180 degrees until he'd see me. The kids at school made fun of us both because we were together so much. Somebody saw me dragging him by the hand one time home from school, so after that everybody called us boyfriend and girlfriend and sometimes made kissy noises so loud the teachers could hear.

The teachers didn't do anything and I stopped expecting they would.

Except for the kids bugging, I didn't mind Wade. He needed somebody and I was the only somebody left. When Mom left for her Hollywood, Dad turned into a ghost and sat all the time in front of the tube, watching talk shows and how-to programs on the public channel. He stopped brushing his hair. It stuck together and shot in all directions, it was so oily. He let his beard grow out too and would sit rubbing his hand across his face, making that sandpaper sound I can't take for a minute. He only moved for the bathroom. He'd make it to bed at night sometimes but usually he stretched out on the couch and cloaked himself with that ratty black afghan. He was like an invalid, he loved Mom that much.

I tried not to notice but our house was falling apart, creaking and complaining anytime you'd move. The barn got a big hole in the roof and let in rain. Wade and I had to take care of the cows but we stopped shoveling their shit every single day. One heifer would stare at us and bawl when she couldn't find a warm place. I used to take pride that we didn't live in one of those cheap Tobo trailers but after Mom ran off that pride shriveled up to nothing.

That's when I got the idea to look for where Mary Alice Bunt died. Finding it wasn't easy. First Wade and I tried piecing together pictures from the news and the papers. We spent whole afternoons zigzagging from our farm to Tobo and the Tunnel Bridge further downstream. It was exhausting even though our river was more like a creek. You only needed twelve steps to get from one bank to the other.

When mine and Wade's searching didn't work we tried talking to Tobo kids. The ones I asked acted like they never heard of Mary Alice. Her living seemed as forgettable as the plastic milk jug some were kicking around because they didn't have a ball. A part of Mary Alice — a memory, I mean — had to be somewhere. After all she'd lived her life there, under those stupid pink and yellow and green pool-party lights hung from the trailers that tried to fool you into thinking Tobo was a happy place.

Mary Alice's little brother was the one finally that showed us the way. We didn't know it was him at first so he was a lucky find, sitting in the street, pushing a toy submarine across gravel. He was eight or nine and dusted white from the shale. Wade said to him, "Do you know where they found that dead girl?" and I looked at Wade queer for saying it that way but that's when the boy nodded and told us he was the dead girl's brother.

"Can you show us where they found her?" I asked.

He led us down to the river like we were visiting tourists who'd never been before. I watched the thick band of dirt around his neck when he ducked under briars and jumped over the black logs in our way. Wade had trouble keeping up because he was tall and sort of large and said a couple times that he was gonna go back. "Shut up, Wade," I said. And he did.

The boy took us to a place where the river snaked hard around a bend. Three gray trees leaned at the water, their roots and the bank had been worn away so. You could tell there'd been the flood even though the high water was gone. A lawn chair with all the stringing busted out sat up straight in the shallows. In other spots fallen branches made it look like somebody'd been trying to build a bonfire the way the branches had stacked themselves. The boy ran for the chair and kicked it over into the water.

"There's where," he said. He pointed with his submarine at a small green island halfway across the river. He was proud to be showing us.

Wade ran ahead too and bent over the lump of land. He was wearing his cutoffs and creek-shoes and at its deepest, the water came up to Wade's knees. "I think this is where her head was. I can see her skull-print," he said.

I followed him, looked to where he meant, but he was seeing what he wanted to see, trying to impress me. His face was wrinkled and stupid with excitement. I wanted him to go away. Suddenly all I could think about was that: how I wanted to be alone. In this place where Mary Alice Bunt had spent the last seconds of her life I wanted to be by myself. The small green island probably not much bigger than Mary Alice had been was somehow mine.

"No, that's not it," I said. "The boy's lying."

This was all it took for Wade to shove Mary Alice's brother. "I'll teach you for lying," Wade said. He snatched the submarine and zoomed it through the air high above the squealing boy's head.

"Give it back to him," I said. Wade looked at me ashamed. Finally he gave the toy back then yelled after Mary Alice's brother, who ran off toward Tobo.

I looked at the green island, the size of a coffin, and imagined Mary Alice there face-down like the newspaper mentioned. I imagined her underwear yanked to her ankles, her shirt pulled up over her head, her goodies — as my mother called them — showing. I wanted to be alone with her. What was it like, living and dying in your pretty body? I wanted to ask.

The next day after school I told Wade I was going for a walk without him. "Why, Connie? Why?" he asked.

I told him I was sick of him hanging around all the time. I told him I needed space and that I didn't want to be his girlfriend anymore.

He was about to turn on the waterworks so I walked off quick enough so I didn't have to see. I heard him following, so I ran. "Go away! Leave me alone!"

In Tobo four kids were playing Maypole with snapped clothesline and the pole it was tied to. They ducked in and out of one another's way until they tangled and ended up arguing over whose fault it'd been. I could hear the sound of the river humming just under their angry voices.

Across the street two boys my age were rolling tires around a car they'd set up on blocks. They had their shirts off so I could see the tattoos on their arms. They watched me, stopped what they were doing and watched me. I stared them straight in the eyes.

The one boy's face looked like you were supposed to see it from one side. The other half was all messed up and pushed together like it'd been smashed by a brick. His mouth had space where teeth were supposed to be and when he smiled a black nothing spread between his lips.

The other boy's face was wide open like a book and red with freckles that matched his hair. His right arm was bigger than his left. "Woo-hoo," he whistled. I just stared at him, thinking how easily he could've been the one that'd killed Mary Alice, thinking *you are the one you are the one you are the one* until the boys and their car were no longer in sight. Until I'd walked so far they disappeared along with their litterbox trailers.

I got to the spot where the river turned. The chair Mary Alice's brother kicked over was still on its side. Small crayfish scooted when my shadow came near. The only difference was that one of the three leaning trees had finally given up and fallen. Its branches speared down into the water a few feet from Mary Alice's island.

The water was cold and I could feel mud and pebbles squishing inside my creek-shoes. The water swallowed me to my knees but I didn't care. Mary Alice's island was in front of me, so bright and green and with a single strand of blue chicory that looked more a silk flower than real poking up for the sun. I lay down like the island was a bed I hadn't slept in before. I could feel it resist me, me resisting it until I stopped caring about mud and dirt and resistance dropped away.

Putting together the lost life of a pretty girl, I started with her killer. Was he fat? Thin? Bald? Tall? All the men I'd ever seen flashed in my head. It was like choosing the right color to paint a room. Lighter or darker? Brown? Black? Or red? Red, yes it would be red, and I thought of the boy fixing the car. Not the boy with the smashed face. The pretty girl's murderer would not be so ugly. He could be plain but not so ugly as to be scary and not so scary as to make the last moments of her life unbearable.

So I thought of the red-haired boy. He was easy to make in my mind. I had him standing over me: his face dripping red gums dripping red freckles dripping. He was hurrying to undo his pants with his thin arm. He pushed me down. He told me he was going to kill me and that I might as well enjoy it. I might as well enjoy it while it lasted and ride the rest of my life out in a limousine. His hands were on me pressing together my breasts, his fingers fumbling. I was there on the point of something when he turned me over and pressed my face into the green-grass island, into the fish silt and the smell of the river and I couldn't breathe anymore. Inside my head I was screaming: "You're dead, Connie. Now you're dead."

My hands were where his hands had been and for a second my heart stopped. It wasn't a complete stop but more like my heart couldn't decide whether or not to keep on beating, like somebody waving her arms to keep balanced on a circus wire.

After that first time at the river I'd been murdered many times. And never the same murderer twice.

There was a big man covered with thick hair across his chest and down his back. Dark eyebrows lowered like feathers over his eyes.

There was a man with a hump.

A man with twisted teeth.

A man who whistled the entire time it happened.

They'd all tell me what they were going to do before they did it.

They weren't horrible men as people might imagine. They were just men.

When I couldn't get to the river I'd stretch out on my bed, turning my head into the pillow and breathing it in like it was Mary Alice's island. Once Wade walked in on me when I was being murdered. It was raining. The river was so far away in the colored party lights of Tobo. I was on my bed and waiting to die. Mr. Farris, second-period algebra, had forced me onto my stomach right away. He held me by the hair. I knew with one flip of his wrist he could push my face into the mud and make me breathe the river into my lungs. He made me repeat again and again that I loved him, that I'd never leave him, that I'd follow him anywhere. I kept thinking of his hand clutching my hair, his gold watch wrapping his wrist just below that hand, the gold watch I had to notice every time he bent over my desk smelling good or wrote on the board. I heard that watch tick-ticking in my ears. "You're dead, Connie," I started to say when he finally pushed my head into the mud.

That's when Wade walked in. I'm sure I looked strange to him, my nightgown pulled over my head, my legs swim-kicking at the bedroom air.

"Help me," I said to him, before the river found its way to my throat, before it drowned my voice.

He pulled my arms, slid the pillow from under my face, but he was too late. I told him so. "I'm dead," I said. "You let me die."

"What are you talking about, Connie? What?" His breathing was hard. He was staring at my breasts.

For a crazy second I started memorizing Wade's face. His fat nose. His marble-blue eyes. His open mouth that could change from pain to pleasure in a second. He'd never yet been one of my murderers. I felt him taking shape in my mind. But the more I looked at him the more impossible he seemed and I said "No." Wade couldn't be a murderer no matter how hard I imagined.

Then came word from Mother. The postcard she sent was plain white and said GENERIC POSTCARD on the front and on the back along with our address she'd scratched a message in big letters. She was reading for several things, she said. Quite a few "independent films," she said. "Acting is hard life," she said. She signed the card

Francine Barlowe. Meaning her the actress. Not Francine Pratt my mother.

I got a sheet of paper and pen to write her and tell her all the things that'd happened. Like how Dad was going out nights. Or how Wade's teacher sent home that note saying he wasn't progressing like he should. Then I remembered Mom hadn't told us where she was going exactly; Hollywood was all. I looked on the postcard, thinking she'd squeezed her new address into a corner. The only thing I found was the postmark — Norristown, PA, not Hollywood, CA — smudged over the stamp of an orange-bellied bluebird.

I shoved that postcard way back in the kitchen junk drawer — behind the Scotch tape and screwdrivers and worn-out batteries — so no one would ever have to know about it but me.

One day, on our way home from school Wade and I were walking along the road, kicking up gravel. We walked to school every day just so we wouldn't have to ride the bus with those Tobo kids. I was listening to him tell about how he'd been the only one left at dodge ball during gym and no matter who threw the ball he'd been quick enough to dodge it. The game couldn't start over until he was got, so this guy came running at him — into the circle where he wasn't allowed! — and blasted the ball into Wade's face. Wade got a bloody nose, had to go to the nurse, but the game kept on going. "No harm done," was what Wade's gym teacher said.

I was staring at Wade's bandaged nose and thinking how it could mean *No harm done* when Arnold Berry drove up beside us and honked. Wade jumped in his skin but I'd seen Arnold coming. It was hard to miss his dark green Thunderbird skulking along the empty road.

"You want a ride?" he said wagging his hand out the window to get our attention. He was a senior at our school, the kind of person like me and Wade you passed in the hall for four years but wouldn't take good notice to. The funny thing was I'd noticed him. He'd killed me before. I don't remember how he did it but I know I was staring into his pimply face and feeling his wild sideburns scratching at my skin. He had nice green eyes. Which is the main reason I chose him. His eyes made him a standout to me when he was a nobody to everybody else.

"So you want a ride?" he said again. Wade, all of a sudden deaf and dumb, just stared at him. Wade was afraid of older kids, especially seniors who drove their own cars. When I looked at Wade he was shaking his head at me. I knew he was saying "No no no no" inside but I told Arnold "Yes."

Wade climbed into the back seat where two giant speakers spit out loud music. I looked at him in the side mirror, could see him covering his ears, so I decided not to look anymore.

"You like Bon Jovi?" Arnold said to me.

"Sure," I said though I couldn't tell a Bon Jovi from a Whitesnake, a Whitesnake from a Poison. I started to bob my head too like I was into it.

Arnold drove with one hand on the steering wheel, the other hand behind my shoulder, his arm propped along the back of the front seat. I kept waiting for him to grab me but he didn't. I guess because Wade was in the back.

Arnold didn't say anything the entire ride home. I figured out he smoked from all the cellophane wrappers on the floor. They crunched every time I'd move my foot. The pine air freshener hanging from the rearview mirror had faded. The car windshield was filthy except for two half-circles where the wipers had washed clean. Arnold chewed at something and kept leaning out the window to spit. He would've been the worst boyfriend but as a murderer he was fine.

When he dropped Wade and me off at our lane I stalled a few minutes by the car door. Arnold just kept chewing whatever it was that was in his mouth and looked straight ahead at the road.

"You want something?" he said finally. He turned his head like he was watching the words form inside me.

"I want you for a date," I told him, "but you have to ask me first."

Arnold's eyebrows raised up a bit but lowered then like he was enjoying the taste of what I'd said. I could see Wade fidgeting at the side of the road. Finally Arnold nodded. "OK. How 'bout Saturday?" he answered me, his voice thick.

"One o'clock," was all I said back, as if it were the most natural thing in the world.

When Arnold drove away I knew that I'd be going somewhere I'd never gone before. No going back. Wade asked me to explain it to him but I couldn't. He'd never understand.

On Saturday Arnold came only fifteen minutes late. I could tell he'd tried to doll himself up. His straggly hair was greased back and he was wearing a shirt I was sure his mother'd pressed for him. "Sorry I'm late," he said.

"No biggee," I told him and got into the car. I'd spent all morning getting ready. I wanted everything to be perfect: the short skirt, my underwear.

My father didn't even argue when I told him I was going out. Before Mom left he would've pitched a fit if he knew his twelve-year-old daughter was going on a date with a senior. But not this version of my father. He didn't even get up from his couch to wave goodbye. He just raised a glass of pop to his mouth, held an ice cube between his lips, then spit it back into the glass.

Wade followed me out to the car. I know he was wanting to go along or not wanting me to go at all but I said "Bye" and that was that. When Arnold drove me away I could see Wade trying to hide himself behind the maple tree in our front yard.

Arnold and I went mini-golfing. He was clumsy and not so good at aiming the ball. I played even worse than he did because I didn't want him to feel bad, like he was any less a man. I watched his ropy hands draw the putter back. The ball went bouncing out of bounds. Arnold got frustrated and whacked the ball so hard it almost hit a woman's face. Seeing this I knew he'd be perfect.

We didn't have much to talk about so over ice cream when I told him I wanted to give him my goodies, he looked shocked. "You're crazy," he said at first.

"No, I'm serious." After that he looked at me and smiled like it was what he'd been wanting all along.

I took him down to the river. To my favorite spot I told him. I didn't tell him why. I sat on Mary Alice's island, the grass pushing up under my skirt. I could tell Arnold was thinking that I only wanted kissing. He was sticking his fat tongue into my mouth and grabbing my breasts but he didn't try any of my clothes so I told him to. He started mumbling about not having a rubber.

"I don't care," I said.

That was all he needed. He dropped his pants and I could see the dark stains on his white underwear. This made me think he hadn't planned to get this far, that maybe he'd respected me. But that wasn't what I wanted. I wanted to be Mary Alice. I wanted his rough hands to touch me, to take me from me.

Soon he was rocking back and forth on top of me and it wasn't at all as I'd imagined. He was like a fish floundering and flapping his arms like he didn't have any control. The sharp pain was there as I'd expected but he kept saying love things like "Oh Connie oh Connie."

I said to him what I knew he wanted to hear: "I'll never leave you. You're so beautiful I could never leave you."

His breathing got heavy and he whimpered. Then he altogether stopped. I felt wide and dirty and new and that's when I said it to him. "Kill me." Calm and serious. "I don't care how," though I wanted him to push my head into the island. But really who could tell killers *how* to kill?

"Ha-ha," he laughed.

I repeated myself and he stopped laughing. "You're one crazy girl," he said. He started to put on his clothes that were wet in places from the river.

"You have to," I said again. I didn't move from where his body had left me. I'm sure my print was pressed into the island.

"Are we gonna go?" he asked zipping his blue jeans.

I didn't move and looked at him thinking *you are the one you are the one you are the one.*

"Listen. I can't do it again if that's what you want."

"I want you to kill me."

"Come on. Get up." When I didn't he shook his head, slinging his shirt over his shoulder. "See ya," he said.

"You can't go." I grabbed him by the arm.

He jerked away. I dug in my fingernails, dragging them along his skin, leaving red scratches from his elbow to wrist. He looked at his arm, then at me, and shoved the side of my head. I fell so that my hands and chin pressed into the silt.

All I could do was lie there, my breath hard and caught in my chest like a trapped bird. I thought Arnold was getting ready, wringing his hands, preparing his strength but then I heard walking, his feet shuffling across water and rock. He was leaving. My body expanded but didn't relax.

A car engine started, revving so loud it beat its way into my mother's voice who was saying over and again — chanting almost — that always the pretty ones got killed. I tried to picture her over-hanging a balcony, under hot Hollywood sun, reading for a direc-

tor she might sleep with to become an updated Juliet. "Romeo, Romeo," she would say dragging out the *O*s like she did. I wanted to
see her writing to me and Dad and Wade from a yellow hotel room
where someone important was in her bathroom taking a shower.
But she was somewhere else, somewhere in Norristown, living in a
trailer maybe, reading for no one but herself.

I rolled over to face the horrible sky as the sound of Arnold's car
became smaller and smaller along Tobo Road. "Murderer," I said.
Like it was a proper name.

DAN LEONE

Family

FROM *Literal Latté*

MY BROTHER'S HOUSE would look like all the other houses in that part of the state: one of those prefabricated "snap-together jobbers," he called it. White. Small. Last one on the left after the road turns to gravel, before it ends in a T.

"Dave," I said, "are you sure you don't mind seeing me?"

"You're my brother," he said.

There was a pause. I moved the phone from my one ear to the other. "Thank you," I said.

He gave me permission to go on in; the back door would be open. "I get home from work around six," he said. "If you get there before then . . ." There was another pause, a longer one, which made me think he was really thinking about it. "There're left-overs in the fridge," he said. "Clean towels in the bathroom closet. Movies, music . . . Make yourself at home."

He didn't say anything about a girlfriend, though, and I caught her entirely off-guard in the bathtub. No bubbles.

"Don't hurt me," she screamed, crossing her arms and kicking her legs up in front of her. Water splashed over the edge of the tub.

I jumped back into the hallway and reeled around the corner, out of sight, almost pissing and shitting myself at once.

"Don't hurt me don't hurt me don't hurt me. Money in my purse on the table in there. Oh my god." I could hear her reaching for a towel, water dripping. "Anything you want. Anything. No need to hurt me."

I opened my mouth but nothing came out. My knees were clacking against each other like bowling pins, the road still rolling under me, thunder in my ears.

"Purse on the table. Just take it and go. No sense in hurting me. I won't call the cops. Just get it and go, OK?" She never stopped talking, not even to breathe, which made me consider the possibility that she was planning an ambush, keeping me occupied with her blah blah blah and then, thwack, a toilet plunger through the heart — so I figured I'd better rally the troops and say something.

"Dave's brother," I blurted. "Sorry."

"On the kitchen table. I'll cooperate," she said. "Anything you want. What? What did you say?" she said.

"I'm Dave's brother. I'm not going to hurt you," I said, between breaths. "I'm sorry I walked in on you. He said I could let myself in. I'm sorry."

She didn't say anything.

"I'm really sorry," I said, hands on knees, thinking: I'll kill my brother for this.

She was catching her breath too. After a while she said, "I'm drying off."

"I'm not looking." I closed my eyes. "I'm not a creep or a criminal. I'm just a guy. Just Dave's brother," I said.

"I've met all his brothers," she said. "He didn't tell me he had any more."

"I can explain that," I said. "I'll show you identification if you want. We're brothers. I just fell out with the whole family a long time ago. Years. Before I called, we hadn't spoken to each other in ten years. How long have you — ?"

She stepped out of the bathroom in a short-cut bathrobe with her hands in the pockets, a sheepish half smile on her lips. "My god, I'm so embarrassed," she said. Her wet, brown hair clung to her forehead in girlish curls. I could smell her cleanness and I could feel the warmth of her bath radiating off of her.

"My name's Thomas," I said.

"I'm Ellen." She made a vague motion with her right hand — a wave, I realized too late. My hand was already out there, awkward. We shook hands. It didn't last long, but it was the first human touch I'd felt in at least a week, and the electricity of it stayed with me afterward. "So," she said, "I guess Dave didn't mention me to you any more than vice versa."

I shrugged. "Ten years," I said. "I called from a phone booth in Wyoming. We didn't have much time to talk."

"That's OK," she said, "Are you hungry?"

"More than anything," I said, "I need to use the bathroom. I've been driving for a long time."

"Go ahead." She stepped aside, smiling all the way now. "Careful," she said. "The floor's wet."

She was still wearing the bathrobe when I came out. Instead of getting dressed, she was standing at the counter in the kitchen, making chip-chopped ham sandwiches.

"You like mustard?" she said.

"Sure, but you don't have to feed me."

"I'm hungry too. Sit down," she said.

I walked past her and sat at the kitchen table. There was the purse.

"There's the purse," she said.

"Ah. Where your money is, if I'm not mistaken."

She laughed. It was a sexy laugh. It was a sexy bathrobe. I could see what my brother saw in her. Over sandwiches, with the sinking December sunlight slanting in through the kitchen window, I got a better look at her face. Her cheeks were freckled at the cheekbones, but other than that her complexion was clear as cellophane. She could have been looking out at me from the cover of a magazine on the rack at a gas station, except that one front tooth was chipped and her nose was crooked. She was real and beautiful. There was mustard on her chin.

"So tell me," I said. "How long have you known my brother?"

"Long enough."

"Long enough. What?"

"To know him," she said. "He doesn't tell me stuff. He's Mister Mysterious. So tell me yourself. I won't judge you."

"Tell you what?"

"Why don't I know you? Why your brother — why your whole family would erase you like that. I'm not judgmental."

"Then why do you want to know?"

"To understand," she said. "I feel like we've . . . well, the way we met, I mean." She paused, flashing the same sheepish half smile, and then continued more quickly. "Like we've been through something together I guess. Which gives us a bond, which makes me curious. That's all."

I set my sandwich down and looked out the window. It was a picture window, facing west onto a down-sloping weed yard, a scummy pond, and a stubbled cornfield. If we sat there for long enough, I'd be able to witness my first straight-on, non-rearview-mirrored sunset in days. "Do you live here?" I said.

"We're married," she said.

I looked at her, but I couldn't tell from her look if she was kidding or not.

"Are you kidding?" I said.

She showed me her wedding band, which was sandwiched on the same finger between two prettier, fancier rings.

I didn't know what to say. "Congratulations," I said.

"Thank you. You know what the best thing about getting married is?" She said, standing up and walking toward the sink.

"No," I said.

She picked up a marble rolling pin out of the dish rack and held it up before her like a torch or trophy. "Presents," she said.

"How long," I said, "have you been married?"

"Long enough."

"Uh-oh."

"No. That's not how I meant it." She set the rolling pin down, picked a couple of mugs out of the rack, and took them to the refrigerator. Because of the incoming sunlight, I could see every individual particle of dust in the kitchen air between us. "Do you want some purple Kool-Aid?" she said.

I couldn't believe my brother hadn't told me he was married.

"You guys drink Kool-Aid?" I said.

"Mostly Dave," she said. "Do you want some? Or can I get you something else? Water? Juice? Beer?" It was one of those vertically split refrigerator-freezers, and she was speaking into the refrigerator half of it. "Well?" she said.

"I'm thinking. I'm thinking," I said.

She closed the refrigerator door and opened the freezer. Steam poured out and around her bare feet and all the way up while she was getting ice cubes.

Wine, I thought. Red wine and candles and classical music. But I was afraid to say so because what kind of wine, if any, would purple Kool-Aid drinkers be likely to have on hand?

"Tell you what," I said. "I brought you a bottle of my favorite wine from California. What say we crack it open?"

"You brought Dave a bottle," she corrected.

"And you," I said. "Only I didn't know about you yet is all." I pushed back my chair and stood up just as she was sitting back down. "I'll go out to my van and get it," I said. "And when I come back, I want to hear how you and Dave met each other."

"It's not much of a story," she said.

"I'm no critic," I said.

The back door opened from the kitchen onto a homemade wooden porch with two barbecue grills, a couple of slat-backed plastic chairs, and a cat. On my way down the stairs the cat, timing its steps perfectly, walked from the railing onto my shoulder, then curled around my neck. I wore it like a scarf across the yard and around the corner of the house to where my van was parked. The cat wanted in, of course, but enough was enough; I shook him off at the sliding side door. There was too much trouble in there for a cat to get into.

As for me, the trouble was everywhere else. Going into the van, with all its smells and other oddities, was like snuggling back under the covers and into a good dream after a midnight run through the cold, hard facts of life in the bathroom. I was tempted to slip into the driver's seat and go, call my brother from Indiana, maybe try again to see him on the way back across.

But it was a passing thought. When you're on the road, if you're me, you're not on the interstate, first of all, so you'll occasionally catch a fleeting glimpse of some little domestic scene, such as two brothers playing driveway basketball, or a man and a woman sitting at a table in the window, drinking coffee and talking. If you've been traveling for any amount of time, like me, you might even be inclined to envy them. But if that man and woman are as typical as the next man and woman, at least one of them is noticing your car whiz by, wistfully, envying you.

The train whistle is always blowing, in other words, and so is the tea kettle.

Or, for our purposes, the van, all my things in it, my music, my mess, the mattress on the loft in back, the card table, the travel mugs and bags of sunflower seeds . . . it was mighty inviting, all of it; but so was a bottle of wine and dinner and a good night's sleep on my brother's couch. Hot shower, thermos of coffee, a couple of hugs, and I'd be off bright and early in the morning . . . catching fleeting glimpses into other people's homes, no doubt — no doubt wishing I was still in bed somewhere, or enjoying a leisurely home-cooked breakfast, or playing basketball with my brother in our driveway.

Is that life, or what?

"We met in a muffler shop," Ellen informed me while I was pouring the wine into a couple of juice glasses.

"Wait a minute," I said. My brother — I knew this much — had always been the academic type, aspiring, last I heard, toward an advanced degree in anthropology. "Dave was working in a muffler shop?" I knew as soon as I'd let it loose that it was a dumb question.

"No. I was," she said.

"I'm sorry," I said.

"For what?"

"To assume that since it was a mechanical job —"

"Oh, I wasn't a mechanic." She showed me her fingernails, which were clean and long and perfectly manicured. "I worked the register."

"Oh. OK," I said. "I'm sorry I interrupted you. Go on."

"End of story," she said. "You didn't interrupt me. I was done."

I laughed.

"No, really. That's all there was to it."

"So let's review the basic tenets of the story," I said. "You met in a muffler shop."

"He needed a muffler," she said. "I rang him up. He asked me out. I said yes."

"And next thing anyone knew . . . " I said.

"Happily ever after." She twisted the three rings all together.

I lifted my glass to clink with her. She didn't return the gesture. "I'd like to propose a toast," I said. Then she caught on. "To your story," I said.

"And to yours," she said. "Whatever it is."

We clinked and drank and Ellen said that she liked the wine and I said yes, wasn't it lovely? It was my favorite "cab." I had a couple of cases of it in the van. Don't worry, though, ha ha, I never opened a bottle until after I was done with the day's driving. Ha ha ha.

"You could still be a killer, you know," she said.

"Excuse me?"

"It occurred to me when you went for the wine." She took a sip of it without taking her eyes off me, but there was no fear, not even genuine distrust in them. "Maybe you looked us up in the phone-book. Maybe you saw his name on a piece of mail. For all I knew, you were going to come back in here with a gun or something and rape me."

"What are you talking about?" I reached into my pocket for my wallet.

"I don't need to see your credentials," she said. "If you were going to rape and kill me you'd've done it by now. I know. I'm sorry. I didn't mean to insult you or anything. I was just telling you how it was, in my head. You don't look very much like Dave."

"No. I never did."

"Are you nervous to see him?"

"Yes. I almost left," I admitted. "I thought about it."

"I wondered if you were going to do that," she said. "But then I'd've known you were a killer. So tell me: What is your story? Where do you live? Where are you going? What do you do? I still can't believe that he never even told me about you — anything. That you existed, for example."

"He's not much of a talker, is he?"

"No," she said, shaking her head. "He's certainly not."

"I live in Seattle," I said. "I'm between jobs right now. I used to work in a print shop, but I quit."

"So where are you headed? Anywhere in particular?"

I thought about it. "No," I said. "Not really. I mean, I know I'm going to New York City, and I know I'm going back to Seattle, and I know I'm taking the scenic route. But it's not just a vacation, either. What do you call it, like in a fairy tale, when —"

"Honeymoon?"

"Honeymoon? No," I said. "You know, like 'slay the dragon,'" I said, "or 'bring me the broom of the Wicked Witch of the West,' or East."

"A quest?"

"Yeah, that's what it's pretty much turned into, I guess. For me. This trip." I took the last drink of my wine and poured myself an-other glass, then topped off hers too.

She looked confused. "So," she said, "what is the quest of your quest?"

"I don't know."

"You have to know," she said, "if you want to call it that."

"I don't know if I can tell you. I mean, I don't know if I know. Exactly."

"Oh." She looked disappointed. She looked down, but then almost immediately her eyes bounced back up, charmingly, disarmingly hopeful. "You can tell me," she said.

And the way she said it, the way she looked at me, saying it, the simplicity of her conclusion and its expression, led me to believe that I *could* tell her.

"I won't tell anyone," she said. "I can keep a secret. I promise. And anyway there's always someone, isn't there, some good witch or imp or elf or woodchuck or something who helps the hero out? Nothing serious, just a little information or advice, or a good-luck charm, or the right weapon."

I thought: Woodchuck?

"Maybe I can help you," she said. "That's all I'm saying."

I didn't say anything for a long time. Neither did she. I looked around at all the walls for something to look at. I looked at the refrigerator, and I looked at the countertops. No art, no pictures, nothing but a plain old institutional clock on the wall above the stove. "I don't know," I said, looking into my glass.

But by the time we finished that bottle of wine I was thinking that maybe she could help me, sure, although I couldn't have put into words any specific way in which I needed help. I invited her to come out to the van with me to get another bottle.

"We should save some for Dave," she said.

"I've got plenty," I said.

"Let's go then," she said, and when she stood up I could tell she'd probably had enough to drink already.

"You might want to put something on," I said. "It's pretty cold out there."

"I'm OK," she said. "I can handle it." She picked her purse up off the table and brought it with her. "How long can it take to get a bottle of wine?" she said.

I didn't know what to say to that. I didn't know that I was going to do what I did, but of course I did, or else why would I have wanted her to come out there with me? I opened the side door and she climbed in and knelt on the floor, looking around at everything, smiling like a kid.

"Home," she said, lifting one of the curtains and peeking out the window at her own house. "It's homey in here."

I crawled past her to the back of the van. With trembling fingers I unlocked the lock on the wooden door I'd built under the loft, and I showed her my growing collection of thrift store wedding dresses. They were hanging on a stretch of rope, kept separate from each other from the waist up while the bottoms flowed together into a churning, foamy sea of white lace, tulle, polyester, and satin. The smell alone was enough to bring tears to your eyes, but Ellen dipped into the white with both hands, feeling the fabric, and she almost lost consciousness. She tilted from her knees onto her side and then back. The purse landed under the card table and her robe fell open.

"Are you OK?" I said, trying to avert my eyes while she righted herself.

"I got dizzy," she said. "The wine. I'm OK. So," she said, "this is your quest?"

I said, "No. Not really. I mean —"

"Do they fit you?"

"They don't have to," I said. I grabbed another bottle of wine. "Let's get back inside," I said. I helped her out of the van and closed the sliding door just as the cat was about to sneak in. He gave me one of those half-eyed if-looks-could-kill cat looks, and slinked underneath the vehicle. I wondered if I'd run over him on my way out in the morning.

"So, have you been raiding people's attics, or what?" Ellen asked once the wine had been poured.

It occurred to me that we'd left her purse in the van.

"No," I said. "I've been hitting thrift stores."

"Are they expensive?"

"Sometimes."

"Do people look at you funny?"

"Yes."

"Do you enjoy it?"

"The funny looks?"

"Yes."

"Yes."

"How many do you have?"

"Nine or ten."

How many do you want?"

"Hundreds."

She laughed, pleasantly, understandingly even, and went on asking the easy questions. The sun went all the way down, however, without her ever asking why, and I loved my sister-in-law for that.

It must have been about time for my brother to come home, about six, when she said across the table to me, "I have one." The second bottle was half empty, at least, and the room was almost all the way dark. "It's in the closet," she said. "Want to see it?"

"Sure. Why not?"

She flicked on a light on her way out of the kitchen and I closed my eyes so as not to have to see anything too clearly. I could hear the clock ticking and I could hear metal hangers sliding in another part of the small house. I wondered what Dave's car would sound like in the driveway, what kind of car he would drive, how he would feel if he came home to his wife showing me her wedding dress. Hopefully bad. It would serve him right, not inviting me to his wedding.

I thought she was going to just show it to me, but more time than necessary passed and I had to open my eyes and look at the clock. It was six-fifteen.

"Hey, I need you in here," she called from across the house.

I emptied my glass and took the bottle with me.

My brother's wife was standing in front of a full-length mirror in their bedroom. Our eyes met in the glass. "Zip me up," she said.

I set the bottle on the bureau and walked to her and zipped her up.

"Now step back," she said.

I went back to the bureau and picked up a small black statue of a crow welded together out of scrap metal. It was skinny and scary, but it was the only decorative touch I'd seen in all I'd seen of their house, and I liked it.

"Believe it or not," Ellen said, fitting the veil onto her head, "I've actually lost weight since I got married. How often does that happen?"

"I don't know," I said, exchanging the crow for the bottle. "Does it feel loose?"

"A little bit," she said. She whistled a measure or two of "Here Comes the Bride." Then, turning to face me, she cut herself off, saying, "This is pretty much what I looked like." She curtsied. She looked cute.

"Sorry I missed it," I said.

"Me too," she said. She smiled. I took a hit of wine. "Dave's going to get it for this," she said.

"No no no no no no," I said, handing her the bottle. "It's my own fault."

She took a drink and handed it back.

"You know what I'm thinking?" she said.

"No."

"I think it might fit you," she said. "You're only a little bit bigger than me."

"You know what I think?" I said.

"What?"

"It's not going to happen," I said. "There's not enough wine in the world, let alone my van, let alone this bottle —"

"Come on," she said. "For the look on Dave's face."

I laughed. "For the look on his face," I said, "while he's booting me out of the family all over again."

"Not this time," she said. "I won't let it happen. I'm the family now. We're family, you know. You can wear what you want."

I sat down on the edge of their bed. I didn't want to wear wedding dresses. I didn't know what I wanted. "Was it a big wedding?" I said.

"Pretty big." She took the wine from me and took a slug, then held it in her hand at her side, turning this way and that, checking herself out in the mirror.

"Do you have any pictures?" I said.

"Yes."

"Where?"

"I'll show you in a minute," she said. "Hold on." She struck a pose. "Here you have the real thing." She smiled into the mirror at me. Even with the bottle dangling from her hand, she looked heavenly.

I smiled back. "Was everyone there?" I said.

"Pretty much," she said. "Except for you."

"But the rest of my family? Yours? Friends? The whole nine yards?"

"Yeah, we did it up."

"That's nice," I said. "Live band?"

She came to the bed and offered me the bottle, then her hand. "Would you like to dance?" she said.

"I'd love to, but I feel I'm on thin ice with my brother as it is. Something's telling me you ought to get out of that get-up before he comes home."

"Why?"

"I don't know. It might look like we were trying to get at him, to make some sort of a point or something. And that's the last thing in the world I want to do is make any points. After ten years."

"I don't get it," she said, sitting on the bed next to me.

"It might make him feel bad," I said. "There's nothing to get, really. I don't get it either. I just have a bad feeling about it."

She dropped back onto her back, behind me. The dress rustled. "Tell me what you did," she said.

"What?"

"To deserve this," she said. "Why did they disown you?"

"Get out of the dress," I said. "We'll go back in the kitchen and talk about it."

"Too late." She sat up, calmly, and put her hand on my knee. Outside, a car door slammed. "He's here."

I didn't say anything. I just stood up, wavered for one second, and went without her into the kitchen.

He was just then coming in the back door.

"Dave," I said, stepping from around the corner.

We stood staring at each other. He was a bald giant in a three-piece suit and a fat tie with goldfish on it. He had wet, puffy lips, tiny eyes, and an overall end-of-the-day redness to his skin, as if he walked through fire for a living.

"Who the fuck are you?" he said.

"Honey?" Ellen called from the bedroom. "Dave?"

I was in the wrong house.

"Honey?" Ellen said, rustling down the hall.

A light came into Dave's eyes then and he lunged for me. Next thing I knew, I was flying through the picture window. Next thing I knew, I was outside in the grass, the cat on top of me, pawing into my chest.

I pushed it off, stood up, and looked in through the broken glass. The man in the suit had Ellen, still in her wedding dress, by the throat, both hands. He had her up against the far kitchen wall, off her toes.

Between her sputters and gasps and his unbroken string of spit-shouted curses and the sound of her still-veiled head tapping against the wall, I had no trouble sneaking back in and cracking his head with the rolling pin. Somewhere, somehow, all three of us had taken some mighty wrong turns.

Ellen, unconscious, folded over on top of her husband. I dragged her off and away from him before checking her pulse. She was still alive, but not exactly breathing. I wasn't sure if I knew CPR or not, but I figured if a cat could do it, I had better well have it in me. I pushed into her ribcage a few times and plugged her nose and blew into her mouth.

She breathed. She didn't open her eyes. She squeezed them shut tighter and shook her head from side to side, as if trying to lose something.

"Don't worry, sweetie," I said. "You're going to be just fine. It's all over now." And I picked her up in my arms and carried her outside to the van. Both Dave and I had bled onto her wedding dress, but I reckoned one of mine would fit her well enough.

"The wine," she said.

"Don't you worry," I said. "My brother lives around here some-where."

THOMAS LYNCH

Blood Sport

FROM *Witness*

MOST TIMES the remembrance was triggered by color — that primary red of valentines or Coca-Cola ads — the color of her toenails, girlish and perfectly polished. He remembered her body, tiny and lifeless and sickeningly still as she lay opened and autopsied on the prep room table. He could still bring to mind, these many years since, the curl of the knot in the viscera bag the pathologist had tied, with all of her organs examined inside, and the raw edge of the exit wound in her right leg and the horrible precision of the hole in her breast where the man who murdered her put the muzzle of the gun.

And he remembered the dull inventory of detail, the hollow in her mother's voice the morning she called him at the funeral home.

"Elena's been shot, Martin. Up in Baldwin. She's at the Lake County Morgue. Go and get her, Martin. Bring her home."

Elena had been only fifteen when her father died — the darkly beautiful daughter of a darkly beautiful mother and a man who'd had cancer. He was laid out in an eighteen-gauge metal casket. The funeral was huge. Martin could remember standing between them, Elena and her widowed mother, when they'd come to see the dead man's body. He figured he was ten years older than the daughter, ten years younger than the mother. He had asked, as he'd been trained to ask, if everything was "satisfactory." It was the failure of words that always amazed him.

"He got so thin."

"Yes."

"At least he's not suffering anymore."

"No."

"Thank you, Martin."

"Yes."

And he remembered how Elena, after trying to be brave for her mother, after standing and staring at the lid of the casket as if she could tough it out, as if she could look but not see, had let her gaze fall on the face of her dead father and cried, in one great expiration of pain, "Oh Daddy! Please, no," and nearly doubled over at the middle holding her tummy and how her knees buckled and how he grabbed her before she fell to the floor. And how she had pressed her sobs into his shirt and how he'd hugged her close and felt her holding on and could smell her hair and feel the form and perfect sadness in her shaking body and how he'd said that everything would be all right because he really didn't know what to say. It made him feel necessary and needed and he wanted to hold her and protect her and make everything better, because she was beautiful and sad and though he could not fix it he would not let her go until she could stand on her own two feet again. And he thought that being the only embalmer in town was no bad thing when you stood among the widowed and orphaned and they would thank you for the unhappy work you'd done on their people.

Five years after that and it was Elena, killed by her husband with a gun.

Martin could not get his mind off how mannish the violence was, how hunter-gatherly, how very do-it-yourself, for the son of a bitch to stand on the front deck of their double-wide out in the woods while she loaded the last of her belongings in the car — her boom box and a last armful of hanging things — how he must have carefully leveled the rifle, his eyes narrowing to sight her in. He put the first bullet through her thigh. An easy shot from fifteen yards.

He must have wanted to keep her from running.

"The way you would with any wild thing," the fat pathologist, smelling of stale beer, had told Martin in the morgue, taking the cigar out of his mouth to hold forth like an expert. "You hobble it first, then you don't have to chase a blood trail through the woods all night." He warmed to his subject. "Bow hunters go for the heart or lungs most times. They don't mind chasing through swamps and marshes after a wounded buck. It's part of the sport to them. But shooters go for the head shot or the legs."

And as she lay in the thick leaf-fall beside the car, bleeding from the severed femoral artery, he'd walked over, put the barrel to her left breast and squeezed off another round.

"She'd have bled to death either way," the pathologist said. The sight of that fat hand with the cigar touching the spot on Elena's thigh where the bullet tore its exit out sickened Martin. And when the same hand pulled the sheet back to show the terrible carnage to her torso — the postmortem incisions very loosely stitched up and the black and blue and red little wound where her killer must have reckoned her heart would be, Martin quickly moved his stretcher beside the morgue tray, covered her body and took charge before the pathologist carried his hapless lecture any further. He signed the log book beside Elena's name and case number, got the death certificate marked "gunshot wounds to leg and chest" in the section that asked for the cause of death and "homicide" where it asked for manner and had her name and date of death, all of it scrawled in the sloppy hand of the pathologist, and got her out of there.

All the way home he tried to imagine how it must have happened — if anyone could have heard it, the small caliber outrage of it, as if she'd been a doe feeding among the acorns or come to the salt lick, her large brown eyes full of panic and stillness. He wondered if she knew he was dangerous. He wondered if she realized, after the first shot, that he was going to kill her. He wondered if she died with fear or resolve. He wondered if bleeding from the first wound, she might have passed out, and never saw the face of her killer or the barrel of the gun or felt it on her body or saw his eyes as he pulled the trigger.

Taken as a thing itself, undistracted by his professional duties, considered as a bit of humanity, the aberration was incomprehensible. How could someone kill someone so coldly, someone with whom you had made plans, had sex, watched television, promised love? It left him with a functional ambiguity. Martin tried to assemble a reasonable sentence in which the last line went like *and then he shot her, twice, because . . .* but he was always unsuccessful.

He looked in the rearview mirror at the length of the stretcher in

the back of the hearse with its tidy blue cover under which Elena's
body was buckled in, her head on the pillow, a small bag with her
bloodied clothes, her jewelry and personal effects beside her. He
tried to connect this horror with his remembrance of a sad, beautiful girl sobbing at the graveside of her dead father a few years before, waiting for the priest to finish with his prayers.

The morning was blue and sunlit, the buds of maples just busting loose, the men who'd been pallbearers lined up on one side of
the grave, Elena and her mother and grandmother on the other.
And all around, a couple hundred who'd come to pay their respects — women who worked with Elena's mother at the real estate
office, men who worked with her father at the shop, parishioners
from Our Lady of Mercy and kids from the freshman class of the
high school. And after the priest had finished, Martin had nodded
to the pallbearers to remove their gloves and solemnly place them
on the casket — a little gesture of letting go. And then, from the
pile of dirt next to the grave, under the green grass matting, he'd
given a small handful of dirt, first to the dead man's mother, then
to the dead man's wife, and then to Elena; and at his direction,
each stepped up to the casket and traced a cross on the top with the
dirt that Martin had given them. He put a hand on their elbows as
they stepped on the boards in a gesture of readiness and ever-vigi-
lant assistance. And after that, Martin made the announcement he
had practiced saying out loud the night before.

"This concludes the services for Mr. Delano."

He reminded himself to speak slowly, to enunciate, to articulate,
to project.

"The family wishes to thank each of you for your many kind-
nesses — for the floral tributes and Mass cards and most especially
for your presence with them this morning."

He took a breath, tried to remember what part came next.

"You are all invited to return now to Our Lady of Mercy Parish
Hall where a luncheon has been prepared in Mr. Delano's memory. You may step now directly to your cars."

At this direction, people began to move away, relieved at the end
of the solemnities, talking freely, trading news and sympathies.
Martin had been pleased with the performance. Everything had
gone off just as he'd planned — a fitting tribute, a good funeral.
The pallbearers walked away as a group, looking official. Someone

assisted the grandmother from the grave. Elena's mother, her eyes tired and red, took Martin's arm as they walked to the limousine, holding the rose Martin had given her, the crowd of people parting as they made their way. And Martin was thinking this is no bad thing for people to see what a dependable man their new funeral director was — a reliably upright, lean-on-me kind of man — less than a year out of mortuary school, mortgaged to the eyes for the business he'd bought from the widow of the man who'd been here before, but clearly a responsible, dependable citizen, someone to be called on, night or day, if there was trouble.

At the door to the car Mrs. Delano stopped, turned toward Martin with a brave smile, tilted her head slightly, opened her arms, and Martin, sensing that she wanted him to, without hesitation bent to embrace her. She was saying, "Thank you, Martin," and "I could never have made it through this without you," loud enough for bystanders to hear and he was patting her back professionally, all caring and kindness as you would with any hurt or wounded fellow human, saying to her, "You did good; he'd be proud of you," and she was patting his shoulders and then, once the hug was over, holding the hankie to her eyes, she quickly disappeared into the back seat of the car in a rush of grief and relief and gratitude, and Martin straightened up and held the door.

Elena, who'd been following Martin and her mother to the limousine, holding two roses she'd picked from her father's casket spray, paused at the car door and, perhaps because she was following her mother's lead, perhaps thinking it was the proper thing to do, looked Martin in the eyes and said, "Thank you, thank you for everything," and reached up to lock her hands around Martin's neck and just as Martin was starting to say, in a voice all caring and kindness, "You're very welcome, Elena," she rose on her tiptoes, pressed her body firmly against his and kissed him squarely on the mouth. Martin could feel her chest on his chest, her small hands holding the sides of his face, and her soft mouth opening and the wet tip of her tongue on his lips. He let go of the door handle and held her at the waist, first pulling her toward him, then opening his eyes, gently pushing her away, and when she stopped kissing him, he could feel his face reddening and he was wondering if the priest and the pallbearers and the townspeople could see his blush and the flash of desire he could feel in himself and the wish beginning to form in his mind that everyone would disappear so that he could hold her and touch her and comfort her and have her and then, before he could pat her on the back professionally, before he could say, "There, there, everything is going to be all right," before he had a chance to restore the air of solemnity and order, Elena proffered, with a brave smile, one of the roses she was holding. He took it from her, and as her mother had, Elena disappeared head first into the back of the long black Cadillac, which then drove away.

There was a safety in dealing with only the parts — the arteries and chemistries, the closure of eyes and lip lines, the refitting of cranium and sternum, the treatment of cavities and viscera, the placement of hands, the suturing of wounds and incisions, the rouge and lipstick and nail polish, the dressing and hairdo and casketing. Duty had a way of separating Martin from what it was he was doing. Stuffing the opened cranium with cotton, fitting the skull cap back in place and easing the scalp back over the skull (thereby restoring the facial contours), and minding the tiny stitches from behind one ear to behind another were only part of the process of embalming and embalming was only part of the process of laying out the dead which was only part of the process of the funeral and the funeral was only a part of the larger concept of a death in the family and a death in the family was a more manageable prospect, more generic somehow, than the horror — round and witless and recognizable and well beyond his professional abilities — of a lovely girl, grown lovelier as a woman, who leaned on him and counted on him and had kissed him once as if she meant it and who moved away and then got shot like an animal in the woods by a man about whom Martin knew next to nothing.

For months after her father's funeral, Martin kept an eye out for Elena. Her mother came to pay the bill, and pick up more holy cards and thank-you notes. And then she came to order a stone. "Beloved Husband and Father" is what it said. Martin had advised her against a double marker. She was young and would surely remarry he thought.

And Martin would always ask, "How is Elena doing?" in his most professional, caring voice.

"She's having some trouble with her schoolwork. She doesn't sleep well. I'm a little worried."

Martin gave Elena's mother a list of grief support groups, run by the local hospice and area churches. He reminded her that there used to be "a year of mourning" and said that Elena's feelings were probably "very normal" and that "time heals all wounds."

"Yes," said Elena's mother. "It's just so hard."

She thanked Martin again for everything and said she hoped he'd understand if she said she hoped she wouldn't be seeing him again.

Martin smiled and nodded and said he understood completely.

The next June, Martin read in the local paper how Elena had been captain of the debate team that went to the regional finals in Ann Arbor, and the year after that she had gone to Italy on a Rotary Exchange Scholarship, and in her senior year she was pictured on the front page smiling in her prom dress beside the son of the man who owned the Lincoln-Mercury dealership in town, over a caption that read "A Night to Remember" and Martin remembered how very happy she looked, how very pretty. After that he pretty much lost track of her.

"After her father died," Elena's mother told Martin when she came in to pick out a casket and arrange the funeral, "she seemed a little lost."

Martin listened and nodded as Elena's mother, looking so much older now, outlined the details of her dead daughter's life. She'd finished school, applied to college, spent the summer after graduation waitressing in a bar-restaurant in western Michigan, to get out on her own and earn a little money.

"She met him there. At the Northwoods Inn." He worked for the county road commission and came in weeknights after work and weekends after fishing or hunting. He was handsome and chatty. He had a trailer in the woods. He gave her compliments and brought her flowers and bought her beer and cheeseburgers. And when it came time to go to the university, to get the education her father had saved for, she called her mother and told her that she was moving in with this man.

"I didn't approve but what could I do, Martin? Her father would never have allowed it. But what could I do?"

Martin shook his head and nodded.

"I told her she was throwing her life away on a summer fling, but she said she loved him. She loved him and he killed her, shot her like a damn dog, Martin."

Elena's mother's sobs grew heavy. Martin poured her a glass of water, moved the box of Kleenex nearer to her. "Thank you, Martin," she said. "I'm sorry."

"Not at all," he said. "It's OK."

"In no time she was pregnant and he said he wanted to 'do right' by her. I told her he would always feel trapped, or always feel like he had done her a big favor, always feel like he was such a big man and she was just nothing without him, but she said she loved him and maybe it was all meant to happen like this and what could I do, Martin? What could I do? Her father would have gone up there and brought her home, but I had no one, no one."

They were married in the county offices in a civil ceremony, Elena wearing her prom dress and her new husband wearing a cowboy hat and a blue jean jacket and a string tie.

Elena's mother took the wedding snapshot out of her purse and told Martin, "Cut him off of there and use that picture for the paper and the holy cards. She was so happy then."

Elena miscarried in her third month and took a job working dispatch for the sheriff's office. By the following midsummer things were getting bad. Her husband's appetite for Budweiser and blood sport hadn't abated.

"She'd call home crying, Martin. He still went to the bar weeknights and came home boozy and, well, unpredictable. And he spent the weekends tramping through the woods shooting small game which he'd bring home for her to clean and cook.

"He'd go out at night and snag spawning salmon and bring them back to freeze and smoke and put up in jars.

"Her letters home got so sad, Martin. 'He doesn't bathe enough,' she wrote me once. 'He seems so angry.'"

She had taken from her purse a packet of pink envelopes and was holding them and rocking a little in the chair across the desk from Martin.

"She had such beautiful handwriting."

Martin nodded, smiled, understood.

"She called me crying horribly once and I asked her if he'd hit her but she said no, no. He had killed a fawn, right outside their trailer. It had come with its mother to feed at the pile of carrots he baited them with. They were in bed. Sunday morning. He sat up, walked to the window, went to the door where he kept his rifle. It was months before the legal season. He shot it right from the door. The fawn, Martin. The little fawn."

She was shaking now again, sobbing and rocking in the chair.

"Do you know what he told her, when she yelled at him for shooting the fawn?"

Martin shook his head.

"He told her it couldn't live without its mother anyway."

Now she was sobbing and shaking fitfully and Martin reached across the desk to take hold of her hands in which she held the packet of her daughter's letters.

"We don't have to do this now," Martin told her.

But she wanted to go on, to get it out, to get this part behind her.

After he killed the baby deer, Elena applied to the state university in Mt. Pleasant, using as return address the sheriff's office. When the letter came from the admissions department, beginning "Dear Ms. Delano: Congratulations!" she made a copy and mailed it home with a note asking her mother if there was still money left for her education.

"Of course is what I told her," Elena's mother told Martin. "I wanted her to get her education before she settled down. After she lost the baby, she had no reason to stay with him. And he was drinking and depressed. He worked and drank and grew more distant. She could see she had made a big mistake. I could tell she wasn't happy."

Elena told her mother how she gave her husband back his leather coat and the tiny diamond ring and said she would always care about him but that she had been too young and she felt she owed it to her father to return to school and get her life on track and she would always treasure their time together but she really had to go. She thought it would be the best thing for them both. She was sure he wasn't happy either.

The night before she had planned to leave, she did her hair and polished her nails and cooked him pheasant and they ate by candlelight — "for old times' sake" she had told her mother when she called to say she'd be home tomorrow. She really wanted no hard feelings. It had been her mistake and she was sorry to have involved him in it. Surely, they would always be friends.

"He's OK with it. He doesn't like it but he's OK with it" is what

she told her mother when her mother asked her how he was taking it.

And, near as the coroner and the sheriff could piece it together,
it was after everything she owned had been loaded in the car,
the trunk full of books and photo albums, the back seat packed
with her stereo and a rack of hanging clothes and the front passenger seat with the one suitcase full of toiletries and socks and
underwear; maybe she was turning to wave goodbye before going, or maybe he'd been drinking Budweiser all night, or maybe
he'd helped her and then went berserk but whatever happened,
whether it was passion or calculation, before she sat into the
driver's seat, he got the rifle from wherever he kept it. Near as they
could figure by the angle of the wound, he stood on the front
porch, aimed and fired, then walked over to where she lay in the
leaf-fall beside the car and shot her again, in the breast.

This was the part that Martin could never imagine — the calculation of shooting her in the leg, then slowly, deliberately walking
over and pressing the barrel against her left breast and pulling
the trigger. Wouldn't such madness in a man give signs before?
Wouldn't the first gunshot wake him from the dream?

Elena's mother was rocking in the chair across from Martin, sobbing quietly, clutching the letters, staring at the snapshot of her
daughter on the desk standing next to the man who had just killed
her.

"You pick out the casket, Martin. I can't do it. Something like her
father's. Please, Martin. You do it."

He used the cherry casket with the moss pink velvet interior and
though it was considerably more costly than what Elena's father was
buried in, he charged the same and thought it was the least he
could do.

And now, twenty years since, nearing fifty, he could still not shake
the sense of shame, that the men in her life had let her down badly.
The father who died too young, the husband who murdered her,
even the embalmer who could only treat her viscera with cavity
fluid, inject her arms and legs and head, stitch the horrible incisions of the postmortem — from left shoulder to breastbone,
breastbone to right shoulder, then breastbone to pubic bone —
the little bulge in her tummy where the bag full of organs made her
look almost expectant, then cover the stitches with cotton and ad-

hesive. And then put a little blush on her cheeks, brush her lipstick on, curl and comb her hair. He had dressed her in the sweater and jeans her mother brought in and lifted her into the casket, put her First Communion rosary in her hand, a crucifix in the head of the casket and put an arm around her mother when she came to look.

"Oh no, no, no," she sobbed, her shoulders rising and falling, her head shaking, her body buckling at the sight of her daughter's dead body. Martin held her at the elbows, whispering, "Let it go; I'm so sorry," because he never could think of the right thing to say.

Over time Martin learned to live with the helplessness and the sadness and the shame. He quit trying to figure the right thing to say. He listened. He stayed.

Still, all these years since, whenever the right shade of red turned up, he could see the fat old pathologist and his cigar and stupid tutorial manner there in the morgue with its cold smell of disaster and formalin, and the hearse that he drove up to get her that October. And the way they lay in coolers in the corner of the room, the two bodies in trays beside one another — Elena and the son of a bitch that shot her.

He had shot himself, after killing her. He walked back in the house, sat on the edge of the bed and taking the muzzle of the rifle in his teeth pulled the trigger with his thumb, dividing his face at the septum in the process.

"Isn't that always the way?" the old pathologist had said, yanking the tray out with Elena's body on it. "It's love sickness. A man kills his wife then kills himself. A woman kills her man then does her nails."

Martin hated those sentences and couldn't forget them. That they rang true sometimes and false at others had never been a comfort.

Eventually, after the wake and Mass, her body was buried beside her father's, leaving another grave on the other side for her mother. It was all Martin could do — to get her where she was supposed to be. Her mother had a stone cut that read "Beloved Daughter" with a rose between her dates and another with her own name on it and her year of birth and a dash and had it placed over the empty plot beside her husband. She moved away some few years after that. Martin never heard from her again.

DAVID MEANS

Carnie

FROM *Witness*

THE CARNIE ROSE slowly, a ragged display that no one seemed to
notice until it was completely up; at least his daughter didn't notice
it until, passing on the way home from school (John picked her
up most days when he was working the night shift buying and selling power for the local utility), she spotted the Ferris wheel and
begged him to take her, to let her go. You'd have thought it was the
first time she'd seen a Ferris wheel, the way she went on about it, he
told his wife later. Carnivals were risky affairs, with their inept
machinery, assembled in haste, and above all the hawkers and
roadies, half-wits and assorted drunks, riffraff who had traveled to
the ends of the earth and were worse for wear. He saw them come
through town when he was growing up in Illinois: souls lost to the
tedium of taking tickets and standing hours in the hot sun helping people on and off rides. Deep inside (it is safe to say) John had
a healthy respect for them, a high regard for the silence which
roadies were seemingly able to put up with. He loved the dusty,
half-mown fields where they usually set up, the way late-afternoon
light drove through the tangle of equipment.

But his respect wasn't enough to put his fears aside.

Consider Ned Alger. Ned manned one of two machines, depending on what his partner, Zip Jones, felt like working; if Zip was running the merry-go-round, Ned would take his shift at the Romper
ride, a wide spider of metal fatigue flinging kids in sloppy circles.
None of the rides worked at full speed. If you were to look, you'd
see Ned standing with an absent, empty look on his face watching

the machine run; you'd see his nervous tic of crossing his arms over each other, up high across his chest, and heaving great bellows of air in and out, as if he'd just lifted himself from an exhausting swim. He suffered from the cigarette dangling off his lips. If you were to spend a day watching the two of them go from one ma- chine to the other — silently changing places with an unspoken commitment to breaking up the tedium — you'd wonder what cur- rents exactly kept Zip and Ned together. What bonds — sacred and otherwise — held them fast? Truth was, they were linked simply by their point of departure; both joined the carnie when it was passing through a small town in Ohio. Zip was hitching aimlessly from the west and needed some cash. Ned, born and raised in the town, saw a help-wanted flier in a laundromat and decided it was his chance to see the world.

More than that, though; the long-simmering nothingness of the fields beyond the edges of the towns in which they set up; bluegrass and timothy and planted hay and corn dried to a brittle song; the endless, almost needless horizon. They came from that, both men, two years of passing town to town.

The kid was begging and he agreed to take her. Simple as that. Later, he had to see it that way.

Zip was halfway through a bottle of gin. The workday was done and most of the roadies were lounging about the campers, smoking, mulling. A bit of corn had lodged between his front teeth, and he was working his tongue against them, taking pleasure in the effort, unwilling to use his fingers except as a last resort. He'd made a kind of testimony to himself this evening — working at the corn — about some things he had done a few towns back, in Pennsylvania; *some things* was how he thought of them, although if he wanted he could conjure up exact memories: break-ins of houses in the after- noons when most suburban folk were off earning their two-income keep, jimmying a door or kicking in a basement window and low- ering himself into the damp, cobwebbed basement of some sod buster's estate. In Ohio — two years ago — he copped a couple of off-the-cuff fondles in the bushes; he could remember the wet mouth beneath his palm as he pushed hard to smother the words trying to come out. Working at the corn in his own mouth he began to speak to himself — as he often did — in his own manner: a few tidbits of Biblical cadence and phraseology — thou arts, therefores — blended in with what the other guys called Zip-speak, or Zip-talk, because he had his own peculiar way of talking.

Don't know likely what the bejezuse you'd be doing to be doing what you are is a good example. Or: *Fuck that fuck I'm gonna fuck him until he wishes he were fucked.*

Now he held his head back, way back, and let a little moan slide from his gullet. The gin was settled into the base of his gut, not enough to warm him but enough to make more necessary.

Yeah, there are myths about this kind of thing, and one wants to avoid stereotypes — plenty of good folk working the road even to this day, the very end of the century, anachronistic as all hell but there, smoking, trying to work out the general situation. So be it. This is his story. This is what happened in this particular incident.

It was the other one, Ned, who did the real wandering. Late at night when all was shut down and the dormant machines stretched their weary metal joints (you could hear them sigh in the wind), he might steal off for a walk, a journey, a venture, a poke-around-town, working his way stealthily through fence gaps and along the backsides of hedges, toeing his way through the night-blue shadows. His travels took him along the topologies of night: garbage cans resting silently on the curb, awaiting pickup; toys left outside to gather shawls of dew; stray dogs and cats slinking on their betrayed hind legs. He walked through expensive backyards with gas grills and swimming pools and elaborate alarm systems and sensors that he was able to evade, except for once, in Canton, Ohio, when a loud siren went off and lights came on and he was chased like a fugitive (as he told it later to Zip), like Tommy Lee Jones in the movie — caught and put in the tank overnight with nothing to prove he'd actually done anything; his radar was off, he thought, he wasn't paying his usual attention — because if there was one thing he did do, and knew he did, it was to mind, to pay heed to what was before him; it was his Indian shit, he told Zip, not getting into the details — that he'd been raised by a squaw, his old lady, old-school Indian stuff, a real squatter who'd crammed his soul with so much junk he could hardly stand to feel it there; he was a tiptoer; he'd seen it growing up — men able to find ways into the darkness, to tread lightly.

One would like to know exactly what it was that filled Ned when he walked through yards and places unspoken for by the light; perhaps it was the way he felt growing up, in the little squat in Petoskey, a patch of land they'd claimed as their own by parking the old bullet-shaped Airstreams side by side. Behind them sat the Chief's yellow-tarnished Winnebago. And behind that, almost hidden in the wind-blind of pines, stood the two teepees, trying to make it official.

You see, there are varieties of darkness. It's as simple as that. All day pitching the ride and smoking and looking up into the hard, ungiving eye of the sun while kids got on the Romper and rested their little rumps to be flung up and down. The eyes of the parents glimmered with their love, big, wide love, because what else would compel them to buy three fifty-cent tickets for a measly five minutes of being spun around on old rusted equipment? Neon bulbs worn out to a damp glow; music, once supplied by a real, air-piped organ, now the same crappy tunes from the Sony boom box he propped in the center of the merry-go-round. Every thirty minutes he had to go turn the tape over.

There are fears so deep and dark that to admit them is to feel the universe slip out from under your own feet; or so John thought. If touched upon too long, these fears would flower out over your skin — the very skin of your life — like a huge wart. He'd seen photographs in a porn magazine of untreated growths flowering like mushrooms from the skin. Guys in the break room were passing it around, and he sat in stunned submission to what he was seeing: a giant, cauliflower growth in the crack of a man's ass. To think that it could go like that untreated. He stared so hard and long at the photo that finally Rick, who had bought the magazine and felt it was his to stare at long and hard like that, took it back. The next Sunday he went to church and spoke to God in the hope of never having to face any such thing in his own life; he wasn't asking for protection; his hope was that God would forget him, pass him over, allow him to walk through his life untouched.

When, in retrospect, he saw the guy on the merry-go-round stumble back to change the cassette; when he saw the guy then move back to hold onto the pole directly behind his daughter; when he saw the way the guy was looking at his daughter, and the droop of the faded Wranglers: when he thought back and retraced everything, he was sure he should have *seen it:* there were wide-open empty spots all over the ride. The first swellings of a skin growth, he should have spotted it.

One theory might be that carnivals provide a natural outlet for a darker need we all have to play ourselves against the forces of transience; a neatly polished road show would go against that need. Rejects, freaks, washaways run the rides. The state inspector — half-blind with foggy cataracts — comes in for a show of civilized examination; he holds his clipboard and checks the joints of the Ferris wheel, and maybe watches the men work lug nuts onto bolts. But he avoids inspecting the undersides of the men's souls.

Strangely enough, the paths of John and Ned had crossed before, on a beach in northern Michigan, near the encampment in which Ned grew up. (No one was really sure how he got the name Ned, or even Alger, his mother going by Alger but also the Indian name of Walk Moon; and there was the man who was supposed to be standing in as his father, Jack-somebody, who came in at night with his belt already undone.) Two women sat on the beach in Petoskey State Park, at the cusp of Little Traverse Bay. It was an unusually cool midsummer day and the beach was almost empty — both women sat watching their sons play, far up, near the waterline. Of course John didn't remember that day, amid countless other days going to the Midwest to visit his grandparents at their summer cottage, but he did remember the ragtag encampment of residual beings where Ned was reared, the warnings his grandfather had given him to stay away; a shaggy little creek wove through the myrtle along the side of the road there, loaded with broken gin bottles and potato chip bags, and through the weeds one could see the old trailers, men and women in lawn chairs drinking beer, and so on . . .

The idea of blind chance put a hole in John's gut; he refused it outright as an available explanation. It just wouldn't do. John made a vow that he would never admit in any way that the *whole* thing hinged on brutal good luck (from Ned's vantage) and bad luck (from his vantage) and nothing else. The fact that his daughter had been at the carnival that day and taken a twirl (sixteen rotations) on Ned's ride allowed him to make the connection between the two that led to a legal conviction; but that was all. Although when he tried to visualize it he came up with the image of a huge arc, a bolt of raw, blue charge going from his house to that ride. A bolt fired by fate, by forces begun by his own actions. After wandering around, Ned found himself beneath her window, hunched in the thickness of the hydrangeas, eyeing the partway-open window and getting his Exacto knife out to slice through the nylon screening with only the faintest of zips, the blade easing through the squares the way a very hot scoop curled back ice cream. Then with both hands spread out, he lay his palms on the underside of the window and lifted it slowly (the window grooves had been recently waxed to reduce friction, which caused brain-deadening lead dust), softly enough so the sound of it was actually nothing more or less than the usual movements of night: trees rasping each other in the gentle upheaval of breeze, or a raccoon scuffing the side of an overturned garbage can. He lifted himself acrobatically into the window — his footfalls on landing softened, he felt, or dreamed, by all of history, his imagined forefathers tiptoeing the wooded trails along the shore of Lake Michigan.

Jesus expelled the demons from the freaks and then sent the fuckers into a herd of swine and drove them headlong over a cliff, John read a year later, trying to find his way into some kind of answer: attending a Bible study at the local evangelical church; reading the passage and then saying fuck this and getting up and walking out to the back of the building where kiddie swings made movements in the wind; he heard the soft squeals of the pigs in the air as they made lopsided motions over the edge, the thuds as they hit the ground. They read somewhere else, too, that driving out the demons only leaves a large, vacant recess into which more evil slips.

You see to tell it as a story or even a series of actions would be to make sense of it and to lend it some kind of orderly function in the world; that's why it is only referred to as *the incident* by the media — the girl's name, of course, withheld to protect her future; and her muteness, her silence, around the event was part of that withholding. In the horrifying darkness Ned went in and *did what he did,* and it was the basics which held sway in the public mind: the entering of the dark room, the violation of the safe, almost sacred silence of night, the pink ruffle curtains and the canopy bed.

*

Zip sensed right away that Ned had gone and *done it* again, something mighty bad. Dawn was pink along the horizon. A brush of high ice clouds licked the sky. Both men hunched beneath blankets, unwilling to leave the herringbone, slip-proof surface of their beloved merry-go-round. They heard the tink, tink of metal adjusting to the cold and, when the wind rose, a rattling of the Ferris wheel guy wires. *Might as well be any place on earth as being in this town,* Zip said, softly. The talk was like that, soft, with a fibrous quality. *Smell somethin' bad coming in this air, Ned,* he said. Off far in the trees, like a bit of lint in a comb, there was the sound of sirens — the rescue crews and cops, all the attendant caregivers coming to open the girl up with their interviews. He knew it would take them a while to pry out the story from her scared soul — if the truth were told, he had, for a small second, a flick of remorse for the other side of the world (as he thought about it): the dark brooding spirits that his grandmother used to mutter about through her leathery lips *there is a darkness in the whiteness of that world that I shouldn't bother with if I were you, boy. You're a fucking Indian squat, nothing more, and don't forget it.* So he got his rucksack from the trailer, stuffed it as quickly as he could, gave Zip a kiss on the mouth, and went off to find the Interstate, where if he was lucky he might catch a hitch to someplace else. He'd change his name and identity, find a new way of showing himself to the world, and then hook back up with the carnie the way he had before, just shaving off his beard and getting his hair cut short in the back and then going right up to Nate and asking for work (Nathan knew damn well it was Ned with another name and face). The carnie was heading west, he knew, and would hit a few pathetic state fairs as sideshow backup and then a few Ohio town festivals before the tremendously boring hinterland towns of Indiana (that's where he would finally reunite with his beloved Zip).

Working backwards, John went over the events of that day and made diagrams, flow charts resembling those intricate schematics of computer innards. He examined the whole day from the very start when he woke her up, nudged her softly, and gave her breakfast of frozen waffles; one thing leading to another which led eventually to that ride (because Ned had been captured, finally, in Albany, after an APB went out on him over fax machines. Irrefutable proof in the form of hair samples found on her sheets and in Ned's trailer linked the crime to the carnie, as had been John's first gut feeling). A crew of jaded cops and medics and social workers hung around long after the event to give some assurance to the family that they were doing all they could in every way. It was no use. Behind him John felt the web of events untangled, like an old used-up fishing net washed ashore; it was all there, in the past, gone, lost. Nothing would ever change it. And yet he felt it might be changed. He pondered it for a year, for another year, for the rest of his life. He lived simply outside the world of rational thought. He kept his toes in the magic. He pondered the electric spark and went on with his life; he even, a few years later, took her to another carnie as a way of going through the pain (as was suggested by the social workers).

The carnie went on to Indiana, to Laketon, where it set up for another firemen's fundraiser. With rheumy eyes, the crew got the rides up during an afternoon that was as brown and hard as peanut brittle, heaving parts from the flatbed, working slowly with a bored somnolence, hammering with wooden mallets, making what used to be music to a kid's ear but now went unheard mostly behind car windows. The edge of the town simmered with insects. To the left of the lot there was nothing but a flat field that married the horizon; to the right of them was the last house in town, in which an old man lived alone. Staring at it, Zip could tell an old fart lived there, the weathered clapboards and the rusting tools on the wooden bench out back. Indeed, the old man came out, unfolded a lawn chair, took a pipe and wedged it into his teeth. He watched them for hours on end with a blank expression. There, Zip thought. I was right.

An old codger working his way through the last of his days. His visions were coming more often since Ned had been caught, and his Zip-speak was even stranger, more fanatic, mostly incomprehensible babble to the other roadies, who avoided him completely if they could. *You can't Christ-all this fucking nothingness,* he said. *He's going to hell-fuck 'fore I get to fuck him myself.* Some even admitted they were scared of the guy. For a moment, resting his back against a canopy support beam of the merry-go-round, which he was assembling himself (there were a few bolts missing), he had one of his visions again — the old man with a blade between his eyes, lodged deep, thunking the way you'd meet a piece of soft wood. In honor of Ned, I just might make this one vision come to pass, he said aloud; then he shook the thought off the way you'd shake away an ice cream headache. The carnie was going up piecemeal. A real half-assed job. It would be inspected by a bribed official of the state, who just happened to be passing through the town to visit his great aunt. It would have the usually dusty light bulbs strung from feeble infrastructure, and the people would arrive sensing the dubiousness of the whole affair, as if it were nothing but a holding pen for the castoffs of the universe. That's what they liked about it, essentially. It gave them a sense of being ripped off, betrayed, denied. They hated it but loved it. Hoards came through the gate on opening night. Stayed a few hours. Left glad to leave. It was Zip who got to stay alone with his bottle, sprawled back on the cold plate steel, watching the old man's house shrouded in darkness, stark against the dark horizon like a cardboard prop. It wasn't real enough. It stood as a testament of the unreality of the world.

KENT NELSON

Tides

FROM *The Georgia Review*

ON A LATE AFTERNOON in May, sun angles across the Intracoastal Waterway to the island and through the open doorway and
high windows of the marina lounge. I maybe should have gone
home, but I'd settled a case in Charleston that afternoon, and Edie
and the children weren't expecting me yet, so I stop in to see Billy
and Purvis. My eyes adjust to the separating light and shadow,
but in one corner it's all sunlight where Billy Prioleau and Pope
Gailliard are playing cribbage and drinking rum and Coke. Purvis
looks on, silhouetted against the masts of sailboats beyond the
open doorway. Pope and Billy are sixty-something, gray haired.
Purvis is in his late forties now, though he stands old — askew and
on one foot, his left hand always in his pocket. I've known them
since I was a kid, from the early days of the island when my father
was still alive.

Four crabbers with pitchers of beer eye the two women in shorts
drinking margaritas at the bar. One of the women is brunette,
maybe thirty, chewing gum a mile a minute. The other's a curly
blonde with wide eyes, halfway pretty. The way Donna, the bartender, is huddled with them, I assume they're all friends.

I sit down a couple of stools away, between the women and the
cribbage game.

"All I know is I don't feel safe anywhere," the brunette says.

"They haven't caught the bastard, either," Donna says. She
comes over, but doesn't say hello.

"Sam Adams draft," I say.

"Hey, Scotty," Pope says.

Purvis waves, and I wave back. Billy doesn't look up from his cards.

Donna squints through her cigarette smoke as she tilts the enamel handle of the tap. "You hear anything about that shooting?" she asks.

"People are talking about it," I say. "The family was from Illinois. I heard the boy was drawing a picture when he died."

"You think it was a colored man did it?" Pope asks.

"You mean, do I think it was racial?"

"'Course it was racial," Donna says. She sets my beer down and writes on my tab. "You saying it was an accident?"

"It could have been a stray bullet — someone hunting."

"It ain't hunting season," Donna says.

"Nothing is an accident," Billy says to Pope, "except your mother's having you. It's your goddamn crib."

Pope turns over the crib cards and counts, "Fifteen two, fifteen four, and trips is ten." He moves his peg, and Billy gathers the deck and shuffles.

Light shimmers across the water, and toward the city the sky yellows through sea haze and city smog. Just about ten years ago, after I finished law school, Edie and I rented a house here on the backside marsh. She was from Atlanta, and at first she thought the island too isolated, but once the children were born — Carla is eight now, and Blair is six — she liked it. She could walk them to the playground, and there were other young mothers with whom she traded babysitting. Of course I was from here, and when my practice took hold as expected, we bought a house on the beach — four bedrooms, a kitchen that looks out to the ocean, and a wraparound deck. Now she wouldn't live anywhere else.

A noise draws our attention to the front of the lounge. The Rupert brothers, Shem and Marvin, jostle each other coming through the door. Marvin's heavyset, jowly, gray-brown hair in a ponytail. Shem's thinner and taller and has a gold chain around his neck. "Pour us two shots, Donna. Make it Jack Daniel's. And give everyone a round, especially the pretty ladies."

The Ruperts stride to the bar as if they own the place.

"And give Scotty two," Marvin says. "Damn right."

"Absolutely," Shem says. "Two for Scott. Without Scotty we'd have been up shit creek without a paddle."

"I just did my job," I say, more to Billy than to the Ruperts.

Billy doesn't look over.

"You saved us all that money on taxes," Shem says. He looks at the brunette chewing gum. "Scotty's the best lawyer in Charleston."

Donna sets up two shot glasses on the bar and pours Jack Daniel's.

The Ruperts are old-timers, too — odd-jobbers and boat painters. My father never liked them much — too pushy even then — but when they came to me, what was I supposed to do? Lawyers give advice.

Donna sets the shots in front of them and fills a pitcher for the crabbers.

"I don't want a rum and Coke from them," Billy says.

Shem nudges Marvin. "I told you he saw us," he says.

Marvin nods. "He was awfully slow closing the bridge for us."

Then Shem turns to me. "Hey, Scotty, you see our new Lincoln?"

"We got the Town Car," Marvin says. "It's out front next to Billy's little bug."

Donna tops off the pitcher and carries it around the bar. "What are y'all going to do with a Lincoln Town Car?" she asks. "Ride around like the Mafia?"

"We're going to travel," Shem says.

"Like where?" asks the curly blonde. "Maybe Janine and me'll go with you."

"Miami. Maybe the Bahamas. Where do you girls want to go?"

"How're you going to drive to the Bahamas?" Janine asks.

"We'll buy a boat."

"Did you boys win the lottery or something?" the blonde asks.

"If it was the lottery," Pope says, "Billy wouldn't have a problem with that."

Donna pours two glasses of Sam Adams and sets them in front of me.

The Ruperts slouch down with the women, one on either side, and Marvin swivels his stool toward Billy. "Your wife still taking the bus to town?" he asks. "She still ride with the colored maids and gardeners?"

There's silence. Pope stops dealing the cards. Purvis looks over at me. I should step in, but instead I watch Billy as he turns slowly toward Marvin. Then he jumps up, and the cards and cribbage board go flying. Chairs clatter. He rushes Marvin like a mad dog. Purvis intercepts him, but only succeeds in throwing him off-target. Billy careens into the two women, who fly sideways and backward onto the floor with Billy on top of them.

Shem and Marvin laugh as Billy untangles himself and gets up swinging his fists.

It isn't a fight, really, just that one lunge. Donna comes around the bar with a baseball bat, and I get hold of Billy and wrestle him out onto the terrace. I'm twice as big and half his age.

Outside, Billy shakes himself free of my grip. "You can't solve anything by fighting," I say, "especially not at your age."

"What's my age got to do with it?" Billy glares at me, his eyes sharp blue, his grizzled jaw shaking.

"What'll Arlene say?"

"She isn't going to know."

"I could tell her."

"You won't," he says. "You haven't got it in you."

"If I helped the Ruperts, I might do almost anything."

"Bullshit," Billy says.

"Calm down now, Billy. Just calm down."

Purvis comes to the door as if to ask what we're going to do. Billy turns away toward the marina. He doesn't want to go in and see the Ruperts again.

"Why don't we go out in the boat," I say. "Let's go see the fish camp."

The johnboat is a sixteen-foot, snub-nosed piece of tin with dents and scrapes. Billy steps down and, without holding on, maneuvers over the fishing gear and the two coolers in the center — one with bait in it, one with beer we bought at Gruber's. He sits in the stern, and I push off and hop in with the bow line. It's my father's old boat, but I don't have the time to use it, so Billy does.

One pull on the Evinrude, and we're under way. He steers around the moored sailboats toward the harbormaster's office where Purvis is waiting with his hand in his pocket.

Purvis stopped talking at fourteen, when his father left for the Piedmont. He dropped out of school and worked on shrimp trawlers until he was thirty, when he caught his hand in a winch. He still lived with his mother then. A year later she died, and I helped him convert the crab shed in back of her house into an apartment so he could rent the main house and have an income.

Purvis squints into the sun, holds his good hand up to shade his eyes. His expression asks a question, *yes or no,* or maybe just says, *please.* Billy angles the boat in to the dock.

Purvis moves the fishing rods and sits on the bait cooler. Billy gives gas, and in a few minutes we're out of the marina and heading up the inland waterway. Purvis twists two Pabsts from the six-pack in the cooler and passes one each to Billy and me. We drink beer and ride the choppy water, moving north.

The steel drawbridge where Billy works comes closer. It's down, and the evening traffic from Charleston hums across to the island. To one side of the center is a pillbox lookout where the operator sits, and Billy pulls an imaginary horn as a joke for the operator to open the span for us. Billy waves, and the silhouette of the operator waves back.

We slide underneath, and traffic rumbles in the sky above us. Then we're past, and the sound fades. The paling blue sky opens out again. No one says anything — Purvis because he won't, and I because I don't know what to say. Billy is a mystery.

For a half mile we beat against the outgoing tide, and then Billy veers the johnboat off the waterway into a side creek. Behind the pale green reeds, a new world takes hold — quieter, slower, as if we've gone back in time. Billy eases off on the gas, and the tin boat glides over the glassy backwater, past mudflats and oysterbanks exposed by the ebb. A mudhen croaks, and a breeze we can't hear for the motor moves across the reeds. Around another bend, a white egret rises like an apparition from a tidal pool and throbs on rounded wingbeats low over the marsh.

"You think they were lying in wait?" Billy asks.

I know what Billy's talking about — that boy who was killed.

"Whoever it was probably didn't know a car was there."

"They shot at the car for no reason."

"Nobody knows that."

"White people live out there, too," Billy says. "Why would they shoot a kid?"

He cuts the engine farther, and we crawl up the winnowing creek. The headland in front of us is a scalloped dark green canopy of live oaks muted by the humid air, both close and far away in the evening light — a half mile, maybe, but longer by way of the serpentine curves. We pass a sailboat sunk in 1989 by Hurricane Hugo, and around another bend a night-heron on the bank watches us ease by.

Purvis looks at Billy. *How far?*

"All the way up," Billy says.

Nearer the headland, the main channel splits into smaller rivulets. Billy squirms the boat across pluff mud into one last pool, then cuts the gas and tilts the Evinrude out of the water. We coast into the mud bank.

Billy finishes his beer and opens another, and we sit for a moment in the quiet. The wind is discernible now, keeping the gnats down, rattling the grass. Hermit crabs bubble and pop along the bank. Rails squawk farther away in the marsh.

"Is it low tide?" I ask.

"Fifteen, maybe twenty minutes," Billy says.

Purvis looks at Billy again.

"You're right," Billy says. "We could have picked a better time."

Purvis gets out in rubber boots and draws the boat higher onto the flat, then wades through the pluff mud toward the trees. The sky broadens with the low sun tinting the clouds orange. Billy looks as if he's expended his last bit of energy getting here, and now he can't move.

He seems to draw inward to memory, and though I can't go with him, I'm pretty close. Maybe Billy's thinking of how he camped here with his father every weekend and brought along my father, who was Billy's age, and how later they brought Edgar and me. We fished from the dock, gigged flounder, and caught sheepshead and drum in the snags on the beach on the other side of the island. The remains of the old dock are still visible — parallel rotten posts two abreast in the reeds.

Billy's father had got the land in 1926, before the island had a bridge to it, in exchange for hauling a bargeload of polo ponies to Palm Beach — sixty acres of shell mounds, palmettos, live oaks, and tick-infested underbrush. At the time, everyone laughed at Billy's father, but now they don't. The Ruperts just sold their abutting thirty-five acres for 2.8 million dollars.

"You want to walk up to the Indian mound?" I ask finally.

"I like the view from here," Billy says.

"Me too." I get two more beers from the cooler and hand one to him.

"Besides, we only got one pair of boots."

I open my beer and sip.

"You know what I'd buy?" Billy asks.

"Is that what you're thinking about?"

"Mixing bowls."

"Mixing bowls?"

"Arlene wants mixing bowls. And a new bed. For forty years we've slept on a damned old mattress that sags in the middle."

The sun lowers, and the orange in the clouds shades to pink. A warbler sings in the closest live oak, then forages in the Spanish moss that drifts in the breeze. Another egret flies over.

Billy throws his empty beer can into the bottom of the boat and cracks open the new one. "You wear the boots," he says, and steps out into the mud in his tennis shoes.

Purvis is back in the trees somewhere, invisible as usual. Billy slogs away toward the headland, *slop slop slop*. I take off my wingtips, pull on the rubber boots, and get out of the boat.

Each step in pluff mud is a pull and a grunt. Ahead of me, Billy pauses and picks a burr from his jeans. Toward high ground the mud isn't so deep, and walking's easier. I know it's there, but still it's a surprise — the mound of oyster shells, ten feet high, where we always pitched the tent.

The Indians used the site the same way we did, as a fish camp, and over hundreds of years built that mound of shells. I say I haven't been to this place for a long time, but that's not true. I haven't forgotten. My father and I sat here the last time we were alone together, and I still hear his voice. He was telling me I should take care of people and not want more than my share, and I hear my own voice saying, "What do you mean you're going to die soon?"

"And you have to take care of Billy," he says. "Arlene takes care of him at home, but that's not the same."

"You aren't going to die," I say.

But in two months he was dead. When I came back to Charleston, I tried to take care of Billy as much as Edie allowed, as much as Billy let me. Early on, before I got so busy at work, we took the johnboat to the jetty for bluefish or into the creeks for sea trout. We cast for shrimp in the shallows behind Mount Pleasant and put down crab pots off the dock at Purvis's. Sometimes, with Pope Gailliard, we towed the boat to John's Island, where Pope had friends.

Edie understood our excursions had a meaning she didn't appreciate, and for a while she accepted my being gone. But after Carla and Blair were born, I couldn't go out with Billy as often. And my law practice assumed a bigger portion of my time, too. I was absent as many hours as before, but with a more permissible reason.

Billy kicks mud from his tennis shoes and walks the last few yards to the tideline. Once we're on higher ground and look back, the Intracoastal Waterway reappears beyond the marsh. Car headlights move through dusklight on the causeway; two TV towers blink red against the darkening sky.

Purvis emerges from the brush a little way down, and I give him a sign. We have arranged this moment without conspiring — getting Billy where he is now, by himself near the live oak. He drinks his beer, sets the can gently on the ground, and looks around at us, as if to make sure we're still there. Then he steps forward under the canopy of the oak and kneels at the grave of his son.

On the way back I take the tiller — no problem with shallows with the tide coming in. In the waterway, the flashing markers guide me — red, right, returning. All the way, Billy drinks beer in the bow.

At the boat landing, I back the truck and trailer down, and Purvis, standing knee-deep in the water, hooks the cable onto the boat. I winch the boat up while Billy watches.

"The one thing I like about you, Scotty, is your truck," Billy says.

"I'm glad there's something."

We leave the boat on the trailer in the lot and drive around to the lounge to get Billy's car. The Town Car is gone, and there are more pickups. Donna's making drinks for a younger crowd. I don't see her women friends.

Purvis opens the door of the cab. "You better drive the VW," I say.

"I can drive," Billy says, but he hands Purvis his car keys and slides over to the open window on the passenger side.

Billy's house is a yellow bungalow just off Coleman Boulevard in Mount Pleasant. Moss grows on one side of the roof. The lights are on inside, and I pull onto the lawn while Purvis drives the beetle into the carport. The street light throws out a purplish glow over the house and the empty lot next door.

We get the coolers from the back of the pickup, and while Billy puts the bait shrimp into the freezer, I hose the coolers out and turn them over on the lawn.

"We could at least have come home with some fish," Billy says.

Arlene hears the commotion and opens the side door. "There you are," she says.

She's a small, plumpish woman with short hair. Barefoot. Her flowered dress is unbuttoned at the top, and in the carport bug light, her gray hair looks yellow-blue. I can't tell whether Arlene's relieved or angry seeing Billy.

He closes the freezer and gazes at her. He's a sight — jeans caked with mud, hair sticking straight up from his head. He breaks into a grin and dances over to her singing, "Five foot two, eyes of blue, has anybody seen my gal?" He takes her hands, pulls her off the step and into his arms, and twirls her across the cement. "Could she love? Could she coo? Could she, could she, could she coo? Has anybody seen my gal?"

Arlene dances a few steps, then shakes him away. "You stop that," she says.

Billy drops his arms and staggers a little.

"It's my fault," I tell her. "We bought some beer and took the boat out."

"I got in a fight," Billy says.

His words are a prideful variation on the truth. He and Arlene gaze at each other for a moment, and then she climbs back onto the step in front of the door. "It's been a long day," she says. "I'm tired." She glances at me. "Should I call Edie and tell her you're on your way?"

"That's all right."

Arlene opens the door.

"They weren't shooting at him," Billy says. "It was a stray bullet."

Arlene pauses, holding the door open, and looks at me again. "What's he talking about?"

I shake my head, shrug.

"How would you like some mixing bowls?" Billy asks. He dances out of the carport, sidesteps the truck, weaves across the grass. Halfway to the street, he loses a tennis shoe and his wet muddy sock dangles from the end of his foot. He pirouettes under the street lamp, still singing.

*

When I get home Carla and Blair are asleep. The house is dark. Edie's in bed, too, though she must have heard the truck pull in. I mount the steps to the deck, but instead of going in I walk around to the ocean. The beach is pale in the half moonlight; the waves, visible as oblique white lines, rush against the sand. Beyond them, barely distinguishable from the sky, is the endless dark water.

I think of the boy riding in the back seat behind his mother and father. He's drawing on a tablet, and suddenly there's an explosion. He feels what? Pain? A numbness? Blood spurts from his leg. Maybe he screams, or cries. Maybe he faints. He loses blood fast. The parents look around into the back seat . . .

"Scott?" Edie comes out through the sliding door in a white nightgown.

"Right here."

She crosses the deck to the railing several feet from me. The breeze lifts her nightgown around her bare legs. "Where were you?"

"With Purvis and Billy. We went up-island in the boat."

"Fishing?"

"No, we didn't fish."

She stares straight out at the sea. "Where were you, really?"

"I've got pluff mud all over me. You can call Arlene, if you want."

"I didn't mean that."

Then she says nothing for a long minute. The half-moon drifts behind clouds miles out over the ocean.

"How are the children?" I ask.

"Fine. Carla went to soccer after school. Blair still wants a bicycle to ride in the dunes."

"He can't ride in the dunes."

"I know, but try to tell him that."

"I'm sorry I was late."

Again there's silence for too long.

Finally she turns toward me. "Come to bed, Scott. It's cold out here."

For several days after that, I prepare for a trial up in Myrtle Beach — depositions, interviews with witnesses, case research. Is a woman liable for a man's illness allegedly caused by her breaking their engagement? Evenings on my way home I drive by Billy's house, then across the causeway and under the drawbridge, past the marina lounge. Billy's car isn't at any of those places.

One evening late I stop by Purvis's. It's dark, but his door is open to the warm breeze. A small television on the counter flicks colors into the air. I say hello through the screen and knock after.

Purvis opens wide the screen door. Inside, there's the smell of tomato and onion and garlic in the air. He's cooking spaghetti and heating up sauce from a can. On the kitchen table is a foot-high stack of library books.

Purvis turns off the television and motions toward the pot of spaghetti on the stove.

"Edie's expecting me," I tell him. "I was wondering how Billy is. Have you seen him?"

Purvis shakes his head and stirs the sauce. He doesn't know any more about Billy than I do. But the moment is more complicated than that. We're used to not speaking, but there's an awkwardness, as if we share a loss we refuse to recognize. He knows I'll go home to my family and have crabcakes and salad, review the children's day at school, maybe quiz them on arithmetic. Carla likes science and math, and Blair collects bird bones on the beach. And I know Purvis will read. I scan the titles of his library books — Hardy Boys mysteries, *Daniel Boone, Boy Frontiersman,* two of the Harry Potter series Carla reads. I envy his time, and he envies mine.

The next day, after a deposition, I stop in at Huguley's on King Street where Arlene works. She's in greeting cards, wall prints, and Southern cookbooks, and when I come in, she's helping a customer pick out a picture of a plantation house with azaleas along the driveway. Edie's birthday is two months off, but I sort through cards and messages.

When the other customer leaves, I bring a card to the cash register. "You look nice," I say. "That dress is pretty."

She's wearing a brown smock with a gold-plated pin on her lapel. "Thank you." She takes the card and scans the bar code. "Is it Edie's birthday again already?"

"How's Billy doing?" I ask.

"He's all right. He's been working nights so I'm asleep when he comes home, and he's asleep when I leave."

"I haven't seen his car."

"Two dollars and eleven cents," she says.

She puts the card in a brown bag, and I give her a five. "He could call me," I say.

"Scotty, he's going through something. I don't know what, but we have to let him. I learned that a long time ago."

"I just want him to know —"

"He knows," she says, and hands me my change.

That afternoon my trial's postponed at the plaintiff's request, so I stop at the marina lounge on my way home. Pope and Purvis are on the terrace watching a fifty-foot powerboat being wedged into a berth. The captain guns the engine and the boat creeps forward; then he revs it in reverse, then forward again. Diesel smoke pours into the air.

Donna comes out with a draft. "They just arrested somebody in the shooting of that boy," she says. "It's on the news."

"Who was it?" Pope asks.

"The last person you'd ever imagine," Donna says. "A twelve-year-old white girl."

We all go inside and stand behind the barstools and look up at the television. A reporter is speaking into a microphone in front of the courthouse downtown. "It's not clear at this time whether the suspect knew the rifle was loaded," she says. "The girl's parents were not home at the time of the shooting."

Details are sketchy. The girl came home from school and found her father's deer rifle and took it into the woods. The girl's quoted as saying she "wanted to see whether it would shoot." There's nothing about intent — whether she loaded the rifle or aimed it at anything, whether she shot at the car deliberately, whether she meant to shoot anyone.

"Jesus H. Christ," Donna says. "What the hell was she thinking?"

On the screen is a replay of the girl's arrival at the courthouse — a police car drives up, an officer gets out, someone holds a coat up in front of the girl's face. The girl has shorts on, and her skinny legs are visible under the coat.

"How did they catch her?" Pope asks.

"They were questioning people," Donna says. "Even your friends only protect you for so long."

The television switches to the area where the shooting occurred — a deserted rural road, paved, with a ditch along it and, just a few feet back, brush and pines. Then it shows the car — a late-model blue compact parked in a police lot — and a close-up of the bullet hole in the rear door.

"Weird shit," Donna says.

"What'll they do to her?" Pope asks.

"They ought to fry her," Donna says. "And her parents, too."

"We don't know the facts," I say.

They all look at me.

"You know, where she was standing in relation to the car, what she could see. Did she know how far a bullet would travel? Did she even see the car? We don't know what really happened."

"A kid's dead," Donna says. "We know that."

Edgar Prioleau was eleven when he died. I was nine. We were at the fish camp on a Sunday. My father was making lunch, and Billy was taking Edgar and me to the beach to cast in the surf. I was carrying a rod and an empty pail, Edgar two rods, and Billy the bait cooler. It was warm and sunny. I don't remember what we saw on the trail or what we said. Edgar walked ahead of me; Billy came behind, because the cooler was heavy. Everything was familiar — the palmettos, the vines, the overhanging live oaks dappled in sunlight. The only thing unusual was how the trail ended at the beach. I mean, it always ended there, but that day I noticed how dark the woods were and how bright the light was on the beach. I noticed the light because Edgar had on a red shirt, and when he ran out of the trees and up the dune, his shirt looked like a kite in the air.

I followed him up the dune, struggling for footing in the sand. Billy shouted, "Wait up, now," but Edgar was already at the top, and he ran down the other side. I heard the wind in the sea oats and the sea behind the dunes, and then at the crest I saw the sea itself. I skittered part of the way down the steep sand and stopped, out of breath. Edgar had already put down the fishing rods and was racing toward the horizon.

That's how I remember him — a boy caught against the whole ocean. He leaped into the froth of the waves and waded out into the sunlight. By the time Billy reached the top of the dunes behind me, Edgar had disappeared.

The next Monday around eleven, Billy shows up in my office wearing a blue suit. He's shaved, and his hair is plastered down with something unspeakable. "I have a meeting with Latimer," he says.

"Is that the only suit you have?"

"What's wrong with it?" He brushes the lapel, the shoulder.

"It's not ironed. It's probably mildewed. What's the meeting about?"

"Did you know the Ruperts bought a sailboat?"

"I heard about it."

Billy examines my law degree hanging on the wall and, beside it, my admission to the bar. "Latimer has a permit to dredge for a new marina," Billy says. "The Army Corps of Engineers caved in. Now he wants to build a second golf course."

"What's he going to do with two?"

"You can't have enough golf courses." Billy steps around the ladder and along the floor-to-ceiling shelves of books and gazes out the window at Broad Street. "If you were me, would you sell?"

"It isn't my property."

"If I gave it to you?"

"I can't answer hypothetical questions. Where are you meeting Latimer?"

"The Mills House."

"You want me to come along?"

Billy gives me a sidelong glance. "Do you know what it's like to ride the bus to town every day?" he asks. "Sometimes I meet Arlene at the bus stop because she can barely walk from being on her feet all day." He pauses. "If I sell, Arlene can quit her job."

"You two can ride around together in a Town Car."

"Don't be smart with me."

"Don't wallow in self-pity."

He looks at me and nods. "You can come with me if you want."

But as we're walking out of the office, a call comes in from a distraught client, so Billy goes ahead. When I get to the restaurant, he and Latimer are hunkered down like golfing buddies, drinking martinis. I make my way toward them through tables elegantly covered with white linen and set with silver and crystal. Next to Billy, Latimer looks like an altar boy — ruddy cheeks, short hair, wet shiny eyes — though I know from representing the Ruperts that he's a sweet-talker who believes God is money. He's dressed in a gray suit and gray tie, and he wears gold cuff links and a tie pin. He's surprised to see me, though I don't know whether Billy intended not to tell him I was coming or simply forgot.

"Scotty!" He stands and shakes hands.

"Hello, Kevin." I sit down without being asked.

"Billy, do you know Scott Atherton?"

"Scotty's my lawyer," Billy says.

Latimer rolls with this. "Have a martini," he says to me.

A waiter in black tie arrives from nowhere with a menu for me and another martini, which he sets on the white tablecloth in front of Billy. "The soup of the day is New England clam chowder," he tells me. "Entrée specials are grilled salmon with lobster sauce, and pork medallions served with shiitake mushrooms and a browned garlic. Would you care for a cocktail?"

"No, thank you."

Latimer raises his glass to Billy. "Here's to mutual success," he says. He drinks, then turns to me. "I was just telling Billy the Ruperts might have sold early. The lots on the interior of the island are going faster than we'd anticipated, so we're discussing accelerated acquisition."

"You mean if they'd waited, they'd have got more?"

"Who knows? In any event, Billy's land has become more valuable."

The ghost waiter appears and takes our orders — salmon for Billy and Latimer, a seafood salad for me.

"And another martini," Billy says.

During the meal, Latimer argues his case. His company, Coastal Amenities, owns every parcel — except Billy's sixty acres — from the beach to the marsh. Plans for development have already been approved. The company has donated five acres for a new grade school to encourage age-group diversity. "Our marina goes in first," he says, "so yachtsmen can access the restaurant and country club."

"Billy can take his johnboat to the club for lunch."

"And play golf," Latimer says.

Billy sips his martini and sets down the glass. "If I sell," he says, "I want three times as much money as the Ruperts."

After lunch I leave Billy and Latimer in the lobby of the hotel. Billy wants to see the development plans — where the houses will be, the golf course, the swimming pool — and promises not to make any decision without consulting me.

I walk back to my office down Broad Street, crossing over into the shadow of St. Michael's, whose white steeple shines above the gray and pastel storefronts. A gust of wind blows a newspaper along. The unfolding scenario goes through my mind — not the one between Latimer and Billy, but the whole future of the island. As trees are felled, roads cut, and houses built, the middle of the woodland becomes the edge. Trees once protected by other trees are made vulnerable to storms. The air changes. Birds requiring space and cover — sparrows, thrushes, warblers — give way to more adaptable grackles, mockingbirds, and starlings.

And even if Billy doesn't sell, his land will abut a dozen houses. At the oyster mound, he'll hear car doors slamming, golf balls teed off, domestic quarrels. At night, car headlights and street lamps will shine into palmettos and pines and oaks that have never known another light besides the moon and stars.

I tell my secretary "no calls," and for the rest of the afternoon, because I can't concentrate, I bill hours at half rate. All I can think of is Latimer's arrogant assumption that Billy is a fool.

Around three, Sylvia looks in. "You said no calls, but it's your wife. She says it's an emergency."

I click a button and say hello.

"Billy's here," she says.

"What for?"

"He wanted to see the view from our deck."

"He had three martinis at lunch. Is he okay?"

"I think so. I gave him a Coke, and he's been telling me about his sex life."

"I hope you haven't been telling him about ours."

"What's to tell? Anyway, he hasn't asked. Did you know he and Arlene are almost seventy, and they still make love three times a week?"

"Did he say whether he's going to sell the fish camp?"

"Are you listening to me, Scotty?"

"I'm listening."

"He says, 'You look beautiful, Arlene,' and she says, 'I think you'd better get to work.'"

"We need signals?" I ask.

"We need more than signals. Time goes by, Scotty. People change. What was good before is not necessarily what's good now."

"I'm coming home," I say. "I'm leaving right now."

I pack my briefcase and put on my suit jacket. On my way out, Sylvia asks whether I've finished the reply brief for the Ruisdale case. "I can take it by the courthouse when I leave," she says.

"Oh shit, I forgot."

"I assumed that's why you didn't want to be disturbed," Sylvia says.

I retreat to my office, taking an hour to write the conclusion, and when I get the brief to Sylvia it's after four.

"Arlene Prioleau called," Sylvia says. "I told her you went home."

"Did she say what she wanted?"

"No, but she sounded upset."

"Call Huguley's. See if she's still at work."

Sylvia dials, gets the manager, and hands me the phone.

"That woman," the manager says, "she walked out the door as if we weren't here. We're a service company. She knows better than that."

"Maybe she won the lottery," I say, and hang up.

I drive north in traffic over the Cooper River Bridge. Behind a truck at the apex of the second span, a flock of white ibis flies in a V close above the girders, the birds' down-curved red bills and the black tips of their white wings illuminated from beneath by the sun. The sudden beauty of their precise flight and their ignorance of themselves heighten my unease, as if the random moment of their passage mocks our tangled human relationships. I don't believe in omens, but I'm sure Arlene's leaving work early has to do with Billy.

In Mount Pleasant, I make the familiar right on Magnolia Street. Billy's car isn't at the bungalow. The shades are drawn on the windows, but I stop anyway and knock on the door. No one answers, so I circle the house. A couple of plastic chairs with rainwater on the seats face each other on the back patio. In the yard, blossoms of azaleas and roses wither, though Arlene's recently weeded vegetable garden flourishes against the back fence.

I peek in the kitchen window. Inside there's evidence of turmoil — a chair turned over, cabinets open, a skillet and two pots on the floor, along with boxes of cereal, lettuce, tin cans. A purse I assume is Arlene's sits on the table.

The knob turns in my hand, and I push the door open.

"Arlene?"

The purse contains glasses, a hairbrush, a bus pass, but no wallet.

I step over the debris and into the dimly lit living room. Cushions from the sofa and cut-up newspapers are strewn around, along with a pair of tennis shoes and Billy's jeans.

"Billy?" I pause. "Arlene?"

I edge to the bedroom, afraid of what I'll find, but it's empty, neat, the bedspread tucked over the sagging mattress. The only unusual item is a newspaper clipping, which I pick up off the bed and hold up to the window light: a child's primitive drawing of a beach with the wide blue sea and the sun going down into the waves. The caption says,

> Brett's Vision. Edisto Beach State Park where the Herzberger family camped the night before Brett was shot.

The colors are blue, yellow, tan. The sun has no reflection on the water, and a single bird is drawn in brown at the tideline. There's no erratic line indicating an interruption in the movement of his hand, no splotches of blood on the picture. Are these the boy's last thoughts? Maybe he looked up an instant before he was shot and saw the dark woodland, or maybe he thought of a friend in Illinois. Maybe he remembered a harsh word his mother said to him ten miles earlier or wondered how to draw other birds at the shoreline. Who can know?

I backtrack to the kitchen, pick up the phone, and call Edie.

Carla answers. "Hi, Daddy. I thought you were coming home early."

"Is your mother there?"

"What's wrong?" Carla asks.

"Just get your mother."

Edie comes on. "What's going on, Scott? Where are you?"

"Is Billy still there?"

"No, he —"

"Did he say where he was going?"

"To work, I think."

"Tell Carla I'm sorry I was short with her. I'll see you later. We'll talk."

I take McCants to the causeway. At the intersection, a line of cars waits to merge with the commuter surge going toward the beach, but no one's moving. Horns honk. A few cars squeeze through the traffic and turn left. On the main road, people crane from their car windows for a view ahead, but no cars are coming the other way from the island because the bridge is open.

I wheel around the dozen cars in front of me, inch through the congestion at the intersection, and instead of turning left toward the city, I turn right into the empty oncoming lane. A mile ahead the highway's tilted into the air, and in front of the raised span police lights swirl across the tops of the waiting cars.

On either side of the causeway is salt marsh. A few cars turn around and come toward me, and I scrape the oleanders on the berm to get by, still paralleling the stopped cars on my right. Then, up ahead, I see Arlene behind two unmoving dump trucks. She strides along the pedestrian path with her arms pumping. She has on a print dress and a straw hat with a wide brim, and sturdy black shoes. She disappears behind a dump truck and reappears behind a Mercedes. I slow down, lean across the cab seat, and roll down the passenger window: "Arlene!"

She turns, sees me, and veers through the line of cars over to my truck. I snap open the door for her, and she gets in. "He's up in the pillbox," she says. "He won't close the bridge, and he won't come down."

"How do you know?"

"His supervisor phoned me at work. I called you, but your secretary said you'd gone home."

Then I notice the boats. On either side of the bridge dozens of masts stick up in the air — the bridge is open enough to block the cars, but not enough to let boats through.

Arlene says, "Did you see the boy's drawing in the paper?"

"Just now at your house. He sure tore up the place."

A policeman on foot ducks among the cars ahead of us, talking to the drivers. As we approach, he holds up his hand, and I stop.

He comes up to Arlene's window and squats down. "You can't go up there," he says, looking up. "What do you think you're doing?"

"I'm Billy's wife," Arlene says.

"Billy who?"

"The man in the lookout," she says, "Billy Prioleau."

The policeman looks at me.

"Scott Atherton. I'm his lawyer."

"We think the guy has a rifle," the officer says.

"Billy doesn't own a rifle," Arlene says.

"It's not hard to get one," the officer says. "That's what he told the newspaper, and we believe him. I was just alerting people to that fact."

"It's not fact," I say. "It's supposition."

"Can we talk to him?" Arlene asks.

The officer gets on his walkie-talkie. "I've got the man's wife here," he says, "and his lawyer."

Two navy helicopters roar in over the marsh, and the noise startles egrets and herons from the reeds.

"The sergeant says to come ahead," the officer says. "If I were you, I'd keep down."

The closer we get, the fewer the cars coming the other way. We pass more dump trucks and several suburban assault vehicles stopped in line. The raised roadway tilts up and away, a sloping stretch of ungainly metal against the blue sky. The sailboats are clearer, too — sloops, yawls, ketches, a trimaran — anchored in the waterway. The helicopters hover above the pillbox.

Billy's Volkswagen is parked in the turnout at the foot of the bridge, along with the police cars and television vans. Four cruisers have their red lights whirling, and several marksmen crouch behind the fenders with high-powered rifles. I pull up beside the nearest car, where the sergeant is leaning against a rear tire. Up in the pillbox, the venetian blinds are pulled down against the sun. Billy isn't visible, even as a shadow.

Arlene gets out and stands in the breeze, holding the brim of her hat. "What's this about a rifle?" she asks. She has to shout above the noise of the helicopters.

"Stay down," the sergeant shouts back.

"I'm his wife," Arlene says.

"He's just as likely to shoot you as anyone else," the officer says. "Maybe more likely."

"Has he said what he wants?" I ask.

"You have to stay down," the sergeant says.

Arlene takes off her hat and throws it into the truck cab, skirts the highway barricade, and heads toward the metal catwalk at the side of the bridge.

"Ma'am?" the officer calls. "Ma'am, stop. Please."

A helicopter drops to the window level of the pillbox, a man poised with a rifle in the passenger seat.

Arlene doesn't stop, and I go after her. I follow her along the grating of the catwalk.

"If he's going to get himself shot," she says, "I want to say good-bye."

"He's not going to get shot."

"That boy did," she says.

The waterway beneath us is choppy, and the breeze rocks the moored sailboats. Swallows dart around the bridge girders. To the north, past the sailboats, the waterway recedes in a wide blue triangle that narrows and evens out in the distance. The border of the waterway is marsh grass, and farther away on the headland, billowing trees.

At the end of the catwalk a metal ladder leads up to an anteroom beneath the pillbox. Arlene holds a rung in her hand and steps up. "Billy?" she calls up. "Billy Prioleau, you listen to me!"

The helicopters are so noisy, Billy can't possibly hear a word.

"You go up there, Scotty," she says.

She issues this instruction as if there's no danger. It's what she would do if she could.

"What should I say?"

"Just talk to him. What do you say when you're fishing?"

I look up at the pillbox. "They should back off on the helicopters. Let him have some breathing room."

"I'll tell them."

"Do you think he has a rifle?"

Arlene takes my two hands in hers and squeezes. "He loves you, Scotty. You bring him down."

She turns and walks back along the catwalk.

The helicopters hover, but I climb the ladder to the windless anteroom.

The noise is still loud, though muffled, and I wait to see whether the helicopters move off. Beside the trapdoor is a keypad, but they're just numbers to me. Finally I shout up, "Billy, it's me, Scotty. Are you in there?"

A few seconds go by. Outside the reinforced storm windows, the sailboats loll on their anchors, hatches open, crews hidden below-decks. Another sloop, unknowing, motors toward the bridge with its sails furled. The captain in the cockpit holds in one hand what I imagine is a gin and tonic.

"Billy?"

He's already dead is what I think. He opened the bridge and then keeled over from a heart attack. The police in their siege mentality have invented the scenario of a lunatic holed up with a rifle.

"Come on, Billy, open up. It's me."

Finally the roar of the helicopters diminishes, and an occasional car horn sounds in the distance.

I hear scraping above me. "Who?" Billy says.

"Let's talk about Edgar."

There's another long pause.

I take a risk to say this, but it makes sense. I've drawn the same connections Billy has, though of course not in the same way. He cut out the boy's drawing from the newspaper; he wanted to see the view from the deck of my house. I imagine what Billy saw that day when he was taking Edgar and me fishing — he climbed the dunes and saw the ocean and the beach spread out before him, but he didn't see Edgar. He saw me.

The trapdoor hums open slowly, and the inside of the pillbox appears — space rather than detail — and then a wedge of Billy's forehead, his blue eyes, gray hair. From so little, I can't tell whether he's drunk or angry or deranged.

"I'm alone," I tell him. "Arlene —"

The door opens wider, and I climb into the pillbox.

The room is spartan, surprisingly cool. Except for the venetian blinds on the west side, the windows are open, and a breeze flows through. There's a control panel for the bridge hydraulics, a chair, a table with binoculars on it. Billy's splayed out on the floor with a six-pack of Pabst — one left — and he's holding a rifle.

"It's a pellet gun," he says. "I want them to think I'm serious."

I slide down next to him and take the last beer. "Serious about what?"

"You know as well as I do."

His eyes hold mine. He's not deranged, but he's had three martinis and most of a six-pack.

I kneel and crane my neck to look out over the sill. Light's fading from the blue triangle of the waterway. The motor sailer is closer. To the east, beyond the island, the blue sea spreads wide and flat to the horizon. To the south, where the helicopters have retreated, the city skyline patterns the horizon in jagged shapes. Gulls fly leisurely above the houses on the island.

I pick up the binoculars and focus on a tern hovering over a tide pool, then swing the glasses to the marina lounge. "There's Purvis," I say. "And Donna and Pope and some other people watching us from the terrace."

"They haven't seen anything yet," Billy says.

I scan the cars and trucks backed up along the causeway and in both directions on Center Street. The dump trucks on the island are empty. I follow the marsh up-island to the live oak tree, but from such a distance I can't see the oyster mound.

"Did Latimer show you what he's planning to do?"

"He's started filling in the ponds," Billy says. "That's what gave me the idea. All these dump trucks are Latimer's."

I lower the binoculars. "So you stopped him by opening the bridge?"

"And one of the boats down there belongs to the Ruperts."

"Which one?"

"I can't remember," Billy says. "How many are there now?"

"Dozens. And a Coast Guard cutter is bringing in reinforcements."

I focus the glasses on the cutter entering the waterway from the harbor. The sun whitens the sky above the trees, and clouds drift across the blue. The air is humid; a sunset threatens.

"We need more beer," Billy says, shaking his empty can. He pulls the phone toward him and dials a number. "We'll get room service."

"Maybe we should eat something."

"Donna, it's me, Billy. Listen, Scotty and I need a case of beer. Yeah, we're up on the bridge. Sam Adams is good. A case. And a half-dozen corn dogs. What else have you got there? Some beef jerky and onion chips — put it on Scotty's tab." He listens a moment. "Purvis can deliver it, but he'll have to take a boat to get across the waterway." Another pause. "Now, yes, right now. We're thirsty."

He hangs up and hands me the phone. "You're my lawyer," he says. "Tell the police to let Purvis up here."

The number for the newspaper is written on a pad in Billy's scrawled hand, and I punch it in, figuring that if Billy called once they'll have someone ready. Sure enough, they switch me to their mobile unit right away. "It's Scott Atherton. I'm with Billy Prioleau in the pillbox. I need to talk to the police."

I stand up, hold back the venetian blinds, and see a man get out of a media van and run across to one of the police cruisers. In another few seconds, the sergeant comes on the line.

"It's Billy's lawyer," I say. "Billy wants the dump trucks off the causeway."

"He wants what?"

"He doesn't like the dump trucks. And we've ordered some food from the lounge over at the marina. A friend of ours, Purvis Neal, will be bringing it from the island. And Billy wants to talk to his wife."

"No, I don't."

"She's right here," the sergeant says.

I hand the phone to Billy.

"Hello, Arlene," he says.

I'm close enough to hear Arlene's voice. "Are you all right?" she asks. "What are you and Scotty doing up there?"

"Not much so far."

"I want you to come home."

"I can't right now," he says. "Maybe in a while."

"You have to get to work, Billy."

"I will," he says. "You're beautiful."

She says something else I can't hear, and then he hands the phone to me.

The sergeant is back on the line. "Are you making any progress?" he asks.

"Billy hasn't offered to surrender his weapon yet," I say, "but we're talking."

"We want to defuse the situation," he says. "We want this traffic to get moving again."

"Start with the dump trucks," I tell him. "And the food. Let me have your cell phone number so I can be in touch when we have other demands."

He gives me the number.

"Don't do anything rash," I say. I lay the receiver in the cradle.

In a few minutes the dump trucks start to turn around on the causeway. On the island, they disappear behind the Episcopal church on Center Street. It takes twenty minutes, and just about when the last truck disappears, Purvis comes out of the marina in a skiff. He maneuvers through the maze of anchored sailboats in the waterway and crosses to the bridge pilings. A police officer helps him offload the case of beer and the food.

"You still think it was an accident about that boy?" Billy asks.

"I don't know."

"What's an accident?" Billy says next. "When you think about it, everything's an accident. Life is an accident."

"You mean Edgar's drowning."

"Up here I watch the seasons change, the years go by," he says. "I watch the tides flow in and out of the creeks . . ."

"Is that what you think about?"

"It's not thinking," Billy says. "It's feeling."

We hear a noise below, and Billy opens the trapdoor slightly. It's Purvis in the anteroom, and Billy opens the door wider. The beer's still on the catwalk, but Purvis has looped a rope around it and tied the rope to his belt. He tosses up the food with his good hand, and I pull him up after into the pillbox. Then I hoist up the beer.

Billy passes me a Sam Adams and takes one for himself. "Help yourself, Purvis," he says.

Purvis isn't a drinker, but he takes one and sits down crosslegged beside Billy. Billy doles out corn dogs.

I pull up the venetian blinds. The helicopters are poised off the end of the island, cars and boats in limbo wanting to get somewhere, the Coast Guard cutter at anchor near the marina. The sun's in the trees now, and rays of pink shoot out into the clouds. Sky colors — all we can see — brighten everything around us.

I join Billy and Purvis on the floor. For a while we don't say anything. Billy and I finish our beers and open two more. Purvis munches on his corn dog.

The beer loosens me up, and I like the new ground it takes me to. Billy will want immunity from prosecution, or at least a reduced charge if he agrees to counseling. He'll need assurance the highway department won't fire him. A transfer, maybe — they can't be expected to let him back up here. These items are negotiable, but the other demands won't be so easily met — to stop the dredging and filling, to end the cutting of trees and the building of roads, to purify the air, cleanse the water, keep the rich from getting richer. We want Edgar's grave undisturbed.

The pink clouds fade to gray, and the pillbox darkens. I rock forward and look out again. The causeway is silent, nearly deserted now, except for the police and the media. Across the harbor, Charleston glimmers in the dusk. The horizon still burns, though the marsh is dark and the creeks and tide pools are silver-gray, tinged with red.

"They still there?" Billy asks.

"They aren't going away," I say. "I guess I should call Edie to let her know where I am."

"She knows where you are," Billy says. "You're with me and Purvis."

Billy opens another beer and passes it over. He chews a piece of beef jerky. "You know the oyster mound?" Billy says. "Guess what Latimer says that's going to be." He waits a moment. "The fifth tee."

Billy laughs. Purvis grins and drinks his beer. Then we're quiet again. The sun makes a last burst from the trees, dances into the clouds — its deep orange and red lighting up the pillbox, even as the darkness comes down over us.

JOYCE CAROL OATES

The Girl with the Blackened Eye

FROM *Witness*

THIS BLACK EYE I had, once! Like a clown's eye painted on. Both
my eyes were bruised and ugly but the right eye was swollen almost
shut, people must've seen me and I wonder what they were thinking, I mean you have to wonder. Nobody said a word — didn't want
to get involved, I guess. You have to wonder what went through
their minds, though.

Sometimes now I see myself in a mirror, like in the middle of
the night getting up to use the bathroom, I see a blurred face, a
woman's face I don't recognize. And I see that eye. Twenty-seven
years. In America, that's a lifetime.

This weird thing that happened to me, fifteen years old and a sophomore at Menlo Park High, living with my family in Menlo Park,
California, where Dad was a dental surgeon (which was lucky: I'd
need dental and gum surgery, to repair the damage to my mouth).
Weird, and wild. Ugly. I've never told anyone who knows me now.
Especially my daughters. My husband doesn't know, he couldn't
have handled it. We were in our late twenties when we met, no
need to drag up the past. I never do. I'm not one of those. I left
California forever when I went to college in Vermont. My family
moved, too. They live in Seattle now. There's a stiffness between us,
we never talk about that time. Never say that man's name. So it's
like it never did happen.

Or, if it did, it happened to someone else. A high school girl in
the 1970s. A silly little girl who wore tank tops and jeans so tight
she had to lie down on her bed to wriggle into them, and teased
her hair into a mane. That girl.

When they found me, my hair was wild and tangled like broom sage. It couldn't be combed through, had to be cut from my head in clumps. Something sticky like cobwebs was in it. I'd been wearing it long since ninth grade and after that I kept it cut short for years. Like a guy's hair, the back of my neck shaved and my ears showing.

I'd been forcibly abducted at the age of fifteen. It was something that could happen to you, from the outside, *forcibly abducted*, like being in a plane crash, or struck by lightning. There wouldn't be any human agent, almost. The human agent wouldn't have a name. I'd been walking through the mall parking lot to the bus stop, about 5:30 P.M., a weekday, I'd come to the mall after school with some kids, now I was headed home, and somehow it happened, don't ask me how, a guy was asking me questions, or saying something, mainly I registered he was an adult my dad's age possibly, every adult man looked like my dad's age except obviously old white-haired men. I hadn't any clear impression of this guy except afterward I would recall rings on his fingers which would've caused me to glance up at his face with interest except at that instant something slammed into the back of my head behind my ear, knocking me forward, and down, like he'd thrown a hook at me from in front, I was on my face on the sun-heated vinyl upholstery of a car, or a van, and another blow or blows knocked me out. Like anesthesia, it was. You're out.

This was the *forcible abduction*. How it might be described by a witness who was there, who was also the victim. But who hadn't any memory of what happened because it happened so fast, and she hadn't been personally involved.

It's like they say. You are there, and not-there. He drove to this place in the Sonoma Mountains, I would afterward learn, this cabin it would be called, and he raped me, beat me, and shocked me with electrical cords and he stubbed cigarette butts on my stomach and breasts, and he said things to me like he knew me, he knew all my secrets, what a dirty-minded girl I was, what a nasty girl, and selfish, like everyone of my *privileged class* as he called it. I'm saying these things were done to me but in fact they were done to my body mostly. Like the cabin was in the Sonoma Mountains north of Healdsburg but it was just anywhere for those eight days, and I was anywhere, I was holding onto being alive the way you would hold onto a straw you could breathe through, lying at the bottom of deep water. And that water opaque, you can't see through to the surface.

He was gone, and he came back. He left me tied in the bed, it was a cot with a thin mattress, very dirty. There were only two windows in the cabin and there were blinds over them drawn tight. It was hot during what I guessed was the day. It was cool, and it was very quiet, at night. The lower parts of me were raw and throbbing with pain and other parts of me were in a haze of pain so I wasn't able to think, and I wasn't awake most of the time, not what you'd call actual wakefulness, with a personality.

What you call your personality, you know? — it's not the actual bones, or teeth, something solid. It's more like a flame. A flame can be upright, and a flame can flicker in the wind, a flame can be extinguished so there's no sign of it, like it had never been.

My eyes had been hurt, he'd mashed his fists into my eyes. The eyelids were puffy, I couldn't see very well. It was like I didn't try to see, I was saving my eyesight for when I was stronger. I had not seen the man's face actually. I had felt him but I had not seen him, I could not have identified him. Any more than you could identify yourself if you had never seen yourself in a mirror or in any likeness.

In one of my dreams I was saying to my family I would not be seeing them for a while, I was going away. *I'm going away, I want to say goodbye.* Their faces were blurred. My sister, I was closer to than my parents, she's two years older than me and I adored her, my sister was crying, her face was blurred with tears. She asked where was I going and I said I didn't know, but I wanted to say goodbye, and I wanted to say *I love you.* And this was so vivid it would seem to me to have happened actually, and was more real than other things that happened to me during that time I would learn afterward was eight days.

It might've been the same day repeated, or it might've been eighty days. It was a place, not a day. Like a dimension you could slip into, or be sucked into, by an undertow. And it's there, but no one is aware of it. Until you're in it, you don't know; but when you're in it, it's all that you know. So you have no way of speaking of it except like this. Stammering, and ignorant.

Why he brought me water and food, why he decided to let me live, would never be clear. The others he'd killed after a few days. They went stale on him, you have to suppose. One of the bodies was buried in the woods a few hundred yards behind the cabin, others were dumped along Route 101 as far north as Crescent City. And possibly there were others never known, never located or identified. These facts, if they are facts, I would learn later, as I would learn that the other girls and women had been older than me, the oldest was thirty, and the youngest he'd been on record as killing was eighteen. So it was speculated he had mercy on me because he hadn't realized, abducting me in the parking lot, that I was so young, and in my battered condition in the cabin, when I'd started losing weight, I must've looked to him like a child. I was crying a lot, and calling *Mommy! Mom-my!*

Like my own kids, grown, would call *Mom-my!* in some nightmare they were trapped in. But I never think of such things.

The man with the rings on his fingers, saying, There's some reason I don't know yet, that you have been spared.

Later I would look back and think, there was a turn, a shifting of fortune, when he first allowed me to wash. To wash! He could see I was ashamed, I was a naturally shy, clean girl. He allowed this. He might have assisted me, a little. He picked ticks out of my skin where they were invisible and gorged with blood. He hated ticks! They disgusted him. He went away, and came back with food and Hires Diet Root Beer. We ate together sitting on the edge of the cot. And once when he allowed me out into the clearing at dusk. Like a picnic. His greasy fingers, and mine. Fried chicken, french fries and runny cole slaw, my hands started shaking and my mouth was on fire. And my stomach convulsing with hunger, cramps that doubled me over like he'd sunk a knife into my guts and twisted. Still, I was able to eat some things, in little bites. I did not starve. Seeing the color come back into my face, he was impressed, stirred. He said, in mild reproach, Hey, a butterfly could eat more'n you.

I would remember these pale-yellow butterflies around the cabin. A swarm of them. And jays screaming, waiting to swoop down to snatch up food.

I guess I was pretty sick. Delirious. My gums were infected. Four of my teeth were broken. Blood kept leaking to the back of my mouth, making me sick, gagging. But I could walk to the car leaning against him, I was able to sit up normally in the passenger's seat, buckled in, he always made sure to buckle me in, and a wire wound tight around my ankles. Driving then out of the forest, and the foothills I could not have identified as the Sonoma hills, and the sun high and gauzy in the sky, and I lost track of time, lapsing in and out of time but noticing that highway traffic was changing to suburban, more traffic lights, we were cruising through parking lots so vast you couldn't see to the edge of them, sun-blinded spaces and rows of glittering cars like grave markers: I saw them suddenly in a cemetery that went on forever.

He wanted me with him all the time now, he said. Keep an eye on you, girl. Maybe I was his trophy? The only female trophy in his abducting/raping/killing spree of an estimated seventeen months to be publicly displayed. Not beaten, strangled, raped to death, kicked to death and buried like animal carrion. (This I would learn later.) Or maybe I was meant to signal to the world, if the world glanced through the windshield of his car, his daughter. A sign of — what? *Hey, I'm normal. I'm a nice guy, see.*

Except the daughter's hair was wild and matted, her eyes were bruised and one of them swollen almost shut. Her mouth was a slack puffy wound. Bruises on her face and throat and arms and her ribs were cracked, skinny body was covered in pus-leaking burns and sores. Yet he'd allowed me to wash, and he'd allowed me to wash out my clothes, I was less filthy now. He'd given me a T-shirt too big for me, already soiled but I was grateful for it. Through acres of parking lots we cruised like sharks seeking prey. I was aware of people glancing into the car, just by accident, seeing me, or maybe not seeing me, there were reflections in the windshield (weren't there?) because of the sun, so maybe they didn't see me, or didn't see me clearly. Yet others, seeing me, looked away. It did not occur to me at the time that there must be a search for me, my face in the papers, on TV. My face as it had been. At the time I'd stopped thinking of that other world. Mostly I'd stopped thinking. It was like anesthesia, you give in to it, there's peace in it, almost. As cruising the parking lots with the man whistling to himself, humming, talking in a low affable monotone, I understood that he wasn't thinking either, as a predator fish would not be thinking cruising beneath the surface of the ocean. The silent gliding of sharks, that never cease their motion. I was concerned mostly with sitting right: my head balanced on my neck, which isn't easy to do, and the wire wound tight around my ankles cutting off circulation. I knew of gangrene, I knew of toes and entire feet going black with rot. From my father I knew of tooth-rot, gum-rot. I was trying not to think of those strangers who must've seen me, sure they saw me, and turned away, uncertain what they'd seen but knowing it was trouble, not wanting to know more.

Just a girl with a blackened eye, you figure she maybe deserved it.

He said: There must be some reason you are spared.

He said, in my daddy's voice from a long time ago, Know what, girl? — you're not like the others. That's why.

They would say he was insane, these were the acts of an insane person. And I would not disagree. Though I knew it was not so.

The red-haired woman in the khaki jacket and matching pants. Eventually she would have a name but it was not a name I would wish to know, none of them were. This was a woman, not a girl. He'd put me in the back seat of his car now, so the passenger's seat was empty. He'd buckled me safely in. OK, girl? You be good, now. We cruised the giant parking lot at dusk. When the lights first come on. (Where was this? Ukiah. Where I'd never been. Except for the red-haired woman I would have no memory of Ukiah.)

He'd removed his rings. He was wearing a white baseball cap.

There came this red-haired woman beside him smiling, talking like they were friends. I stared, I was astonished. They were coming toward the car. Never could I imagine what those two were talking about! I thought *He will trade me for her* and I was frightened. The man in the baseball cap wearing shiny dark glasses asking the red-haired woman — what? Directions? Yet he had the power to make her smile, there was a sexual ease between them. She was a mature woman with a shapely body, breasts I could envy and hips in the tight-fitting khaki pants that were stylish pants, with a drawstring waist. I felt a rush of anger for this woman, contempt, disgust, how stupid she was, unsuspecting, bending to peer at me where possibly she'd been told the man's daughter was sitting, maybe he'd said his daughter had a question for her? needed an adult female's advice? and in an instant she would find herself shoved forward onto the front seat of the car, down on her face, her chest, helpless, as fast as you might snap your fingers, too fast for her to cry out. So fast, you understand it had happened many times before. The girl in the back seat blinking and staring and unable to speak though she wasn't gagged, no more able to scream for help than the woman struggling for her life a few inches away. She shuddered in sympathy, she moaned as the man pounded the woman with his fists. Furious, grunting! His eyes bulged. Were there no witnesses? No one to see? Deftly he wrapped a blanket around the woman, who'd gone limp, wrapping it tight around her head and chest, he shoved her legs inside the car and shut the door and climbed into the driver's seat and drove away humming, happy. In the back seat the girl was crying. If she'd had tears she would have cried.

Weird how your mind works: I was thinking I was that woman, in the front seat wrapped in the blanket, so the rest of it had not yet happened.

It was that time, I think, I saw my mom. In the parking lot. There were shoppers, mostly women. And my mom was one of them. I knew it couldn't be her, so far from home, I knew I was hundreds of miles from home, so it couldn't be, but I saw her, Mom crossing in front of the car, walking briskly to the entrance of Lord & Taylor.

Yet I couldn't wave to her, my arm was heavy as lead.

Yes. In the cabin I was made to witness what he did to the red-haired woman. I saw now that this was my importance to him: I would be a witness to his fury, his indignation, his disgust. Tying the woman's wrists to the iron rails of the bed, spreading her legs and tying her ankles. Naked, the red-haired woman had no power. There was no sexual ease to her now, no confidence. You would not envy her now. You would scorn her now. You would not wish to be her now. She'd become a chicken on a spit.

I had to watch, I could not close my eyes or look away.

For it had happened already, it was completed. There was certitude in this, and peace in certitude. When there is no escape, for what is happening has already happened. Not once but many times.

When you give up struggle, there's a kind of love.

The red-haired woman did not know this, in her terror. But I was the witness, I knew.

They would ask me about him. I saw only parts of him. Like jigsaw puzzle parts. Like quick camera jumps and cuts. His back was pale and flaccid at the waist, more muscular at the shoulders. It was a broad pimply sweating back. It was a part of a man, like my dad, I would not see. Not in this way. Not straining, tensing. And the smell of a man's hair, like congealed oil. His hair was stiff, dark, threaded with silver hairs like wires, at the crown of his head you could see the scalp beneath. On his torso and legs hairs grew in dense waves and rivulets like water or grasses. He was grunting, he was making a high-pitched moaning sound. When he turned, I saw a fierce blurred face, I didn't recognize that face. And the nipples of a man's breasts, wine-colored like berries. Between his thighs the angry thing swung like a length of rubber, slick and darkened with blood.

I would recall, yes, he had tattoos. Smudged-looking like ink blots. Never did I see them clearly. Never did I see him clearly. I would not have dared as you would not look into the sun in terror of being blinded.

He kept us there together for three days. I mean, the red-haired woman was there for three days, unconscious most of the time. There was a mercy in this. You learn to take note of small mercies and be grateful for them. Nor would he kill her in the cabin. When he was finished with her, disgusted with her, he half-carried her out to the car. I was alone, and frightened. But then he returned and said, OK, girl, goin for a ride. I was able to walk, just barely. I was very dizzy. I would ride in the back seat of the car like a big rag doll, boneless and unresisting.

He'd shoved the woman down beside him, hidden by a blanket wrapped around her head and upper body. She was not struggling now, her body was limp and unresisting for she too had weakened in the cabin, she'd lost weight. You learned to be weak to please him for you did not want to displease him in even the smallest things. Yet the woman managed to speak, this small choked begging voice. Don't kill me, please. I won't tell anybody. I won't tell anybody don't kill me. I have a little daughter, please don't kill me. Please, God. Please.

I wasn't sure if this voice was (somehow) a made-up voice. A voice of my imagination. Or like on TV. Or my own voice, if I'd been older and had a daughter. *Please don't kill me. Please, God.*

For always it's this voice when you're alone and silent you hear it.

Afterward they would speculate that he'd panicked. Seeing TV spot announcements, the photographs of his "victims." When last seen and where, Menlo Park, Uriah. There were witnesses' descriptions of *the abductor* and a police sketch of his face, coarser and uglier and older than his face which was now disguised by dark glasses. In the drawing he was clean-shaven but now his jaws were covered in several days' beard, a stubbly beard, his hair was tied in a ponytail and the baseball cap pulled low on his head. Yet you could recognize him in the drawing, that looked as if it had been executed by a blind man. So he'd panicked.

The first car he'd been driving he left at the cabin, he was driving another, a stolen car with switched license plates. You came to see that his life was such maneuvers. He was tireless in invention as a willful child and would seem to have had no purpose beyond such maneuvers and when afterward I would learn details of his background, his family life in San Jose, his early incarcerations as a juvenile, as a youth, as an adult "offender" now on parole from Bakersfield maximum security prison, I would block off such information as not related to me, not related to the man who'd existed exclusively for me as, for a brief while, I'd existed exclusively for him. I was contemptuous of "facts" for I came to know that no accumulation of facts constitutes knowledge, and no impersonal knowledge constitutes the intimacy of knowing.

Know what, girl? You're not like the others. You're special. That's the reason.

Driving fast, farther into the foothills. The road was ever narrower and bumpier. There were few vehicles on the road, all of them minivans or campers. He never spoke to the red-haired woman moaning and whimpering beside him but to me in the back seat, looking at me in the rearview mirror, the way my dad used to do when I rode in the back seat, and Mom was up front with him. He said, How ya doin, girl? OK. Doin OK, huh?

Yes.

I'm gonna let you go, girl, you know that, huh? Gonna give you your freedom.

To this I could not reply. My swollen lips moved in a kind of smile as you smile out of politeness.

Less you want to trade? With her?

Again I could not reply. I wasn't certain what the question was. My smile ached in my face but it was a sincere smile.

He parked the car on an unpaved lane off the road. He waited, no vehicles approaching. There were no aircraft overhead. It was very quiet except for birds. He said, C'mon, help me, girl. So I moved my legs that were stiff, my legs that felt strange and skinny to me, I climbed out of the car and fought off dizziness helping him with the bound woman, he'd pulled the blanket off her, her discolored swollen face, her face that wasn't attractive now, scabby mouth and panicked eyes, brown eyes they were, I would remember those eyes pleading. For they were my own, but in one who was doomed as I was not. He said then, so strangely: Stay here, girl. Watch the car. Somebody shows up, honk the horn. Two-three times. Got it?

I whispered yes. I was staring at the crumbly earth.

I could not look at the woman now. I would not watch them move away into the woods.

Maybe it was a test, he'd left the key in the ignition. It was to make me think I could drive the car away from there, I could drive to get help, or I could run out onto the road and get help. Maybe I could get help. He had a gun, and he had knives, but I could have driven away. But the sun was beating on my head, I couldn't move. My legs were heavy like lead. My eye was swollen shut and throbbing. I believed it was a test but I wasn't certain. Afterward they would ask if I'd had any chance to escape in those days he kept me captive and always I said no, no I did not have a chance to escape. Because that was so. That was how it was to me, that I could not explain.

Yet I remember the keys in the ignition, and I remember that the road was close by. He would strangle the woman, that was his way of killing and this I seemed to know. It would require some minutes. It was not an easy way of killing. I could run, I could run along the road and hope that someone would come along, or I could hide, and he wouldn't find me in all that wilderness, if he called me I would not answer. But I stood there beside the car because I could not do these things. He trusted me, and I could not betray that trust. Even if he would kill me, I could not betray him.

Yes, I heard her screams in the woods. I think I heard. It might have been jays. It might have been my own screams I heard. But I heard them.

A few days later he would be dead. He would be shot down by police in a motel parking lot in Petaluma. Why he was there, in that place, about fifty miles from the cabin, I don't know. He'd left me in the cabin chained to the bed. It was filthy, flies and ants. The chain was long enough for me to use the toilet. But the toilet was backed up. Blinds were drawn on the windows. I did not dare to take them down or break the window panes but I looked out, I saw just the clearing, a haze of green. Overhead there were small planes sometimes. A helicopter. I wanted to think that somebody would rescue me but I knew better, I knew nobody would find me.

But they did find me.

He told them where the cabin was, when he was dying. He did that for me. He drew a rough map and I have that map! — not the actual piece of paper but a copy. He would never see me again, and I would have trouble recalling his face for I never truly saw it.

Photographs of him were not accurate. Even his name, printed out, is misleading. For it could be anyone's name and not *his*.

In my present life I never speak of these things. I have never told anyone. There would be no point to it. Why I've told you, I don't know: you might write about me but you would respect my privacy.

Because if you wrote about me, these things that happened to me so long ago, no one would know it was me. And you would disguise it so that no one could guess, that's why I trust you.

My life afterward is what's unreal. The life then, those eight days, was very real. The two don't seem to be connected, do they? I learned you don't discover the evidence of any cause in its result. Philosophers debate over that but if you know, you know. There is no connection though people wish to think so. When I was recovered I went back to Menlo Park High and I graduated with my class and I went to college in Vermont, I met my husband in New York a few years later and married him and had my babies and none of my life would be different in any way, I believe, if I had not been "abducted" when I was fifteen.

Sure, I see him sometimes. More often lately. On the street, in a passing car. In profile, I see him. In his shiny dark glasses and white baseball cap. A man's forearm, a thick pelt of hair on it, a tattoo, I see him. The shock of it is, he's only thirty-two.

That's so young now. Your life all before you, almost.

T. JEFFERSON PARKER

Easy Street

FROM *Easy Street*

I

IN THE SUMMER of that year, Clay Canfield accepted a transfer from the Bureau's Atlanta office to Orange County, California. He'd been working bank robberies, and he was good. He was thirty-two years old, dark haired, presentable, and had always lived his life on the square.

He left Atlanta with minor regrets: his small part in the arrest of the Olympic bomber suspect who turned out to be innocent, and his season tickets for the Braves at home.

On the plus side it was a convenient way to break off with the woman he was seeing. Marie. And there was southern California, where he'd grown up. His parents had long ago moved away but his little brother Sonny was still there. When Clay thought of Sonny he pictured him surfing big crunchers at Rockpile in Laguna Beach. It would be good to see Sonny again. That town, too.

Clay read the in-flight magazine out of Atlanta, ate the neat little lunch, looked down at the Texas desert. He thought about the years he'd spent in Atlanta, told himself it would be nice to miss something or someone. But he didn't. Ditto Washington, Miami, and Dallas.

Sonny met him at the airport. He'd put a little weight on but it looked like muscle. Blond hair buzzed short for summer, beer on his breath. Flip-flops and a Hawaiian shirt with palm trees on it, worn out to hide his hip rig. Sonny was an officer with the Laguna Beach PD, had a new girlfriend last Clay had heard.

Sonny snapped one of Clay's suspenders, straightened his neck-tie, and grinned. "Fed-Man."

"That's me."

"You look good."

"So do you."

Sonny took Clay by the arm and angled him into the terminal bar.

"Meet Laurel," he said.

Laurel had blue eyes and freckles and smelled like suntan oil. Yellow dress, good legs. A small smile, straight dark hair, sunglasses propped up on her head. Sonny's type, all the way.

"Sonny left me here to guard his drink," she said. Her handshake was firm and dry. "So I drank it."

"Can't keep her out of anything," said Sonny.

"Cuff me."

"I'll get us another one," said Clay.

They sat on stools at a high table in the back of the bar. They each had two. Sonny told him how Orange County had grown in the ten years Clay had been gone: more roads, more houses, more people, and more on the way.

"And one pretty bold bank robber," said Clay.

"He's hit eight banks in eight weeks, all in north county," said Sonny. "Small takes, nobody hurt yet. The Bike Bandit."

Laurel said, "Polite, soft-spoken. Long golden hair and a big gun. Just gets on his motorcycle and speeds away. I hope you don't shoot him."

"Laurel's romantic," said Sonny.

"He's dashing," she said. "Like Joaquin Murrietta or Robin Hood. Extremely handsome."

"He's still got his helmet on in all the pictures," said Sonny. "Visor down. All they have to go on is his hair sticking out the back."

"I can tell."

"We can get his height with photogrammetry," said Clay.

"He loses himself quick on the motorcycle," said Sonny.

"He completely vanishes," said Laurel. "The tellers watch him speed away, but after that nobody sees him. That's dashing."

"Maybe he's got help," said Clay.

"What kind of help?" asked Laurel.

"Some woman who thinks armed robbery is romantic."

"Fed-Man just called me some woman, Sonny."

"You are some woman."

Laurel smiled at Clay then, a big smile this time, and her eyes laughed as she raised the plastic cocktail cup to her lips, tilting the liquid back into her mouth, middle finger extended.

Clay sat in the FBI conference room with his new partner in bank robbery and the agent-in-charge of the Orange County field office.

Salena Mendez was the partner. He'd met her once at Quantico, a few years back. Then, she'd been bright and compact and a little distracted. She still was. She showed him pictures of her children, then slipped them back into her wallet like he was going to make off with them. She tapped the tabletop with stout fingers, questioning Clay about Atlanta in a tone that confirmed how little she cared about his answers.

The agent-in-charge of the Orange County field office, Bob Tuvale, was slender and slow-moving, either subtle or colorless or both. He looked soft.

Close to retirement, Clay figured.

Tuvale ran down the county bank robbery stats for the year-to-date. There had been thirteen in all, eight attributable to the so-called Bike Bandit. Tuvale had printed out a run comparing the annual numbers going back ten years, warning Clay that if you adjusted this year's rate to account for the active holiday season to come, bank robberies would be up a whopping 20 percent.

More robberies, of course, he said: more people, more banks, more bank robbers.

"But the Bike Bandit is single-handedly ruining our curve," he said. "Violent crime down to a two-decade low nationwide, and this guy's making it look like the James gang is back in Orange County."

"Once a week for eight weeks," said Mendez. "He can't keep up that pace and not get himself caught."

Tuvale nodded, unconvinced. "We don't have a single eyewitness except for the bank employees and customers present at the time of the jobs," he said. "He drives that motorcycle out of the immediate area and gets lost in the traffic."

"He completely vanishes," said Mendez.

Clay listened for some of the tone of pride that Laurel had had when speaking those identical words the afternoon before. But he didn't hear pride. He heard exasperation.

Tuvale huffed up from the table, turned off the lights, and stead-

ied the beam of an overhead projector onto the blank wall in front
of them.

Clay listened to the fan. A Thomas Guide map of the county
sharpened into focus. Tuvale had marked the Bike Bandit's scores
with angry red Xs. The light from the projector caught Tuvale's
face from the bottom and made him look like a craggy old man.
Like a gravedigger bending over his lantern, thought Clay. Something he'd seen in a children's book a thousand years ago.

"Clay, we put all the local PDs and the sheriffs on a direct alert
status after the third job," said Tuvale. "So we're radioed along with
the first response. Now, you and Sal can't get to north county from
here in time to do any good. Too much distance. Too much traffic.
So it's probably going to be a local takedown. That's fine with us,
right?"

"I don't care who takes him down," said Clay, although he did.
You could swallow your pride for the record, for the press and the
public and local enforcement, but you couldn't swallow it with your
heart. Nobody did.

"I'd like to see the sites," he said.

"I've already done that," said Mendez. "Freeway close, busy locations so the cash is there, less windows the better."

Clay thought about this and wondered why some people, even
Bureau people, were content doing a mediocre job.

"I'd still like to see them. And I'd like to have the photogrammetry done back in Washington. Any good stills from the surveillance videos?"

Mendez's eyes flashed anger. "The stills suck. The bank videos
are either old, broken, or turned off."

Clay enjoyed other people's anger, because it drew off his own
and opened a big cold space inside. Marie had said the same about
love.

"May I see the bad ones, then? Goodin in Image Enhancement
can work with almost anything."

He did all eight sites that day. The north county traffic was bad
but it wasn't anything like Miami or Washington. Californians still
don't know how good they have it, he thought.

After viewing the heist sites he found that the Bike Bandit was
choosing wisely. Salena Mendez had culled the obvious: quick freeway access, busy branches, few windows.

But there was more: they were hit late morning or early afternoon when the customers were thin but the cash drawers were full.
He wasn't waiting around for safe money — just the cash drawers
then out of there. Average time from initial demand to exit: fifty-
eight seconds.

They were small, freestanding buildings on the borders of residential neighborhoods, thus easier to control and lacking armed
security.

They were far away from local PD headquarters or Sheriff's sub-
stations.

They were all built with the parking areas to the side or back, offering the Bike Bandit anonymity until he was inside the building,
and again until he had sped away.

They were all at least fifteen years old, increasing the chances of
out-of-date or out-of-repair surveillance cameras.

And in every one the Bike Bandit had chosen a young woman
teller, rather than an older one, or a male, both statistically more
likely to offer resistance or the dye-pack bag, even though instructed by the robber not to.

Of course by the third heist, every teller in every bank was hitting
the hot button the second the golden-haired, helmeted bandit
strode into the branch.

Until the third heist, only two bank customers had even been
aware that an armed robbery was going on right beside them.

On the fifth and seventh jobs he'd been offered dye-pack bags,
but he knew one when he saw one and declined both deals. He'd
told teller number five that the only ink he needed was already in
his pen.

A man with a sense of humor.

Clay wondered about the exclusively north county locations. Was
he working his own neighborhood, taking advantage of home turf?
Or was he working from out-of-area, keeping his own litter box
clean?

Clay guessed the latter because, for an armed robber, the Bike
Bandit was careful. He was smart enough to hide his face. To obscure. To evade. Out-of-area, Clay thought.

Driving back toward Sonny's place that evening he passed the
soot-stained Disneyland Matterhorn on I-5, wondered if Mr. Toad's
Wild Ride was still there. His favorite as a kid. Sonny, age eight,
had slithered past his restraint bar, hopped out of the car, and run

amok through the hallucinogenic ultraviolet landscape for twenty minutes, until security dragged him struggling from the exit. The brothers got lectured, got their parents called down to fetch them. As a ten-year-old, Clay had been responsible for Sonny as well as himself, and he received the bulk of his father's wrath. On the long drive home, Clay told his mother and father he'd like to be security someday, help people in trouble, and he actually half meant it. The other half was BS to get himself off the hook. Sonny had skipped the BS, as always, and told them next time he'd like to jump ship inside the Pirates ride, help out looting the port.

He went back to the field office, chose a still photograph of the Bike Bandit and got it ready for Image Enhancement in Washington. They weren't as bad as Mendez had made it sound, though the focus was too fuzzy for anything but photogrammetry. You weren't going to read an arm tattoo from any of these, or a prison gang number, or get the name of a school off a ring.

He'd just need to stop by the robbed branch the next day and measure some of the key contents of the photograph: the height of the teller counter, the distance of the clock in the background from the floor, the distance from the camera to the clock, etc.

Goodin would draw the lines and make the extrapolations to tell them — within half an inch or so — how tall the Bike Bandit was.

Sonny and Laurel put up Clay in the garage apartment of their Laguna Canyon house until he found a place to live. The house was a semineglected rental, but Sonny seemed happy with it. It wasn't easy for a Laguna Beach cop to live in Laguna because the town was so expensive. Sonny told Clay he liked the idea that Tim Leary's Brotherhood had distributed LSD from a house just up the street. It gave the place character.

The apartment was small and drafty at night, but Clay had a view of the tree-shaded neighborhood, a couch that made into a bed, a bathroom, and a refrigerator. A pepper tree gave it shade. One of the windows was stained glass — a hummingbird dipping its beak into a hibiscus flower — which gave the room a muted glow when the sun was right.

On his first night there a huge raccoon looked through the window, stared at him, then lumbered away. Clay's take-home Bureau Ford was covered with pink pepper hulls that first morning, but

Sonny had his van in the little one-car garage. Clay liked the way the hulls blew off when he accelerated up Laguna Canyon Road, like he was driving through a pale pink storm.

Sonny worked night patrol, so he'd be gone before Clay got home. Laurel taught at a private elementary school so she'd be there when Clay was.

Second night, she made drinks and they sat in wooden patio chairs in the little front yard, in the shade of the pepper tree, watching the tourist cars creeping into town for the annual art festivals.

"You could find a place in Laguna," she said. "It's a good place to live."

"I got the paper to check the rentals. Awful high."

"It's two grand a month for this dump."

"I like it."

"It's small."

"Could you get something better?"

"For twice the money. Things are tight. I don't make much. Sonny's place on Canyon Acres burned flat in the big fire of 'ninety-three. Way underinsured. He got a lump sum that would just about cover a new foundation and that was all. Split the lump with his ex."

"He said it was a lot of money."

"Not enough to rebuild a home in Laguna Beach. So he blew a lot of it, betting. The fire was bad, but the divorce was worse. He's got a big heart, your brother. But his steering wheel goes out sometimes. That's all over now. He quit. But we're still digging out. There's a shopping bag full of bills in there that barely get paid. Some of the credit cards it's been months. We'll get there. It's under control."

Clay said nothing. There was no divorce. It wasn't his business what Sonny told his girlfriend, or what he didn't.

But Clay had no idea that Sonny was gambling. "What, college basketball, football?"

"Everything. All legal, Fed-Man. We'd fly out to Vegas every other weekend, he'd play the sports book at Caesar's. We'd drag our sorry asses home Sunday night, get up on Monday and start again. Fun. But it's over now."

Clay thought about this, said nothing. Sonny had called and written only sporadically. He'd made it sound like his divorce was the best thing that had ever happened to him. Like the insurance money was beyond his wildest dreams. Like life was just so damned good. Sonny had always obscured his troubles with bluff and optimism.

"It looks to me like he's got it good here," Clay said.

"Of course he does. He's got a live-in girl he doesn't have to marry, a job, and a bungalow in Laguna Beach."

She was wearing a pair of cutoffs and a sleeveless blouse. Blue eyes and freckles. As much as Clay wanted not to have noticed, he noticed she was without a bra. She still smelled like the suntan oil that made him think of California in the summer. It was some kind of perfume for all he knew.

"Why doesn't he have to marry you?"

"Won't marry."

"How do you know that?"

"You get a sense of things. I'm twenty-four."

"You want that?"

She looked at him, smiled, ran her fingers through her hair to get it away from her face.

"I grew up in a desert town so small it didn't make the maps. Filthy and hopeless. What I want is to never go back."

"Looks like you've got it pretty good here, too."

"I want the best I can get. For now, this is it."

She stood. "I'll make us dinner."

"I'm going to visit some of the old haunts tonight."

"Then I'll eat alone."

She walked back toward the house with her drink in her hand. Clay saw where the chair slats had left straight red bars across her thighs.

Clay walked into town in the twilight. The hills were tan and crisp against the darkening July sky and the houses sat on the ridgeline with specific bearing, sun turning their windows bronze.

Tour buses lined the road. The visitors poured out and swirled like liquid toward the festival entrances, the crosswalk, the sidewalk, the street.

Clay fell in with a big group and headed down Broadway. Past the playhouse he could smell the eucalyptus and the ocean and the canyon sage and the tourist perfumes and the car exhaust all mixed together and it was a smell he'd never found anywhere else in the world.

He crossed Coast Highway and walked up to Heisler Park to look down on the Rockpile break where he and Sonny had learned to surf. The roses in the park made red and white marks on the Pacific behind them. He looked down at the water and the rocks.

You went a long way, Fed-Man, he thought, and then you came back. Thank you, Bike Bandit.

He had a beer at the Marine Room, dinner at what used to be the old Ivy House, another drink at the Saloon.

Night had fallen soft and damp and Clay was standing at the corner of Coast Highway and Forest when the white and blue LBPD cruiser pulled to a stop and Sonny smiled at him from behind the wheel. The window was down.

"Get in, creep."

"Glad to."

Clay slid onto the rigid bench and slammed the door. Sonny punched the car into the traffic and headed north.

"You gotta get rid of those white shirts and suspenders."

"I know. My life's in storage. By the way, I'll get somewhere to stay the next day or two. I'm not going to flop in your apartment for the rest of my life."

"Stay a year if you want. Two. I'll charge you a third of the rent and make out good. See that old fart with the white hair right there? He's one of Leary's guys from the Brotherhood. Runs a leather shop now, you know, purses and sandals and belts and shit."

Sonny pulled the cruiser over and leaned across Clay to the window. "Hey you old drug addict! What colors you seeing right now?"

"Sonny! I'm clean as ever. Go bust somebody with a leaf blower, man!"

"Stay clean, you depraved old lizard. We still got room in jail for you."

"Praise the Lord!"

"You better, brother. You need Him."

Sonny pulled back, checked his rearview and chirped the car back into the traffic.

"We got a city ordinance against leaf blowers now."

"I gathered."

"You can blow your buddies in the Boom-Boom bungalows, but you can't blow leaves. Go figure. It's small-town stuff, Clay, but I love it. See that apartment up there, the one with the plants on the balcony?"

"The girl. I remember that."

"We finally got a conviction on the boyfriend. Fourteen years later, we finally got him. That's where he did her."

"I was a senior that year."

"I was a sophomore. Remember how pissed off you were when I quit the baseball team to surf?"

"My whole point was you could have done both."

"I didn't want to goddamn do both. I wanted to surf, brother. Look, that son of a bitch in the Lexus is drunk."

"Maybe he's just old."

"They ought to lower the driving age to sixty. You wouldn't believe these old Elmers coming out from Dayton to see art in California. Scarier than the Nightstalker, if you ask me. How do you work in suspenders, anyway?"

"Jesus, Sonny, they just hold my pants up."

Sonny cackled and gunned the car north toward Emerald Bay.

"No, really, I understand. You just operate on a higher level than me. You can be comfortable and stylish. Little gel in the hair. You don't have to be a city cop wearing a blue uniform that's half polyester all summer in the heat."

"Get cotton."

"Half poly doesn't wrinkle. You even carry anymore?"

"I work bank robberies, Brother. I carry."

"What?"

"A Smith nine."

"Pussy gun. I still use the .45 for maximum stopping power."

"Ever stopped anybody with it?"

"Hell no. I've never even drawn it. You know something? It's good to have you back. Did you miss this place?"

Clay thought about that. "I didn't think I did. But now that I'm back I'm not so sure."

"You never were very decisive. But you have a disadvantage."

"What's that?"

"You're a Libra. The scales. You can always see it one way, then see it another. So it takes you five years to decide something most people decide in a second."

"Astrology — you've been in California too long."

"Laurel make you something to eat?"

"She offered. But I wanted to come down here, maybe run into my little brother."

"What do you think of her?"

"Well, she's pretty. Bright. I think she loves you. You should marry her, make her happy."

Sonny laughed. "I don't know if I can afford her."

"Expensive tastes?"

"Not so much that, but yeah, on what I make. She's just hard to keep up with. She outdrinks me, outscrews me, outtalks me. Needs about four hours of sleep a night and I crawl out of bed after eight, still need a nap before the shift. You get a twenty-four-year-old woman who grew up poor, thinks she knows what she wants, better look out."

"Maybe she's just trying to make you happy."

"Well, whatever, Clay. What about you? What about this Georgia peach you left heartbroken in Atlanta?"

"I left her the Braves tickets, too."

"Why not bring her out here?"

"Clean break. Fresh start. I don't know."

"You don't know. Who does?"

"Don't start that again."

The Bike Bandit hit a Wells Fargo branch in Fullerton the next morning at 11:25.

Salena Mendez had taken the morning off, so Clay flew down the steps of the field office building, hustled to his car, and drove fast the whole way there, got there twenty-one minutes later. He was sweating hard even with the air on high, hadn't rolled on a live alarm in five weeks now. The closer he got the harder he scanned the streets around him for a sight of the golden-haired Bike Bandit snaking his way to an on-ramp.

The Bandit was gone. Fullerton PD was already on scene, six officers and a sergeant who accommodated Clay with feigned disinterest. Par for the course.

The bank employees were giddy and talked fast, relieved to be alive and to have been robbed of only impersonal money — par for the course, too. The Bandit was polite and soft-spoken. The Bandit was obscured by his helmet and visor. The bandit "seemed handsome and calm." The Bandit had refused the dye-pack again. The Bandit had taken down $11,450, a little better than his average.

Clay collected the videotape, glad to see the recorder was a new one, hoping he could get something more revealing than what they'd gotten so far.

He listened in on the police interviews, then did his own. He used a tape recorder and a notepad so nothing would get past him. The target teller told him that the Bandit's gun hand was shaking as he made his demand.

What were his exact words?

All your money real fast, hon. Don't touch the button, don't touch the dye. Quick! Quick! You gotta be quick!

Two hours later Clay stood in the bank parking lot. This one was behind the building, away from the entrance windows and foot traffic — like the others. An assistant branch manager had mustered enough foolish courage to follow the Bandit out of the building and watch him make his escape. She described the motorcycle as mostly black, some yellow maybe, with a high-pitched scream, "not very big." She showed Clay the parking space.

Clay looked for a departure skid: no. He looked north up Pinehurst, the direction the Bandit had gone, checked where the street met the lot for skids — it was often a good place because gutter water helped tires to chirp. No.

He walked up Pinehurst five blocks just looking at the innocuous street, which turned from light commercial to residential in less than a quarter mile. Apartments, condos, some single residences.

He knocked on doors. Talked to some kids. Found a seniors complex where there were always plenty of people home. Nobody had seen a motorcycle except for a young boy eager to help. He'd have told Clay he'd seen a spaceship if that's what Clay had asked. He wanted to hold Clay's badge — against Bureau procedure — but Clay let him anyway.

Only one person noticed something out of the ordinary. Older woman, sharp, clear eyes, floral print dress, and support hose thick as a sweater.

What she saw on her morning walk was a ResCom Cable van parked along the street, half a block from her unit. It was 11:15 when she noticed it and it made her think of the bad picture she was getting on QVC. At 11:35 she was back home and saw it leave.

"What's unusual about that?" Clay asked.

"The motorcycle driving into it's unusual," she snapped.

"Explain."

"Just did. They rode a motorcycle into the back of it, up some kind of ramp. Then the ResCom Cable van drove away. What's even more unusual, Mr. FBI, is that we're all on Comcast Cable here, no *reason* for no ResCom."

Clay smiled and said nothing for a moment. There it was: the break.

He spent another hour grilling the woman. Her name was Gladys Forbes.

She couldn't describe the motorcycle driver, didn't remember any long golden hair, couldn't remember if he — or she, Ms. Forbes warned him with a stern finger — had on a backpack or not.

Couldn't describe the motorcycle.

Couldn't describe the van other than white with the ResCom Cable sign on the side.

Couldn't figure out what ResCom Cable was doing in this part of the county anyway.

But she could show him exactly where it was parked. She led him there in her floral print dress, blinking in the hot sunshine. Clay examined the oil-stained asphalt for tire tracks. He checked the street from all four directions because the angle of the sun can obscure or expose the faint markings left by tires on hard surfaces.

Nothing.

"I swear it was there," said Gladys.

"I believe you," said Clay.

"No reason to be, but it was there."

"You've been a terrific help."

From the bank he called information for the ResCom number, figuring he'd start with their head of security. No such company in Fullerton, Irvine, Newport Beach, Tustin, Santa Ana.

No such company anywhere in Orange County, the directory operator told him.

None in L.A., San Bernardino, or San Diego counties either.

Clay confirmed by checking the bank's current collection of phone books: zip for ResCom.

Just a couple of cheap magnetic signs, he thought: check the local signmakers for the ResCom order.

He called Tuvale but had to talk to Salena instead. She seemed miffed that he'd been on the case for two days and made more progress than she'd made in eight weeks. She'd taken the morning off because her head was killing her. She told him she'd cover the sign makers, suggested he double-check the street because track indentations can be invisible when the light is wrong. Clay told her to check DMV for what they had on handicapped persons' vehicles equipped with ramps — not lifts — for getting wheelchairs in and out. He figured the Bank Bandit had probably rigged the thing himself, but the DMV was worth a try. Salena said she'd see what she could do.

Clay hung up and knocked on doors for two more hours, took more notes, learned nothing that seemed useful.

Then he drove to the bank that was hit last week and measured off the photographic elements for Image Enhancement. Next, to the post office in Irvine to make the overnight mail to D.C.

Oddly happy and a little giddy and for some reason thinking of Marie, Clay stopped by the Law Enforcement Firing Range in Anaheim and burned off some clips of wadcutters from his nine. One hundred and twenty rounds. Gray residue on his cuffs. Pussy gun or not, his right wrist was tender and both ears were ringing faintly and his nostrils were scented with gunsmoke on his drive back down to Laguna.

Always liked that smell.

2

Sonny had gotten up early that morning, just after he heard Clay's Ford crunch down the drive. While Laurel was in the shower he went into the bathroom to brush his teeth. He scrubbed the night's breath away, looking at her through the glass shower door. Her head was tilted back into the spray, arms raised, her pale underarms glistening almost white with the water. She moved her head level and peeked at him.

"Ambush?"

He nodded and smiled around the toothbrush.

"Oh, goodie."

He lay in bed and thought about her. She came out with a towel still wrapped around her head. He took that and her robe off and pulled the sheet over them against the canyon chill.

"You're up early this morning," she said, running her hand down him. "In more ways than one."

"Busy day."

"Don't hurry through the good things."

"Nope, nope."

He got on top of her and in. Skin on cool skin but inside heat on heat. A low voltage shook up through him and he felt the sheet on his gooseflesh. He pushed himself up and looked down. Her eyes were gray on gray mornings, blue on blue. Blue today. He could smell her soap and shampoo and see the furrows the big pink comb had left in her hair. She ran her fingers up and down the low of his back.

Sometimes when she looked at him her face was relaxed and her eyes clear and Sonny had no idea what she was thinking. He never asked because he believed that privacy was the nest for secrets and that secrets were the center of the soul.

But they had made a habit of carrying on conversations like this, and so they did:

"What's your day today, police guy?"

"Clean out the garage, drive the van around the block to keep the battery good . . . oh, *my* . . . things like that."

She laughed, trailed her nails down his skin. He pushed hard and she pushed back.

"Go to the bank, pick out that new holster. *Ummm.* You?"

"We got a field trip to that new kids' museum up in Santa Ana. They got a bed of nails they can lay on. Some laser stuff. Let me turn over."

She rolled over and got her knees under her. She gasped lightly when Sonny pushed in and set a rhythm.

"I'll get some groceries," he said. "We're low."

He reached forward and cupped her breasts, then kneaded her fanny with his hands. She groaned as he dug his thumbs into the big muscles. With her face sideways on the pillow he could see her in profile and she could look at him with one astonishingly clear blue eye. Like a playing card, he thought: queen of something.

Sonny leaped back and let his middle do the work. Arms out like wings, fingers spread like endfeathers.

The body electric.

"God*damn* that feels good."

She groaned in time with the sharp slap of their bodies.

"I love you," he said.

"Well sure you do *now.*"

"But when we're done I will too."

"Oh . . . oh . . . oh. Hey . . . when you get to Lucky's pick up some . . . oh . . . make sure you pick up some . . ."

"Eggs?"

"Got those. *Oh.*"

"Wine?"

"Got . . . oh . . . that."

"What?"

"Cash back. *Ohhh . . . yesss.* We need cash."

When she started shaking he spread his hands on her hips and pulled her in, let her out, pulled her in, let her out. He gently pushed her down and covered her with all his weight, all of it forward on that one thing. A riot of nerves in her then, a series of detonations big and small like fireworks and he wondered why his was a rhythm and hers more like chaos.

Her quivers had just started to slow when his stomach felt like he'd stepped over a cliff.

Then the long sweet fall.

"Hey sweetie," she whispered in profile. His face was right up against hers. "I'm gonna be late."

When she was gone Sonny dressed and ate a big breakfast, drank a shot of Cuervo gold to take off the edge. His stomach had gone from the long freefall with Laurel to the tight, slightly aching tension he always felt on a workday.

He read the paper, did the breakfast dishes, had another drink. He got the key from the bottom dresser drawer and went outside.

The morning was warming now, with the sun well over the eastern ridgeline. Sometimes the way the sun came up so bright over the hills made Sonny feel like it was looking for him. Buzzards circled in a canyon updraft. He smelled the sage and pines as he unlocked the padlock on the garage and lifted the door.

He backed out the big panel van, made sure there was plenty of gas, then slid off the old vinyl seat and locked the garage door shut again. He checked the oil and coolant and tire pressure, and got the control pad from the console, underneath a half-empty bottle of Cuervo.

Then he walked ten steps behind the vehicle, hit the control pad and watched the back doors open. A ramp lifted, then slid from the cargo floor. It was two feet wide and eight feet long. It groaned into position on the driveway. When it came to a rest against the asphalt he could heard the hard-working little motor stop, its servo-gear disengage.

Sonny had bought the entire rig at a police auction believing it would become handy someday, no idea how. It was once property of a middle-management cocaine distributor with a penchant for Harley Davidsons, a guy Sonny'd taken down on a bust right here in Laguna Canyon. The police band scanner was already in.

He'd reworked the motor and gearing so it was fast. It took seven seconds for the doors to open and the ramp to come out, seven seconds to get them back in place.

He'd bought it with money from a good weekend at the sports book — one of the few things he had left from those days, besides the debts.

It was just after ten when he left to do his errands.

He stopped off at the storage rental in Santa Ana and walked the little 200cc street bike up the ramp and into the back of the van. Turning it around was always kind of a pain.

He was sweating good by the time he had it aimed right, fastened the straps tight so it wouldn't tip over when the van made a turn.

It was already ninety degrees according to the bank sign he passed back on 17th Street. He got the helmet and the bag of gear and the magnetic signs for the vehicle, the Velcro strap to fasten the control module to the handlebars of the bike. A nip from the Cuervo in the console.

Then on to Fullerton, his nerves jacked tight and everything around him so clear and acute it seemed to Sonny like the kind of vision a hawk would have, or a big predatory cat. The adrenaline made you see things you never knew were there: the sparrow lost in the sparrow-sized leaves of a cottonwood, the old man with the wrinkled neck watching you from the dark of his garage.

Now to park. Critical that he have twelve feet of clearance behind the van — eight for the ramp and at least four feet to turn onto it. Best was a straight shot, park the van at a corner where nobody could park behind him. And critical, too, that he park in a place where there wouldn't be people lined up to see him: an industrial zone where workers punched the clock, a moribund parking lot for an out-of-session school or failing business, upscale neighborhoods where people had views of something better than the street. You needed some privacy, but enough activity around so a van wouldn't seem out of place. Sometimes it took him fifteen minutes just to find the right spot.

Today was a tough one. Nothing looked right. Crowded side-streets, apartments, and houses too close to the road. The further you got from the site, the more risk you'd get seen.

He circled outward from the bank, further and further, finally settling five blocks from the branch, northbound on Pinehurst. A nice stretch of open curb, then a fire hydrant behind it, which left him a guaranteed thirty extra feel. Looked like an old-folks complex up the street half a block, but at least he wasn't right in front of someone's window. That was fine with Sonny because he liked old people, thought they deserved respect, and had been convinced early in life that he himself would never become one. What happened to his wife seemed to confirm this idea.

He put on the backpack and unfastened the straps that held the bike. It was uncomfortable because he couldn't stand up all the way. It felt good to sit on the little motorcycle and take the handlebars in his gloved hands, feel the beautiful balance of his weight over the tires. He reached down to the console and took the Cuervo.

He could feel his heart slamming against his shirt and the dry roar of blood in his ears. And that funny taste far back in the throat, like steel. And everything so clear, so bright and actual.

He started the bike and let the engine scream inside the sheet-metal cave of the van, then pushed the control pad dangling on the right handlebar. On with the helmet, first shaking back the blond wig he'd Superglued to the inside.

Brightness. Daylight. Noxious exhaust rolling out the opening doors. Visor down. Ramp extending, touching the asphalt seven seconds later. Like a bridge that would lead him away.

Down the ramp and onto the street. Out of himself and into the world. Sonny pushed the control pad again. But he didn't look backward and he didn't check the side mirror because he knew it would work, because all of his focus was in front of him, all his resources aimed only at the here and the now.

He was bulletproof.

The next thing Sonny knew he was coming in for his landing. Time had just begun to pass again, the world starting to turn after a long pause.

This was his favorite part of the whole thing. He hit the control module. He lined up the front tire of his screaming motorcycle with the back of the van. He downshifted and braked a little, paid out the seven seconds in second gear, felt the heft of the backpack behind him, felt his awareness of things begin to return. Saw the ramp settle into place on the street.

Parked OK.

Cute teller.

All your money real fast, hon. Don't touch the button, don't touch the dye. Quick! Quick! You gotta be quick!

Hands shaking, revolver heavy, this roar like the roar of an Amtrak train going through his head . . .

Sonny hit the ramp just after it touched down. The little bike climbed the steep angle and as soon as it leveled off inside he hit the control pad again, then the kill switch by his left thumb. Strapped the bike fast. The ramp settled into place and the door swung inward.

He took the helmet off, hooked it to the handlebar and climbed across the console and into the driver's seat. Less than ten seconds later he was moving north on Pinehurst, the bike behind him jiggling tautly against the ties, the backpack with gun and cash on the floor, the bottle of Gold clamped between his thighs.

Sonny hit the air conditioner, then the police band scanner, picked up Dispatch sending units to the Wells Fargo branch in east Fullerton.

He took a deep breath and headed toward the freeway. He could already feel the first numbing warmth of exhaustion starting to spread inside him.

He took a sip of Gold and wondered how long it would take Clay to arrive on scene. Terrible luck to have things work out like that, he thought, but what could you do? You couldn't very well turn out your brother because you had a business conflict with him.

But Clay would be out of the apartment soon. Everything would be back to normal. And before long he'd have the bills paid off and enough for a down on a dream home somewhere, on the beach, plenty of square feet, a wall around it.

It seemed to Sonny like he deserved a little time on Easy Street.

When Sonny got out of bed late that afternoon Clay was already home, talking with Laurel in the kitchen. He hadn't even heard them come in. But the postjob exhaustion and the tequila always put him down hard for a few hours.

He'd dreamed that he was a flying squirrel, gliding from treetop to treetop on nifty gray wings.

"Hi, kids," he said. He was still woozy from everything, still in his boxers.

Laurel was ironing one of his uniform shirts, her cocktail glass wobbling on the board with each stroke she made.

"The Bike Bandit's using a van to get away in," she said.

Sonny watched Clay raise his eyebrows: that was what you got for bringing your work home.

"Hope it's not mine," Sonny muttered. He headed for the coffee pot.

"He robbed a bank in north county today," said Laurel. "Clay didn't see him but he found out about the van. From this old lady."

Sonny poured some coffee. "He's got a getaway driver?"

"I don't think so," said Clay. "I think he's working alone."

Sonny pondered this, sipped the black, hot coffee, looked through the steam at his brother. "Plates?"

"I wish."

"Anybody hurt?"

"Just the FDIC. Eleven grand, plus."

"You Feds can afford it. Just a little less money for suspenders."

Laurel snapped one of Clay's suspenders. "I like 'em."

"You would," said Sonny. He didn't like leaving them now. Not that he didn't trust them, nothing like that at all, but he wished Clay was working nights and he could be alone with his girl. The jobs always made him tired and horny.

Sonny spent the first hour of his shift helping one of the cadets direct the festival traffic. The poor girl looked frantic, standing in the crosswalk while the pedestrians scurried by and the irate drivers ignored her whistle chirps and hand commands.

Rough town, he thought.

After that he talked down a furious husband on a domestic dispute call, sat around with the couple and shot the breeze about Laguna in the old days for a while before telling them they'd both go to jail if he ever had to come back here.

Okay, Sonny, we're sorry man, this'll never happen again . . .

Quiet night, overall. When the tourists were gone the streets were mostly empty. The ocean air made the car windows slick with mist and he could see the damp air swirling around the streetlamps. He got a drunk and disorderly call to the Sandpiper nightclub, booked the shitbird.

Then a peeper reported up on Cliff, couldn't find him but with his flashlight saw footprints in the flower bed outside the window, right where she said he was standing. The right shoe looked normal. The left was oversized, like a prosthetic device or a cast. Gave Sonny the creeps. The girl was a pretty college student, June. He told her he'd have a detective call in the morning, maybe make a cast, set up a way to catch the perv.

Up to Newport. Newport was way out of jurisdiction, of course, but bills weren't the only thing Sonny was having trouble with these days. While running up losses at Caesar's in Las Vegas he'd been trying to cover them on the side with a bookie named Bobby up here in Newport. That kind of worked and kind of didn't. Two months ago he was into Bobby for about thirteen large, and since then he'd paid that off but run up another sixteen on some incredible bad luck with Women's World Cup Soccer. He hadn't seen any way on Earth that our girls could beat the Communists.

Sonny guided the cruiser up Coast Highway. To his left the Pacific glittered black in the moonlight. The trailer park at El Morro swept by, then the cottages at Crystal Cove.

He found Attila at Snug Harbor bar. Attila was a huge, unflabby man given to wild aloha shirts and expensive cigars. He was on the collection side of Bobby's business. Attila struck Sonny as a reasonable enough guy, but you didn't want to make a promise you couldn't keep.

Sonny hated him on principle but most of his principles were gone. Gambling did that. And Bobby had tangled him up with phone recordings and a clandestine videotape, as insurance against Sonny's law enforcement position. Sonny had it in his mind that he could claim a sting operation if they ratted him, though it probably wouldn't work.

And he also figured that if the banks were giving him marked bills, it would be quite a surprise to Attila and Bobby when they got popped with them. With so much cash going through their hands, it would be tough to trace them back to him.

Attila didn't acknowledge Sonny when he walked into Snug Harbor, but ten minutes later the big man came out, heaving himself along the sidestreet toward his Jaguar. His shirt was blue with tigers all over it.

Like a whole goddamned jungle coming at you, thought Sonny, starting up the car.

He pulled up parallel with the Jag, no lights, no way he wanted to get caught out of jurisdiction, try to explain shaking down some big hood for not signaling a lane change.

Attila opened the Jaguar trunk. Sonny tossed in the shopping bag sealed with masking tape and Attila used one fat finger to press down the lid, the convenience motor kicking in with a hum and latching it into place.

"That's nine. The rest next week."

"That would be seven, plus one more for the time."

"I know the goddamned formula."

"You should. Bobby says hello."

"Tell Bobby to go fuck himself. While you're at it, fuck yourself, too. Maybe you'll have a heart attack and I won't have to look at your shirts anymore."

"Sonny, you're a funny guy."

"I'll see you next time."

Sonny held the cruiser to sixty, heading back down Coast Highway. Felt better. Relieved. Relaxed.

It was good to know that the two grand he'd held back would go toward the household bills bag, and the down payment bag. He was up to almost fifteen thousand for the dream house. Still a little way to go, he thought. Could double that in one bet on the All Star Game. The American League had the pitching, Martinez would get the start. No. Money was money, but that was a different kind of money. When he had, say . . . fifty or a hundred grand, then he'd lay it on Laurel and they could start looking.

He felt tired then, and it was getting close to midnight. But it was a good tired, an earned one, knowing that you'd worked hard to provide for your girl, your future.

3

On Sunday they celebrated Clay moving out. He'd found a good rental right there in Laguna and he could move in next week. Then he'd have time to look inland for something to buy if he wanted to.

But today, the beach. After a brief argument between Sonny and Laurel, they decided it made sense to take the van. Clay thought Sonny was a little more on edge every day: probably just sick of the intrusion. Didn't blame him. They piled in with three of Sonny's old boards and a cooler, towels, and beach chairs. Headed for Rockpile. Since there were only two seats in the thing, Laurel volunteered to ride back with the cargo.

"Hang on, kids!" said Sonny, starting his right turn on PCH.

Clay turned and offered a hand as Sonny took the corner fast. Laurel grabbed it and hung on, and the cooler slid out from under her and left her sitting midair, still holding Clay's hand, until she plopped to the floor.

Her legs spread into an awkward position and it was just her bathing suit black under the cover-up but Clay saw the blush come to Laurel's face and he was glad that she felt that way.

"Watch it, man," she screamed, more for humor than alarm. "I just flashed your brother."

"Sorry, kids."

Clay watched her get the cooler back under her, then brace herself against the van body, arms extended.

"Not going anywhere now," she announced, smiling at Clay. "So slow down, jerk-wad."

Clay saw that the cooler bottom wouldn't grip the smooth piece of metal on the floor.

"Sonny, what's all that machinery back there?" Clay asked.

"A wheelchair ramp and a motor to run it. I got this thing cheap at the auction. I didn't need the ramp, but the van was clean."

"It gets about two hundred yards per gallon," said Laurel. "Besides being the ugliest thing on wheels."

"It comes in handy for stuff like this, though. That's why I bought it."

Clay looked back at Laurel again, then at the ramp. He thought of the white ResCom van in which the Bike Bandit had made his escape.

"It's like the setup the Bike Bandit uses."

"You'd have to rob banks to pay the gas for it," said Laurel.

"Hope he doesn't use his in a high-speed chase," said Sonny. "Past fifty, these things'll turn over in a breeze."

"That corner *felt* like fifty back here," said Laurel.

Clay turned and smiled at her and she spread her legs and lifted the cover-up, smiling back.

"I just flashed Fed-Man again. This time because I wanted to."

"Slut," said Sonny.

"You sweet-talker, you."

It was early enough that they had the break to themselves. A little south had pushed up from Mexico and the waves were building on the rocks and breaking off in steep walls.

Clay could hardly get himself up and balanced before getting knocked off. He remembered being a lot faster in the water when he was a kid. He'd lifted some weights since then, and gained some muscle, but he felt heavy and dopey in the water. *Feds don't surf.* It didn't matter. Just being out was enough, with the sun warm on his skin and the water cold around him. There was just something about this: the hiss of a board on the sea, the smooth velocity.

But Sonny seemed to have retained his talent: Clay watched him carving up and down the wave faces, then crouching low to power through the tubes. Then he'd exit with an exaggerated kick-out, board and body twisting skyward, connected by the leash, ending with a scream and a splash.

Clay looked back at Laurel on the beach, upright in a portable chair, reading a magazine, the cooler beside her. She waved and he waved back. He tried to get a big wave, maybe show off a little, but he slipped on the takeoff, got pitched headfirst and thoroughly pummeled.

A few minutes later he looked back again and she was pinned beneath Sonny, struggling to get away. Clay could hear her screams. He watched her slip past him, run for the water. A minute later they both came splashing out and capsized him, then a fight for the board broke out. It ended with them three across like puppies, breathing hard, and eyeing a silent five-footer suddenly rolling toward them from the horizon. They abandoned ship and dove for the bottom.

Later Clay bought wine and beer and ice cream. Sonny sprung for three enormous live Maine lobsters, which Laurel named Spike, Mike, and Ike. They got the pots and barbecue going in the little front yard and cracked some beers.

They ate early and drank a lot. Clay was a little surprised how fast Sonny could drink a six-pack, most of a bottle of wine, and three very stiff margaritas. Caught him downing a shot of Cuervo in the kitchen when he thought nobody would see.

Clay got a little shellacked himself. He was sitting in the shade of the pepper tree when Sonny wobbled into the house and didn't come back out. Then Laurel followed him and she didn't come back out either. A few minutes later Clay heard them in the bedroom. Ten, fifteen minutes after that they were still at it.

He gathered up two handfuls of pink pepper hulls, wondering how much they weighed. Not much. He thought of Marie, dialed her on his cell phone and told her answering machine he'd arrived OK, hoped she was fine.

What a *putz*, he thought.

When Laurel came back her hair was brushed out neat and she smelled like a fresh dose of suntan oil. She was barefoot, walking with just enough hesitancy that he knew she was drunk. She sat down on a patio chair.

"Sorry," she said.

"It's OK."

"He gets that way sometimes. Just shitfaced. Then he gets weepy and wants to do things."

"He loves you."

"He's fucked up, Clay. I know it."

"I guess I don't see him that way."

She pushed herself up, went into the house, came back a minute later. She set a big twine-handled paper shopping bag on his lap.

"What way do you see this?"

Clay set the bag between his feet, leaned over and pulled out of the envelopes. A quick check: bills, bills, and more bills. All overdue, canceled this and that, referred to collections, blah, blah, blah.

"What's the total?"

"Thirty, forty grand. I don't know. He had fifteen credit cards going at one point. I do know the interest piles up about as fast as our paychecks. Those are the ones we're waiting on. The ones were paying on, that's a whole other bag."

"No toys. Where'd it all go?"

"Where do you think?"

"You said he quit."

"Robbed Peter to pay Paul. That's Peter between your feet, patron saint of the cash advance."

Clay dropped the handful of bills back into the bag.

"I don't know if it started with Suzanne. You know about that."

"Yeah."

"I do too, but he never told me. I wondered if you would. One of his partners thought I deserved to know, since I was sharing a bed with him by then."

"Yes."

"Yes, well, if I'd been married a year and my husband died in a car crash, I might spin out, too."

Clay thought of the long coma, the days he'd spent with Sonny and the parents and Suzanne's brothers in the IC ward, then the critical care ward, then the regular ward, then the cemetery. The diminishing gradients of hope. It was so hard, just to look at her.

He'd understood what Sonny was going through, feeling so much of it himself. Then the fire destroying his house. And nowhere near enough insurance. Like God Himself had put the black hand on Sonny, some kind of test or curse or payback. Clay had lost his easy faith in a good and righteous God then, never gotten it back. He wondered if Sonny was trying to get it back when he bet on something, giving Him a chance to change His mind. But he knew that Sonny was trying to get Suzanne back, because Laurel looked a lot like her, right down to the freckles, the dark straight hair and blue eyes. Same age as Suzanne was when Sonny married her. Same sweet, fuck-the-world attitude.

"Or I might try to find somebody else like her," said Laurel. "Look, I'm drunk. I'm going to go lay down for a while."

She picked up the unpaid bills bag, looking down at him from close.

"We're different, you and me," she said. "But a couple of times the last week I've wondered what it would have been like to meet you first. That's not a come-on. It's just me talking to you. You wonder that?"

Clay felt a great desire to stand and hold her, to take her. He didn't want to feel it, but he couldn't control it any more than he could make himself miss Marie or Atlanta or Dallas.

"There's some things you don't allow yourself to think."

"That's a lie if I ever heard one."

"Well, yes. And yes."

"What did you come up with?"

"I wish we had. I wish I could take you in that bedroom right now and not come out for about five years. That's not a come-on. It's just me talking to you."

She smiled down at him. "Fed-Man has feelings."

"And what did you come up with?"

"I'm actually embarrassed to say. But I won't try to tell you I didn't allow myself to think it."

"Cough it up."

"No."

"You're not playing fair."

"You just got suckered is all."

She reached down and touched his cheek. It felt to Clay like a matter-of-fact touch, a way of making sure he was what she thought he was. "I'll see you later, Clay. I'm going to go be with Sonny."

In the bird-chirping twilight Clay cracked another beer while he studied the back of his brother's van. It was locked up and he didn't want to bother them for the keys, but he wanted to get a feel for how the Bike Bandit was making his getaways.

The method made sense: it was quick and it changed his appearance, like a disguise. Once inside he was almost safe. Speed was the key, so there must be some motorization involved. It would take too much time to park the bike, open the van doors and pull out the ramp, then drive up it, retract the ramp, etc.

But it was easy enough to motorize a ramp and a set of vehicle doors — handicapped vans like Sonny's were retrofitted that way all the time.

Yes, the right rig would keep the Bike Bandit out of sight after just a few critical seconds for loading. That was why no witnesses had seen the bike further than a block or two away from the banks. A good parking place was essential. The downside was that someone would finally see him make the entry or the exit, and Gladys Forbes, out for her morning walk, had done just that.

He sipped his beer, looked through the driver's side window. There wasn't much to see in the dim light. When he looked at the ramp he saw Laurel sitting midair before she collapsed onto it, then that look on her face.

Clear your head of her, he thought. Fun is fun but poison is still poison.

Tuesday Goodin called from Washington, said Clay's work on the photograph was perfect. The suspect in the picture was between five-nine and five-ten, approximate weight 185. His backpack was a No Fear brand now popular with young people on both coasts. The helmet was a Bell, common and probably impossible to trace.

"Get me a clear picture of his shoes," said Goodin. "I do good things with shoes."

"I'll try."

On Wednesday Salena Mendez told him that she'd found the maker of the ResCom vehicle sign: Signs of the Times in Santa Ana. They were a mom and pop shop but they remembered the ResCom order. It was placed on May 10 of this year, filled May 18. The customer's name was Ed Presley, and Mr. Presley left an address and phone number that Salena determined to be fictitious. No state or Federal jacket on an Edward or Ed Presley living in California. He paid $38.88 cash for two signs that read ResCom Cable Services, followed by a phone number that turned out to be that of a funeral home in San Clemente.

"White male, medium height, medium weight, short hair," said Mendez, staring past Clay's shoulder at God knew what. "Thirty to early thirties. Wore a shirt with palm trees on it when he placed the order. The owner remembered because he's got the same shirt. Alone both times. Never saw his vehicle."

Clay collated the data while his heart fluttered, then steadied. Presley was Sonny's age, height, and weight, had short hair and a shirt with palm trees on it. Sonny had a white van with a motorized ramp in it. Sonny owed money but bought sixty dollars' worth of lobster for dinner.

On the flip side, there was no motorcycle, and the fact that Sonny was a brother and a cop, and a good one. More on the flip side was common sense, and, if it came down to it, the simple truths revealed by faith in a brother, which was faith in yourself.

"A pretty common shirt, then," he said, hearing the relief in his voice.

"Common enough the owner had the same one."

"How old is he?"

"Sixty, heavy, short. Forget him. He's not being cute."

And that was when the hot line rang and Placentia PD reported a robbery in progress, B of A branch off Kraemer Blvd.

They were rolling in less than a minute, Clay burning rubber out of the parking lot and Salena choosing this steady moment to check the clip in her .357.

Nine minutes of high-speed blur, Main to I-5 to the 55 and off on Kraemer, the traffic sparse and Clay flying, the police radio squawking backup to the branch.

Salena knew this part of the county and guided him in without a map. They sped up Kraemer northbound, and Clay saw the light bars flashing up ahead, the black-and-whites scattered along the boulevard, the dart of uniforms through the halted traffic.

He screeched to a stop and bailed out, badged the PD commander. The commander said a patrolman had been one block away when the teller hit the button, and the bank bandit had grabbed a customer hostage when the cruiser rolled up. The Bike Bandit was still inside, they didn't want to rush the door with all the people, hostage team on the way, but nobody was coming out and that didn't look good, *get the fuck down will you he's armed!*

Clay assessed: police cars clustered, guns braced on car hoods and open doors, a SWAT sniper leaning against the hood of a cruiser with the tripod of his scoped M-16 steady on the paint and his face tight to the butt, horns blaring from far back in the stalled traffic but around the cop units a brittle silence in the clear, hot morning.

"Here he comes. He's coming out!"

Clay saw him, hands up, helmet and visor still on, long blond hair and a slow, short stride. He feinted left then dodged right and hopped a low wall into the parking lot.

The guns roared and dust popped off the wall and Clay could see him weaving between the cars, down low, then springing in one mad leap over a grape-stake fence and into someone's yard.

The commander screamed cease fire.

Clay said, "Let's go."

He went left and wide, through an alley behind a liquor store, then along the sidewalk. He figured the Bike Bandit would stick to the backyards as long as he could, heading away from the boulevard, then try something desperate like grab a motorist out of his car at a stop sign, maybe take a hostage.

Clay saw him jump another fence, heard the dog bark, then snarl. He crossed the street, gun drawn now and Salena behind him, crouching low through the front yards, guessing himself parallel with the bandit on the other side of the neat suburban homes.

The last yard ended at a wide sidewalk and a street corner. A streetlight. A high curb. Clay rounded it just as the Bike Bandit dropped to the sidewalk thirty feet away.

Clay braced his nine, spread his legs, and aimed at the chest. *"FREEZE, FBI!"*

The helmet turned. The blond hair swung back. A turn of the bandit's hand and a flash of metal.

"Sonny, *NO!*

Then an explosion behind him. Three more, quick. The smack of bullets in meat and bone. The Bandit grunted then dropped out of Clay's sight picture.

Fuck, she killed him, he thought, glancing once behind at Salena still in her kneeling stance, breathing hard and loud, the magnum auto aimed down at her crumpled target.

Motherofgod, she was whispering, *motherofgod.*

They approached him slowly, guns extended, but Clay lowered his when he saw the bad upward angle of the helmet, the blood pouring onto the sidewalk, the stainless frame revolver three feet from the Bike Bandit's right hand. He could smell the cordite and the metallic scent of the blood.

Salena kicked the revolver away and Clay knelt down to pull off the helmet.

He knew it wasn't. He knew it couldn't be. You don't do that to brothers, no matter who you are.

When he pulled off the helmet the hair went with it and Clay looked into Sonny's clear and sightless eyes.

"Sonofabitch," said Salena. "Motherofgod. You all right?"

4

Clay sat in the shade of the pepper tree and called his parents. He felt no emotions inside except hopelessness. No matter what he looked at in the world around him all he saw was something else.

Her heard Laurel's old car pull in, the parking break ratcheting up, the engine dieseling. The door slam. Footsteps.

He looked at her as she came through the little gate. She stopped and studied his face and said nothing.

She brought out a beer for him and one for her. When she was seated in the patio chair across from him he told her.

She sat very still, not drinking, for almost an hour. Clay registered sounds but not sights. His eyes saw what they saw but his brain wasn't interested in them. Objects passed his vision like words in an unknown language.

But he heard every birdsong in the neighborhood and every car engine on Laguna Canyon Road, and he could hear the sound of blood in his ears and the sound of Laurel breathing.

She got up and went into the house. When she didn't come back he got worried and went in to check on her. He heard the shower, made a strong drink of tequila and water, and took it outside.

By then it was dark. When Laurel came out she had a heavy robe on, even though the night was warm. Hair combed back and shiny, eyes dead in her face.

"I'll do what needs to be done," she said. "You can go if you want."

"All right."

"What does that mean?"

"It means I'll do what needs to be done also."

She got up without another word and went back inside. She was gone another long time. He looked at his watch and saw the numbers but couldn't know the time.

He found her in the bedroom, sitting on the floor against the bed, the lamp on the nightstand giving her a faint orange glow.

"Talk to me, Clay."

"I can't. I'm sorry."

"Just sit and be quiet then."

He sat on the floor across from her, mostly in the dark, with his back against the wall. His glass made a round pool on the old hardwood floor.

She slid a bottle of tequila across to him. He didn't know she had it. He took a long drink, screwed the cap on, and slid it back.

She drank, shuddered quickly, then reached up and turned off the lamp. There was the neighbors' lights and moonlight.

"Stay until you're ready to sleep. Then sleep with me in this bed."

He looked at her in the dark and saw her clearly.

"I know it's not right, Clay. But I believe it could be made to be right. That it's possible."

Clay wasn't sure that the concepts of right or possible applied here. There was a chance you had to make those things yourself, out of thin air, and this gave him no comfort. He had never aspired to do that. He had become a tool of the law to not have to make those kinds of things for himself. But he understood what he had to do, even if he didn't know where the understanding came from.

"First I'm going to sit in the yard and finish the bottle," he said.

"I'm going, too. Leave the lights off. Every one. The dark's light enough for tonight."

BILL PRONZINI

The Big Bite

FROM *The Shamus Game*

I LAID A red queen on a black king, glanced up at Jay Cohalan through the open door of his office. He was pacing again, back and forth in front of his desk, his hands in constant restless motion at his sides. The office was carpeted: his footfalls made no sound. There was no discernible sound anywhere except for the faint snap and slap when I turned over a card and put it down. An office building at night is one of the quietest places there is. Eerily so, if you spend enough time listening to the silence.

Trey. Nine of diamonds. Deuce. Jack of spades. I was marrying the jack to the red queen when Cohalan quit pacing and came over to stand in the doorway. He watched me for a time, his hands still doing scoop-shovel maneuvers — a big man in his late thirties, handsome except for a weak chin, a little sweaty and disheveled now.

"How can you just sit there playing cards?" he said.

There were several answers to that. Years of stakeouts and dull routine. We'd been waiting only about two hours. The money, fifty thousand in fifties and hundreds, didn't belong to me. I wasn't worried, upset, or afraid that something might go wrong. I passed on all of those and settled instead for a neutral response: "Solitaire's good for waiting. Keeps your mind off the clock."

"It's after seven. Why the hell doesn't he call?"

"You know the answer to that. He wants you to sweat."

"Sadistic bastard."

"Blackmail's that kind of game," I said. "Torture the victim, bend his will to yours."

"Game. My God." Cohalan came out into the anteroom and began to pace in front of his secretary's desk, where I was sitting. "It's driving me crazy, trying to figure out who he is, how he found out about my past. Not a hint, any of the times I talked to him. But he knows everything, every damn detail."

"You'll have the answers before long."

"Yeah." He stopped abruptly, leaned toward me.

"Listen, this has to be the end of it. You've *got* to stay with him, see to it he's arrested. I can't take any more."

"I'll do my job. Mr. Cohalan, don't worry."

"Fifty thousand dollars. I almost had a heart attack when he told me that was how much he wanted this time. The last payment, he said. What a crock. He'll come back for more someday. I know it, Carolyn knows it, you know it." Pacing again. "Poor Carolyn. High-strung, emotional . . . it's been even harder on her. She wanted me to go to the police this time, did I tell you that?"

"You told me."

"I should have, I guess. Now I've got to pay a middleman for what I could've had for nothing . . . no offense."

"None taken."

"I just couldn't bring myself to do it, walk into the Hall of Justice and confess everything to a cop. It was hard enough letting Carolyn talk me into hiring a private detective. That trouble when I was a kid . . . it's a criminal offense, I could still be prosecuted for it. And it's liable to cost me my job if it comes out. I went through hell telling Carolyn in the beginning, and I didn't go into all the sordid details. With you, either. The police . . . no. I know that bastard will probably spill the whole story when he's arrested, try to drag me down with him, but still . . . I keep hoping he won't. You understand?"

"I understand," I said.

"I shouldn't've paid him when he crawled out of the woodwork eight months ago. I know that now. But back then it seemed like the only way to keep from ruining my life. Carolyn thought so, too. If I hadn't started paying him, half of her inheritance wouldn't already be gone. . . ." He let the rest of it trail off, paced in bitter silence for a time, and started up again. "I hated taking money from her — *hated* it, no matter how much she insisted it belongs to both of us. And I hate myself for doing it, almost as much as I hate him. Blackmail's the worst goddamn crime there is short of murder."

"Not the worst," I said, "but bad enough."

"This *has* to be the end of it. The fifty thousand in there . . . it's the last of her inheritance, our savings. If that son of a bitch gets away with it, we'll be wiped out. You can't let that happen."

I didn't say anything. We'd been through all this before, more than once.

Cohalan let the silence resettle. Then, as I shuffled the cards for a new hand, "This job of mine, you'd think it pays pretty well, wouldn't you? My own office, secretary, executive title, expense account . . . looks good and sounds good, but it's a frigging dead end. Junior account executive stuck in corporate middle management — that's all I am or ever will be. Sixty thousand a year gross. And Carolyn makes twenty-five teaching. Eighty-five thousand for two people, no kids, that seems like plenty but it's not, not these days. Taxes, high cost of living, you have to scrimp to put anything away. And then some stupid mistake you made when you were a kid comes back to haunt you, drains your future along with your bank account, preys on your mind so you can't sleep, can barely do your work . . . you see what I mean? But I didn't think I had a choice at first, I was afraid of losing this crappy job, going to prison. Caught between a rock and a hard place. I still feel that way, but now I don't care, I just want that scum to get what's coming to him. . . ."

Repetitious babbling caused by his anxiety. His mouth had a wet look and his eyes kept jumping from me to other points in the room.

I said, "Why don't you sit down?"

"I can't sit. My nerves are shot."

"Take a few deep breaths before you start to hyperventilate."

"Listen, don't tell me what —"

The telephone on his desk went off.

The sudden clamor jerked him half around, as if with an electric shock. In the quiet that followed the first ring I could hear the harsh rasp of his breathing. He looked back at me as the bell sounded again. I was on my feet, too, by then.

I said, "Go ahead, answer it. Keep your head."

He went into his office, picked up just after the third ring. I timed the lifting of the extension to coincide so there wouldn't be a second click on the open line.

"Yes," he said, "Cohalan."

"You know who this is." The voice was harsh, muffled, indistinctively male. "You got the fifty thousand?"

"I told you I would. The last payment, you promised me . . ."

"Yeah, the last one."

"Where this time?"

"Golden Gate Park. Kennedy Drive, in front of the buffalo pen. Put it in the trash barrel beside the bench there."

Cohalan was watching me through the open doorway. I shook my head at him. He said into the phone, "Can't we make it someplace else? There might be people around. . . ."

"Not at nine P.M."

"Nine? But it's only a little after seven now —"

"Nine sharp. Be there with the cash."

The line went dead.

I cradled the extension. Cohalan was still standing alongside his desk, hanging onto the receiver the way a drowning man might hang onto a lifeline, when I went into his office. I said, "Put it down, Mr. Cohalan."

"What? Oh, yes . . ." He lowered the receiver. "Christ," he said then.

"You all right?"

His head bobbed up and down a couple of times. He ran a hand over his face and then swung away to where his briefcase lay. The fifty thousand was in there; he'd shown it to me when I first arrived. He picked the case up, set it down again. Rubbed his face another time.

"Maybe I *shouldn't* risk the money," he said.

He wasn't talking to me so I didn't answer.

"I could leave it right here where it'll be safe. Put a phone book or something in for weight." He sank into his desk chair, popped up again like a jack-in-the-box. He was wired so tight I could almost hear him humming. "No, what's the matter with me? That won't work. I'm not thinking straight. He might open the case in the park. There's no telling what he'd do if the money's not there. And he's got to have it in his possession when the police come."

"That's why I insisted we mark some of the bills."

"Yes, right, I remember. Proof of extortion. All right, but for God's sake don't let him get away with it."

"He won't get away with it."

Another jerky nod. "When're you leaving?"

"Right now. You stay put until at least eight-thirty. It won't take you more than twenty minutes to get out to the park."

"I'm not sure I can get through another hour of waiting around here."

"Keep telling yourself it'll be over soon. Calm down. The state you're in now, you shouldn't even be behind the wheel."

"I'll be OK."

"Come straight back here after you make the drop. You'll hear from me as soon as I have anything to report."

"Just don't make me wait too long," Cohalan said. And then, again and to himself, "I'll be OK."

Cohalan's office building was on Kearney, not far from where Kerry works at the Bates and Carpenter ad agency on lower Geary. She was on my mind as I drove down to Geary and turned west toward the park: my thoughts prompted me to lift the car phone and call the condo. No answer. Like me, she puts in a lot of overtime night work. A wonder we manage to spend as much time together as we do.

I tried her private number at B & C and got her voice mail. In transit probably, the same as I was. Headlights crossing the dark city. Urban night riders. Except that she was going home and I was on my way to nail a shakedown artist for a paying client.

That started me thinking about the kind of work I do. One of the downsides of urban night riding is that it gives vent to sometimes broody self-analysis. Skip traces, insurance claims investigations, employee background checks — they're the meat of my business. There used to be some challenge to jobs like that, some creative maneuvering required, but nowadays it's little more than routine legwork (mine) and a lot of computer time (Tamara Corbin, my techno-whiz assistant). I don't get to use my head as much as I once did. My problem, in Tamara's Generation X opinion, was that I was a "retro dick" pining away for the old days and old ways. True enough; I never have adapted well to change. The detective racket just isn't as satisfying or stimulating after thirty-plus years and with a new set of rules.

Every now and then, though, a case comes along that stirs the juices — one with some spark and sizzle and a much higher satis-

faction level than the run-of-the-mill stuff. I live for cases like that;
they're what keep me from packing it in, taking an early retirement. They usually involve a felony of some sort, and sometimes a
whisper if not a shout of danger, and allow me to use my full com-
plement of functional brain cells. This Cohalan case, for instance.
This one I liked, because shakedown artists are high on my list of
worthless lowlifes and I enjoy hell out of taking one down.

Yeah, this one I liked a whole lot.

Golden Gate Park has plenty of daytime attractions — museums,
tiny lakes, rolling lawns, windmills, an arboretum — but on a foggy
November night it's a mostly empty dark place to pass through on
your way to somewhere else. Mostly empty because it does have its
night denizens: homeless squatters, not all of whom are harmless
or drug-free, and predators on the prowl in its sprawling acres of
shadows and nightshapes. On a night like this it also has an atmosphere of lonely isolation, the fog hiding the city lights and turning
street lamps and passing headlights into surreal blurs.

The buffalo enclosure is at the westward end, less than a mile
from the ocean — the least-traveled section of the park at night.
There were no cars in the vicinity, moving or parked, when I came
down Kennedy Drive. My lights picked out the fence on the north
side, the rolling pastureland beyond; the trash barrel and bench
were about halfway along, at the edge of the bicycle path that paral-
lels the road. I drove past there, looking for a place to park and
wait. I didn't want to sit on Kennedy; a lone car close to the drop
point would be too conspicuous. I had to do this right. If anything
did not seem kosher, the whole thing might fail to go off the way it
was supposed to.

The perfect spot came up fifty yards or so from the trash barrel,
opposite the buffaloes' feeding corral — a narrow road that leads
to Anglers Lodge, where the city maintains casting pools for fly
fishermen to practice on. Nobody was likely to go up there at night,
and trees and shrubbery bordered one side, the shadows in close
to them thick and clotted. Kennedy Drive was still empty in both directions; I cut in past the Anglers Lodge sign and drove up the road
until I found a place where I could turn around. Then I shut off my
lights, made the U-turn, and coasted back down into the heavy
shadows. From there I could see the drop point clearly enough,

even with the low-riding fog. I shut off the engine, slumped down on the seat with my back against the door.

No detective, public or private, likes stakeouts. Dull, boring, dead time that can be a literal pain in the ass if it goes on long enough. This one wasn't too bad because it was short, only about an hour, but time lagged and crawled just the same. Now and then a car drifted by, its lights reflecting off rather than boring through the wall of mist. The ones heading west might have been able to see my car briefly in dark silhouette as they passed, but none of them happened to be a police patrol and nobody else was curious enough or venal enough to stop and investigate.

The luminous dial on my watch showed five minutes to nine when Cohalan arrived. Predictably early because he was so anxious to get it over with. He came down Kennedy too fast for the conditions; I heard the squeal of brakes as he swung over and rocked to a stop near the trash barrel. I watched the shape of him get out and run across the path to make the drop and then run back. Ten seconds later his car hissed past where I was hidden, again going too fast, and was gone.

Nine o'clock.

Nine oh five.

Nine oh eight.

Headlights probed past, this set heading east, the car low-slung and smallish. It rolled along slowly until it was opposite the barrel, then veered sharply across the road and slid to a crooked stop with its brake lights flashing blood red. I sat up straighter, put my hand on the ignition key. The door opened without a light coming on inside, and the driver jumped out in a hurry, bulky and indistinct in a heavy coat and some kind of head covering; ran to the barrel, scooped out the briefcase, raced back and hurled it inside; hopped in after it and took off. Fast, even faster than Cohalan had been driving, the car's rear end fishtailing a little as the tires fought for traction on the slick pavement.

I was out on Kennedy and in pursuit within seconds. No way I could drive in the fog-laden darkness without putting on my lights, and in the far reach of the beams I could see the other car a hundred yards or so ahead. But even when I accelerated I couldn't get close enough to read the license plate.

Where the drive forks on the east end of the buffalo enclosure, the sports job made a tight-angle left turn, brake lights flashing again, headlights yawing as the driver fought for control. Looping around Spreckels Lake to quit the park on 36th Avenue. I took the turn at about half the speed, but I still had it in sight when it made a sliding right through a red light on Fulton, narrowly missing an oncoming car, and disappeared to the east. I wasn't even trying to keep up any longer. If I continued pursuit, somebody — an innocent party — was liable to get hurt or killed. That was the last thing I wanted to happen. High-speed car chases are for damn fools and the makers of trite Hollywood films.

I pulled over near the Fulton intersection, still inside the park, and used the car phone to call my client.

Cohalan threw a fit when I told him what had happened. He called me all kinds of names, the least offensive of which was "incompetent idiot." I just let him rant. There were no excuses to be made and no point in wasting my own breath.

He ran out of abuse finally and segued into lament. "What am I going to do now? What am I going to tell Carolyn? All our savings gone and I still don't have any idea who that blackmailing bastard is. What if he comes back for more? We couldn't even sell the house, there's hardly any equity . . ."

Pretty soon he ran down there, too. I waited through about five seconds of dead air. Then, "All right," followed by a heavy sigh. "But don't expect me to pay your bill. You can damn well sue me and you can't get blood out of a turnip." And he banged the receiver in my ear.

Some Cohalan. Some piece of work.

The apartment building was on Locust Street a half block off California, close to the Presidio. Built in the twenties, judging by its ornate facade, once somebody's modestly affluent private home, long ago cut up into three floors of studios and one-bedroom apartments. It had no garage, forcing its tenants — like most of those in the neighborhood buildings — into street parking. There wasn't a legal space to be had on that block, or in the next, or anywhere in the vicinity. Back on California, I slotted my car into a bus zone. If I got a ticket I got a ticket.

Not much chance I'd need a weapon for the rest of it, but some-

times trouble comes when you least expect it. So I unclipped the
.38 Colt Bodyguard from under the dash, slipped it into my coat
pocket before I got out for the walk down Locust.

The building had a tiny foyer with the usual bank of mailboxes. I
found the button for 2-C, leaned on it. This was the ticklish part; I
was banking on the fact that one voice sounds pretty much like another over an intercom. Turned out not to be an issue at all: the
squawk box stayed silent and the door release buzzed instead, almost immediately. Confident. Arrogant. Or just plain stupid.

I pushed inside, smiling a little, cynically, and climbed the stairs
to the second floor. The first apartment on the right was 2-C. The
door opened just as I got to it, and Annette Byers put her head out
and said with excitement in her voice, "You made really good —"

The rest of it snapped off when she got a look at me; the excitement gave way to confusion, froze her in the half-open doorway. I
had time to move up on her, wedge my shoulder against the door
before she could decide to jump back and slam it in my face. She
let out a little bleat and tried to kick me as I crowded her inside.
I caught her arms, gave her a shove to get clear of her. Then I
nudged the door closed with my heel.

"I'll start screaming," she said. Shaky bravado, the kind without
anything to back it up. Her eyes were frightened now. "These walls
are paper thin, and I've got a neighbor who's a cop."

That last part was a lie. I said, "Go ahead. Be my guest."

"Who the hell do you think you are —"

"We both know who I am, Ms. Byers. And why I'm here. The reason's on the table over there."

In spite of herself she glanced to her left. The apartment was a
studio, and the kitchenette and dining area were over that way. The
briefcase sat on the dinette table, its lid raised. I couldn't see inside
from where I was, but then I didn't need to.

"I don't know what you're talking about," she said.

She hadn't been back long; she still wore the heavy coat and the
head covering, a wool stocking cap that completely hid her blond
hair. Her cheeks were flushed — the cold night, money lust, now
fear. She was attractive enough in a too-ripe way, intelligent enough
to hold down a job with a downtown travel service, and immoral
enough to have been in trouble with the San Francisco police before this. She was twenty-three, divorced, and evidently a crank-

head: she'd been arrested once for possession and once for trying to sell a small quantity of methamphetamine to an undercover cop.

"Counting the cash, right?" I said.

" . . . What?"

"What you were doing when I rang the bell. Fifty thousand in fifties and hundreds. It's all there, according to plan."

"I don't know what you're talking about."

"You said that already."

I moved a little to get a better scan of the studio. Her phone was on a breakfast bar that separated the kitchenette from the living room, one of those cordless types with a built-in answering machine. The gadget beside it was clearly a portable cassette player. She hadn't bothered to put it away before she went out; there'd been no reason to, or so she'd have thought then. The tape would still be inside.

I looked at her again. "I've got to admit, you're a pretty good driver. Reckless as hell, though, the way you went flying out of the park on a red light. You came close to a collision with another car."

"I don't know what —" She broke off and backed away a couple of paces, her hand rubbing the side of her face, her tongue making little flicks between her lips. It was sinking in now, how it had all gone wrong, how much trouble she was in. "You couldn't have followed me. I *know* you didn't."

"That's right, I couldn't and I didn't."

"Then how — ?"

"Think about it. You'll figure it out."

A little silence. And, "Oh God, you knew about me all along."

"About you, the plan, everything."

"How? How could you? I don't —"

The downstairs bell made a sudden racket.

Her gaze jerked past me toward the intercom unit next to the door. She sucked in her lower lip, began to gnaw on it.

"You know who it is," I said. "Don't use the intercom, just the door release."

She did what I told her, moving slowly. I went the other way, first to the breakfast bar, where I popped the tape out of the cassette player and slipped it into my pocket, then to the dinette table. I lowered the lid on the briefcase, snapped the catches. I had the case in my hand when she turned to face me again.

She said, "What are you going to do with the money?"

"Give it back to its rightful owner."

"Jay. It belongs to him."

I didn't say anything to that.

"You better not try to keep it for yourself," she said. "You don't have any right to that money . . ."

"You dumb kid," I said disgustedly, "neither do you."

She quit looking at me. When she started to open the door I told her no, wait for his knock. She stood with her back to me, shoulders hunched. She was no longer afraid; dull resignation had taken over. For her, I thought, the money was the only thing that had ever mattered.

Knuckles rapped on the door. She opened it without any hesitation, and he blew in, talking fast the way he did when he was keyed up. "Oh, baby, baby, we did it, we pulled it off," and he grabbed her and started to pull her against him. That was when he saw me.

"Hello, Cohalan," I said.

He went rigid for three or four seconds, his eyes popped wide, then disentangled himself from the woman and stood gawping at me. His mouth worked but nothing came out. Manic as hell in his office, all nerves and talking a blue streak, but now he was speechless. Lies were easy for him; the truth would have to be dragged out.

I told him to close the door. He did it, automatically, and turned snarling on Annette Byers. "You let him follow you home!"

"I didn't," she said. "He already knew about me. He knows everything."

"No, you're lying . . ."

"You were so goddamn smart, you had it all figured out. You didn't fool him for a minute."

"Shut up." His eyes shifted to me. "Don't listen to her. She's the one who's been blackmailing me —"

"Knock it off, Cohalan," I said. "Nobody's been blackmailing you. You're the shakedown artist here, you and Annette — a fancy little scheme to get your wife's money. You couldn't just grab the whole bundle from her, and you couldn't get any of it by divorcing her — a spouse's inheritance isn't community property in this state. So you cooked up the phony blackmail scam. What were the two of you planning to do with the full hundred thousand? Run off somewhere together? Buy a load of crank for resale, try for an even bigger score?"

"You see?" Annette Byers said bitterly. "You see, smart guy? He knows everything."

Cohalan shook his head. He'd gotten over his initial shock; now he looked stricken, and his nerves were acting up again. His hands had begun repeating that scoop-shovel trick at his sides. "You believed me, I know you did."

"Wrong," I said. "I didn't believe you. I'm a better actor than you, is all. Your story didn't sound right from the first. Too elaborate, full of improbabilities. Fifty thousand is too big a blackmail bite for any crime short of homicide, and you swore to me — your wife, too — you weren't guilty of a major felony. Blackmailers seldom work in big bites anyway. They bleed their victims slow and steady, in small bites, to keep them from throwing the hook. We just didn't believe it, either of us."

"We? Jesus, you mean . . . you and Carolyn . . .?"

"That's right. Your wife's my client, Cohalan, not you — that's why I never asked you for a retainer. She showed up at my office right after you did the first time; if she hadn't, I'd probably have gone to her. She'd been suspicious all along, but she gave you the benefit of the doubt until you hit her with the fifty-thousand-dollar bite. She figured you might be having an affair, too, and it didn't take me long to find out about Annette. You never had any idea you were being followed, did you? Once I knew about her, it was easy enough to put the rest of it together, including the funny business with the money drop tonight. And here we are."

"Damn you," he said, but there was no heat in the words. "You and that frigid bitch both."

He wasn't talking about Annette Byers, but she took the opportunity to dig into him again. "Smart guy. Big genius. I told you to just take the money and we'd run with it, didn't I?"

"Shut up."

"Don't tell me to shut up, you son of —"

"Don't say it. I'll slap you silly if you say it."

"You won't slap anybody," I said. "Not as long as I'm around."

He wiped his mouth on the sleeve of his jacket. "What're you going to do?"

"What do you think I'm going to do?"

"You can't go to the police. You don't have any proof, it's your word against ours."

"Wrong again." I showed him the voice-activated recorder I'd had hidden in my pocket all evening. High-tech, state-of-the-art equipment, courtesy of George Agonistes, fellow P.I. and electronics expert. "Everything that was said in your office and in this room tonight is on here. I've also got the cassette tape Annette played when she called earlier. Voice prints will prove the muffled voice on it is yours, that you were talking to yourself on the phone, giving yourself orders and directions. If your wife wants to press charges, she'll have more than enough evidence to put the two of you away."

"She won't press charges," he said. "Not Carolyn."

"Maybe not, if you return the rest of her money. What you and baby here haven't already blown."

He sleeved his mouth again. "I suppose you intend to take the briefcase straight to her."

"You suppose right."

"I could stop you," he said, as if he were trying to convince himself. "I'm as big as you, younger — I could take it away from you."

I repocketed the recorder. I could have showed him the .38, but I grinned at him instead. "Go ahead and try. Or else move away from the door. You've got five seconds to make up your mind."

He moved in three, as I started toward him. Sideways, clear of both me and the door. Annette Byers let out a sharp, scornful laugh, and he whirled on her — somebody his own size to face off against. "Shut your stupid mouth!" he yelled at her.

"Shut yours, big man. You and your brilliant ideas."

"Goddamn you . . ."

I went out and closed the door against their vicious, whining voices.

Outside, the fog had thickened to a near drizzle, slicking the pavement and turning the lines of parked cars along both curbs into two-dimensional black shapes. Parking was at such a premium in this neighborhood, there was now a car, dark and silent, double-parked across the street. I walked quickly to California. Nobody, police included, had bothered my wheels in the bus zone. I locked the briefcase in the trunk, let myself inside. A quick call to Carolyn Cohalan to let her know I was coming, a short ride out to her house by the zoo to deliver the fifty thousand, and I'd be finished for the night.

Only she didn't answer her phone.

Funny. When I'd called her earlier from the park, she'd said she would wait for my next call. No reason for her to leave the house in the interim. Unless —

Christ!

I heaved out of the car and ran back down Locust Street. The darkened vehicle was still double-parked across from Annette Byers's building. I swung into the foyer, jammed my finger against the bell button for 2-C and left it there. No response. I rattled the door — latched tight — and then began jabbing buttons on all the other mailboxes. The intercom crackled; somebody's voice said, "Who the hell is that?" I said, "Police emergency, buzz me in." Nothing, nothing, and then finally the door release sounded; I hit the door hard and lunged into the lobby.

I was at the foot of the stairs when the first shot echoed from above. Two more in swift succession, a fourth as I was pounding up to the second-floor landing.

Querulous voices, the sound of a door banging open somewhere, and I was at 2-C. The door there was shut but not latched; I kicked it open, hanging back with the .38 in my hand for self-protection. But there was no need. It was over by then. Too late and all over.

All three of them were on the floor. Cohalan on his back next to the couch, blood obscuring his face, not moving. Annette Byers sprawled bloody and moaning by the dinette table. And Carolyn Cohalan sitting with her back against a wall, a long-barreled .22 on the carpet nearby, weeping in deep, broken sobs.

I leaned hard on the doorjamb, the stink of cordite in my nostrils, my throat full of bile. Telling myself it was not my fault, there was no way I could have known it wasn't the money but paying them back that mattered to her — the big payoff, the biggest bite there is. Telling myself I could've done nothing to prevent this, and remembering what I'd been thinking in the car earlier about how I lived for cases like this, how I liked this one a whole lot . . .

PETER ROBINSON

Missing in Action

FROM *Ellery Queen's Mystery Magazine*

PEOPLE GO MISSING all the time in war, of course, but not usually nine-year-old boys. Besides, the war had hardly begun. It was only the twentieth of September, 1939, when Mary Critchley came hammering on my door at about three o'clock, interrupting my afternoon nap.

It was a Wednesday, and normally I would have been teaching the fifth-formers Shakespeare at Silverhill Grammar School (a thankless task if ever there was one), but the Ministry had just got around to constructing air-raid shelters there, so the school was closed for the week. We didn't even know if it was going to reopen, because the idea was to evacuate all the children to safer areas in the countryside. Now, I would be among the first to admit that a teacher's highest aspiration is a school without pupils, but in the meantime the government, in its eternal wisdom, put us redundant teachers to such complex, intellectual tasks as preparing ration cards for the Ministry of Food. (After all, *they* knew what was coming.)

All this was just a small part of the chaos that seemed to reign at that time. Not the chaos of war, the kind I remembered from the trenches at Ypres in 1917, but the chaos of government bureaucracies trying to organize the country for war.

Anyway, I was fortunate enough to become Special Constable, which is a rather grandiose title for a sort of part-time dogsbody, and that was why Mary Critchley came running to me. That and what little reputation I had for solving people's problems.

"Mr. Bashcombe! Mr. Bashcombe!" she cried. "It's our Johnny. He's gone missing. You must help."

My name is actually *Bascombe,* Frank Bascombe, but Mary Critchley has a slight speech impediment, so I forgave her the mispronunciation. Still, with half the city's children running wild in the streets and the other half standing on crowded station platforms clutching their Mickey Mouse gas masks in little cardboard boxes, ready to be herded into trains bound for such nearby country havens as Graythorpe, Kilsden, and Acksham, I thought perhaps she was overreacting a tad, and I can't say I welcomed her arrival after only about twenty of my allotted forty winks.

"He's probably out playing with his mates," I told her.

"Not my Johnny," she said, wiping the tears from her eyes. "Not since . . . you know . . ."

I knew. Mr. Critchley, Ted to his friends, had been a Royal Navy man since well before the war. He had also been unfortunate enough to serve on the fleet carrier *Courageous,* which had been sunk by a German U-boat off the southwest coast of Ireland just three days ago. Over 500 men had been lost, including Ted Critchley. Of course, no body had been found, and probably never would be, so he was only officially "missing in action."

I also knew young Johnny Critchley, and thought him to be a serious boy, a bit too imaginative and innocent for his own good. (Well, many are at that age, aren't they, before the world grabs them by the balls and shakes some reality into them.) Johnny trusted everyone, even strangers.

"Johnny's not been in much of a mood for playing with his mates since we got the news about Ted's ship," Mary Critchley went on.

I could understand that well enough — young Johnny was an only child, and he always did worship his father — but I still didn't see what I could do about it. "Have you asked around?"

"What do you think I've been doing since he didn't come home at twelve o'clock like he was supposed to? I've asked everyone in the street. Last time he was seen he was down by the canal at about eleven o'clock. Maurice Richards saw him. What can I do, Mr. Bashcombe? First Ted, and now . . . now my Johnny!" She burst into tears.

After I had managed to calm her down, I sighed and told her I would look for Johnny myself. There certainly wasn't much hope of my getting the other twenty winks now.

*

It was a glorious day, so warm and sunny you would hardly believe there was a war on. The late-afternoon sunshine made even our narrow streets of cramped brick terrace houses look attractive. As the shadows lengthened, the light turned to molten gold. First, I scoured the local rec where the children played cricket and football, and the dogs ran wild. Some soldiers were busy digging trenches for air-raid shelters. Just the sight of those long, dark grooves in the earth gave me the shivers. Behind the trenches, barrage balloons pulled at their moorings on the breeze like playful porpoises, orange and pink in the sun. I asked the soldiers, but they hadn't seen Johnny. Nor had any of the other lads.

After the rec I headed for the derelict houses on Gallipoli Street. The landlord had let them go to rack and ruin two years ago, and they were quite uninhabitable, not even fit for billeting soldiers. They were also dangerous and should have been pulled down, but I think the old skinflint was hoping a bomb would hit them so he could claim insurance or compensation from the government. The doors and windows had been boarded up, but children are resourceful, and it wasn't difficult even for me to remove a couple of loose sheets of plywood and make my way inside. I wished I had my torch, but I had to make do with what little light slipped through the holes. Every time I moved, my feet stirred up clouds of dust, which did my poor lungs no good at all.

I thought Johnny might have fallen or got trapped in one of the houses. The staircases were rotten, and more than one lad had fallen through on his way up. The floors weren't much better, either, and one of the fourth-formers at Silverhill had needed more than fifteen stitches a couple of weeks ago when one of his legs went right through the rotten wood and the splinters gouged his flesh.

I searched as best I could in the poor light, and I called out Johnny's name, but no answer came. Before I left, I stood silently and listened for any traces of harsh breathing or whimpering.

Nothing.

After three hours of searching the neighbourhood, I'd had no luck at all. Blackout time was 7:45 P.M., so I still had about an hour and a half left, but if Johnny wasn't in any of the local children's usual haunts, I was at a loss as to where to look. I talked to the other boys I met here and there, but none of his friends had seen him since the family got the news of Ted's death. Little Johnny Critchley, it seemed, had vanished into thin air.

At half past six, I called on Maurice Richards, grateful for his offer of a cup of tea and the chance to rest my aching feet. Maurice and I went back a long time. We had both survived the first war, Maurice with the loss of an arm and me with permanent facial scarring and a wracking cough that comes and goes, thanks to the mustard gas leaking through my mask at the Third Battle of Ypres. We never talked about the war, but it was there, we both knew, an invisible bond tying us close together while at the same time excluding us from so much other, normal human intercourse. Not many had seen the things we had, and thank God for that.

Maurice lit up a Passing Cloud one-handed, then he poured the tea. The seven o'clock news came on the radio, some such rot about us vowing to keep fighting until we'd vanquished the foe. It was still very much a war of words at that time, and the more rhetorical the language sounded, the better the politicians thought they were doing. There had been a couple of minor air skirmishes, and the sinking of the *Courageous,* of course, but all the action was taking place in Poland, which seemed as remote as the moon to most people. Some clever buggers had already started calling it the "Bore War."

"Did you hear Tommy Handley last night, Frank?" Maurice asked.

I shook my head. There'd been a lot of hoopla about Tommy Handley's new radio program, "It's That Man Again," or "ITMA," as people called it. I was never a fan. Call me a snob, but when evening falls I'm far happier curling up with a good book or an interesting talk on the radio than listening to Tommy Handley.

"Talk about a laugh," said Maurice. "They had this one sketch about the Ministry of Aggravation and the Office of Twerps. I nearly died."

I smiled. "Not far from the truth," I said. There were now so many of these obscure ministries, boards, and departments involved in so many absurd pursuits — all for the common good, of course — that I had been thinking of writing a dystopian satire. I proposed to set it in the near future, which would merely be a thinly disguised version of the present. So far, all I had was a great idea for the title: I would reverse the last two numbers in the current year, so instead of 1939, I'd call it *1993*. (Well, *I* thought it was a good idea!) "Look, Maurice," I said, "it's about young Johnny Critchley. His mother tells me you were the last person to see him."

"Oh, aye," Maurice said. "She were round asking about him not long ago. Still not turned up?"

"No."

"Cause for concern, then."

"I'm beginning to think so. What was he doing when you saw him?"

"Just walking down by the canal, by old Woodruff's scrap yard."

"That's all?"

"Yes."

"Was he alone?"

Maurice nodded.

"Did he say anything?"

"No."

"You didn't say anything to him?"

"No cause to. He seemed preoccupied, just staring in the water, like, hands in his pockets. I've heard what happened to his dad. A lad has to do his grieving."

"Too true. Did you see anyone else? Anything suspicious?"

"No, nothing. Just a minute, though . . ."

"What?"

"Oh, it's probably nothing, but just after I saw Johnny, when I was crossing the bridge, I bumped into Colin Gormond, you know, that chap who's a bit . . . you know."

Colin Gormond. I knew him all right. And that wasn't good news; it wasn't good news at all.

Of all the policemen they could have sent, they had to send Detective bloody Sergeant Longbottom, a big, brutish-looking fellow with a pronounced limp and a Cro-Magnon brow. Longbottom was thick as two short planks. I doubt he could have found his own arse even if someone nailed a sign on it, or detect his way out of an Anderson shelter if it were in his own backyard. But that's the caliber of men this wretched war has left us with at home. Along with good ones like me, of course.

DS Longbottom wore a shiny brown suit and a Silverhill Grammar School tie. I wondered where he'd got it from; he probably stole it from some schoolboy he caught nicking sweets from the corner shop. He kept tugging at his collar with his pink sausage fingers as we talked in Mary Critchley's living room. His face was flushed with the heat, and sweat gathered on his thick eyebrows and trickled down the sides of his neck.

"So he's been missing since lunchtime, has he?" DS Longbottom repeated.

Mary Critchley nodded. "He went out at about half past ten, just for a walk, like. Said he'd be back at twelve. When it got to three . . . well, I went to see Mr. Bashcombe here."

DS Longbottom curled his lip at me and grunted. "Mr. Bascombe. *Special* Constable. I suppose you realize that gives you no real police powers, don't you?"

"As a matter of fact," I said, "I thought it made me your superior. After all, you're not a *special* sergeant, are you?"

He looked at me as if he wanted to hit me. Perhaps he would have done if Mary Critchley hadn't been in the room. "Enough of your lip. Just answer my questions."

"Yes, sir."

"You say you looked all over for this lad?"

"All his usual haunts."

"And you found no trace of him?"

"If I had, do you think we'd have sent for you?"

"I warned you. Cut the lip and answer the questions. This, what's his name, Maurice Richards, was he the last person to see the lad?"

"Johnny's his name. And yes is the answer, as far as we know." I paused. He'd have to know eventually, and if I didn't tell him, Maurice would. The longer we delayed, the worse it would be in the long run. "There was someone else in the area at the time. A man called Colin Gormond."

Mary Critchley gave a sharp gasp. DS Longbottom frowned, licked the tip of his pencil, and scribbled something in his notebook. "I'll have to have a word with him," he said. Then he turned to her. "Recognize the name, do you, ma'am?"

"I know Colin," I answered, perhaps a bit too quickly.

DS Longbottom stared at Mary Critchley, whose lower lip started quivering, then turned slowly back to me. "Tell me about him."

I sighed. Colin Gormond was an oddball. Some people said he

was a bit slow, but I'd never seen any real evidence of that. He lived alone and he didn't have much to do with the locals; that was enough evidence against him for some people.

And then there were the children.

For some reason, Colin preferred the company of the local lads to that of the rest of us adults. To be quite honest, I can't say I blame him, but in a situation like this it's bound to look suspicious. Especially if the investigating officer is someone with the sensitivity and understanding of a DS Longbottom.

Colin would take them trainspotting on the hill overlooking the main line, for example, or he'd play cricket with them on the rec or hand out conkers when the season came. He sometimes bought them sweets and ice creams, even gave them books, marbles, and comics.

To my knowledge, Colin Gormond had never once put a foot out of line, never laid so much as a finger on any of the lads, either in anger or in friendship. There had, however, been one or two mutterings from some parents — most notably from Jack Blackwell, father of one of Johnny's pals, Nick — that it somehow *wasn't right,* that it was *unnatural* for a man who must be in his late thirties or early forties to spend so much time playing with young children. There must be something not quite right in his head, he must be up to *something,* Jack Blackwell hinted, and as usual when someone starts a vicious rumour, there is no shortage of willing believers. Such a reaction was only to be expected from someone, of course, but I knew it wouldn't go down well with DS Longbottom. I don't know why, but I felt a strange need *to protect* Colin.

"Colin's a local," I explained. "Lived around here for years. He plays with the lads a bit. Most of them like him. He seems a harmless sort of fellow."

"How old is he?"

I shrugged. "Hard to say. About forty, perhaps."

DS Longbottom raised a thick eyebrow. "About forty, and he plays with the kiddies, you say?"

"Sometimes. Like a schoolteacher, or a youth-club leader."

"Is he a schoolteacher?"

"No."

"Is he a youth-club leader?"

"No. Look, what I meant —"

"I know exactly what you meant, Mr. Bascombe. Now you just listen to what *I* mean. What we've got here is an older man who's known to hang around with young children, and he's been placed near the scene where a young child has gone missing. Now, don't you think that's just a wee bit suspicious?"

Mary Critchley let out a great wail and started crying again. DS Longbottom ignored her. Instead, he concentrated all his venom on me, the softie, the liberal, the defender of child molesters. "What do you have to say about *that*, Mr. Special Constable Bascombe?"

"Only that Colin was a friend to the children and that he had no reason to harm anyone."

"*Friend,*" DS Longbottom sneered, struggling to his feet. "We can only be thankful you're not regular police, Mr. Bascombe," he said, nodding to himself in acknowledgment of his own wisdom. "That we can."

"So what are you going to do?" I asked.

DS Longbottom looked at his watch and frowned. Either he was trying to work out what it meant when the little hand and the big hand were in the positions they were in, or he was squinting because of poor eyesight. "I'll have a word with this here Colin Gormond. Other than that, there's not much more we can do tonight. First thing tomorrow morning, we'll drag the canal." He got to the door, turned, pointed to the windows, and said, "And don't forget to put up your blackout curtains, ma'am, or you'll have the ARP man to answer to."

Mary Critchley burst into floods of tears again.

Even the soft dawn light could do nothing for the canal. It oozed through the city like an open sewer, oil slicks shimmering like rainbows in the sun, brown water dotted with industrial scum and suds, bits of driftwood and paper wrappings floating along with them. On one side was Ezekiel Woodruff's scrap yard. Old Woodruff was a bit of an eccentric. He used to come around the streets with his horse and cart yelling, "Any old iron," but now the government had other uses for scrap metal — supposedly to be used in aircraft manufacture — poor old Woodruff didn't have any way to make his living anymore. He'd already sent old Nell the carthorse to the knacker's yard, where she was probably doing her bit for the war effort by helping to make the glue to stick the aircraft together. Old mangles and bits of broken furniture stuck up from the ruins of the scrap yard like shattered artillery after a battle.

On the other side, the bank rose steeply toward the backs of the houses on Canal Road, and the people who lived there seemed to regard it as their personal tip. Flies and wasps buzzed around old Hessian sacks and paper bags full of God knew what. A couple of buckled bicycle tires and a wheelless pram completed the picture.

I stood and watched as Longbottom supervised the dragging, a slow and laborious process that seemed to be sucking all manner of unwholesome objects to the surface — except Johnny Critchley's body.

I felt tense. At any moment I half expected the cry to come from one of the policemen in the boats that they had found him, half expected to see the small, pathetic bundle bob above the water's surface. I didn't think Colin Gormond had done anything to Johnny — nor Maurice, though DS Longbottom had seemed suspicious of him, too, but I did think that, given how upset he was, Johnny might just have jumped in. He never struck me as the suicidal type, but I have no idea whether suicide enters the minds of nine-year-olds. All I knew was that he *was* upset about his father, and he *was* last seen skulking by the canal.

So I stood around with DS Longbottom and the rest as the day grew warmer, and there was still no sign of Johnny. After about three hours, the police gave up and went for bacon and eggs at Betty's Cafe over on Chadwick Road. They didn't invite me, and I was grateful to be spared both the unpleasant food and company. I stood and stared into the greasy water a while longer, unsure whether it was a good sign or not that Johnny wasn't in the canal, then I decided to go and have a chat with Colin Gormond.

"What is it, Colin?" I asked him gently. "Come on. You can tell me."

But Colin continued to stand with his back turned to me in the dark corner of his cramped living room, hands to his face, making eerie snuffling sounds, shaking his head. It was bright daylight outside, but the blackout curtains were still drawn tightly, and not a chink of light crept between their edges. I had already tried the light switch, but either Colin had removed the bulb or he didn't have one.

"Come on, Colin. This is silly. You know me. I'm Mr. Bascombe. I won't hurt you. Tell me what happened."

Finally, Colin turned silently and moved out of his corner with his funny, shuffling way of walking. Someone said he had a club-foot, and someone else said he'd had a lot of operations on his feet when he was a young lad, but nobody knew for certain why he walked the way he did. When he sat down and lit a cigarette, the match light illuminated his large nose, shiny forehead, and watery blue eyes. He used the same match to light a candle on the table beside him, and then I saw them: the black eye, the bruise on his left cheek. DS Longbottom. The bastard.

"Did you say anything to him?" I asked, anxious that DS Long-bottom might have beaten a confession out of Colin, without even thinking that Colin probably wouldn't still be at home if that were the case.

He shook his head mournfully. "Nothing, Mr. Bascombe. Honest. There was nothing I *could* tell him."

"Did you see Johnny Critchley yesterday, Colin?"

"Aye."

"Where?"

"Down by the canal."

"What was he doing?"

"Just standing there chucking stones in the water."

"Did you talk to him?"

Colin paused and turned away before answering "No."

I had a brief coughing spell, his cigarette smoke working on my gassed lungs. When it cleared up, I said, "Colin, there's something you're not telling me, isn't there? You'd better tell me. You know I won't hurt you, and I just might be the only person who can help you."

He looked at me, pale eyes imploring. "I only called out to him, from the bridge, like, didn't I?"

"What happened next?"

"Nothing. I swear it."

"Did he answer?"

"No. He just looked my way and shook his head. I could tell then that he didn't want to play. He seemed sad."

"He'd just heard his dad's been killed."

Colin's already watery eyes brimmed with tears. "Poor lad."

I nodded. For all I knew, Colin might have been thinking about *his* dad, too. Not many knew it, but Mr. Gormond senior had been killed in the same bloody war that left me with my bad lungs and scarred face. "What happened next, Colin?"

Colin shook his head and wiped his eyes with the back of his hand. "Nothing," he said. "It was such a lovely day, I just went on walking. I went to the park and watched the soldiers digging trenches, then I went for my cigarettes and came home to listen to the wireless."

"And after that?"

"I stayed in."

"All evening?"

"That's right. Sometimes I go down to the White Rose, but . . ."

"But what, Colin?"

"Well, Mr. Smedley, you know, the Air-Raid Precautions man?"

I nodded. "I know him."

"He said my blackout cloth wasn't good enough and he'd fine me if I didn't get some proper stuff by yesterday."

"I understand, Colin." Good-quality, thick, impenetrable blackout cloth had become both scarce and expensive, which was no doubt why Colin had been cheated in the first place.

"Anyway, what with that and the cigarettes . . ."

I reached into my pocket and slipped out a few bob for him. Colin looked away, ashamed, but I put it on the table and he didn't tell me to take it back. I knew how it must hurt his pride to accept charity, but I had no idea how much money he made, or how he made it. I'd never seen him beg, but I had a feeling he survived on odd jobs and lived very much from hand to mouth.

I stood up. "All right, Colin," I said. "Thanks very much." I paused at the door, uncertain how to say what had just entered my mind. Finally, I blundered ahead. "It might be better if you kept a low profile till they find him, Colin. You know what some of the people around here are like."

"What do you mean, Mr. Bascombe?"

"Just be careful, Colin, that's all I mean. Just be careful."

He nodded gormlessly, and I left.

As I was leaving Colin's house, I noticed Jack Blackwell standing on his doorstep, arms folded, a small crowd of locals around him, their shadows intersecting on the cobbled street. They kept glancing toward Colin's house, and when they saw me come out, they all shuffled off except Jack himself, who gave me a grim stare before going inside and slamming his door. I felt a shiver go up my spine, as if a goose had stepped on my grave, as my dear mother used to say, bless her soul, and when I got home I couldn't concentrate on my book one little bit.

By the following morning, when Johnny had been missing over thirty-six hours, the mood in the street had started to turn ugly. In my experience, when you get right down to it, there's no sorrier spectacle, nothing much worse or more dangerous, than the human mob mentality. After all, armies are nothing more than mobs, really, even when they are organized to a greater or lesser degree. I'd been at Ypres, as you know, and there wasn't a hell of a lot you could tell me about military organization. So when I heard the muttered words on doorsteps, saw the little knots of people here and there, Jack Blackwell flitting from door to door like a political canvasser, I had to do something, and I could hardly count on any help from DS Longbottom.

One thing I had learned both as a soldier and as a schoolteacher was that, if you had a chance, your best bet was to take out the ringleader. That meant Jack Blackwell. Jack was the nasty type, and he and I had had more than one run-in over his son Nick's bullying and poor performance in class. In my opinion, young Nick was the sort of walking dead loss who should probably have been drowned at birth, a waste of skin, sinew, tissue, and bone, and it wasn't hard to see where he got it from. Nick's older brother, Dave, was already doing a long stretch in the Scrubs for beating a night watchman senseless during a robbery, and even the army couldn't find an excuse to spring him and enlist his service in killing Germans. Mrs. Blackwell had been seen more than once walking with difficulty, with bruises on her cheek. The sooner Jack Blackwell got his call-up papers, the better things would be all around.

I intercepted Jack between the Deakins' and the Kellys' houses, and it was clear from his gruff "What do you want?" that he didn't want to talk to me.

But I was adamant.

"'Morning, Jack," I greeted him. "Lovely day for a walk, isn't it?"

"What's it to you?"

"Just being polite. What are you up to, Jack? What's going on?"

"None of your business."

"Up to your old tricks? Spreading poison?"

"I don't know what you're talking about." He made to walk away, but I grabbed his arm. He glared at me but didn't do anything. Just as well. At my age, and with my lungs, I'd hardly last ten seconds in a fight. "Jack," I said, "don't you think you'd all be best off using your time to look for the poor lad?"

"Look for him! That's a laugh. You know as well as I do where that young lad is."

"Where? Where is he, Jack?"

"You know."

"No, I don't. Tell me."

"He's dead and buried, that's what."

"Where, Jack?"

"I don't know the exact spot. If he's not in the canal, then he's buried somewhere not far away."

"Maybe he is. But you don't *know* that. Not for certain. And even if you believe that, you don't know who put him there."

Jack wrenched his arm out of my weakening grip and sneered. "I've got a damn sight better idea than you have, Frank Bascombe. With all your *book* learning!" Then he turned and marched off.

Somehow, I got the feeling that I had just made things worse.

After my brief fracas with Jack Blackwell, I was at a loose end. I knew the police would still be looking for Johnny, asking questions, searching areas of waste ground, so there wasn't much I could do to help them. Feeling impotent, I went down to the canal, near Woodruff's scrap yard. Old Ezekiel Woodruff himself was poking around in the ruins of his business, so I decided to talk to him. I kept my distance, though, for even on a hot day such as this, Woodruff was wearing his greatcoat and black wool gloves with the fingers cut off. He wasn't known for his personal hygiene, so I made sure I didn't stand downwind of him. Not that there was much of a wind, but then it didn't take much.

"Morning, Ezekiel," I said. "I understand young Johnny Critchley was down around here yesterday."

"So they say," muttered Ezekiel.

"See him, did you?"

"I weren't here."

"So you didn't see him?"

"Police have already been asking questions."

"And what did you tell them?"

He pointed to the other side of the canal, the back of the housing estate. "I were over there," he said. "Sometimes people chuck out summat of value, even these days."

"But you did see Johnny?"

He paused, then said, "Aye."

"On this side of the canal?"

Woodruff nodded.

"What time was this?"

"I don't have a watch, but it weren't long after that daft bloke had gone by."

"Do you mean Colin Gormond?"

"Aye, that's the one."

So Johnny was still alone by the canal *after* Colin had passed by. DS Longbottom had probably known this, but he had beaten Colin anyway. One day I'd find a way to get even with him. The breeze shifted a little and I got a whiff of stale sweat and worse. "What was Johnny doing?"

"Doing? Nowt special. He were just walking."

"Walking? Where?"

Woodruff pointed. "That way. Towards the city center."

"Alone?"

"Aye."

"And nobody approached him?"

"Nope. Not while I were watching."

I didn't think there was anything further to be got from Ezekiel Woodruff, so I bade him good morning. I can't say the suspicion didn't enter my head that *he* might have had something to do with Johnny's disappearance, though I'd have been hard pushed to say exactly why or what. Odd though old Woodruff might be, there had never been any rumor or suspicion of his being overly interested in young boys, and I didn't want to jump to conclusions the way Jack Blackwell had. Still, I filed away my suspicions for later.

A fighter droned overhead. I watched it dip and spin through the blue air and wished I could be up there. I'd always regretted not being a pilot in the war. A barge full of soldiers drifted by, and I moved aside on the towpath to let the horse that was pulling it pass by. For my troubles I got a full blast of sweaty horseflesh and a pile of steaming manure at my feet. That had even Ezekiel Woodruff beat.

Aimlessly, I followed the direction Ezekiel had told me Johnny had walked in — toward the city center. As I walked, Jack Blackwell's scornful words about my inability to find Johnny echoed in my mind. *Book learning.* That was exactly the kind of cheap insult you would expect from a moron like Jack Blackwell, but it hurt nonetheless. No sense telling him I'd been buried in the mud under the bodies of my comrades for two days. No sense telling him about the young German soldier I'd surprised and bayonetted to death, twisting the blade until it snapped and broke off inside him. Jack Blackwell was too young to have seen action in the last war, but if there was any justice in the world, he'd damn well see it in *this* one.

The canal ran by the back of the train station, where I crossed the narrow bridge and walked through the crowds of evacuees out front to City Square. Mary Critchley's anguish reverberated in my mind, too: *"Mr. Bashcombe! Mr. Bashcombe!"* I heard her call.

Then, all of a sudden, as I looked at the black facade of the post office and the statue of the Black Prince in the center of City Square, it hit me. I thought I knew what had happened to Johnny Critchley, but first I had to go back to his street and ask just one important question.

It was late morning. The station smelled of damp soot and warm oil. Crowds of children thronged around trying to find out where they were supposed to go. They wore nametags and carried little cardboard boxes. Adults with clipboards, for the most part temporarily unemployed schoolteachers and local volunteers, directed them to the right queue, and their names were ticked off as they boarded the carriages.

Despite being neither an evacuated child nor a supervisor, I managed to buy a ticket and ended up sharing a compartment with a rather severe-looking woman in a brown uniform I didn't recognize, and a male civilian with a brush mustache and a lot of Brylcreem on his hair. They seemed to be in charge of several young children, also in the compartment, who couldn't sit still. I could hardly blame them. They were going to the alien countryside, to live with strangers, far away from their parents, for only God knew how long, and the idea scared them half to death.

The buttoned cushions were warm and the air in the carriage still and close, despite the open window. When we finally set off, the motion stirred up a bit of a breeze, which helped a little. On the wall opposite me was a poster of the Scarborough seafront, and I spent most of the journey remembering the carefree childhood holidays I had enjoyed there with my parents in the early years of the century: another world, another time. The rest of the trip, I glanced out of the window, beyond the scum-scabbed canal, and saw the urban industrial landscape drift by: back gardens, where some people had put in Anderson shelters, half covered with earth to grow vegetables on; the dark mass of the town hall clock tower behind the city center buildings; a factory yard, where several men were loading heavy crates onto a lorry, flushed and sweating in the heat.

Then we were in the countryside, where the smells of grass, hay, and manure displaced the reek of the city. I saw small, squat farms, drystone walls, sheep and cattle grazing. Soon, train tracks and canal diverged. We went under a long noisy tunnel, and the children whimpered. Later, I was surprised to see so many army convoys winding along the narrow roads, and the one big aerodrome we passed seemed buzzing with activity.

All in all, the journey took a little over two hours. Only about ten or eleven children were shepherded off at the small country station, and I followed as they were met and taken to the village hall, where the men and women who were to care for them waited. It was more civilized than some of the evacuation systems I'd heard about, which sounded more like the slave markets of old, where farmers waited on the platforms to pick out the strong lads, and local dignitaries whisked away the nicely dressed boys and girls.

I went up to the volunteer in charge, an attractive young countrywoman in a simple blue frock with a white lace collar and a belt around her slim waist, and asked her if she had any record of an evacuee called John, or Johnny, Critchley. She checked her records, then shook her head, as I knew she would. If I were right,

Johnny wouldn't be here under his own name. I explained my problem to the woman, who told me her name was Phyllis Rigby. She had a yellow ribbon in her long wavy hair and smelled of fresh apples. "I don't see how anything like that could have happened," Phyllis said. "We've been very meticulous. But there again, things *have* been a little chaotic." She frowned in thought for a moment, then she delegated her present duties to another volunteer.

"Come on," she said, "I'll help you go from house to house. There weren't that many evacuees, you know. Far fewer than we expected."

I nodded. I'd heard how a lot of parents weren't bothering to evacuate their children. "They can't see anything happening yet," I said. "Just you wait. After the first air raid you'll have so many you won't have room for them all."

Phyllis smiled. "The poor things. It must be such an upheaval for them."

"Indeed."

I took deep, welcome breaths of country air as Phyllis and I set out from the village hall to visit the families listed on her clipboard. There were perhaps a couple of hundred houses, and less than fifty percent had received evacuees. Even so, we worked up quite a sweat calling at them all. Or I did, rather, as sweating didn't seem to be in Phyllis's nature. We chatted as we went, me telling her about my schoolteaching, and her telling me about her husband, Thomas, training as a fighter pilot in the RAF. After an hour or so with no luck, we stopped in at her cottage for a refreshing cup of tea, then we were off again.

At last, late in the afternoon, we struck gold.

Mr. and Mrs. Douglas, who were billeting Johnny Critchley, seemed a very pleasant couple, and they were sad to hear that they would not get to keep him with them for a while longer. I explained everything to them and assured them that they would get someone else as soon as we got the whole business sorted out.

"He's *not* here," Johnny said as we walked with Phyllis to the station. "I've looked everywhere, but I couldn't find him."

I shook my head. "Sorry, Johnny. You know your mum's got a speech impediment. That was why I had to go back and ask her exactly what she said to you before I came here. She said she told you your father was missing in action, which, the way it came out, sounded like missing in *Acksham,* didn't it? That's why you came here, isn't it, to look for your father?"

Young Johnny nodded, tears in his eyes. "I'm sorry," he said. "I couldn't understand why she didn't come and look for him. She must be really vexed with me."

I patted his shoulder. "I don't think so. More like she'll be glad to see you. How did you manage to sneak in with the real evacuees, by the way?"

Johnny wiped his eyes with his grubby sleeve. "At the station. There were so many people standing around, at first I didn't know . . . Then I saw a boy I knew from playing cricket on the rec."

"Oliver Bradley," I said. The boy whose name Johnny was registered under.

"Yes. He goes to Broad Hill."

I nodded. Though I had never heard of Oliver Bradley, I knew the school; it was just across the valley from us. "Go on."

"I asked him where he was going, and he said he was being sent to Acksham. It was perfect."

"But how did you get him to change places with you?"

"He didn't want to. Not at first."

"How did you persuade him?"

Johnny looked down at the road and scraped at some gravel with the scuffed tip of his shoe. "It cost me a complete set of 'Great Cricketers' cigarette cards. Ones my dad gave me before he went away."

I smiled. It would have to be something like that.

"And I made him promise not to tell anyone, just to go home and say there wasn't room for him and he'd have to try again in a few days. I just needed enough time to find Dad . . . you know."

"I know."

We arrived at the station, where Johnny sat on the bench and Phyllis and I chatted in the late afternoon sunlight, our shadows lengthening across the tracks. In addition to the birds singing in the trees and hedgerows, I could hear grasshoppers chirruping, a sound you rarely heard in the city. I had often thought how much I would like to live in the country, and perhaps when I retired from teaching a few years in the future I would be able to do so.

We didn't have long to wait for our train. I thanked Phyllis for all her help, told her I wished her husband well, and she waved to us as the old banger chugged out of the station.

It was past blackout when I finally walked into our street holding Johnny's hand. He was tired after his adventure and had spent most of the train journey with his head on my shoulder. Once or twice, from the depths of a dream, he had called his father's name.

I could sense that something was wrong as soon as I turned the corner. It was nothing specific, just a sudden chill at the back of my neck. Because of the blackout, I couldn't see anything clearly, but I got a strong impression of a knot of shifting shadows, just a little bit darker than the night itself, milling around outside Colin Gormond's house.

I quickened my step, and as I got nearer I heard a whisper pass through the crowd when they saw Johnny. Then the shadows began to disperse, slinking and sidling away, disappearing like smoke into the air. From somewhere, Mary Critchley lurched forward with a cry and took young Johnny in her arms. I let him go. I could hear her thanking me between sobs, but I couldn't stop walking.

The first thing I noticed when I approached Colin's house was that the window was broken and half the blackout curtain had been ripped away. Next, I saw that the door was slightly ajar. I was worried that Colin might be hurt, but out of courtesy I knocked and called out his name.

Nothing.

I pushed the door open and walked inside. It was pitch dark. I didn't have a torch with me, and I knew that Colin's light didn't work, but I remembered the matches and the candle on the table. I lit it and held it up before me as I walked forward.

I didn't have far to look. If I hadn't had the candle, I might have bumped right into him. First I saw his face, about level with mine. His froth-specked lips had turned blue, and a trickle of dried blood ran from his left nostril. The blackout cloth was knotted around his neck in a makeshift noose, attached to a hook screwed into the lintel over the kitchen door. As I stood back and examined the scene further, I saw that his downturned toes were about three inches from the floor, and there was no sign of an upset chair or stool.

Harmless Colin Gormond, friend to the local children. Dead.

I felt the anger well up in me, along with the guilt. It was my fault.

I shouldn't have gone dashing off to Acksham like that in search of Johnny, or I should at least have taken Colin with me. I knew the danger he was in; I had talked to Jack Blackwell before I left. How could I have been so stupid, so careless as to leave Colin to his fate with only a warning he didn't understand?

Maybe Colin *had* managed to hang himself somehow, without standing on a stool, though I doubted it. But whether or not Jack Blackwell or the rest had actually laid a finger on him, they were all guilty of driving him to it in my book. Besides, if Jack or anyone else from the street *had* strung Colin up, there would be evidence — fibers, fingerprints, footprints, whatever — and even DS bloody Longbottom wouldn't be able to ignore that.

I stumbled outside and made my way toward the telephone box on the corner. Not a soul stirred now, but as I went I heard one door — Jack Blackwell's door — close softly this time, as if he thought that too much noise might wake the dead, and the dead might have a tale or two to tell.

ROXANA ROBINSON

The Face-Lift

FROM *The Atlantic Monthly*

THIS HAPPENED in San Salvador, not long ago. My friend Cristina
was coming back from lunch at a restaurant downtown with her
mother, Elvira, and her mother's friend, Consuela. They were in
Cristina's big car, and all three sat in the back. The driver was alone
in the front seat.

Cristina was dropping her mother and Consuela off at her
mother's house. Her mother lives on a narrow street lined with
high stucco walls and solid gates. Everyone in that neighborhood
has big heavy gates controlled by electricity. The car drives up to
the gate, the chauffeur pushes a remote control button, the gates
open inward, the car drives inside, and the gates close after it. The
walls in San Salvador have always been high. In the past broken bottles were cemented into the tops of them — a row of glittering
teeth to keep people from climbing over. Now electrified wires
have replaced the broken bottles. El Salvador has always been like
this, but since the revolution security has become more of a problem.

Cristina's car pulled into Elvira's clean, quiet street. All the
houses there were tidy, all the high stucco walls freshly painted, all
the gates tightly closed. They drove slowly down the block toward
Elvira's house. A car, which no one noticed, was parked halfway
down the block. At her mother's house Cristina told the driver to
pull over to the sidewalk, to let her mother and Consuela out. They
didn't go in through the big gates because Cristina was continuing
on from there. The two women would get out at the little street
door, right next to the sidewalk.

"Por aquí, por aquí, por aquí," Cristina said rapidly to the driver. Cristina says everything rapidly; she moves quickly and talks fast. She is quite beautiful, with thick black-brown hair and large, bright, dark eyes. She has an oval face and a short, straight nose. Her eyelids are slightly droopy, which gives her a drowsy, aristocratic look. She was my roommate in boarding school.

Cristina and I went to the same girls' school, outside Philadelphia, on the Main Line, but we came from very different worlds. I grew up in the country, in western Pennsylvania. My mother was the librarian at my elementary school, and my father was a doctor. We lived in an old stone farmhouse, rather dark inside, with small windows. I was an only child. Every night the three of us sat down to dinner at the round wooden table in the kitchen. We bowed our heads, and then my mother said grace over the food. After we raised our heads, I poured each of us a glass of water. The pitcher was made of dark blue china. My father spoke very little at meals, and our house was quiet inside. Outside were smooth rolling fields. At night I could feel the three of us in our small lighted house, alone in all that empty land, set among the dark fields.

I was brought up to be good and obey the rules, and I was, and I did. I couldn't imagine violating those beliefs that grown-ups held: that rules were important, that lies were intolerable, that being good was the correct way to be. At school I was good. I wasn't good enough to be a star at anything (I was a mediocre student), but I wasn't bad. The worst thing I ever did was to sneak out on Halloween and go trick-or-treating through the darkened streets of Bryn Mawr, carrying a pillowcase and knocking timidly at front doors. I never lied to teachers or sneaked out to meet boys or cheated on tests or smuggled in alcohol or smoked marijuana or did anything wrong. Those things were beyond me somehow, out of my reach. The rules I'd been given held me within their bounds.

But Cristina came from a large family and a fiery-hot place that was unimaginable to me, and she broke any rule she felt like breaking. She kept vodka in our room at school, right on her bureau. It was in a Phisohex bottle, in full view of the housemother. Cristina looked straight into teachers' eyes and lied about where she was going for the weekend. She lied about how she was getting there and whom she was seeing. She did all this with a bold and absolute certainty that I admired: she was utterly sure of the rules she wanted to break and of the things she needed to do. She didn't care about her grades or about honesty or about living up to people's expectations. All that was immaterial to her. The things she did need to do were things like going off to Princeton for the weekend. The things she didn't need to do were things like homework.

After we graduated, I went on to college and Cristina went back to El Salvador. In school she had laughed when I asked her about college.

"Are you kidding?" she said. "You have no idea what it's like down there. No one I know goes to college."

"But what do you do instead?" I asked.

"We do our hair, and then we do our nails." She looked up at me and laughed again. "What we do is visit each other. We go and stay with friends in their country places; then they come and stay with us at our beach houses. We go to someone's ranch in Argentina. We go down to Rio sometimes. We're busy! This takes up all our time."

"Then we get married," she added.

While she was telling me this, Cristina was sitting on her bed with no clothes on, a thick maroon towel wrapped around her head. She had a bigger, thicker towel wrapped around her body, tucked in on itself at her left armpit. Her legs were shaved perfectly smooth. She was painting her toenails, very meticulously, and she had tiny puffs of cotton separating her toes. She had a bottle of scarlet nail polish, and undercoat, and overcoat, and bottles of other luxurious things — emollients and oils and lotions. It looked as if a professional had just stepped out of the room for a moment, in the middle of doing a job on Cristina's toes.

I never did my toenails at school. Even today I've never done my toenails. My feet are large and rather homely. Putting scarlet shimmer on my big, square nails would be an error, and I can't help knowing this. I loved the way Cristina put shimmer on her toes, the way she put shimmer anywhere, everywhere, wherever she wanted.

Cristina got married two years after we graduated from boarding school. She invited me to the wedding, but it was during my final exams, and I couldn't go. In fact, I never went down to see her. We wrote to each other for a few years, but Cristina is not much interested in writing. After the letters stopped, she sent Christmas cards, and each year I would examine her family photograph: there was Cristina, looking wonderful, tanned and gleaming, with her delicious, smooth caramel skin and her thick, dark hair and sleepy eyes, standing beside her husband, who was very handsome. Cristina had always said she would marry only a handsome man. His name was Carlos, which she pronounced "Car-los," with a wonderful sort of gargle between the syllables. Car-los was tan too, with a square face, dashing low eyebrows, big, brilliant black eyes. The children looked like Cristina, exactly. Two girls and a boy. I watched them on the Christmas cards, turning more and more like Cristina each year, their chins pointed, their small, perfect bodies supple and alert, their features neat and animated. I knew their names: Analisa, Jorge, Elenita. Sometimes when I was thinking about Cristina, I would say those names in a whisper to myself: Analisa, Jorge, Elenita. They had such a crackle, such a lilt. That seemed to be the way Cristina's life was.

After college I got married, and in the beginning I thought I would have children too. I sent Cristina Christmas cards, sometimes seasonal pictures of reindeer or snowy forests and sometimes snapshots of Mark and me. Every year I hoped I would be able to put a note on our card: "Next Christmas there'll be three of us!" I imagined writing the notes. I imagined different ways of making my announcement, something lively or funny or clever. A photograph of the two of us with a note next to it: "How many people are in this picture? Wrong."

Cristina didn't come to my wedding, because she was pregnant with her first child. She was too big to travel, she told me. She couldn't move, she told me. I smiled as I read this, trying to imagine Cristina as big as a house, lying like a languorous whale on a sofa out on a veranda, long-leafed plants in giant urns at each end. I liked the image of her sleepy and swollen. This is what it's like, I thought to myself, with a little thrill of anticipation. Soon I would know about this: morning sickness, fatigue, swollen ankles.

When I learned that she had become pregnant again, three years later, I felt a jolt. It seemed unfair that she should be pregnant for the second time before I was for the first. Then it happened a third time. I saw her swollen belly on the Christmas card photograph that year, with a casual hand laid on top of it, and I felt betrayed and abandoned, as though some promise to me had not been kept.

I loved Cristina, and I didn't begrudge her having children. But when she did, I felt the absence of my own.

Cristina always asked on her Christmas cards when I was going to come down and visit them, and I thought for years that I would. But I never found a good time to do it, so I just kept Cristina and Carlos and the three tiny Cristinas in my head. I imagined them living luxuriously in a low colonial city with stone buildings, wide colonnaded avenues, palm trees, and scarlet flowers erupting everywhere.

When I heard about the revolution, about assassinations and hostages and *desaparecidos*, I worried. I wrote Cristina twice, but she didn't reply. I hoped they had moved to Guatemala, where Carlos had family and business interests, or somewhere else less dangerous. Carlos and Cristina came from very rich families, and it seemed that everyone they knew was rich. Being rich had originally seemed like a great shining carapace of protection over them, shielding them from everything: from having to go to college, having to wake up in the night with a crying baby, having to carry money, having to stand in line at the supermarket, having to find a parking place. But during the revolution being rich took on another aspect. It seemed like a signal they gave off continually and involuntarily, which made them terrifyingly vulnerable, as if they were targets for heat-seeking missiles that followed them no matter how they twisted and turned, no matter what they tried to do to save themselves.

I hoped that Cristina and her family were somewhere safe, and I found out later that they were. They had gone to Guatemala.

Then one year they turned up in New York, the whole family, for a week before Christmas. Cristina called me, and we made a plan to meet for lunch. She looked just as appealing as she always had — vivid and exotic, her clothes a little brighter than a New York woman's, her jewelry a little more brilliant. She held my shoulders tightly in her hands and kissed me on both cheeks.

"Julie!" she said. "You look wonderful!"

I didn't look wonderful. I knew that. I'm plain, with pale, freckled skin. I've put on a middle, and I wear my skirts below the knee. My hair is just as it was at boarding school, shoulder length, and held back from my face with a tortoise-shell band. Even when I remember to wear earrings, as I did that day, they look as though

I've borrowed them from someone. I've always looked like this. I never had the nerve to wear clothes that were tight and spangled, jazzy and stretchy. When I was at school, wearing clothes like that seemed wrong. I felt I had to make a moral choice, and that somehow I was coming down on the right side. I think I believed in some long-term goal, as though later on I might get an award for Discreet Dressing. Now I can't change; this is the only way I know how to dress.

I'm divorced now. Mark has remarried and lives in San Francisco, where he works for a software company. He has two children — boys, I think. I haven't heard from him in years. We have no reason to talk ever again. Nothing connects us now but pain. Looking back at that time we were together is like looking into a black tunnel of grief — tumultuous, endless, without solace. Just thinking of his name brings back the memory of that misery.

I'm used to living on my own, though I'd hoped not to. I live in a small apartment in Murray Hill. I run a family arts foundation that specializes in music education, and we give away $50,000 a year in small grants. We review the recipients very carefully. We visit the sites, we interview the participants, we talk to other people in the field for references. We want to feel that we are rewarding the people who most deserve it. I want to give them their due.

I've always tried to be fair, and to be responsible. I once thought that was the way the world worked, the way everyone worked. At school I was always amazed that Cristina got away with what she did. I confess that at times I almost hoped Cristina would get caught at something. In those moments I resented her astonishing bravado.

I remember her one Friday afternoon during our junior year. Cristina stood coolly in the handsome front hall of the school, on the Oriental rug, next to the big Spanish chest. She was wearing a new orange suit and was waiting for a taxi to come and take her to the train with her suitcase.

"Now, let me see, Cristina. This is your uncle's name, Alfredo Pacheco?" Mrs. Winston, the housemother, held Cristina's weekend form, which she had duly filled out. Mrs. Winston was a pleasant woman, tall and lean and attractive, with black-rimmed glasses, perfectly curled-under gray hair, and a perfectly straight back.

"That's right, Mrs. Winston," Cristina said. She smiled dazzlingly at the housemother. Cristina's shoes and pocketbook matched, both dark brown. Her hair was glossy and full of bounce. She had a brown and orange silk scarf at her throat.

"And he lives in Philadelphia, at this address?" Mrs. Winston looked at the form.

"That's right," Cristina said. "I put down his phone number. That's where I'll be." She was going to Princeton for House-parties Weekend.

"All right," Mrs. Winston said, looking again at the form. "This seems fine." The taxi drew up to the door, and Cristina picked up her suitcase. "Have a nice time," Mrs. Winston called, and Cristina waved as she got into the taxi. She looked out at me and waved again, her smile to me slightly different. She never got caught; I never went to House-parties Weekend.

But in New York that day, when she grabbed me and hugged me, I was caught up again by her energetic intimacy, won over by her charm.

"Tell me everything," Cristina said, sitting down again, "and let's get something to drink — or at least I hope you'll have a drink. Everyone has stopped drinking. And smoking. Do you mind?" She looked at me solicitously, holding up a cigarette.

"I don't mind," I said, "but the restaurant won't let you." We were in a small Italian place in the East Seventies, just off Madison. She couldn't smoke there or in any New York restaurant; it was now illegal.

Cristina waved her hand. "Oh, they don't mind if I smoke," she said. "I've already talked to the waiter." Someone had put an ashtray next to her, and she flipped open her lighter and lit up. I was surprised by this. I had not seen anyone smoke in a restaurant since the law was passed, and I looked nervously over at the waiter, but he walked right by our table with a bottle of wine, ignoring us completely. I wondered if Cristina had to obey any rules at all.

"What's happened to everyone?" Cristina asked, drawing hard on her cigarette, sucking in her cheeks for a long, disreputable pull. She exhaled, shaking her head and expelling a bluish cloud. "I go away for a couple of years and all of a sudden the entire population of New York has turned into goody-goodies. What is it?" She grinned at me. "I bet *you* don't smoke, do you?" she said, cocking her head.

"No," I admitted, "but I never really did."

"No, that's right," Cristina said, remembering. She leaned back in her chair and took another luxurious drag on her cigarette. She grinned again. "You never did. You never broke any of the rules. You made me feel like such a bad girl! I felt like a felon!" She laughed and shook her head. "But now you're a big success, eh? I hear you're the head of your foundation! *¡La Exigente!*"

That's how Cristina talks — all exclamation points and big scarlet smiles. Anything is more fun when she tells it. Listening to her, and watching her smoke, I found myself being torn, as I always had been, between simply adoring her and wishing grumpily that somehow she wouldn't get away with everything.

"You look terrific," I said, which was true.

Cristina pulled in her chin and gave me a knowing look. *"Please,"* she said extravagantly, rolling her eyes. She put down her cigarette and turned sideways, thrusting her head out and stretching out her neck. A tiny swag of skin hung below her chin. Cristina patted the top of her hand against it. "What about this horror? But it's going," she announced. She turned back to face me and touched a line between her eyebrows. "And this."

I dropped my voice. "You're having your face done?" I asked, impressed.

Cristina shrugged elaborately. "I wouldn't call it *done,*" she said. "Only the chin, the line in the forehead. A few little alterations — but hey! nobody's perfect." She picked up her cigarette again and added, "Except this surgeon, I hope. He's supposed to be a genius. He's in Brazil." There was another pause while she grinned. Then she added, "I'll probably come out looking like a monkey."

I confess that when I heard this, about having a face-lift, I felt a tiny surge of moral triumph. Scarlet nails were one thing, I thought, but a face-lift was something else. A face-lift, I thought, was wretched excess — now she had gone too far. Makeup seemed to me fundamentally different from surgery, and self-respect should keep us all from the latter. A line had to be drawn, and it involved integrity and honesty and probity. Face-lifts were definitely on the other side, the far side, of that line. That women debased themselves in trying to fight the biological fact of aging seemed clear. Women who struggled were acting foolishly, I believed, and women who didn't struggle were acting with dignity and self-confidence. So when she told me what she was going to do, I felt a thrill, as though I had at last bettered Cristina at something. I felt a jolt of self-righteousness.

"You know we've moved back to El Salvador?" Cristina asked. She took another long pull on her cigarette. "Last summer. Everyone's moving back there."

"Is it safe?" I asked.

"Well. We have armed holdups, hijackings, and murders, but no rapes. Which is to say that San Salvador is safer than New York City." She smiled and then shrugged her shoulders. "It's home. It's where I grew up. The revolution is over. Everyone is going back."

Cristina's troubles were over. She was back at home, after the revolution, with all three children and her handsome husband, and she was still rich. And in another few weeks she'd look twenty-eight again, instead of forty-two. I found myself wondering if she would go on forever getting away with things. But I knew this was mean-spirited, and I dislike that side of myself. So what I said to her was that I was glad she could go home now, and I meant what I said. I do love Cristina, and I don't like my uncharitable side. I told her I was glad the danger was over.

"Well," Cristina said, and paused again. "It's not really over. It's never really over, right?" She stubbed out her cigarette and gave me her big flashy smile. "And who cares?"

That day in San Salvador, Cristina told the driver to pull over to the side of the street, behind the car that was already parked there. For some reason the driver was taking a long time to pull in behind the other car, which was where he had to go to be right next to the street door, so that Elvira and Consuela could step across the sidewalk, through the door, and into Elvira's courtyard.

"*Ándale, ándale, ándale,*" Cristina said rapidly, leaning forward. The driver started to say something to her, but Elvira spoke at the same time, and Cristina turned back to her mother. Their car pulled in behind the other and stopped. Consuela opened her door but didn't get out; she was waiting for Elvira, who was asking Cristina about a piece of silver she was going to return.

"OK, OK, OK," Cristina was saying, very rapidly. "OK, Mama, you're right. *Claro que sí.* I'll do it tomorrow. I don't know why I didn't do it before. You're right, the sooner the better. OK," she said again. And just then all three women realized that something was happening.

The door that Consuela was holding nearly shut was suddenly pulled open, and Consuela herself, gray-haired, in a sleek gray dress, and carrying a black bag, was yanked out by her arm. Frightened, she fell onto the grass strip along the sidewalk. The man in the doorway was holding a gun that was bigger than his face, and he grabbed at Elvira, pulling her out as well. The whole time he was talking fast, fast, fast.

Get out, he was saying. Get out or I'll kill you. Get out, he said to the driver. I'll kill you all, get out, get out. He kicked Elvira as he pulled her out. She staggered a bit and then sat down unintentionally on the grass next to Consuela, who was leaning over, holding her knee. No one was on the street; the sidewalks were empty. All the houses were hidden behind high walls and closed electronic gates.

Get out, get out, get out, the man said, pointing the gun at the driver. The driver turned his face away at once, as though that would make him safer. Then he ducked down and climbed out of the car, sinking to his knees. All these things happened quickly — the two older women sitting heavily on the grass, the driver in his dark uniform crawling on his knees along the hard paved road.

The man with the gun was wearing a dark shirt and pants, no jacket. He had dark skin and black hair, and his face was pock-marked. His black eyes were enraged, as if hatred and wildness were the only things inside him. He pulled Cristina out of the back seat and held on to her arm as she stood next to him on the grass. He held her tightly as he pulled open the front passenger door. He was watching Elvira and Consuela then, and he pointed his gun at them. I'll kill you, I'll kill you, he promised over and over, and his voice was filled with such wildness, such heat, such fury, that no one doubted him. He slid into the front seat, pulling Cristina in after him, keeping his gun pointed at the two older women. Don't move or I'll kill you, he chanted.

Then it was like a movie, everything happening without anyone's being able to stop it — him moving into the car, the chauffeur crawling farther and farther away along the street, Cristina's eyes brilliant as the man held his elbow around her neck in the front seat. And just as in a movie, everyone could see how things were going to unfold — that this was how it happened, how one became *desaparecida*. Cristina could see that she was not going to be helped. She saw herself getting into the car with this man and his gun, leaving her mother and her children and Carlos, and the man muttering in a steady, violent stream that he would kill them all.

And then something else happened. Elvira, who was struggling to stand up, realized that Cristina had been pulled back into the car with the gunman, and she turned and ran the few steps across the grass to the hood of the car and threw herself across it, her gold earrings glinting against the hard shine of the black car.

"Don't take her!" Elvira screamed. *"Don't take her, she's a mother! ¡Es una madre! ¡Tiene tres niños! Take me!"* Elvira banged her thin old-woman's arms against the hood in a horrible, unsettling, embarrassing way. "Take me!" she screamed, her voice high and demanding. "Take me! Don't take her! She has three children! Take me!" She clambered up the hood in her beautiful silk-print dress, beating at it with her fragile fists, her gold bracelets jangling on the metal and her wild, screaming face looming through the windshield.

The gunman was trying to organize himself — to hold on to Cristina with his arm hooked around her throat, to hold the gun cocked in the air, and to pull the driver's door shut and find the key and turn it in the ignition and ignore the terrible screaming of the old woman who was flailing on the hood in front of him.

He leaned out the window to shout at her. "We don't want an old woman," he yelled contemptuously. "We want the young one."

When he said that, it was as though everything stopped for Cristina, just for one moment. Everything crystallized slowly and perfectly in her mind. She heard the gunman's shout, and she could see what would happen next: She could see the car driving off, with her mother thrown onto the street, weeping and flinging her hands up in the air. She could see herself being driven to the place where the gunman's friends waited. She knew the pain that was waiting for her there among them. She could see that she would die, that they would kill her. She meant nothing to them, and once her body was still, they would throw it from the car. It would be found by the side of a road, and later it would be taken, bruised and discolored, to her family. Then her mother would weep in earnest. It was that thought — the thought of her mother when they found her body, and of her children sinking moment by moment into the profound darkness of grief, that changed everything for Cristina.

As the gunman held her close to his body, his mind distracted, and leaned out the driver's window to shout at her mother, who was screaming at him through the windshield, Cristina bent her arm and brought it down as hard as she could, the point of her elbow driving — as hard as she had ever imagined doing anything — deep into the soft place where the gunman's legs met his body. What she did was smooth and exact, as in a dream, as though she had practiced that one stroke all her life, in preparation for this moment.

The gunman's face dropped like a stone toward the place where her elbow had hit him. His whole body seemed to turn in on itself, as if it now had some secret business, rolling tightly and deeply into itself with a grunt. And even before the gunman's head started going down, almost before she felt him start to crumple, Cristina found herself moving, sliding across the front seat, opening the door and spilling herself out onto the grass.

Outside the car things had changed: Elvira was pulling herself off the hood, Consuela had managed to stagger to her feet, and from the corner of her eye Cristina could see the houseman, alerted by all the commotion, by her mother's furious pounding and demands, standing in the open doorway of the house.

"Porfirio!" Cristina yelled to him at the top of her lungs. "Call the police! Kidnappers! Thieves! Call the police!" Now it was her turn, now she was yelling over and over, anger and wildness in her voice. The gunman clambered out of the car and began running toward the other car, which was idling in front of him. The chauffeur thought he was being pursued, so he lay on the street without moving, as if he were already dead, so that he wouldn't be shot. The gunman pulled open the back door of the other car and jumped in, and before the door was even shut again, the car fishtailed and skidded and roared and gunned off down the street. It was a red sedan, an old, beat-up American car. It was never found.

Cristina told me all that while we were having lunch. The restaurant we were in was chic, and full of women with streaked blond hair, wearing snappy tailored suits and gold earrings. The Italian waiters wore white aprons over black pants and long-sleeved white shirts with the sleeves rolled up.

Cristina told me the story the way she tells everything, with exclamation points and pauses, rolling her eyes. She told it as though it were both extravagant and hilarious, as though the gunman, holding her desperate throat in the crook of his brutal arm, were funny; as though her three children, poised on the verge of endless grief, were funny; as though her mother, beating her frail old arms on the car's hood and shouting crazily through the windshield, were funny; as though her own brilliant and daring and courageous escape were funny — as though the whole world were spread out before her in a series of wild and hilarious adventures, which she chose to see as absurd although she knew exactly how dangerous and serious they really were. She talked as though boldness and certainty and a fearless readiness to break rules, any rules at all, were all normal traits — common, insignificant, negligible. She talked as though challenges were there for her amusement, as though they were simply things for her to respond to, like a swimmer lofting herself miraculously over the crests of great waves.

And I forgave Cristina the vodka, the House-parties Weekends, the smoking, the face-lift, the children. I forgave her everything.

JOHN SALTER

Big Ranch

FROM *Third Coast*

ALTHOUGH FREE to walk around, Anna Lee never left the island of brittle grass on which the cabin, barn, and bunkhouse sat. There was no point. She had been told more than once that a high steel fence surrounded the ranch, a fence wired to a series of iron rods planted up and down the spine of the Sierras. Hank had flipped open the encyclopedia and shown her just how often lightning struck the earth. Sometimes, the sky demonstrated this to her, and while she'd never seen the fence, not even through Hank's spotting scope, during storms she thought she could hear the metal sizzling.

And even without the electricity to worry about, there were cougars beyond the fence, and bears. The ranch was too remote for television signals but there was a big-screen Sony and VCR and a stack of movies that grew every time Hank and his guests came up to hunt and fish. One of the movies was about a huge grizzly that wandered into a summer camp and devoured everyone except a beautiful blind girl and a counselor with bulging muscles not unlike Hank's. Bullets could not stop the grizzly, as an unfortunate game warden discovered, but the counselor and the blind girl, both excellent swimmers, lured it into the river, into the rapids. The grizzly went over a waterfall and died, although Hank said it would probably turn up again, in a sequel. Bears similar to the one in the movie had been spotted trying to burrow under the fence, Hank added, and they had a preference for eating Indian girls.

So the safest place to be was in her quarters, in the old bunkhouse, with its heavy oak door and massive dead bolt for which only

Hank had a key. The windows were small, up near the ceiling, designed more for venting the body heat of sleeping cowboys than adoring the view of the pasture, the dark screen of trees, the mountain peaks. To see out, Anna Lee had to stand on her rocking chair, on two encyclopedias, with her fingers curled over the sill for balance. Still, she was happy she didn't live in an airy canvas tent, like those in the movie, vulnerable to sharp claws and teeth.

She stood in the doorway and watched Hank drive in, slowly, his tanned arm dangling from the window and bisecting the gold *King Lumber Security* star painted on the door. The star was lined with scratches from driving on narrow, brush-crowded dirt roads. For a while, Hank had been driving a new pickup every couple years, but this one, a battered Chevrolet with a deep crease in the rear bumper, had been around so long the other trucks appeared in Anna Lee's memory as simple smears of color, like blurred faces from her past. The one time she'd asked when he was getting a new truck, after it wouldn't start one chilly November morning, Hank had just laughed. "Not until they find a way to make big timber grow faster."

He honked and waved. She waved back. She had known he was coming soon. She was down to only two Diner's Delight microwave dinners, both macaroni and cheese, her least favorite, but Hank had never allowed her to run out of food. She was on a schedule: dinner, her big orange vitamin, the little white baby pill, and an hour with her exercise videotape before bathing and going to bed. If she skipped even part of the routine, Hank often warned her, everything would go to hell. The vitamin wouldn't work without food, and without the exercise, the food would just sit in a pile in her stomach. She would die.

She started for the driveway, to help unload the pickup. Hank always came up a day or two before bringing guests, to stock the cabin and check things out. Sometimes he brought tools and lumber, and made repairs. Once in a while, though not often, he showed up very late at night, smelling of smoke and beer, and slept with her in the bunkhouse. On these strange nights she did not get much rest because Hank twitched, swore, jerked, and cried, snoring loudly through it all.

Without speaking, they carried in cases of Budweiser and Corona, frozen steaks, mesquite chicken breasts, Pepsi and coffee, milk and eggs. Toilet paper. For her, more microwave dinners. Her freshly laundered nightgown and underwear in a plastic bag. Kotex.

They sat on lawn chairs, on the porch. Hank smoked, watched a hawk wheeling in the sky far above the pasture. He turned his fingers into a pistol and shot it. He looked at her. "Anybody come around, last couple of weeks?"

"Yes," she said. "A Jehovah's Witness." She recalled the dusty green sedan, the smiling, dark-skinned man ambling up the driveway clutching a brochure.

Hank laughed. "That's ambition." He squinted at her. "Anything you need to tell me about that?"

From the bunkhouse, she'd watched the Jehovah knock on the cabin door, then peek in the windows through cupped hands before coming toward her. Because of the angle she'd lost sight of him, but with her ear pressed against the heavy door heard him whistling, heard the scuffing of his shoes on the steps. The Jehovah had rattled the latch. Later, back at her window, she'd seen him going to his car, pausing to urinate on the dry grass with his head tilted back, his eyes closed.

"No," she said. "He wasn't here very long."

"Good."

"Was he a test?"

"Doesn't matter," Hank said, reaching down to squash his cigarette butt under his cowboy boot heel.

"You never tell me. I wish I knew when it was a test."

"No, you don't. You get that grill cleaned up like I told you? All that grease?"

"Yes," she said. "We need more propane, I think. The tank was easy to lift."

Hank nodded. "Be three of us coming up tomorrow. Me plus two."

"Is Grant coming?"

Hank stared at her. His eyes were watery blue, the corners webbed with lines. She had told him once, after they watched *Cool Hand Luke*, that he looked like Paul Newman, only older. "Well, he's Jewish," Hank had said, but seemed pleased. Now he grinned. "You liked that boy, didn't you? Grant."

She nodded. Grant had not fucked her. He'd asked only for a pencil, and on the sheet rock wall above her bureau drew a picture of her while she sat on the floor with her legs straight out and her hands planted behind her. From time to time he'd walked over to rearrange her long hair, or tilt her head. She still remembered the feel of his smooth, warm hands under her chin. Grant had a wife, he'd said, and a baby named Paige. He didn't like working for King Lumber. He wanted to teach high school art, something he'd gone to college for. Anna Lee had broken a rule, then, one of Hank's big rules: *Never talk about yourself, even if they ask.* She'd told Grant about an art project in seventh grade, a vase she made for her aunty on the pottery wheel, one of only a few pieces in the class to survive the kiln firing. While carefully penciling in her eyes, Grant asked where she'd gone to school and Anna Lee froze up, suddenly afraid it might be one of Hank's tests. But Grant hadn't pressed the matter. "Have you ever seen the ocean?" he'd asked. She hadn't, except in movies. So Grant drew the Pacific Ocean on the wall, too, along with a sailboat and gulls. She was worried Hank would make her wash it off, but so far, he hadn't.

"Well," Hank said. "Grant won't be coming back."

"He won't?"

"He's not with the company anymore. Be me and Pink and another guy —"

"Is he teaching high school?" she asked.

Hank shrugged, stood abruptly. "Come inside. I need to be getting back pretty soon."

After, she stood naked before him, hands down at her sides. Hank reached out from the edge of the bed and pinched her hip. "What is this shit?"

She looked down. Her hip bore his fingerprints, a trail of fading white circles on her brown skin.

"You been doing your tape?"

"Every night," she said.

"Getting too easy for you?"

"No. I burn."

"You bored with the Fonda? They got new ones now. All kinds."

"I like Jane."

"Well." Hank motioned with his finger for her to turn around. "Someday I'll enlighten you about Hanoi Jane. Tighten up now."

She tensed her muscles. Felt his rough hands on her rear, poking, squeezing. He turned her sideways, leaned back, sighted along her belly. Lifted her breasts, let them flop down. He sighed. "Anna Lee, you're getting old. No doubt about it."

"I am?"

"You are." He pushed himself up from the mattress, slapped his own belly, mounding over the waistband of his boxers. "We all are."

She laughed and squeezed his bicep. It was hard, the skin over his Navy tattoo still taut although the color had faded even in the ten years she'd known him. Hank regarded her fingers. The room was very quiet; the low afternoon sun striped them both in shadows from the trees in the yard beyond the big picture window. He covered her hand with his own. Their eyes met and he looked away. "Try to fix those nails up before tomorrow night."

On cool evenings, whenever she made a fire in the tiny sheepherder's stove in the bunkhouse, Anna Lee remembered, saw her uncle Raymond whirling her aunt Aletha in a sweeping circle, throwing her against the orange-hot stove in their company house on Indian Hill. Saw her aunty flopping on the metal, arching her back, her lips pulled back in a smile that wasn't a smile, saw Raymond stomping his wife with his knobby logging boots, hitting the floor half the time because he was sloppy drunk, shaking the house, vibrating the windows, knocking Anna Lee's vase from the shelf, sending ceramic puppies toppling over the edge. She remembered reaching out from her hiding place under the coffee table to rescue them, her uncle grabbing her thin arm. Saw herself slipping past him, out the door, almost running into Hank's pickup as he churned up the muddy road from the mill. Hank pulling her into the backseat, saying down, down, down. Hank taking her away, up to the ranch, while she stayed on the floor like he'd told her. "Good girl," he'd said. "Good girl."

She sprayed a cloud of Elizabeth Taylor's White Diamonds into the air and walked briskly through it, something she'd seen done in a movie. She put on her black kimono and perched on the edge of the bed, and waited. She knew it could be ten minutes or it could be an hour. Or not at all. Sometimes, Hank said, men weren't interested. People were complicated, he said. That would explain the men who sometimes broke into tears afterward, or the men who kept their eyes closed the whole time, or men like Grant who drew pictures on the wall.

She picked up an encyclopedia but put it down right away. She studied her freshly painted fingernails. China Rose, the color was called. She looked around the room. She wished that she smoked, so she would have something to do while Hank and Pink and the other man, whom she hadn't seen yet, sat on the front porch drinking and talking about hunting, lumber, Japan, Sacramento, Washington. It was always the same talk. The other man was new so he would be first. Pink would be tomorrow night. She was glad. She didn't like Pink. Pink was mean, called her names the whole time.

The door opened. A fat man wearing a floppy camouflage hat with a snap-brim came inside. He dropped his duffel bag. Blinked. Took off his glasses, wiped his sweaty face with his sleeve. Turned to look back outside. Hank and Pink were laughing, the sound fading out as they walked back to the cabin.

"My, my," the fat man said. He took a long drink from his Corona. "Hank said the bunkhouse wasn't such a bad place to sleep."

Anna Lee smiled, patted the bed.

Under mounds of flab, through the grunting, the stink of nervous sweat and alcohol, Anna Lee found a shaft of fresh air drafting through an ancient nail hole in the wall. She thought of *Bridge on the River Kwai*, William Holden breathing through a reed. Or was it another movie? She couldn't remember. The fat man was having trouble. This had happened more times with more men than she could remember and she had learned ways to help, "rope tricks," Hank called them, but the fat man pushed her away. He lowered his heavy feet to the floor and leaned forward as if his belly hurt. Anna Lee turned on the bedside lamp. Sometimes it helped if they could see her.

The fat man kept his eyes on his knees. "What are you looking at?" he hissed.

Another rule: *Never give up*. She smiled, crawled over to him, ran her fingernails along his thigh. Nothing. He grabbed his Corona from the nightstand and stood, walked over to the wall. The fat man regarded Grant's picture, licked his thumb, rubbed at one of the gulls until it was a black smudge, a dead raven. "Piece of shit," he said. "Where did Hank find you, anyway?"

Anna Lee sprang from the bed, came up behind him, gripped

his puffy, pale shoulders. She pressed her cheek against his back. "Want a massage? Loosen you up."

He spun around, slapped her ear. She hit the floor. He moved fast for someone his size. He grabbed her hair, jerked her up to the bed, pushed her face into the pillow. She felt the rim of his Corona bottle, icy wet, running down her back. She shivered. The fat man was panting. His entire weight seemed to be on his left forearm, against the back of her neck. The bottle went lower. The fat man grunted, screwed it into her roughly. Lightning bolts flashed in her skull. A rule was being broken, though not by her. She thought of Jane Fonda and pushed up mightily. The forearm slipped and the fat man began to roll. He clawed wildly at the air and toppled from the bed. His head struck the corner of the sheepherder's stove with a sound like an ax blade burying itself in green wood. His great, fleshy body shook wildly. The Corona bottle dropped from Anna Lee and rolled across the floor.

"Well, this is a problem," Hank said. He sat on her rocking chair, smoking. He studied the tip of his Salem. "Cover him up, will you?"

It hurt to move, but she dragged her sheet over the fat man. Her blood was on the sheet.

"This motherfucker is a state legislator," Hank said. "Was a state legislator."

"What's that?"

"A big-time mucky-muck. Get dressed now."

"A boss?"

"What? Yes. Big boss."

Pink had come in right behind Hank. Now he was out in the yard, vomiting. Anna Lee pulled on her panties, her jeans. She found her King Lumber sweatshirt but Hank shook his head. "Not that shirt. Wear a plain one."

She put on one of Hank's old white T-shirts. He nodded. They listened for a few moments to Pink retching, swearing, coughing. Hank looked at her and rolled his eyes.

"Is Pink a boss, too?" she asked.

Hank groaned, stood. "Right now, everybody is my boss. The whole goddamn world is Hank's boss, right about now." He prodded the fat man's belly with the toe of his cowboy boot. "Son of a bitch. A beer bottle. What gets into people, anyhow?"

Pink appeared in the doorway. The skin that had given him his nickname was gray now, the color of the weathered antlers mounted above the bunkhouse door. Pink did not look at Anna Lee or the fat man. He glared at Hank. "We're fucked, you know that?"

Hank squatted by the Corona bottle. It looked smaller than it had felt, Anna Lee thought. On the floor, in a pool of beer, it seemed innocent. Incapable of harming anyone. She watched Hank pick it up delicately, with two fingers, and examine it briefly before placing it on the fat man, in a deep crevice in the sheet. "Just relax," he said quietly.

For a moment Anna Lee thought he was talking to the fat man, but then Pink spoke up. "Relax? Are you kidding me?"

"Go inside, have a drink. I'll take care of this."

"You fucking yokel," Pink said. He wiped a string of vomit from his cheek. "You have any idea what's going to happen when this gets out?"

Hank straightened up. His knees popped. "So this drunk bastard took a spill and banged his head. So what?"

"You really believe it's that simple."

"He fell down," Hank said. "End of story."

"You're forgetting about something, Flynn. Someone."

"There is no someone." Hank glanced at her. "Someone doesn't exist. Hasn't for ten years."

Pink's bald head went from gray to pink to red. He jabbed a finger at Hank. "*You* won't exist. I won't exist. King fucking Lumber won't exist if your little Paiute whore ever gets tired of country life."

Anna Lee gazed down at the fat man. "I didn't mean for it to happen."

The men ignored her. Pink threw up his hands. "You swore that when the time came, you'd deal with things."

"I will. I'll move her for a while."

"No."

"You're in this too," Hank said. "It shouldn't all be on me."

"It is on you. You brought her up here. You have the gold star on our truck. Your hands have never been that clean, anyway. What's little more dirt?"

Hank lit another cigarette, glared at Pink. Pink glared back. A long time passed. Anna Lee stared at the wall, at herself, pretty on the beach, smiling at the ocean.

"I'll drive," Pink said.

It was cool in the yard. The sky was clear, the ranch illuminated by stars, the full moon. Hank gripped her by the arm and they followed Pink to the cabin. "When we get back," Pink was saying, "we'll clean everything up and haul that fat fucker down the hill."

"Whatever," Hank said. His fingers tightened on her arm. He yanked her close and for a few steps they walked as one. She smelled his breath, smoky, sweet from brandy. When Pink opened the screen door and went inside, Hank's lips brushed her ear. "Run," he whispered. "Go and keep going."

She ran. Headed for the trees beyond the pasture. She heard Hank cursing, heard the screen door screech open, slam shut. Her rear end was on fire but she bit her lip and kept going. She reached the pasture, tripped on the ragged fringe of weeds, rolled on the ground. She looked back as she scrambled to her feet. Pink was in the yard, with his deer rifle, striding toward her.

Close to the jungle-thick trees, she remembered the fence, ten feet high, the current so strong at times, according to Hank, that birds landing on it burst into flames. She slowed down. Her stomach hurt. Everything hurt. She stopped, turned around. Pink was almost across the pasture. Farther back, Hank was walking in tight circles, hands on his hips, looking up at the sky. Bears, she thought. A grizzly could outrun a horse in a quarter mile stretch. She tried to step into the trees but her legs wouldn't allow it. She did not want to be eaten alive. She closed her eyes and listened to the footsteps getting closer. Maybe, she thought, brightening a little, maybe it was only a test.

NATHAN WALPOW

Push Comes to Shove

FROM *A Deadly Dozen: Tales of Murder from Los Angeles*

THUMPER'S FINISHING MOVE was called The Thump. It started out like a power slam, but then he would twirl his opponent around so the guy would go face-first into the mat. After each match, Thumper's victim would just lie there, and they'd get a stretcher and carry him off. Thumper would act real sorry and walk halfway back to the dressing room beside the stretcher, then suddenly run back to the ring, put his rabbit ears back on, and get a big pop from the crowd.

I got mixed up with Thumper at a TV taping. Each of the job-bers, me included, had at least three matches, so Lou Boone, the promoter, could build up enough tape to keep the fans going for a few weeks. I'd already had my matches, two squashes and one where they let me put on a few martial arts moves before getting my ass kicked.

Thumper's match was after my last one. His opponent was some new guy whose name I never caught. A jobber. They were still build-ing Thumper up to face some real competition.

After the Thumping I watched on the monitor in the dressing room as they carried the guy off. Then I went to take a leak before driving back to the motel. But I walked the wrong way and ended up near an exit. I saw them carry the jobber out through a door into the parking lot and dump him into a car. They were handling him like a sack of potatoes.

I forgot about going to the john and ran back to the dressing room to see what the hell happened. But when I got there, Tommy Bufone said Lou wanted me to take the Thumped guy's place in a tag team with Tommy against the Barrister Brothers. The extra money sounded good. I could find out about the guy later.

The Barristers were major heels, so I got to be a good guy for the only time that night. I put on my good-guy tights. No one in the crowd ever noticed I wore a different outfit depending on who I was against, but I didn't care. It helped me play the part better.

Of course, the payoff was the same. I got beat up and pinned. Tommy got to drag me out of the ring.

After the card was over I started asking around about the wrestler who'd been Thumped. I spotted Joe the Greek Pappas, the heel on the announcing team. "What happened to the new guy?"

Joe caught me with the glare they called the Evil Eye when he was still in the ring. "He's fine," he said.

"Where is he?"

Another Evil Eye. "He should be back next week in Springfield." He pushed open the gray metal exit door and walked out into the rain.

I stared after him for a second, then walked back to get my stuff, and there was Lou holding my duffel bag. He's shorter than he looks on TV, and skinnier, and paler. He tossed the bag to me.

"Good work tonight," he said. "I really liked how you sold that double clothesline from the Barristers. The crowd ate it up."

"Thanks."

Lou held his glasses up to the light like he was checking if they were clean. "What do you think of Thumper?" he asked.

"He's pretty big." I could never think of what to say around Lou.

"The fans like him a lot." Now he was wiping his glasses on his tie. "He's the best thing we've had in a long time. I wouldn't want anything to mess that up."

He put on his glasses and pulled on his raincoat and said, "I was thinking maybe it's time to give you a push."

Talk about something coming out of the blue. I was a jobber. I made my living losing. And I knew I didn't have whatever it was that made some wrestlers go over with the crowd. But that magic word "push" made me forget all that.

"You think so?" I said.

"I just need time to think up a gimmick for you. Probably not by Springfield, but by the taping after that I should have something. Then maybe I'll put you in with Illegal Alien." Illegal was a jobber-to-the-stars. He always beat the regular jobbers, but when somebody got a push Illegal was usually the first one who lost to them.

"There's only one thing," Lou said.

"Name it."

"I want you to forget the new guy." Lou gave me a stare that made Joe's Evil Eye look wimpy.

I thought about it a second. Then I did what any jobber would have done.

"Sure, Lou," I said. "Consider him forgot."

People think it's easy being a jobber. They figure all you have to do is act like you're getting beat up for a while, then you make like you're helpless while the superstar pins you, then you limp out of the ring and collect your pay and go home.

What they don't think about is how you feel outside the arena. You know it's all phony, and your friends and family know, but people on the street don't sometimes. Some of the fans, the ones we call "marks," think this stuff is real. They stop you on the street and say, "You should give it up" or "You'll never win," and they laugh a stupid little laugh and walk off. And you want to call them back and tell them it's all fake, but you can't, because you don't want to mess up their dreams.

When I started, I was just this husky guy who knew a little martial arts and didn't want to work in a lumberyard all his life. I jumped at the chance to be a pro wrestler. Back then, all that losing bugged me a lot. Back then, I worried girls would think I was a loser.

Then one day I realized, the hell with that, if they're so dumb they think it's real I don't want anything to do with them. So I became a jobber, and I do six or seven matches a month, and, with what Sue makes, we have enough to get by.

They aired one of my matches that weekend, and I watched it at home with Sue. They showed the match with the Barristers, and when I took that double clothesline, I took a really poor bump. Even Sue knew it.

"You were falling down before they even touched you," she said. "If they ever did touch you, that is."

I looked into her big blue eyes and told her how Lou said I'd done such a good job of selling it.

She crinkled up her nose and got up for more beers. From the kitchen she said, "You've got to get away from Lou. Find yourself another outfit to work with."

"There's not a whole lot of call for jobbers, Hon," I said. "You go where the work is. That's with Lou."

She came back in and sat on my lap and kissed my nose. Then she downed some of her beer and said, "Let's not worry about it now," and she put her head on my shoulder and got all content like she does. But a minute later wrestling was over and *Gilligan's Island* came on, and I jumped up to turn it off — the clicker was broken — and I dumped her on the sofa. Because I really hate that show.

I didn't tell Sue what Lou had said about a push. I figured I'd let it be a surprise when — if — it happened.

In Springfield the next week they had Tommy Bufone and me against the Barrister Brothers again. But the Brothers had turned babyface in the meantime. Lou was short of good-guy tag teams, so he changed their name to Pro Bono and turned them by having them bounce their manager, Sammy the Muskrat Deegan, around the ring after he lost them a match by interference against Frick and Frack, a couple of jobbers-to-the-stars. So now Tommy and I had to act mean when we were announced, making faces at the crowd and all, then Pearl-Harboring Pro Bono while they were taking their jackets off. Of course, it didn't do any good. Tommy got pinned, and I got knocked out of the ring when I went to rescue him. I sold that bump pretty damn well, if I do say so myself.

I was scheduled for one more match that day, against Man Mountain Beazel, and since he was a heel I changed into my good-guy tights. Then I watched the next match on the monitor. It was Lenny Lemaire against Thumper. Lenny would do stuff like call himself Larry Levine in New York, or Luis Larriva anywhere there were a lot of Mexicans, but that night he was using his real name.

After a couple of minutes Thumper put the Thump on Lenny, and the crowd went wild. They were shaking the dressing room, they were so worked up. I mean, this Thumper guy was over. I'd heard they were setting him up to challenge Beast Benton for the title, and right then I knew it was true. Beast had held the belt for a month, since he'd won it from Terry Casino by using what they liked to call a foreign object, and Lou never liked to let a heel be champ too long.

The monitor showed them carting Lenny out, and Thumper

went with him. Everybody but me was watching Thumper. I was watching Lenny. He wasn't moving at all. Then they did the bit where Thumper runs back to the ring, and Lenny went off camera, but just before he did I saw a guy in the corner of the screen opening a door. It wasn't the door to the dressing room. It led somewhere under the stands.

I slipped out into the corridor, and after a bit found myself in a dark hallway that smelled like old beer. Somebody opened a door that led outside, and I could see someone else sling something over his shoulder. It was Lenny. They threw him in the trunk of a car and slammed the lid. The guy walked back in, and Lou was right behind him. Somebody's headlights shone in through the door, and there I was right in the beam. Lou saw me. He put his hands out in front of him and made a pushing motion, then disappeared into the dark.

I found my way back to the dressing room, and there was Thumper. I'd never seen him up close before. He must've been six foot six. Real buff. Nowhere near the 380 pounds they announced him at, but a solid 300 at least. He was still wearing his outfit, the furry white tights and boots, and he had the damn rabbit ears on his head. His face was real pink, one of those faces that looked like he never had to shave.

He saw me and smiled. "Hey, little buddy," he said, just like the Skipper on *Gilligan's Island.* Now, I'm not usually anyone's little buddy. I'm six-three and 235. So I especially hated when he called me that. "Didja see me Thump?"

I drifted over to the massage table and got it between me and him. "On the monitor."

"I like to Thump," he said. "'Course, sometimes I Thump a little too hard. I used to hate to do that, but now I'm gettin' to kind of like it. 'Cause the fans like it. And Lou, he likes it a lot, too, and Lou says if I keep Thumpin' I might just get to be champ someday."

He pulled off his boots and stripped off his tights and laid them real careful into an army green duffel bag. Then he said, "Better watch out, little buddy. I might just have to Thump you sometime." He grinned, but the grin was all around his mouth. His eyes were little pig eyes in that pink bunny face.

Still wearing his ears, he went off toward the showers. "Don't call me 'little buddy,'" I said.

*

A week later Lou called. "I'm calling about your push," he said. "I haven't figured out all the angles yet, but I just wanted you to know it's still coming."

"That's good, Lou."

He gave this funny high laugh. "Did you see Thumper on TV the other day?"

"I must have missed it."

"Best thing that's happened to this federation in a long, long time."

"Yeah," I said. "Speaking of Thumper, I haven't seen Lenny Lemaire lately."

It was only a second before he said, "Didn't you hear? His mother's real sick, and he's gone back to Alabama to take care of her."

"That's a damn shame," I said.

"That it is." Lou cleared his throat. "Now, we've got a card coming up in Easton . . ."

"Uh-huh."

"You'll job there, but by the next taping I think I'll have a big surprise ready for you."

"That'll be great, Lou," I said. "I like surprises."

Easton was on a Friday night. It was a house card, which meant most of the matches didn't have jobbers in them but instead had heel stars against face stars. There were only two jobbers in the dressing room. I was scheduled to go against Monster Madigan, and Paul Tompkins was up against Thumper.

Paul wore black tights and a mask with big white felt teeth and went on as The Shark. Sometimes we'd be a tag team together, and they let me wear the same getup, and we were The Sharks. I never got around to making a mask with teeth and would always have to scotch tape some on at the last minute. When we were The Sharks, Lou would let us do a little better, actually pound our opponents for a little while, with me getting in some martial arts stuff, before one of us ended on our back — one, two, three.

I found Paul sitting in a corner of the dressing room. He was real sweaty already, even though they had the air conditioning on way high. He filled his cheeks with air and blew it out slow. "You know much about Thumper?"

"Enough," I said.

"Nobody knows his real name," he said. "No one's even sure where he came from."

"Lou must know."

The Michigan Men ambled into the dressing room. They'd just been beaten by Pro Bono. They were laughing and talking about some girl in Cleveland.

"I'm up," Paul said.

"Do good."

He nodded and pulled on his Shark mask and walked through the curtain into the arena. I sat down by the monitor. Funny things, those monitors. During the parts of the show when the folks at home see all the commercials, the monitors still show what's going on ringside. So I watched Paul walk down the aisle, past all the fans who didn't know him from Adam, and on past the broadcasting booth.

Something happened there I'm sure no one but me saw. As Paul walked by the booth, he turned in Joe and Lou's direction. And Lou put his hands out in front of him and gave a little push. After that, Paul walked to the ring a little faster and a little straighter. The thing is, he didn't walk out of it again.

Later I was sitting in the dark in my motel room. I'd just told the guy at the desk to give me a wake-up call at six. That way I'd be home to Sue by one or so the next afternoon. Since it was Saturday, we could have most of the day together.

I was rubbing my right knee, which I'd bruised during my three and a half minutes in the ring with Monster Madigan, thinking about finding some ice to pack around it. Somebody knocked on the door. "It's Lou."

I slowly walked to the door and pulled it open. "It's late, Lou."

"I'll just be a minute."

He came in. He had on that damn raincoat. His eyes scanned the place. "Kind of a pit," he said.

"It's a jobber room."

He nodded and sat on one of the rickety wooden chairs. "Once you get your push, you'll be able to afford better than this."

"And that'll be . . ."

"Next week, at the taping in Grandville. We're going to call you Samson Sanders. You'll come out in this strongman getup."

"Face or heel?"

"I'm not sure yet. Probably face. I've got a couple of contract negotiations in the next few days, and I have to see what the balance is
after that."

I couldn't help myself. This big stupid smile grew on my face.

"There's just one thing," Lou said.

The stupid smile went back where it belonged. "What's that?"

"Nothing much," he said. "I just need you to job once more. It'll
be early in the card. The crowd won't even remember you by the
time Samson Sanders shows up." He got up and walked out without
saying another word.

I got undressed and into bed. I had the radio on low, because
sometimes that helps me fall asleep. A Tom Petty song came on,
and that's when I remembered Lenny Lemaire didn't come from
Alabama. He always used to sing that song. "Louisiana Rain," it was
called.

The getup came by UPS a couple of days later. This fake fur loin-
cloth thing, leather arm and leg bands, and the dumbest wig I'd
ever seen. Sue saw it and got a laughing fit. I put it on, and soon she
was rolling on the floor laughing. Then I went into a muscleman
pose, and she pulled me down on top of her. I kept the wig on
while we did it.

The TV taping was the next Saturday. I let Sue sleep and slipped
out before seven. I drove slow and careful and still got to the arena
with two hours to spare.

I put on my new outfit, checked it out in the crummy old mirror,
and put it away. I sat there in my underwear for a little while, then
put on my bad-guy tights. I just had a feeling I was going to be the
heel in that jobber match.

Joe wandered into the dressing room with the card. Seventeen
matches, enough to feed the TV audience for weeks, enough to
keep the arena crowd happy even if most of the matches were
squashes. I started at the bottom and looked for Samson Sanders.
He wasn't there. I kept scanning until I got to the first match on the
card. There was my name. My real name.

Across from it was Thumper's.

The rest of the gang began to trickle in. Everyone but Thumper.
At three o'clock somebody stuck his head in and called me to the

ring. I zipped up my bag and tossed it on the floor and slowly walked out of the dressing room, then down that long walkway. The place was only about half full, though lots of folks were still streaming in. As I passed the broadcast booth I thought of looking for Lou, then said the hell with it. If he was giving me that damn push sign I didn't want to know about it.

The ring announcer introed me, and I did my heel gig, throwing my fists up in the air, beating my chest, howling at the one or two people who'd noticed me.

The announcer drew in a deep breath. "Ladies and gentlemen," he said, "his opponent, weighing in at three hundred and ninety pounds, from Green Meadow, Nebraska . . . Thump — per!"

He came marching down the aisle, looking more pumped than ever, getting a huge pop from the crowd. They yelled. They screamed. Ladies blew kisses. Men held up their kids.

He came down to ringside, wearing that big Green Meadow smile, the one that stopped somewhere around his nose. He hopped up the metal steps and stepped over all three ring ropes. He glared at me across the ring, pointed his big finger, and shouted, "You're going down, little buddy!"

I said, "Don't call me that." He just laughed.

We started with a collar-and-elbow tie-up. He tossed me away. As the heel, it was up to me to make the first illegal move. Once I did that, he could pound me, and finally Thump me. I locked up with him a couple more times, letting him throw me all the way out of the ring after the last one. I complained to the ref about a hair pull, and he rambled over to Thumper like they always do and told him not to do it again. We tangled again, and I came out of it with my left arm in a wringer.

It was about time to elbow him in the face. I put a little more into it than I had to to sell it, and he got a little surprised expression. Not enough so the crowd would notice. He kicked me in the stomach, and I went down. I got up a little faster than he expected. He threw a couple of lefts, a couple of rights, and I went down again. He body-slammed me and dragged me up by my hair, suplexed me, and pulled me up again. Then he threw me over his shoulder.

"This is it, little buddy," he whispered. "Thumpin' time." He ran forward and started to twist me around so my face would smash the mat.

It was the little buddy stuff that did it.

I broke his neck.

It's easy when you know how. When you've had the right kind of martial arts. While he was tossing me around his head, I just threw out a hand, and then the other, and grabbed and twisted. Nobody in the crowd saw anything except me trying to catch onto something. And they were yelling so loud none of them heard the crack.

I sold the rest of the move and hit the mat just in time to have Thumper come crashing down on top of me. I managed to get both my shoulders down before he hit me like a big sack of cement. Right then, he really did feel like the 380 or 390 or whatever they were saying that week.

The ref didn't know what to do. "Count," I whispered. He finally did — one, two, three, and there it was, Thumper had won. Just like he was supposed to.

And that's what really counts, isn't it?

Contributors' Notes

Jennifer Anderson lives with her husband in Napa, California. "Things That Make Your Heart Beat Faster" is her first published story.

▪ The protagonist of this story is my Emma Bovary, looking for transcendence in fictive, provincial Saint Amelia, a place inspired by humorous police blotters. She also happens to love her husband and to live in a postfeminist era of unfettered options. Sure, she needs health insurance, but she's more excited by the esoteric, transforming knowledge of police work.

I had been reading about mythological descents into Hades and was interested in conflict generated by placing a character, in this case idealistic and abstract in thinking, in a situation opposite her temperament; police work and Dionysus's cold, green vines both represent the same grounded physicality that trips her up. Sight versus insight is a central motif: she sees, she doesn't see, she sees *differently,* and in this the story is primarily about personality, not gender.

Russell Banks is the author of thirteen books of fiction, including the novels *Continental Drift, Rule of the Bone,* and *Cloudsplitter,* and four collections of short stories, most recently *The Angel on the Roof: New and Selected Stories.* Two of his novels, *The Sweet Hereafter* and *Affliction,* were made into award-winning motion pictures. His work has received numerous awards and has been widely translated and anthologized. He is a member of the American Academy of Arts and Letters and is the president of the International Parliament of Writers. He lives in upstate New York with his wife, the poet Chase Twichell.

▪ "Lobster Night" is a fictional transformation of three different stories told to me by three different people, a woman who was struck by lightning, a man who owned a restaurant and one night lost his temper and shot a foraging bear in front of his customers, ruining his business because of it, and another man who, drunk, shot and wounded a bear, which proceeded to tear down the man's cabin and bury him in it. The three stories would seem to have little in common, except perhaps unexpected violence, but somehow to me they connected in that restaurant kitchen on "Lobster Night," establishing the causes, if not the motives, of a murder.

A former reporter and restaurant critic, **Michael Downs** learned to write fiction at the University of Arkansas's Graduate Programs in Creative Writing, where he was a Truman Capote Fellow. He has published short stories in the *Georgia Review,* the *Michigan Quarterly Review,* and *Oxford Magazine.* He teaches journalism at the University of Montana, where he is also at work on two books, both set in his hometown of Hartford, Connecticut. One is a collection of short stories; the other is a book of nonfiction, supported by a grant from the Freedom Forum.

▪ When I worked as a reporter in Montana, one of the biggest news stories was an execution, the Big Sky State's first in decades. A man had raped and murdered a schoolteacher, and he was going to get a lethal injection because of it. I didn't cover his death, but, because it was Montana's first execution in so many years, it warranted lots of ink. I read every word. A colleague covering the execution from behind the two-way glass noted that for the last meal the murderer ordered a tenderloin steak, french fries, orange sherbet, and whole milk. But the good people in the prison cafeteria also sent him a tossed salad; prison officials thought he needed his greens.

That was the beginning of "Prison Food."

Leslie Edgerton is an ex-convict who has changed his ways and is now regularly invited into people's homes, where the silverware is no longer counted after he leaves. He has five books in print, including the novel *The Death of Tarpons* and the story collection *Monday's Meal.* His short stories have been nominated for the O. Henry Award and the Pushcart Prize, among others, and *Tarpons* received a Special Citation from the Violet Crown Book Awards, presented by the Austin Writers' League. Edgerton teaches creative writing online for Vermont College and previously taught online for the UCLA Writers' Program. He also teaches public speaking at St. Francis University and writing for the Ft. Wayne (Indiana) Neighborhood Connection adult education classes. Last year, one of his screenplays was a semifinalist in the Nicholl's Awards and another a finalist in the Writers Guild's "America's Best Screenplays" competition. Edgerton's work has also been nominated for the Edgar Allan Poe Award (short story category) and his collection *Monday's Meal* was nominated for the Texas Institute of Letters's Jesse Jones Award.

▪ "In the Zone" is based rather faithfully on a real-life experience I had while serving time in the state prison at Pendleton (Indiana). I won't reveal which parts are true and which are fictionalized, as there's this statute of limitations thing . . . I think I captured the true spirit and outlook of many of those incarcerated with this story. To survive the hell of prison, a person needs to create his or her own world, à la "the zone," or it becomes madness. You create one insane world to escape the other more devastating and demeaning one.

William Gay's fiction has appeared in *Harper's, The Atlantic Monthly,* the *Georgia Review,* and other magazines, as well as the anthologies *New Stories from the South* and *O. Henry Prize Stories.* He is the author of two novels, *The Long Home* and *Provinces of Night.*

 • I always think of "The Paperhanger" as a sort of gothic fairy tale, and the fact that it is completely a work of the imagination appeals to me. Though it is a very recent story, it grew out of a tale a plumber told me a long time ago concerning a small vicious dog, a pipe wrench, and a handy toolbox.

Jeremiah Healy is a graduate of Rutgers College and Harvard Law School. The author of thirteen John Cuddy novels and two legal thrillers, he's been nominated twelve times for the Shamus Award, receiving it for *The Staked Goat.* Healy has served as president of the Private Eye Writers of America, and he is currently the president of the International Association of Crime Writers.

 • While visiting Chicago, I mentioned to a friend that though my forebears had come from Ireland, everybody with a brogue had died before I was born. She suggested we visit the Irish-American Heritage Center, occupying space in the grammar school she'd once attended. Upon entering the building, I felt strangely "at home," and upon seeing the Center's facsimile of the magnificent *Book of Kells,* I knew I'd been given the kernel of a John Cuddy story as well.

After spending most of his life in the Midwest, **Steve Hockensmith** recently moved to northern California just in time to find his power flicking on and off at random intervals. He is senior editor of *Cinescape,* a magazine devoted to films and TV shows in which spaceships, cars, and/or humans explode. "Erie's Last Day" was his first published mystery story. He shares his home with his wife, Mary, a big yellow cat, and a big black cat.

 • Most detective stories are about helping people. Our hero catches the killer/retrieves the diamond/foils the kidnapping/what have you, thus making the world a better place for all of us. In "Erie's Last Day," I wanted to write about how hard it really is to do good. Does catching the killer always make the world a better place? Can you set out to help someone and end up destroying him? I guess "The road to hell is paved with good intentions" is a heck of a lot pithier than my story, but hopefully I was able to take that basic idea and give it some extra shading.

On the lower West Side of Chicago, **Clark Howard** grew up a ward of the county and habitual runaway who eventually was sent to a state reformatory for being, he recalls, "recalcitrant." He later served in combat in the Korean War as a member of the Marine Corps, and he began writing shortly thereafter. Having written more than one hundred short stories, sixteen novels, and five true crime books, he is an eight-time Mystery Writers of America Edgar nominee in the short story and true crime categories, and winner of the Edgar for best short story. He is also a five-time winner of the Ellery Queen Magazine Readers Award, and has been nominated for the Private Eye Writers of America's Shamus Award, and twice for the Western Writers of America's Spur Award.

▪ A lot of my work is steeped in the streets of Chicago. Despite what many consider to have been an underprivileged and deprived youth, my recollection of it is shot throughout with memories of great fun and fine friends, frayed clothes and a hungry belly at times, but never a day without a challenge, always a damned good run before being caught, and never any regrets looking back. Hard knocks just make the sweet times sweeter. I could not have written "Under Suspicion" without seasoning it with memories of Chicago.

Michael Hyde grew up in Dover, Pennsylvania, and received his B.A. from the University of Pennsylvania in 1995 and M.F.A. from Columbia University in 1998. His fiction has appeared in the *Alaska Quarterly Review, XConnect,* and the *Ontario Review.* Currently he lives in New York City and is at work on a novel.

▪ I like to think that Connie Pratt in "Her Hollywood" is something of what Nancy Drew might have been like, had she been born into different circumstances. Special thanks to Ronald Spatz, Robert Clark, and the *Alaska Quarterly Review.*

Dan Leone comes from Ohio and lives now in San Francisco, where he writes a humorous food column for the *Bay Guardian* and weekly fiction for the *Guardian*'s Web site, www.sfbg.com. He has two books, a collection of short stories called *The Meaning of Lunch* and a nonfiction collection called *Eat This, San Francisco.* He has won the *Paris Review*'s John Train Humor Award and published fiction recently in *Literal Latté* and the *Antioch Review.* When he's not writing or eating, he's usually playing music with his wife, Tami, and his brother, Chris.

▪ I come from a gigantic and very close-knit family: eleven kids, couple of parents . . . fairly functional . . . more wedding dresses than skeletons in our closets, at any rate. I'm not sure how that figures into "Family," the story, but I reckon I'll tip my cap right here to brother #5, Dave, who lives in a "prefab" house on a dirt road in rural Missouri, last house on the left . . . you can't miss it.

Thomas Lynch is the author of three collections of poems, most recently *Still Life in Milford* (1998) and two collections of essays, *The Undertaking* (1997), which won an American Book Award and was a finalist for the National Book Award, and *Bodies in Motion and at Rest* (2000), which won the Great Lakes Book Award. His work has appeared in *Harper's Magazine, The New Yorker, Esquire,* the *New York Times, Poetry,* the *Paris Review,* and elsewhere. He lives in Milford, Michigan, where he has been a funeral director for twenty-seven years, and in West Clare, Ireland, where he keeps an ancestral cottage.

▪ "Blood Sport" is the first fiction I've published and borrows from events I've been involved with over the years as a funeral director in a small town in Michigan. I am struck by the different territories of poetry and essay and story — how each presents essential challenges and delivers essentially different satisfactions. Over the years I have attempted to deal with the dynamics of "Blood Sport" in verse and in nonfiction without success. The comfort — odd word here — of occupying this narrative, for the writing of it, was real.

David Means's second book of stories, *Assorted Fire Events* (2000), was nominated for a National Book Critics Circle Award and won the Los Angeles Times Book Prize. He was born and raised in Kalamazoo, Michigan, before migrating east to New York. Now he lives along the Hudson River.

▪ I've always been interested in those mythic shadow figures moving secretly around American culture: hobos, roadies, circus folk, and the like. Then a few years ago — one hot summer day — a carnie set up in a field near our house. I went with my family and, while we were standing in line, made eye contact with one of the roadies, a mean, scary-looking kid smoking a cigarette (of course it was drooping from his lip) while he handed out tickets. Out of that long gaze, and the deep parental anxiety it sparked, the story arose.

Kent Nelson has written three novels and four collections of short fiction, in addition to more than one hundred short stories published in America's best literary magazines. He has worked as city judge, squash coach, hired ranch hand, and university professor. In 1997 he ran the Pikes Peak Marathon (8,000 feet elevation gain) in his home state of Colorado in 5 hours 53 minutes.

▪ The Ben Sawyer Bridge to and from Sullivan's Island, South Carolina, intrigued me for its simplicity of operation. Years ago I wrote a draft of a story about a troubled bridge operator, but the motivation for what he did in that earlier story was not thorough enough. I hope, in this version, it is.

Joyce Carol Oates is the author most recently of *The Barrens,* a novel of suspense, and *Faithless: Tales of Transgression.* She is a member of the American Academy of Arts and Letters and is a professor of humanities at Princeton.

▪ I've long been fascinated by the effects upon "ordinary" people of sudden, seemingly random acts of violence. My family history was marked, decades ago, by two mysterious events, neither of which has been satisfactorily explained: the violent suicide of a great-grandfather, and the brutal murder of a grandfather. The second event in particular irrevocably changed the course of my family's life.

One of the consequences is that I seem to be under the spell of "mystery," especially conjoined with violence. "The Girl with the Blackened Eye" dramatizes the utterly random way in which a more or less average girl is selected for a horrific fate. She quickly becomes anesthetized to emotion, she adapts to her new situation, she survives, and she will never forget. Yet her horrific situation — raped, assaulted, brutalized by a psychotic killer — somehow becomes for her suffused with a lurid sort of romance: she has learned that she is "special," as in a malevolent fairy tale.

T. Jefferson Parker was born in Los Angeles and has lived in southern California all his life. He has worked as a janitor, waiter, veterinary hospital emergency attendant, newspaper reporter, and technical editor. All of his nine novels are set in southern California. He lives in San Diego County with his wife and two sons. The T doesn't stand for anything.

▪ Jim Seels of ASAP Publishing asked me to write a short story for him, so I did. I'd had the idea of competing brothers for a long time but could never work it into a novel. The crimes are loosely based on a series of bank robberies that took place in Orange County. I like the overt sexuality of the story, the atmosphere of lazy danger, the desperate sense of entitlement that drives Sonny to make things right for Laurel. It reads more like a compacted novel than a true short story.

In a career spanning more than thirty years, native Californian **Bill Pronzini** has published nearly sixty novels, four nonfiction books, ten collections of short stories, and scores of uncollected stories, articles, and essays. He is the recipient of a Lifetime Achievement Award and three Shamus Awards from the Private Eye Writers of America and has been nominated for six Mystery Writers of America Edgar Awards and the International

Crime Writers Association Hammett Award. His most recent novel is a nonseries thriller, *In an Evil Time,* published earlier this year.

▪ Contrary to the opinion of some critics, the Nameless Detective series is not hard-boiled fare. I make a conscious attempt to keep violence and sexual content to an understated minimum. If I had to pin a label on it, I'd say it's "humanist crime fiction with an edge." Even more to the point, it's a multivolume chronicle of the personal and professional life of a detective — all the good, bad, funny, sad, bitter, ugly things that affect and change him in one way or another from year to year, book to book.

From 1967 to 1995 I produced enough short stories featuring "Nameless" to fill two collections, *Casefile* (1983) and *Spadework* (1995). "The Big Bite" is my only short case since the publication of *Spadework.*

Peter Robinson was born in Castleford, Yorkshire. His first novel, *Gallows View* (1987) introduced Detective Chief Inspector Alan Banks, who has since appeared in eleven more books, including *Wednesday's Child* and *In a Dry Season,* both of which were nominated for an Edgar. *In a Dry Season* won both the Anthony and Barry Awards. Robinson's short stories have also been nominated for many awards, including the Edgar, Arthur Ellis, and Agatha. "The Two Ladies of Rose Cottage" won a Macavity. His early stories were collected in *Not Safe After Dark,* published by Crippen & Landru in 1998.

▪ "Missing in Action" is the second story featuring Special Constable Frank Bascombe, about whom I first wrote in "In Flanders Fields." I think the opening of the story really sums up its main theme: that amidst the sanctioned slaughter of war, other crimes are committed that cannot go unpunished. I like Frank as a narrator; he's sarcastic and he doesn't suffer fools gladly, but he is also a compassionate and learned man. I hope to write more stories about him in the future.

Roxana Robinson was born in Pine Mountain, Kentucky, and grew up in Bucks County, Pennsylvania. She attended Bennington College and graduated from the University of Michigan. She is the author of two short story collections, two novels, and a biography of Georgia O'Keeffe. Three of these were named Notable Books of the Year by the *New York Times,* and one, by the American Library Association. Her work has appeared in *The New Yorker, The Atlantic Monthly, Harper's,* the *New York Times, The Best American Short Stories,* and other publications. She has received fellowships from the National Endowment for the Arts, the MacDowell Colony, and the Guggenheim Foundation. She lives in New York.

▪ I'm honored to find myself here, though surprised, since I wouldn't have identified what I do as mystery writing. My modest qualifications are as follows: my father, the head of a small Quaker school, was famous throughout the community — and our family — as a teller of heart-stopping ghost stories. I myself am a long-time admirer of Agatha Christie, Dorothy Sayers, Margery Allingham, Josephine Tey, Ngaio Marsh, and P. D. James.

"The Face-Lift" isn't a conventional mystery story, but I'd be pleased to think it contained a certain suspense, as well as the sort of narrative muscle necessary to the mystery form. To me, the story — a true one — is about alternative endings, about women solving the problem of violence in a brave and unexpected way. But perhaps all serious fiction is a kind of mystery writing, in which author and reader together unravel the tangled knot of confusion that obscures the human heart.

John Salter was born in North Carolina, raised in eight states, and educated at the University of North Dakota. He lives in Minnesota with his wife, Nancy, and their three children. His short story collection, *Alberta Clipper,* will be published in 2002.

▪ When I lived in the northern Sierras, there was a rumor going around about extended Bacchanalian events held at a remote logging company ranch. Looking for this secret property gave purpose to a few otherwise aimless Sunday drives. Roaming around gloomy mountain clear-cuts in my pickup, I got to thinking about the mentality behind these festivities, and how women might become involved. That's how Anna Lee was born. I never found the ranch but I got this little noir story cooking in the back of my mind.

Nathan Walpow began writing at the age of forty-three and is fond of pointing out that, like Raymond Chandler, he published his first novel at fifty. This was *The Cactus Club Killings,* first in the Joe Portugal series, which also includes *Death of an Orchid* and the forthcoming *The Petal Pushers.* He recently completed work on *Steel Cloud,* a suspense novel. His stories have appeared in a variety of speculative fiction publications; "Push Comes to Shove" is his first short crime fiction. Walpow lives in Los Angeles with his wife and inspiration, Andrea Cohen. For more, see www.walpow.com.

▪ I've been an on-again-off-again professional wrestling fan since I was a teenager. About five years ago I saw a call for submissions for an anthology of wrestling-related horror stories. I kicked out an early version of "Push Comes to Shove," but by the time I sent it in the market was already closed. I tried unsuccessfully to place the story a couple more times, then packed it away in my electronic trunk. A couple of days later, my local Sisters in Crime chapter put out a call for stories for a book of members' work. I dusted off "Push" and discovered that it consisted of four thousand words of good story and a thousand of darlings to be killed. I made the cuts and the editors liked what was left.

I'm fond of this story because its protagonist is very different from the urban neurotics who usually populate my work. Just a guy faced with a big problem while trying to do his job. I thought Thumper's costume and persona might be a little over the top, but recent developments in the WWF have proven me wrong.

Other Distinguished Mystery Stories of 2000

BLUE, J. MICHAEL
  The Lady Goes to Marakech. *Blue Murder,* June

COHEN, STANLEY
  A Night in the Manchester Store. *Murder Among Friends,* The Adams Round
    Table (Berkeley)
CURRANS-SHEEHAN, TRICIA
  The Last Trapshoot. *Virginia Quarterly Review,* Summer

DEVEREAUX, GRANT
  Marti's Secrets. *Magnolias and Mayhem,* ed. Jeffrey Marks (Overmountain)
DUBOIS, BRENDAN
  The Summer People. *Ellery Queen's Mystery Magazine,* November

FREEDMAN, J. F.
  The Hunters. *Ellery Queen's Mystery Magazine,* September/October

GATES, DAVID EDGERLEY
  This Little Piggy. *Alfred Hitchcock's Mystery Magazine,* December
GISCHLER, VICTOR
  Xs for Eyes. *Plots with Guns,* June/July
GREENBERG, ELEANOR
  The Categorical Imperative. *Pangolin Papers,* Summer

HEMON, ALEKSANDAR
  The Deep Sleep. *Esquire,* November
HENDRICKS, VICKI
  Gators. *Mississippi Review,* Summer
HOROWITZ, RICHARD M.
  The Public Defender. *Pangolin Papers,* Summer

HOWARD, CLARK
   The Killing Floor. *Challenge the Widow-Maker and Other Stories of People in Peril* (Crippen & Landru)

LEVY, BOB
   Metro. *Other Voices*, Spring/Summer
LIDA, DAVID
   A Beach Day. *Travel Advisory: Stories of Mexico* (William Morrow)
LOTT, BRET
   Rose. *Shenandoah*, Summer

MARTIN, DAN
   Nora. *Blue Murder,* June

NELSON, KENT
   Skyway. *Witness*, vol. 14, number 2

PECK, DALE
   Bliss. *Zoetrope*, Summer
PICKARD, NANCY
   Speak No Evil. *Unholy Orders: Mystery Stories with a Religious Twist,* ed. Serita Stevens (Intrigue)
PLATT, JOHN R.
   Combs. *Crafty Cat Crimes: 100 Tiny Cat Tale Mysteries,* ed. Stefan Dziemianowicz and Martin H. Greenberg (Barnes & Noble)
POWELL, JAMES
   The Flower Diet. *Ellery Queen's Mystery Magazine*, April

RHEINHEIMER, KURT
   Shoes. *Nebraska Review,* Summer
RIHA, JOHN
   The Chaplain's Kachina. *Ellery Queen's Mystery Magazine*, April
ROCK, PETER
   Stranger. *Zoetrope*, Spring

SCHEID, KRISTINE
   Valuables. *Murder Most Confederate,* ed. Martin H. Greenberg (Cumberland)
SILER, JENNY
   Sharks. *Mississippi Review,* vol. 6, number 3
SMITH, ANTHONY NEIL
   Nobody's Killing Anybody Here. *Blue Murder,* February
SUBARTON, DARREN
   The Best Things in Life Are Someone Else's. *Mississippi Review,* Summer

THON, MELANIE RAE
   Ghost Brother. *Five Points,* Summer

THE B·E·ST AMERICAN SERIES ™

THE BEST AMERICAN SHORT STORIES 2001
Barbara Kingsolver, guest editor · Katrina Kenison, series editor

0-395-92689-0 CL $27.50 / 0-395-92688-2 PA $13.00
0-618-07404-X CASS $25.00 / 0-618-15564-3 CD $35.00

THE BEST AMERICAN TRAVEL WRITING 2001
Paul Theroux, guest editor · Jason Wilson, series editor

0-618-11877-2 CL $27.50 / 0-618-11878-0 PA $13.00
0-618-15567-8 CASS $25.00 / 0-618-15568-6 CD $35.00

THE BEST AMERICAN MYSTERY STORIES 2001
Lawrence Block, guest editor · Otto Penzler, series editor

0-618-12492-6 CL $27.50 / 0-618-12491-8 PA $13.00
0-618-15565-1 CASS $25.00 / 0-618-15566-X CD $35.00

THE BEST AMERICAN ESSAYS 2001
Kathleen Norris, guest editor · Robert Atwan, series editor

0-618-15358-6 CL $27.50 / 0-618-04931-2 PA $13.00

THE BEST AMERICAN SPORTS WRITING 2001
Bud Collins, guest editor · Glenn Stout, series editor

0-618-08625-0 CL $27.50 / 0-618-08626-9 PA $13.00

THE BEST AMERICAN SCIENCE AND NATURE WRITING 2001
Edward O. Wilson, guest editor · Burkhard Bilger, series editor

0-618-08296-4 CL $27.50 / 0-618-15359-4 PA $13.00

THE BEST AMERICAN RECIPES 2001–2002
Fran McCullough, series editor · Foreword by Marcus Samuelsson

0-618-12810-7 CL $26.00

HOUGHTON MIFFLIN COMPANY / www.houghtonmifflinbooks.com